HUNTED

THE CHASE RYDER SERIES BOOK 3 (REVISED AND EXPANDED EDITION)

JO HO

*For Matt, for showing me the kind of love
I had only read about.*

SIGN UP TO JO'S NEWSLETTER!

Be the first to hear Jo's news and book releases.

Apply for her ARC teams (she has one for ebooks AND one for
audiobooks) to get free, advanced copies of her
books to read/listen to and review.

Plus, you'll get a free book as a thank you for signing up! What's
not to like?

Sign up and join all the cool kids at
www.johoscribe.com

$$1$$

CHASE

"And the first answer in this Double Jeopardy round… for $1,600, this 1972 novel is about a community of rabbits in Berkshire, England, who set out to find a new warren."

The sound of the announcer's cheerful voice sounded from the iPad that lay propped up on the floor of the wooden deck.

At first glance, the pattern that covered the tablet's foam case seemed an odd design choice. It was only on closer inspection that the millions of tiny depressions that covered the case could be identified as punctures caused by two rows of sharp canine teeth.

Seeing them, my lips curled into a grin as I pictured the much-loved culprit. No matter how carefully he tried carrying it, inevitably, Bandit would grip onto the thing with way too much enthusiasm.

Fact: iPad cases weren't designed to be handled by our four-legged friends.

Then again, I couldn't really blame Apple for the lack of insight: they couldn't know that in addition to regular people, their devices were also being used by a super intelligent, genetically modified dog.

As I stared down at the device, snatches of our eventful journey popped into my mind, filling me with a sense of wonder that still hadn't faded even now, almost seven months to the day since I'd first set foot on this ranch.

Everything that had come before seemed so long ago that the memories were fuzzy, as if they were hidden behind several sheets of material. You know the ones, those long white almost-see-through curtains they always use in trendy New York loft apartments in the movies.

From my time in the trailer park with Mom and Tubs, when I ran away, to the months of surviving by myself, homeless and alone… those memories had faded until they were tiny black and white snippets in my mind. Still, they were unpleasant enough that on the rare occasion when they did surface, I would bury them back in the far recesses of my mind.

I didn't like to focus on bad things… I couldn't see the point of deliberately making yourself feel bad.

Across the spectacular horizon that formed the Montpelier backdrop where Zeb, Sully's dad's ranch was based, red-gold leaves spoke of the approaching fall.

Though the sun still shone brightly in the sky, mornings now came with a chill, one that required a light cardigan over my usual sleepwear of an old tank top and shorts. I even had socks on my feet — reluctantly — as they were something I hated. I was a bare-foot or flip-flop kind of girl, although, during my time on the streets, there were many nights where all I wanted was a pair of socks to warm my frozen toes.

My hands were wrapped around my favorite mug where only the top of the boldly printed slogan could be seen, yet I didn't need to see the words to know what they were: "ACHIEVEMENT UNLOCKED. Fifteen whole years of being awesome."

It was a present from Sully, something he had picked up on one of his trips out of town but which I loved to death. Call me sentimental, but I thought it was kind of wonderful — and true, obviously.

I sipped at my coffee as Bandit lay on the deck before me, his long pink tongue hanging out as his tail thumped an excited rhythm on the floor. The sun glinted off his glossy black, brown, and white coat, which was a far cry from the dirty, dull, and starving appearance he'd had when I'd first met him. Then again, having spent the morning dumpster diving, I probably wouldn't have won any beauty awards myself.

See how much fun it is to go down Memory Lane?

Delicately picking up one of the many stylus pens we had made for him, Bandit tapped "Watership Down" into the iPad. His answer was greeted by loud in-game applause and more tail thumping.

Over the last few months, Bandit had developed an insatiable appetite for books and had read through pretty much all the children's classics, sometimes several in a day. His tastes were broad, but he had a special place in his heart for stories that featured animals.

To the casual — and shocked — outsider, this would seem like he was just having fun, though this was an actual exercise Bandit went through every morning. It was how we regulated his brain to make sure all was working as it should be.

You'd never know it seeing him now, but Bandit had come very close to meeting the Reaper… and that hadn't been the end of our troubles. A pang of shame welled up inside my chest when I thought of how I had become so caught up in my own family drama, how I had believed all that rubbish my mom had spouted, that Bandit had been taken on my watch.

Of all people, I should have known better than to trust her.

She was gone now, having sold me off for one hundred thousand dollars.

Strangely, I didn't feel as bitter as I had expected. I knew I'd never see her again. That kind of money wasn't something she would ever have hoped to see in her lifetime. It afforded her the luxury of changing her miserable life and ditching Tubs, and she wouldn't risk losing any of it for sentimental reasons.

She was gone, and I was pretty OK with that.

I had my own family now, one who actually cared about me, and I would do anything to keep them safe.

Leaning forward, I stroked Bandit's head, mentally affirming that I would never take him for granted again. His eyes flicked up at me before settling back onto the screen. His tail swished a pattern back and forth across the wooden floor. Tails were ridiculous things if you thought about them. I mean, what was their purpose other than to knock things down?

A sound burst out from the iPad, a kind of hallelujah music blast signifying something important. I thought Bandit must have unlocked some kind of in-game trophy, but it was just an announcement that had just popped up on the tablet.

A giant red banner bisected the screen, letting us know that they were giving away tickets for a special charity edition of Jeopardy that would be broadcasting live. Bandit's hopeful eyes raised to my own, his tail thumping harder with excitement. I clicked on the banner only for the small print to appear.

"Sorry, boy. This is happening in Los Angeles. If it was in New York, where the normal shows are filmed, we might have been able to swing it, but that's way too far from us.

He sighed. A long sigh of disappointment that tugged at my heart. I hated to disappoint him, no matter how small. Not wanting to focus on what he would be missing, I pressed the button to start a new round. Bandit instantly perked up again.

"*I love this game!*" he typed into the tablet, grinning at me.

"We know," I said. "We would have moved onto something else by now if you'd let us."

"Has he ever lost an actual game?" Gideon asked, yawning, even though he'd been up at least an hour. He sat across from me, sleep still fogging his eyes. A tuft of his hair stood up awkwardly on his head, and I had to resist the ridiculous urge to smooth it down. We were close, but not *that* close.

"Not that I've seen." He was one of those people who needed *hours* to wake. While we could get him doing simple tasks like early morning pastry runs, his brain didn't really click in until halfway through the morning, usually around ten or eleven.

If only there was an app that could work on him, too.

"Are you going to eat that?" Gideon gestured to the last donut, a frosted cinnamon one that lay on the middle of the table. I stared at the sugary doughy ring of deliciousness.

"I hadn't decided to *not* eat it, but I guess you could have it, if you want. I mean, you did get them and all," I conceded reluctantly.

"Gee thanks, Chase," he said. "It's not like you haven't already had five. Oh wait, yes you have."

"You know I can't control my fast metabolism. Isn't that right, Zeb?"

I looked toward the end of the porch. Zeb sat in his wheelchair, head ducked low, reading the paper, sipping from a cup of coffee. For some reason, he always sat away from Gideon and me, especially in the morning.

"If there is any way I can get out of this by not answering, that would be ideal," Zeb responded without even looking up.

It was coming up to two weeks since Sully and Sam had gone on their honeymoon, during which time Zeb had been drawn into every single one of our disagreements. Judging by the surly tone in his voice, I think he was getting tired of being our referee.

"What time are they calling?" he asked, finally looking up at me over the top of the newspaper.

I glanced down at my watch — a gift from Sam who felt that phones didn't make a suitable equivalent — to check. "Any second now, actually."

As if Sully knew we had been talking about him, Bandit's iPad suddenly started ringing as the familiar Skype icon blinked on-screen.

Dropping his stylus pen onto the floor, Bandit set the iPad on the table. I tapped the answer icon, propping the tablet up against the juice jug so we could all get a good look at them. After a few seconds, the video call connected, and Sully and Sam's happy faces appeared.

"Hey! How's everyone doing?" Sully said, squinting into his phone.

As if he hadn't seen or spoken to him for years, Bandit's entire body shook with excitement as he shoved his face at the screen until his nose filled up the frame.

Chuffing into the iPad, he talked a mile a minute, though, of course, without the tablet to translate, it was pretty hard to know what he was saying. Laughing, I wrapped my arms around him, gently easing his face back so that we could all see Sully and Sam, and they could see more than a shiny, wet nose.

They were crammed into a packed restaurant. People feasted on giant plates piled high with French toast and waffles, fruit salad, sausages and bacon. It all looked so good that I felt a surge of envy even though I had only just eaten.

Outside, large crowds of people milled around, jazz music playing behind them. I tapped the screen's volume arrow, turning it up so we could hear them above the music.

"We're fine as you well know," said Zeb. "There really is no need for you to call every single day. Don't you have better things to do on your honeymoon?"

Beside Sully, Sam laughed. She wore a pretty halter dress with giant sunflowers printed onto the fabric. Her usually tied back blonde hair flowed loosely over her shoulders. There was even a touch of glossy lipstick on her lips. She looked so pretty and happy. Used to Sam in her role as the town's Sheriff, I had never really seen her so girly like this.

It was nice.

"Don't worry, we'll get back on that real soon," Sam laughed, causing a flush to color Sully's face. She pinched his cheeks, laughing. "Never noticed how cute you were when you blushed."

The screen suddenly turned away from her as Sully shifted the phone's perspective to him, pushing Sam offscreen.

"That's enough of that," he said, trying to regain control of the conversation. "Segueing into a topic that isn't going to make me uncomfortable… what's everyone doing today?" he asked.

Munching that last donut, Gideon leaned forward in his seat. "Oh, you know, the usual. I've decided not to fight crime today. Going to hang up the cape and rest my superhero self."

Sully answered without blinking. "Another day off from the garage? Is business that bad?"

Gideon shrugged. "I don't think it's ever really booming. This is Montpelier, after all."

Bandit made a sound between a snort and a chuff in his version of a laugh. Unable to speak since his iPad had been hijacked, he padded off to the grass, retrieving his favorite ball, then very deliberately, he set it onto the table in front of Sully. Sully looked at the red ball and laughed.

"I guess Bandit's day will consist mostly of fetch. What about the rest of you?"

I rolled my eyes.

"Why are you asking this boring question? We're obviously doing nothing exciting. Everything's fine. In fact, it's been boring as heck since you guys left. Can't we just talk about Montréal? Like, are Canadians really that weird? Do they really finish all sentences with "ey"?" Once I'd started, I wasn't able to stop the stream of questions.

"Yes and no," came Sully's short answer. "They're just people, Chase. There's nothing special about them and they don't have any distinguishable traits apart from how they like to speak French for some reason. Sorry to disappoint you."

I must have looked more disappointed than I realized, as he

shot a reassuring grin at me. "Don't worry, we'll come here together one day."

"Not if they keep playing that terrible music we won't. What's wrong with actually carrying a tune?" This had come from Gideon.

A cluster of powdered sugar had caught on his upper lip giving him a comical sugar mustache that clashed with the serious expression on his face (Gideon had a love affair with music but hated anything he deemed pretentious, which apparently included this particular kind of jazz).

"Young people and their inability to appreciate the classics." Zeb shook his head sadly. "Right there is everything wrong with the world."

Sully looked at us, an eyebrow cocked crookedly in question. "We've barely been gone two weeks. What have you done to him?"

My face went immediately bland in that expression I always used whenever I didn't want to admit to causing trouble. Problem was, Sully knew me too well even if Bandit hadn't jumped up, placing his two front paws onto the table to bark at him.

I shot Bandit a dirty look. "You little snitch."

Bandit opened his mouth in a goofy grin that turned into a yawn, dropping back onto all fours. Sully crossed his arms, still waiting for an explanation — one that he could understand. Reluctantly, I translated what my dog had said.

"It's possible that we may have asked him to referee our debates a few more times than he wanted."

"It's important to know that by 'asked' she means 'hounded'," Zeb cut in.

Sully tried not to look amused by the resigned tone in his voice. "We'll be back tomorrow, Dad. Hang in there."

"I'll try, but I'm not promising anything," Zeb said grumpily.

Sam whispered something in Sully's ear that had him standing to attention. It wasn't only Bandit who had the goofy grin on his face now. I figured I would never want to know what it was she had said. Probably something disgustingly cute

"Looks like we should get going."

"Seriously Sully, we're fine. Nothing is going to happen between now and tomorrow. Go and enjoy the last day of your honeymoon. You'll see more than enough of us when you're back," Zeb said.

Sully's eyes roamed over each of us one last time, like he was doing some kind of mental check. Finally, he nodded. "You two behave. Try not to kill my father. We'll see you all tomorrow."

We shouted goodbye — even Bandit, who howled enthusiastically — and then the screen went blank. I got up from the table and went into the kitchen to see if there was any cereal left. Spying the Cheerios box, I picked it up and shook it, relieved to hear the rustling inside. I was pouring the last of it into what was probably a mixing bowl, judging by the size of it, when the doorbell rang.

"Chase, can you get that? I've got laundry to do."

I'd had the spoon in my hand ready to dive in when Gideon's voice called out to me. Sighing, I shot the cereal a sad look and went to answer the door.

Through the frosted glass I could make out the woman outside. She wasn't wearing a suit or carrying any products, so she wasn't a saleswoman of some kind.

I opened the door.

The woman was a little taller than me with a slim dancer's body, long blonde hair and delicate features. No make-up adorned her face yet even without any help, she was naturally pretty, but it was her sapphire eyes that caught my attention, staring at me as they were in utter confusion.

Though I had never met her before, she seemed somehow familiar. She opened her mouth to speak, but no sound came out of it. She only stood there, her birdlike hands gripping onto a rucksack as if they were a lifeline.

I was about to ask what she wanted when it suddenly hit me.

I *did* know who this woman was…

And yet… it couldn't be possible.

The world started spinning around me. My mouth fell open, my face turning slack-jawed. I could feel my heart begin to pound as the blood in my veins turned to ice.

From somewhere in the back of my mind, I heard Zeb call out. "Who's at the door?"

The woman in front of me didn't move or say a word. She only stood there staring beseechingly at me — as if I would be able to explain away this madness.

I didn't know how to respond.

"I think it's best if you come here," was all I managed before my voice died in my throat.

Hearing the shock in my voice, Zeb came over, lines creasing his face. When he arrived beside me, his hands froze on the wheels of his chair.

We stood side-by-side, staring at the visitor, unable to hide the shock from either of our faces.

2

SULLY

At the crack of dawn, we drove the three or so hours back from Montréal in a state of bliss.

After the stress of the last few weeks when I had almost lost not only Sam, but my entire family, the trip away had been exactly what we'd needed.

The first few days of our honeymoon, we'd never even made it out of the hotel.

If it wasn't for the Godly room service — and man, did Montreal know how to make a great brunch — we probably would have starved, no joke.

Around the third day, when we realized we should actually experience the city so that we would have something to report back to the family, we took a lazy boat ride in the Old Port.

Technically, the correct name would be Le Vieux Port, but since I sound like Bandit when he tries to speak with a mouthful of ball whenever I attempt any French words, the world rested easier when I gave in to my native tongue.

After the blue waters had relaxed our souls, we took a leisurely stroll along the boutiques that lined quaint cobblestone streets, picking up the odd trinket or gift for the kids. I was particularly taken by an arts and crafts store where a rainbow of dream catchers hung in the window. Bandit still suffered from the odd nightmare, worrying that the Bad Men would be coming after him again. I got him one of the biggest on display, hoping it would help psychologically if not realistically.

When we'd exhausted the Old Port, we tried visiting RESO, the famous interconnected underground city downtown that ran for some thirty-two kilometers.

Montreal was known for its long and punishing winters, where, for six months of the year, the city would be barraged by icy winds that kept the temperature below freezing, while the streets above would be blanketed in a sea of snow. Its citizens had come up with a creative solution to keep their lives going despite the brutal weather by building an entire city underground, one that connected to their metro system — linking up to ten stations — so that a person could walk the entire length of downtown without ever having to go up to the surface.

Excited to experience this, we'd disembarked at Peel metro and started our shopping spree.

Two hours later, I was already regretting our decision.

While the subterranean mall did not disappoint, filled to the brim with household brands sitting side-by-side with their designer cousins, it turned out shopping was a lot more exhausting than either of us had prepared ourselves for.

Back home, our local shops consisted only of the essentials. With the one grocery store that also doubled as the post office, Warrey's garage, a Dollar General where we picked up most of our household items, and a handful of eateries, we'd had to drive almost an hour to get to the nearest mall, but that was nothing compared to this behemoth.

A kaleidoscope of color assaulted our eyes, while various styles of music boomed out from the store's speakers, clashing with each other in their haste to win the war of the noises.

Then there was the general sound of the people: parents fighting with young kids, and dogs who were much less behaved than Bandit. Even the smells that drifted up from the basement food courts turned my stomach.

It was all too much for us simple folk.

Barely making it to the next metro stop, we admitted defeat, packing it in for craft beer and smoked meat sandwiches at Schwartz's, a place so renowned that it was standing room only.

Sam had discovered it on a food blog during her research where the glowing reviews numbered in the thousands. She had book-marked the eatery, letting me know that we *would* be stopping at it during our honeymoon. After tasting their food for myself, I could certainly see why it was so popular.

I was even giving serious consideration to franchising a branch back home — if only for myself to enjoy.

On hotter days, when the sun warmed the city enough that it seemed summer was lingering around, we strolled through the stunning Botanical Garden with its themed gardens, enjoyed the many outdoor theaters that the city freely offered, and ate until we were fit to burst.

Happy as I was, in love with my new wife as I was, I couldn't help missing the kids back home.

When we passed by a Mclaren showroom, I felt a pang that Gid wasn't there to experience it, loving sports cars as much as he did. We certainly never got those back home where it was all four wheelers and trucks. I took as many pictures as I could, but when the manager started glaring our way; we knew it was time to beat a hasty exit.

Chase was a little tougher to buy for, but not in the usual difficult teenager sense; quite the opposite, in fact. The girl had been given so little that she was grateful for *everything*. No matter how small, or how ordinary, each gift had been so happily received that I had started to doubt if she really liked the presents, or was just so glad to get something. I couldn't tell the difference. And the thing of it was, I wanted her to like the gifts I got her.

I wanted her to be happy.

She'd had so little of it growing up. It felt right that I should spoil her now.

I guess that's what happens when you become a dad. Your life isn't your own anymore. Suddenly, everything has a richer meaning, and the world feels heightened.

At least, that's how it was to me. I knew I was a pretty decent parent, unlike Chase's real mom. To think I'd trusted her to be alone with Chase.

Even now, the anger burned, turning my heart to stone.

The less I thought about her, the better. That woman didn't deserve an ounce of sympathy from anyone.

Sam sang most of the way back in that rich voice of hers, while I joined in, harmonizing perfectly. We sounded good, maybe good enough to enter one of those televised singing competitions that the kids loved to watch if we had been so inclined.

Remembering the spring when Chase, Bandit, and I had to perform on the streets of Atlantic City, I thought about how much more money we would have made if Sam had been there to sing with us. It would be such a different experience if we went there now that we had each other… and money.

Money was king, unfortunately.

Everything that happened before the honeymoon seemed like a fading nightmare. The breakup that had left me reeling, Chase and Bandit being kidnapped, Dad falling into a coma… Through it all, one thing had become clear to me: I knew without a doubt that Sam was my person.

My eyes slid over to her, taking a moment to eat up the sight of her twinkling eyes as she sang a popular country song with gusto. The woman lived her life like that. She wasn't afraid of anything. Her vivacity filled up the holes that had been left in me when I had become a widower much too young.

I was a whole man again, and I liked it.

Fall was starting to encroach on this part of the world and as we drove through Montpelier towards the ranch, the trees had started to turn. Red and gold swallowed what was left of the green. The chill in the air grew more pronounced the closer we got to home.

A snow filled winter was something Bandit had not yet experienced, but it was something Montpelier excelled in. We had attempted to explain what snow was on several occasions, but it continued to perplex him. He couldn't wrap his big old dog head around it. Picturing Bandit careening down a hill on a toboggan while Chase raced after him, I laughed.

Sam looked over at me. "Care to share the joke?"

"It was nothing, just thinking something silly."

She smiled and rested her head on my shoulder.

The miles passed easily until the ranch finally appeared, looking exactly the same as when we had left it. There was something great about that. We were home, and within seconds, we would be surrounded by our loved ones.

I couldn't wait for us to start our new lives. Maybe, if we were lucky, there would be another kid to add to our mix soon...

A baby's face popped into my mind, round and chubby with a mix of our features. I was hit with a longing so strong that I had to hold my breath. We'd briefly discussed the possibility of having our own children, but I knew we were on the same page.

Sam was as keen as I was to get going on it. We'd have to be careful how we broke the news to Chase. Despite how much we loved her, Chase's old insecurities would surface now and then, and a new baby would probably cause some of that angst to surface, until she came around to the idea at least.

When the time came, we'd be treating her with kid gloves.

I parked the car then sprinted to Sam's side. Flinging open her door, I offered my hand.

"Here you go, my lady."

She was tickled pink by my gesture. Taking hold of my hand,

she let me help her out of the car. Her feet barely touched the ground before I scooped her into my arms. Her peals of laughter floated into the sky.

"Put me down before you drop me!"

"What do you mean, drop you? Do you know how much I can bench-press?"

"No. Do you?"

"Of course not. I've never bench-pressed anything in my life. What is it anyway?"

She laughed again and flung her arms around my neck, probably concerned that I really would drop her. Truthfully, my arms were already starting to ache, but I was determined to carry my new bride over the threshold. Some traditions had to be upheld.

"OK, tough guy. Five bucks says you don't make it."

"If we're going to do this, let's make it interesting. Ten bucks… *and* you do my laundry for a week." Sam hated laundry at the best of times. I thought this was a suitable enough punishment for her lack of faith in my manhood.

"You're on." Her eyes breathed life, her lips parted in a big smile.

Digging deep into my core (despite what I'd said, I had known my way around a gym a time or two so the joke was about to be on her), I crossed the distance to the front door, maybe not as easily as I'd like, but at least I got us there.

Briefly, I wondered why the others weren't here to greet us. The way I had imagined our homecoming, Bandit and Chase would dash out of the door long before I even stopped the truck. We never had many visitors in these parts, and you could usually hear a vehicle approaching. They had to have known we were back.

Since no one opened the door for us and I couldn't get it with Sam in my arms, I leaned awkwardly toward it so she could reach over and grab the handle.

She threw open the door.

We saw directly through to the lounge, where Chase sat on the couch beside a blonde woman. The two had been chatting but stopped when the door burst open.

My face broke into a welcoming smile when the blonde woman turned from Chase to look at me… and my world imploded.

It was all I could do not to drop Sam.

I stood, rooted to the spot, my smile frozen on my face.

This couldn't be real.

This couldn't be happening.

Sensing my shock, Sam's eyes darted to me, unable to hide the concern in them. When she couldn't understand what was causing my distress, she twisted back to the blonde.

"What's going on?" She finally asked. "Who is that, Sully?"

I couldn't speak.

My mouth had turned sandpit dry. I wasn't in control over any part of my body. The blood pounded through my temple, threatening to pop a vein.

The blonde got up off the couch and took a step towards us.

"I'm Emma," she said, answering Sam.

"I'm Sully's wife."

3

SULLY

I couldn't move.

In the back of my mind, I could hear a voice speaking into my ear, asking what was going on, but I had shut down, unable to process what was standing in front of me.

The blonde approached us.

With every step, her familiar face assaulted my senses. Those beautiful gem-like eyes and sweet cherry lips were exactly as I had remembered them.

Even her movements were familiar: she'd always had the grace of a dancer, while I seemed as clumsy as an oaf in comparison. She glided toward me, an impossible apparition, and one which I had seen on multiple occasions after her death.

But this time, she was real.

Her chest moved as the breath went in and out of her body. Her golden hair glistened as the light bounced off the strands that tumbled over her shoulder. She was as familiar to me as the air.

The one thing that was odd — other than the fact that my dead wife was standing in front of me — was the confused expression in her eyes, which must have mirrored my own.

I was yet to say a word.

My arm muscles, aching at first, were now cramping up a storm. Unceremoniously — though completely by necessity — I had to set Sam down. She buckled a bit, not ready to be dumped onto the ground so abruptly.

Her eyes flared open, shock radiating through her.

"Emma? But that's not possible..." I barely recognized my voice, pushing toward hysteria as it was.

Was I experiencing a nervous breakdown as a delayed response to losing my wife? Had I imagined everything that had come to pass in the last six months?

And yet, there was Chase coming toward me, as real as anything I had ever seen. In her face shone the sympathy she directed not only at me, but Sam as well. As usual, Bandit was only a few steps behind, whining a greeting that carried his own confusion.

"Sully," Chase began, then broke off as she tried to find the words that were tripping over her tongue. "She turned up here yesterday, after our call..."

She fell silent again, her hands clasped together. Even from here, I could see how white they were. She must have been squeezing them so tight.

"Chase has been trying to explain everything that's happened in the last year and a half, but I can't remember any of it. I don't even remember you," the blonde said in Emma's voice.

My dead wife's voice.

"I need to sit down," Sam said suddenly.

Her eyes were glazed over, her lips had turned white. She was in shock and that scared me. For the time I'd known her, Sam always had her wits about her, so to see her like this...

This had to be real.

Somehow, my wife, the woman who had died some eighteen months ago, whose body had been ravaged by cancer and which I had watched be buried into the ground — was back.

Sam went to the couch.

Taking a seat at the end of the floral couch that my mom had loved, Chase sat beside her, reached over, and took her hand. Sam shot her a quick, grateful look, then flicked her eyes back to Emma.

Searching for something to say, anything I could grab a hold of, I finally addressed *her*. "If you don't remember me, how did you get here?"

"The pictures in the bag. I found them when I woke up," she answered cryptically.

I tried to focus on one thing at a time as everything seemed too difficult right now. What had she just said? "What pictures?"

Emma retrieved a bag that had been sitting on the floor. It was a cheap navy bag, the kind of thing you could pick up at a dollar store, with an orange label. She rummaged inside until she came up with a handful of photographs that she held out to me.

"Here," she said. "Look."

I looked down at the thirty or so pictures she held in her hand, unable to take them from her, as I was afraid to touch her. I didn't want to know how a dead wife — who had returned from the grave — would feel.

Turning my attention downward, the pictures swam into view.

Faces floated up at me, our faces. There Emma and I were on one of our first dates at a local drive-in theater. Taken by a helpful passer-by, the picture framed us in the seats of the battered Ford truck I had driven at the time.

While Zeb and I had patched up our differences now, back then, we hadn't been speaking. My parents were a renowned surgeon and respected medical researcher. With their support and backing, it was always decided that I would follow in their footsteps to become a surgeon myself, but my heart had been drawn to another path...

One that had led to Emma.

I waited for the thought to shift, trying to focus on the memories that sat in her hands. Whether we were in a far-flung location experiencing one of the many exotic vacations we loved to take, hosting barbecues at the clinic during our July 4th celebration, or doing something as humdrum as painting a room in our recently bought house: in all the pictures, we were laughing, blissfully happy and in love.

My head felt like it would explode.

It wasn't only Emma's presence here that was impossible. The very pictures themselves shouldn't have existed: they had turned to ashes in the fire that had consumed the clinic and our home.

But here they were, as solidly in her hand as the woman herself.

I looked up at this woman and saw she was exactly the same as my wife in the pictures.

My hands started shaking. Tears blurred my vision, though I wasn't sure why I was crying. I couldn't tell whether they were tears of happiness…

Or fear.

Chase, who had been respectfully and unusually quiet until now, suddenly spoke.

"Emma doesn't know what happened to her or where she came from. But she woke up not far from here with that bag beneath her head. Aside from those pictures, she had some water and some energy bars."

Her voice broke as if she were struggling to complete her sentence. Tearing my gaze from Emma, my eyes slid over to Chase. She had that grave expression I had only seen a few times before, the last being when her mom had turned up unexpectedly at the door.

"I recognize that bag, Sully," Chase began, her voice heavy with concern. "It was the same one I woke up with when I found myself in the woods."

Sam turned to Chase, her work self kicking in. "What're you saying, exactly?"

Chase's eyes grew round.

"Remember the big experiment Xavier boasted about? I think, somehow, he managed to bring Emma back."

4

SULLY

One year and two months, over ten thousand hours or some six hundred thousand minutes.

That's how long Emma had been dead for, how long she had been buried, six feet under the ground.

Depending on where you went to for your source of information, there were either four or five stages of decay for a body. Suffice to say, either way, there would not be much of my Emma left. My muddled mind clung to these facts, repeating them over and over inside my head.

"How did you know how to find us if you can't remember Sully?"

This had come from Sam.

Some color had come back into her cheeks as she fought to gain some manner of control. Despite the shock we were all feeling, Sam the Sheriff was about to take charge. I couldn't have been more relieved and didn't feel a lick of shame about it.

Emma turned to Sam, looking her up and down, biting her lip, uncomfortable by the question and the tone which came along with it.

"I followed the path, then the signs to the town and showed people the pictures. It wasn't until I came to one man that he told me where you were. He looked at me strangely, but I didn't know why. I didn't like him," she added, her lips pursing into a pout.

"It seems an unlikely thing for someone in town to give a complete stranger our home address." Sam didn't bother to hide the scepticism in her voice. Somewhere in the back of my mind, I felt myself wanting to laugh hysterically. Of all the things that had happened in the last five minutes, *this* is what she questioned?

"Well, he did," Emma said, somewhat petulantly. "He said something about not being surprised, then told me exactly where you would all be."

Through the fog of bewilderment I found myself in, I suddenly knew exactly who she was referring to. "Was he a mechanic? Owns a garage in town?"

Emma nodded. I looked over at Sam. "Warrey. He's never liked me. Probably hoped I lied to you about Emma. He doesn't know she is... about my situation." I finished quickly, not wanting to insult or scare her even though I understood how ludicrous that was, given how pretty damn scared I felt myself right now.

Emma eyed me with the open curiosity of a child, taking in my features. She leaned in so close to me that I felt myself flinching.

"Why can't I remember you? Shouldn't I be able to remember my husband?" she asked, as if I was still hers.

Reaching up, she traced a finger along my jawline, though there was nothing sexy or loving about the gesture. Then her head came up close to my neck as she started to *sniff me?*

A thought jolted through me, filling me with unease. I stepped back away from her. Her fingers fell away from my face.

Feeling suddenly unsteady, I moved away from her, stopping by Chase on the couch.

"What exactly have you explained to her... to Emma?" Her name stick in my throat, thick and cloying.

Chase's expression changed, her lips twisting into a nervous, apologetic smile. "Just that you *were* her husband, but that she's been… gone a while."

My heart sank.

As I suspected, Chase had left the tough talk to me.

"There's obviously some discussion that needs to happen. A lot has changed since you were last… here," Sam said quietly.

"I've been here before? I don't remember this house either?" Misunderstanding Sam's meaning, Emma's eyes swept the area, trying to place the house in her mind.

"That's not what I — Listen, I know this is going to be hard for you to understand, but you still need to hear it: I'm Sully's wife now. We actually just returned from our honeymoon."

Emma's face turned stricken. As the news sank in, another emotion took over. She spun to face me, eyes blazing with heat, crossing the room to me in several quick strides.

"You married another woman? What kind of man does that when his wife disappears? Did you even look for me?"

With every question, she jabbed her finger at my chest until I finally caught her hand in mine, not wanting her to hurt herself. Her hands felt cool to the touch, but they also felt *real*.

They felt alive.

I dropped them as if they were hot coals.

"That's not what happened… You don't understand. You're… You died."

"I'm obviously not dead, am I? I'm standing right here." Emma blinked at me, confusion turning her blue eyes hazy.

"But you did die, Emma. I watched it happen. Buried you myself."

She laughed at me, finding my words ludicrous, but when no one else joined in, her smile faded. I plowed on, knowing what needed to be said, however impossible this conversation might be.

"You had cancer. We couldn't cure it. When you finally passed, the disease had eaten away most of you."

Anger flashed across her face. She glared at each one of us.

"This isn't funny. Why are you people doing this? This is cruel. Just because I don't remember anything doesn't mean you can make fun of me."

"We're not picking on you. He's telling the truth. I just didn't know how to tell you," Chase pointed out gently.

"I grieved for you a long time." I needed her to know that, whatever good that would do.

"Clearly not that long if you married someone else!"

"I didn't meet Sam until a year after you had died."

Tears misted in her eyes as she struggled to accept what I was saying. "So you're saying you thought I was dead for over a year?"

"It'll be two years in December. And you did die. You died right before Christmas."

A gasp came from Chase. I didn't realize she hadn't known this until now. Sympathy poured out of her as Bandit whined his own platitudes. Emma's head shook left and right, unable to accept the news.

"You're not making sense. I didn't die. I can't have died if I'm here."

"Well, we don't really know what you are right now," Sam answered in a gentle tone normally reserved for toddlers.

"*What* I am? So not only am I dead, now I'm not even human?"

Her voice went up a notch, hysteria not far behind.

"That's not what Sam's suggesting. None of us have any answers right now. I don't think we can jump to any conclusions. We all need time to get used to you being here again." Chase sounded far more mature than her years.

Emma's lower lip trembled, those glistening sapphire eyes of hers threatening to spill over with tears.

"I don't remember anything before I woke up, but I know I have feelings for you. You feel familiar to me."

She grabbed my hand, placing it against her heart. I could feel it beating beneath her chest. *Thump… thump… thump…*

And that terrified me.

Wrenching my hands away, I stepped back from her even as she stared at me with such betrayal that I almost fell. The world tilted on its axis. I felt as if the ground might come rushing up to me when I felt a strong presence by my side.

Sam.

She had left the couch and come to my side, where she was now silently giving me her moral and physical support. I sagged against her, taking in her strength as my own.

Bandit stood up and whined. Padding over to Emma, it seemed he wanted to offer some form of comfort, but as he came near her, his steps faltered. He stopped just short of touching her, his nose wrinkling as he sniffed the surrounding air cautiously. Taking out his iPad, he typed.

"She does not smell right."

Emma glared down at him, apparently unsurprised that the dog was communicating with them in such a manner. "Well, you don't exactly smell great either," she snapped before turning her eyes back to the rest of us.

"I came to you for help, not for all these questions or judgement. You need to help me because I've nowhere else to go."

Her eyes glittered with feeling. She was either the best actress I'd ever come across, or she truly was as scared and desperate as she seemed. Sam must have come to the same conclusion as she softened her voice.

"I can go to the office and see if I can dig anything up?" She offered, but I shook my head.

"We're not going to find anything about her. Whoever is behind this isn't going to register her."

The whir of Zeb's wheelchair interrupted our conversation. He came into the room, Gideon at his side.

"Welcome back," Gideon said. "I see you've met our predicament. Seems Zeb spoke too soon when he said nothing would come up before your return."

Gideon's flippant attitude might have raised a few eyebrows, but I didn't rise to it, knowing this was his way of dealing with a pressure filled environment.

My dad shot me a sympathetic smile. "I had hoped to welcome you with better news after your vacation. I'm sorry that this is what you had to come back to."

Hurt flashed over Emma's face as her eyes turned to flint. "You think I want to be here? You people could be crooks for all I know. I came to you for help, but if all you're going to do is stand there being mean to me, then I'm better off alone."

She shoved the photos back into her bag. She was walking toward the exit when the door exploded inward, sending her flying back. She fell onto the floor, her body landing with a thud as a high-pitched ringing sounded in my ears.

Smoke and debris filled the air. I found myself coughing after inhaling a lung full of smoke. "What the hell?"

After making sure that Bandit was safely behind the sofa where he had naturally darted to, Chase sprinted to Emma's side, tugging on her arm to help her up.

Her eyes were glazed over with shock. Other than that, she seemed unharmed, at least from what I could tell by a cursory glance.

Gideon had acted fast, shielding Zeb from the blast with his own body. Recovering faster than I could give him credit for, Gideon sprinted behind cover, pushing Zeb's wheelchair with him, while Sam had darted out of harm's way herself, flattening against the wall, keeping herself out of sight from the entrance where a gaping hole now stood.

All that was left of the front door were the shards of splintered wood that now littered the floor, and the blackened hinges, which swung at an angle, attached to the frame by a single, solitary screw.

Sam and I shared a tense look.

I signaled silently, letting her know that I would move forward to scope out the area. She nodded, though she didn't seem happy by my decision. Using the smoke for cover, I eased my way to the front in a crouch-walk, keeping myself low to the ground.

Through the clouds, I could see movement outside.

First, I could only spot the one figure, but as the smoke began to clear, the hazy figures multiplied at a rapid pace. Fear clutched at my heart when I saw our front yard littered with black-clad men.

And a flashback of my clinic crashed into my head.

In my mind's eye, I saw Forbes' men — led by that ruthless mercenary — come crashing into my clinic armed with shotguns.

Blinking, I forced the memory away, knowing I needed to deal with this new nightmare. Details flew at me. I took in their all-black military-like outfits. Belts made out of bullets and magazine clips were slung casually across their bodies as if they were some kind of utility fashion item. They stood stock still, several feet away, their eyes hidden behind yellow-lensed glasses that made them look like bugs.

Even as I realized this, I wondered why none of the men were moving. Why would they break down our front door only to stand there? What were they waiting for?

Then my gaze lowered to the long range sniper rifles they each held in their hands.

Sniper rifles that they were now aiming into the house.

"Get away from the windows!" I yelled, waving at the others, frantically signaling for them to back away. "Get down!"

"What is it?" Gideon screamed out.

"They have snipers," I managed to warn before my voice gave way to the stark terror that rose up inside. Before, when Forbes's men had come, they had only the one objective — to take Bandit back.

My eyes flicked over to him betraying my thoughts, as Chase immediately sprinted to Bandit's side. Trouble may have loved company, but it seemed to love our beloved dog more. Pulling him behind the couch, they flattened against the floor when a hail of silenced bullets impaled the wall above them. Plaster fell off in chunks, leaving them wearing a coat of white dust.

"That's too close for a warning shot," Sam called over.

"Then what are they doing?" Chase cried, the whites of her eyes looking abnormally bright.

"I think they're trying to kill us," Sam finished.

The hairs on the back of my neck rose. I felt everything as if it were amplified. We were under attack *again*. Though this time, they didn't want Bandit alive.

This time, they wanted him dead.

"Well, let's not make it easy for them." I replied grimly.

Turning to Zeb and Gideon, I gestured to the far wall uttering the three words I had hoped never to say.

"Contingency Plan A!"

5

CHASE

Hearing those words come out of Sully's mouth, I knew we were in trouble.

Big trouble.

The kind we might never be able to get out of.

We had been against this hard place before, and after that first time, then what happened with Mom and Xavier, Sully swore that we'd never be taken by surprise again.

Clearly, he had been wrong on that front.

This time, though, we were at least partially prepared for it.

Over by the west side of the room, Sam's hand was already reaching behind the bookshelf she was using as cover.

I didn't need to carry on watching to see what she would find: I knew the handgun that lived there, nestled in a holster that Sully had fastened to the bookshelf during one long weekend after Xavier had been caught. Before the wedding, when unhappy that he and Sam would be leaving us for their honeymoon, he had decided we would erect secret defenses around the place.

Of course, our weapons hadn't come to much use when Xavier had broken in, since none of us had been here to use them. Zeb had been alone when he had attacked, putting him into a coma that we'd thought he'd never come out of, which, luckily had only lasted a few days.

Tearing my thoughts from the past, I focused on what I needed to do. Bandit's stomach was pressed to the floor in the way Sully had taught him when we'd been going through our contingency plans. Gideon had mocked him at first, sure that our problems were over. Tossing him a look, I saw that he was as glad as I was that Sully had forced us to learn the drill.

We'd practiced only a handful of times, but we seemed to remember what was expected of us. *Only grab a weapon if you can,* came Sam's voice in my head. The safest way to survive an attack was to hide. I was only to fire a weapon if I was forced to fight.

Seeing those black-clad figures outside, the ones who I would still wake up in the middle of the night fearful of, I knew without a doubt that running wasn't an option.

I heard a whimper and thought that it had come from Bandit until his tongue snaked out to lick my hand, offering what comfort he could. There was no time for him to use his iPad. No time for anything other than to find the weapon that was closest to me.

But in the madness of the moment, my brain froze, and I found myself unable to remember where it was.

Snapping around to Sully, I saw he was busy locating his own gun, a rifle that stood upright, half-hidden in the umbrella stand. Gideon was scrambling to the kitchen, where several more hand-guns were hidden in various drawers and cupboards.

My hands felt like claws. I was so scared. The last time I had used a gun, I had killed a man. Though he had deserved it, the memory of it had haunted me for months after. I wasn't sure if I would be able to do it again.

Hearing the weakness in my thoughts, I clamped down on them.

My family needed me! This was no time to be scared. I had to fight for them. I had to protect them, the same way they protected me.

Knowing I'd get strength from Bandit, I turned to him, expecting to see those loving eyes of his on mine. Instead, his attention was on the space beneath the couch: specifically the floor, which he scratched at pretty frantically. I wasted a few precious seconds wondering what he was doing when it suddenly came to me.

Hunkering down, I reached beneath the couch, feeling around the wooden slats until my fingers closed around the Glock that was taped to the underside of the sofa.

This was what my Muttface had been trying to tell me if only I'd been listening.

Taking hold of the gun, I ripped it away. There was a thirty-round mag inserted into the gun. The metal felt cold in my hand and heavy with the weight of the world.

My fingers tightened around the metal. I got back onto my feet into a crouch.

"Stay low," I hissed at Bandit. He nodded, not wanting to make a sound in case it would give our hiding place away. The air was so thick with tension that I could feel it. Our group waited, each of us armed with a weapon except for Emma.

When the door had exploded, she hadn't moved. I hadn't even thought about what I was doing. I just found myself by her side, yanking her down since she seemed unable to do so on her own. She had yelped, startled by my forceful tug, but now that she was down, she had curled into a tight ball, her hands wrapped around her head.

A soft mewling sound came out of her. She sounded like a terrified child.

Silence had fallen in the house. You could hear a pin drop. During our drills, Sully had commanded us not to fire until either he or Sam gave the command. It was always best not to engage if there was any kind of chance that we could escape.

I clutched my weapon, biting my lip until I tasted the rusty iron of blood. I watched, holding my breath, as Sully hesitated. I could see his mind ticking over our options when— *pfffffftttttttttt.*

A silenced bullet hit the television, causing it to explode in a burst of electricity.

More silenced bullets whistled through the air above my head. A lamp shattered, caught by one of the stray bullets. The sound as loud as a thunderclap.

Sully's eyes turned flat.

"Shoot them!"

And with that one command, I aimed my weapon outside and let rip.

6

SULLY

This was it.

This was the end.

The over-powering smell of gunpowder swamped the low-ceilinged room, filling my nose and making my eyes water.

Steel flashing from her eyes, Chase popped up from behind the couch, firing shots through the doorway, before ducking down again.

The extra large magazine she had taped next to her firearm ensured she wouldn't have to reload soon. We made sure that this was the case with every weapon we owned. Sam had taught us that ducking out of view would make it more difficult for any attackers to hit us with their shots. It was one of the first lessons in gun fighting we ever learned.

The longer you stayed in view, the more chance you had of getting hit.

A flash of blonde hair caught the corner of my eye, drawing my attention to the far side of the room where Sam took aim. Her lips were a thin, tight line. A frown creased her forehead, but other than that, she looked impossibly calm and composed.

I knew better than anyone that looks were deceiving.

The more stressed Sam became, the quieter and calmer she seemed. It was a tactic she had cultivated to throw criminals off the scent, and I was sure it was working now. If the men who hunted us outside could see her face, maybe they would be taken aback by her lack of fear.

Maybe they would back away.

Wishful thinking.

Through the chaos, I took in the faces of the people I loved, desperately wishing that we had more time together.

I saw my dad fighting so bravely from his wheelchair, Gideon by his side. He handed Gideon bullets while the boy aimed and took fire for all he was worth.

Bullets sprayed out of his gun and out of the window. Glass smashed, raining onto the floor around his booted feet, but Gideon kept his aim sharp, his eyes glued to the enemy outside.

When one gun was empty, he silently handed it to Zeb to refill while he picked up another of the several handguns he had taken from the kitchen. The old man's sight wasn't great, his aim was even worse, but even with those handicaps, he was making himself useful.

Sam, who was the next closest to the opening, fired again. I felt a grim satisfaction when I heard a man's grunt of pain, followed by the sight of his spray of blood that splashed onto the porch's faded floorboards.

I didn't know why these men wanted us dead, but that they were here at all meant we were enemies. Neanderthal as it may have seemed, it was us or them.

And it sure as hell would not be us.

Someone whimpered close by and I knew instinctively that it was Emma. I turned, searching across the war zone that our living room was fast turning into as plant pots and furniture exploded, showering debris all over the floor.

Emma had crawled behind a table where she huddled, her eyes

wide and frightened like a child. While the rest of us defended our home with everything that we had, Emma only sat hunched over, arms wrapped around her knees, unable to move.

Her terror was palpable, yet I couldn't think about her — not with everything else that was happening. So, I tore my eyes away, to find the face of the woman I now called my wife.

She had stopped firing, realizing that our shorter ranged weapons weren't doing much against their snipers. In fact, it suddenly occurred to me it was stupid to even try.

One wrong move and they would have us in their crosshairs.

Sam suddenly darted to the nearest window and drew the curtains closed.

"Block the windows! They can't shoot us if they can't see us!" she instructed.

Moving as fast as I could, I closed the curtains around the windows on my side of the room while Gideon helped Sam with hers. In the murky half-light that remained, nothing felt real. I was in a nightmare that surely I would wake up from any second now.

A noise came from behind, raising the hackles on my neck.

Spinning around, I raised my gun, ready to blast the scumbag to kingdom come until I saw the two familiar figures sneaking around the kitchen.

Chase and Bandit.

They were scrambling across the kitchen floor, staying low to avoid getting hit. I watched as Chase grabbed a hand towel, shoved it into the sink, then turned the taps on full. The metal of the taps glistened, encased by the flowing water that now flowed around the worktop, soaking the floor tiles.

What was she doing?

Was she was trying to flood the house? What would that solve? The questions ran through my mind until it suddenly occurred to me — she wasn't trying to drown our home. She wanted to protect us in case the men tried to set the place ablaze. She was making sure we wouldn't be trapped inside a burning building.

This thought hadn't come out of nowhere, but from our previous defense of the ranch, when, with our backs up against the wall, we had improved Molotov cocktails using Zeb's prized moonshine.

But we had none of that now.

The moonshine — which had taken Zeb months to perfect — was long gone, but Chase, in her infinite wisdom, was covering the floor with water and giving us an extra chance at survival.

She was buying us time.

My heart swelled with pride even as I knew it was pointless to resist any more. What could we do against a skilled team of killers? We had been lucky to escape the last attack by Forbes's men, but we wouldn't be so fortunate a second time.

"Sam," I called out above the noise. "We need to get out. We'll never survive this."

"They have the front blocked. Pretty sure they'll be pushing us from the back if they haven't started to already," she said.

Bobbing and weaving, I ran to the other side of the room, keeping away from those windows as best I could, knowing that obscuring their vision might not be a foolproof way of protecting us since they could still shoot through the thin material.

The smell of powder hung in the air. Across the front yard, the shooters were moving with urgency, forming a tight semi-circle as they advanced toward us. In addition to their snipers, they now carried riot shields they held out before them in a defensive black wall. The shields were full length, covering them from head-to-toe. Their heads, along with their bodies, were completely hidden from view. With almost no place we could shoot them, things were looking really bad for us.

I racked my brain, trying to come up with a solution that would keep us alive when a hail of bullets tore through the walls and windows. Emma screamed, her cry piercing the air, cutting through my terror.

"Back up," I hissed at my family, reaching out to grab the

handlebars of Zeb's wheelchair. He kept himself bent so low, his head almost touched his knees as I wrestled with his chair, trying to get him as far away from those shooters as possible.

I was almost to the kitchen before I noticed only Gideon and Sam still with me. Chase and Bandit had gone ahead, vanishing from view, but it was the figure crouching beneath a table that caused my heart to leap into my throat.

Emma hadn't moved.

I wasted a moment, scanning my eyes up and down her body, expecting to see blood blossoming from a gunshot wound, but there was no injury that I could find. She was just scared: too scared to come out from there.

Sam read the expression on my face. The blood left her face, leaving her white as a sheet. "No!" she uttered when I bolted toward Emma.

More shots flew in, ricocheting off the walls, eating up a path everywhere they hit. A bullet went past my head, so close that pain exploded in my right ear. All sound dulled in that ear as a high-pitched whine took over.

I knew I must have been hit, but assumed the bullet hadn't done too much damage as I was still standing. Keeping my eyes glued to Emma, I sprinted to her side, taking hold of her hand.

"Come on," I said urgently, tugging her along. But she resisted, using her body weight to pull away from me.

"Leave me alone!" she yelled. "This has nothing to do with me!"

I spared a quick glance at the open doorway. The row of men were seconds from breaching the house. We had to go… *now*.

"We don't have time for this," I hissed through gritted teeth. Hauling her onto her feet, I tossed her over my shoulder as if she wasn't more than a sack of potatoes.

She struggled against me, out of her mind with fear. Although she must have known that I was trying to keep her safe, she resisted every step of the way, pummelling my back with her small fists.

"Let me go!" she screamed until I set her down with the others.

I caught the furious look Sam shot me and turned away. I'd have to deal with her anger later — if there was a later. Looking through the small window in the kitchen, I saw another row of the shielded men.

Jesus.

They were everywhere.

We couldn't go out either end, and since we lived in a ranch, there was no upstairs we could flee to either, even if it would trap us on an upper floor.

We were out of options and time.

My tongue felt thick in my mouth. I was struggling to form the words to our predicament. While we could split up and hide, that would buy us mere seconds at best, and try as I might, I wasn't ready to separate the family. If we were going to die, then it would be together.

My eyes scanned the group, memorizing each beloved face, when I noticed two were still missing.

My heart near stopped by the realization.

"Where are Chase and Bandit?" I asked, a sick feeling in the pit of my stomach.

Shocked silence greeted me, only to be quickly replaced by a furious rumbling from outside.

The house seemed to quake from the ground up as something big and fast came hurtling toward the ranch. Before I had a chance to react, the western wall of the room disintegrated into rubble when an armored truck careened right through it, mowing down several armed men who had just stepped into the house.

Dust and rubble fogged the air, turning it thick and making it impossible to breathe without choking. I coughed, fear clouding my mind as I considered what fresh horror this could be when the driver's door flew open and a familiar - and beloved head - leaned out of it.

"What are you waiting for?" Chase cried. "Get in!"

I gaped at her in astonishment. How the heck had she gotten outside, and where had the truck come from?

"Come on idiots, get in before they come after us!"

Shooting to my feet, I grabbed Zeb's wheelchair and sprinted to her. "In the truck. Now!" I yelled at everyone else.

Despite the stunned faces, they all — even Emma — did as instructed.

We climbed into the truck as Chase slammed the door shut. Stepping on the gas, burning rubber so that the tires squealed, we tore out of the place we called home.

7
____

CHASE

I floored it.

My hands gripped the wheel so tightly I thought my fingers would snap off. I had only driven a few times before - thanks to some lessons with Gideon - so I wasn't entirely comfortable driving this humongous thing, but I was doing my best to keep my concerns to myself, what with the army of bad guys hot on our heels.

Bandit sat beside me, stomach pressed to his seat. He kept his head beneath the window, beneath the line of sight. His intelligent eyes fixed on me, silently urging me on as he pricked his ears and scanned the area, listening for any sign of approaching trouble.

The truck I had stolen was a bit of a beast, made from some kind of reinforced metal that meant it wasn't even dented, not even after ramming into the side of a house. And it wasn't only the outside that was impressive: the inside was a thing of beauty too.

The interior walls were lined with custom shelves that were filled with ammo of all kinds. I recognized the .38 specials that Gideon used in his revolvers, mixed in with .45s, but some grew to wickedly big sizes, almost the same length as my phone. A chill went through me as I wondered why anyone would ever need bullets *that* big: they looked like they could take down an elephant.

Had they been meant for us?

Shoving the horrifying thought from my mind, I looked into the rearview mirror so I could see directly into the attached cabin where the others were doing their best to strap Zeb's wheelchair to one the steel benches, secured to the truck's sides. The benches had extendable seatbelts for extra security. Directly opposite from them was an office of sorts.

There was a metal table where a high-tech looking laptop, that was connected to several flat screen monitors, sat. From my quick glance, I also spotted a weird-looking phone and what seemed to be a map.

Lowering onto a bench, Sam was reaching for her own seatbelt when she saw Emma, struggling to stay upright in the middle of the cabin. There was a glazed look in her eyes, like she wasn't really seeing anything.

I knew she was in shock, though she seemed to have enough of her faculties around her to know that she didn't trust any of us. This apparently led her to the decision to stay as far away from us as she could.

Sam called over to her. "You need to sit down before you hurt yourself."

Emma tossed her a terrified look. "Who are those men? Why are you kidnapping me?!"

Sam's eyes turned bright with annoyance.

"We're trying to keep you safe! Sit down before you get your-self killed."

Emma looked as if she wanted to argue back. She chewed on her lower lip making no move to comply. It was only when the truck went over a rough part of the road, causing her to almost lose her balance, that she took a seat by Sam — though far enough away that there was an empty space between them.

Sam waited, but Emma made no move to secure herself. "You need to strap yourself in," she hissed.

Emma shot her a look of confusion..

"Strap myself into what?"

Gritting her teeth, Sam grabbed the seatbelt that was fixed onto the wall of the truck, wrapping it around the other woman and clipping it into place.

"You don't know how to use a seatbelt?" asked Sam.

Emma's only response was to look down at her hands. It seemed she really hadn't understood what Sam had instructed her to do. Bracing her hands on either side of her, Sam waited for someone to break the silence that smothered the truck.

"At least we can fight back. Should be a while before we run out of bullets," I said over my shoulder, hoping to break the tension between them. Of course, this was a mistake as the truck swerved beneath my hands. My heart plummeted to my stomach as I tried to straighten up. The truck felt so unwieldy, but we didn't have time to stop and change drivers: in the side mirrors, I could see the men piling into three identical trucks.

"Get ready, they're coming," I yelled. *Why couldn't they just leave us alone?*

A deathly silence greeted my warning until Gideon's voice broke it. There was a new stressed tone in it I didn't like.

"I don't have my guns," he admitted.

"Why not?" I cried out, flicking my eyes to him briefly, then wishing I hadn't when I saw the sick look on his face.

"I dropped them to help Zeb."

"I'm empty, too," Sully echoed his words, seeming to shrink before us. Sam was looking his way with a knowing expression.

"He had to drop it when he went to save Emma," she said. Her voice wasn't loud but carried the weight of an anvil that might as well be dropping on my head.

"Are you telling me Sam's the only one with a weapon?"

I pretty much shrieked out the question, but I couldn't help it, having to leave my gun behind when I crawled out of the basement window with Bandit in order to steal the truck.

They didn't bother to ask where mine was, having figured out that I didn't have it. What did it matter where it had gotten to? We had one weapon between the seven of us. Our chance of survival was less than zero at this point.

Suddenly, a barrage of hailstones pelted the truck, leaving crater-like dents in its metal frame. One after the other, they clattered against the vehicle. The awful noise reverberated around the truck, deafening us, causing Bandit to howl next to me. Dogs had much better hearing than we did, so if the noise was affecting me so badly, I can only imagine how painful it was for him.

Examining one dent, Gideon suddenly gasped. "The truck's bullet-proof!" He yelled, his voice filled with a sudden excitement.

Sully reached out his hand to touch the wall when several more dents appeared right beneath his fingertips. He yanked his hand back, but it wasn't necessary — the bullets could not make it through the reinforced metal.

"He's right," Sully said, relief turning his face slack. His shoulders sagged, letting go of the tension that had kept his back ramrod straight. "They can't hit us through the truck."

"Then why are they shooting at us? Wouldn't they know that?" I asked.

A furrow creased Zeb's forehead as he studied the trajectory of the dents. "I think they're trying to get wheels. And maybe Chase too. It's possible the glass isn't bulletproof."

At this revelation, I felt super vulnerable sitting in-between several large panes of glass.

"Not that I want to be the bearer of more bad news," I began, "but we're driving across an open field right now. There aren't even trees that can hide us: there's no way I can lose them."

Sully glanced out of his nearest window, his eyes turning black with seriousness. "We need to stop them from following us."

"I'm not liking our chances of taking potshots at them with only the one gun," Gideon began.

Scanning the cabin, Sully's eyes alighted on a metal box that sat on the desk beside the laptop.

He suddenly smiled, eyes glinting with hardness. "We won't have to. I've a better idea."

8

SULLY

Sprinting to the box, I lifted it carefully from the desk, eyeing the small oval objects with a mix of fear and reverence.

"Chase, I'm going to need you to keep the truck as steady as you can, OK?"

Hearing the gravity in my voice, she tried to crane her head to me.

"No! Keep your eyes up front," I yelled at her. "Keep it steady and straight, you understand? Our lives depend on you doing that.

Chase gaped at me in the rearview mirror. "What's going on? What's happening?"

"Are you thinking what I think you're thinking?" Sam asked, her eyes wide and round as she stared at the box's contents.

"Son?" Zeb asked, a world of understatement in that one-worded question.

"Holy crap," Gideon exclaimed, sending Chase's hackles rising.

"Someone needs to explain what is going on before I totally lose it!" she yelled as Bandit barked in agreement, sounding as peeved as she was.

"Chase, I've found a box of grenades."

She didn't immediately answer. Needing a moment for my words to sink in. I grabbed the box of grenades, carefully handing them to Sam. "Hold on to these a sec."

Moving back to the table, I grabbed the laptop, sliding it to the back of the cabin as I tipped the table onto its side. It was wide enough that it came up to my shoulder. Grabbing onto the corner, I half pushed, half shoved the table across the floor until it was positioned in front of the gate. It wasn't much, but I hoped it would provide some form of protection.

"When I say ready, Gideon, I'm going to need you to slide up the back gate. Sam, keep yourself strapped in, but I need you to hold on tight to my belt, so I don't get tossed if we hit a bump or something."

Chase blinked several times, her face growing paler by the second.

"*That's the plan?* You're going to lob grenades at them? What is this, Call of Duty? What if you miss? What if one of them falls out of your hand and rolls back into the cab with us?"

She was voicing the concerns I had already run through my head, but I needed to keep them all calm — Chase most of all — since she was the one responsible for keeping the ride smooth.

"None of that will happen if you focus on the driving. This is all we have to fight back with Chase, so that's what it's got to be. Sam, Gid, get ready."

"No!" Emma shouted suddenly, sprinting back and forth like a trapped animal. "You're all crazy! I don't want to get blown up. Let me out!"

As if she was going to leap over the seats, she ran towards Chase, but Bandit snapped his head around to her, growling fiercely and baring his fangs in warning. Stopping her short. He was smart enough to know what Emma wasn't — that her panic could distract Chase into crashing the truck.

She shirked away from him, retreating to her corner, scared out of her mind, but at least, out of the way for the moment.

Gideon's fear was palpable as he moved away from Dad and towards the back of the truck. Sam sat back in her seat, her trembling hands indicating her anxiety about my plan; although she knew we had no alternatives, that didn't mean she wanted to do it. She fiddled with the belt buckle until it locked into place.

These men had forced us into a terrible position. They were forcing my hand.

Trying not to think about the devastation I was about to cause, I made my way to the gate. As I ducked behind the table shield, Sam looped her fingers through my belt until she had a strong grip on me. Raising her eyes to mine, she gave me a terse smile.

"Give them hell."

My heart swelled with so much love for her it almost brought tears to my eyes. What a woman.

I spared a look in Chase's direction. "Let me know when you're ready, Chase."

"Oh God, Oh God, Oh God," she chanted in a panic. "Wait! Give me a second."

I kept quiet, giving Chase a few seconds to think, although our time was limited. Our only hope was to take out these criminals as quickly as possible and make our escape. Finally, after what seemed like an eternity, Chase nodded.

"I'm as good as I'll ever be."

I turned my focus to Gideon. "Ready?"

Gideon nodding, not trusting himself to speak. His hands hovered over the switch that would raise the gate. Opening my legs wider, I bent my knees, taking a bigger stance, hoping it would help keep my balance should anything happen.

I took hold of the first grenade and carefully placed it into the pocket of my hoodie, making sure the pin couldn't accidentally be knocked out. The metal was bitingly cold, and the grenade felt a lot lighter than I thought it would.

I'd never had any dealings with these tiny instruments of death, so there was no way of knowing how heavy they were supposed to be, or even, preparing myself for the handling of them.

Everything I knew about them, I had learned from watching Gideon and Chase play those popular video games back when we had visited my old clinic. The new vets who had taken over the place enjoyed playing games, though I would never allow the kids to have a console. They'd had enough dealings with violence to last a lifetime.

Now, of course, I was kicking myself.

I would have put time into the games myself if it meant having a better handle on our current situation.

I loaded up each of my three other available pockets with grenades, then grabbed one in each hand. Nodding at Gideon, I gave the command.

"Now!"

Gideon slammed his hand on the switch. As the gate rose, I pulled the pin out of the first grenade, making sure that I had the safety lever firmly gripped and pressed down to the side. As long as I didn't let go, the grenade would not go off until a few seconds after I released the lever.

I could not afford any mistakes. I would blow us all to smithereens if I did.

A cloud of dust blew up, kicked up by the racing vehicles. The trucks weren't too far away from us, maybe only fifty feet or so, and closing rapidly. Sweat broke out across my forehead as I imagined their snipers focusing their sights on me.

If I were going to do this, I only had seconds before they would inevitably start firing. Seconds before I dropped to the ground with the armed grenade in my hand…

Aiming for the closest vehicle to us, I hurled the first grenade at it.

The world slowed right down. I held my breath, watching as the grenade sailed through the air in a perfect arc. When it started coming down, I knew I had mis-timed my throw as it landed to one side, far enough away that I wasn't sure it would do any damage to the truck behind us.

Was that enough?

Would it have any effect?

I was still wondering when KABOOM!

The grenade exploded, sending forth a wave of debris that fogged the air causing the trucks to swerve wildly to one side. A hole appeared on the road, cracks forming on the rough surface in an ad hoc pattern. They weren't large enough to be a problem for the truck's wheels, but they'd feel it.

Taking another grenade out of my pocket, I primed it when a glint of something moving caught my eye. Ice water filled my veins as I saw the point of one of their snipers sticking out of an open window. At the speed we were traveling, with the uneasiness of the road's surface, I wasn't so much worried over the unlikelihood of a bullet hitting me: I was concerned that it would miss me and get one of the others.

Knowing I couldn't waste another moment, I hurled the second grenade. It flew like a guided missile, twisting through the space between us until it landed a few feet in front of the truck's path.

The driver's expression changed the instant he knew there was no way to get away from the blast. His gaze dropped to the ground as his face filled with terror. His mouth hung open in a voiceless scream as the force of the explosion sent the truck toppling over, scraping several feet along the dirt until it finally came to a grinding stop. The truck behind it was going much too fast to stop. The driver tried to swerve away, but the bumper clipped the downed truck, causing his vehicle to fishtail. They careened into the last truck.

Then all was still.

Gideon whooped behind me as Chase tried desperately not to spin around in her seat.

"Did it work?" she all but cried out the question.

I didn't answer, watching as the men crawled out of the trucks. A few limped out, having to be helped by their friends. Their shirts were torn. I could see cuts and bruises, but the majority of them seemed unharmed.

Which meant I had only delayed them for a moment. As soon as they were able to fix up their vehicles or call in reinforcement, they would be after us again.

Unless I made sure I put a stop to them.

Taking out another grenade, I armed and threw it at the pile-up that now blocked the road. Before that could even detonate, I tossed out the last remaining grenade.

The explosion that came was several times the size of the others. The force was so great; it knocked me backward and onto my butt. The table slid aside. Pain flew up my tailbone.

Thick black smoke swallowed the world. I could barely see two feet in front of me.

"Is everyone OK?" I called into the cab.

A chorus of "yeses" rose in answer, including one very distinctive bark. Only Emma didn't speak, but she stood far enough back to be unaffected by the blast. I'd check on her as soon as I could, but right now, I needed to see what remained of the small army that had come after us.

"Can I stop now? Did you stop them?" Chase asked pretty desperately.

"I don't know. I can't see through the smoke. Keep going," I instructed. "We need to put as much distance away from home as possible. We can't stop and we can't go back."

As the words left my mouth, their message hit home like a ton of bricks. Our lives. Everything we had built over the last half a year, including my mom's little touches that she had imprinted on the ranch before she had passed away… We were leaving it all behind.

For the second time in my life, I was having to flee my home with no warning.

The truck hurtled along as Chase floored the gas. I signaled it was safe for Sam to let go of my belt. She loosened her hands, which had been gripped tightly onto me. With my hands now empty of grenades, I held onto one of the metal brackets that was welded onto the truck, my eyes straining to see behind us.

Finally, I spotted some shapes inside the cloud of black smoke. The trucks were burned out, hollowed husks of themselves. They looked like something out of a movie, their sides eaten away by the blast. I kept my eyes peeled for signs of movement, only to spot two shadowy figures crawling out from the wreckage.

From this distance away, even if the smoke wasn't an issue, I wouldn't have been able to make out their faces. But one man, the taller of the two, with a slimline shape, stood his ground, feet planted on either side of him, staring at us.

Reeking of animosity.

A chill went down my spine, spreading until it froze my feet to the floor. Call it intuition, but in that very moment, I knew without a doubt that we would see those men again.

Only this time, they would bring bigger guns and more manpower.

Needing to erase the image of that shadowy figure watching us, I strode over to Gideon and hit the switch. The gate shuttered down, providing a wall between us and them.

I couldn't see them anymore. Couldn't see the wreckage and destruction I had caused. I had expected to feel vindicated. Instead, I felt sick to my stomach.

Having spent my entire life saving lives, I was horrified by the deaths I had likely caused, even if I had excellent reasons for my actions. I looked at Sam to see the same conflicted emotions across her face. When she caught my stare, she gave me a wobbly smile of support.

Turning, my eyes found Emma where she had slid along the bench until she was as far as possible from the rest of us. The whites of her eyes seemed brighter than they should be. She shiv-ered, arms wrapped around herself.

"Are you okay?" I asked.

In response, she shot me a wild look. "You should have just left me there. You people are completely insane." Curling into a ball, she turned her back to us.

9

CHASE

My fingernails dug into the leather of the steering wheel, my knuckles turning white. The last minute felt like an eternity; as if time had slowed to a crawl, and any wrong move would lead us straight to hell. It was so much pressure that I just was not prepared for.

There was a massive tightness in my chest that wasn't a familiar sensation. I hadn't hit anything. I wasn't injured. Yet there it was, this rapidly rising pressure that threatened to crush me.

A hand fell onto my shoulder — Sully's. That was enough to help me release the breath I had been holding since he had shouted his crazy plan. He squeezed my shoulder, letting me know he was well, then climbed in next to me.

"In just a second, we're going to swap seats. Keep your feet on the gas. I'm going to put my foot on the pedal, then you're going to hop over me to the right while I slide left. Understand?"

The fact we couldn't even stop for a second to change drivers told me we weren't out of danger. My mouth went dry but I nodded. I couldn't wait to be relieved of driving duty — I was pretty sure I'd never volunteer again.

In fact, this entire experience had put me off driving for good. I was done.

"OK… now!" he said, his foot having already stepped onto the gas. The second Sully grabbed hold of the wheel, I released my grip, hopping over him quickly while he took over the reins.

My legs, however, had a mind of their own. Frozen stiff from all the tension, they refused to cooperate. They tangled up with his until I managed to pull myself clear and stumbled, face-first, onto the seat beside Bandit. He lowered his nose to the back of my head, so close that I could feel his breath blowing into my neck.

"I'm fine, boy."

He woofed, satisfied with my answer, and raised his nose to the sky to take in all the scents that were like another language for him. Within those smells, he could determine a million factors that our human brains would never understand.

Sully checked each of the mirrors, making sure we weren't followed while I tried to regain my composure. My heart was still thumping a beat in my chest: I was hoping it would calm soon or I was pretty sure I'd be having a heart attack — at fifteen. I knew it was possible since I'd read it in a magazine once… and we all knew how my photographic memory had a habit of being right.

Bandit laid his head on my lap, his eyes rolling up to look at me. I stroked him, half to comfort him, half for myself. I couldn't believe what had just happened and wasn't ready to deal with any of it yet. I was just happy to sit there petting my dog, pretending that none of that madness had just occurred… but all the while, Sully's eyes burned into me. Even though I didn't want to. Even though I knew some kind of tirade was coming, my eyes slid over to him.

"Have you any idea how much danger you were in?"

He had his bug-eyed look, a look that I'd only seen a handful of times in all the time I'd known him. He wasn't kidding around. Sully was mad as all hell right now and that was on top of being scared for our lives.

"Pretty sure we were all in the same boat," I said, not meaning to sound flippant. My back was up, and truthfully, my pride was taking a beating too. I had got us out of the ranch, hadn't I? We had been sitting ducks in that place. "It wasn't looking particularly good for any of us."

Apparently, common sense had left the vehicle and taken a long trip away.

"So you thought you'd run out there *toward* the men with guns?" Sully demanded, gripping onto the dashboard so hard I thought he would rip it off. Unnerved by his anger, Bandit whined, then shifted his head to Sully's lap in an attempt to comfort him.

"Well, we'd managed to sneak out the last time someone attacked here us. I figured we might get lucky again if Bandit and I took the basement route out. And you know what? I was right. They didn't expect us to be going to them. No one was in the vehicles. No one paid any attention to us until it was too late."

Instead of being impressed by my explanation, Sully only grew angrier. A vein throbbed on his forehead, threatening to burst.

"You shouldn't have gone out there without me. I don't care that you were successful. You were lucky this time, Chase, like you were lucky when you stole the helicopter, but this luck is going to have to run out sometime!"

I was wounded to the quick. Wasn't he going to give me *any* credit for getting us out of there? He sat, a volcano about to blow, while I was burning up a decent rage too.

A hand came over the seat to rest on Sully's shoulder. Followed by dangling ends of blonde hair that crested over the back of the headrest. "It's OK, Sully. It's OK."

She said nothing more than that, but kept her hand on his shoulder. Like magic, Sully's heat faded. Sam was a calming breeze to his rage. When she saw that his anger had receded, she gave him a hug, then sat back down.

"You don't risk yourself, Chase. That's what I'm trying to say."

His voice cracked at the end of the sentence as a weariness came over him. Some of my bravado vanished. I knew he was right, but at the time, all I could think was that they were all in danger. I couldn't stand by and let them all die after everything our family had been through.

"I'm sorry. I didn't really think. I just wanted to get us out of there. We were trapped in that house, and we couldn't even shoot at them with our guns since they were too far away. I know I shouldn't have done it, but I would do it again if it would keep us safe."

I was as stubborn as they came. I also knew that no matter the danger, I would always risk my life for them. They were my people. My family. Bandit was my best friend, and no one was going to kill him. Not while I had anything to say about it.

His eyes became suddenly bright.

"Chase, you still don't get it. You're the kid. I'm the parent. It's on me to keep us safe. Not you."

"Aren't you the one who's always grumbling that you're too young to have all these teenagers?" I tried for brevity, knowing how desperately it was needed right now.

"I risk my life, Chase. Not you. Not ever you," Sully finished, looking stricken.

Feeling the love flow out of him, my lips curled into an apologetic smile. "Sorry."

He nodded. His gruff way of accepting my apology. The car sped along the winding road, the engine roaring like a lion as the wind whipped against my face. I sat in the passenger seat, staring blindly at the countryside rushing past us, reliving every moment of the attack like it was happening all over again. Even when I closed my eyes, I could still see the faces of the men, their eyes full of intention, as the lasers from their guns danced dangerously close to my loved ones.

I don't know how long I stayed motionless, my thoughts a jumble of confusion and distress. I was startled out of my reverie by the sound of a familiar whine. Bandit, my loyal companion, had come to my side, nudging me gently with his wet nose, his eyes filled with concern. He shoved his face into my hands. My fingers wove into his fur, craving the familiarity of his comforting presence.

"Does anyone know who they were?" Sully asked, only to be greeted with a wave of shaking heads. Seemed no one had a clue. Sully turned his attention to Emma — the new unknown in our group.

"But they have something to do with you."

From where she sat across from us, Emma looked at him. "I have never seen them before in my life. Then again, I've never seen any of *you* before in my life."

"But that doesn't change the fact that they turned up hours after you did," Gideon mused out loud, weighing up the facts. Of course, Emma took offense at his words.

"Those men were trying to kill *you*. Why are you trying to blame me? I have nothing to do with any of this. Can you just let me out? It was a big mistake coming to you for help."

"I can't do that. It's not safe." He didn't explain who it wasn't safe for.

"It does seem too big a coincidence that they arrived within a day of you," Sam said. "It seems likely that she led them to us."

"I told you I don't know who they are! I don't even know who I am! Why would I lead them to you when Sully is my only link to this world? How do you know they're not after me?"

The second the question left her lips, the blood drained from her face. "Could they be after me?"

Her only answer was the silence that blanketed the vehicle like a thick fog. The dull buzz of the engine and the occasional crunch of gravel under the tires were the only sounds that penetrated the silence. Twisting to face Sully, she pleaded, "You have to help me! You can't let them kill me. I need to find out who I am and why I'm here."

The poor guy was in complete torture, his gaze sliding between Sam, then Emma, then back to Sam.

I couldn't even begin to understand how he must be feeling. How could anyone have known that his dead wife would come back to life like this? Had this happened last year, when I had just met Sully, this would have been the miracle he had been praying for. But now… So much could change in a year.

"We need to stop. Come up with a plan. Let's pool our resources, see what we have with us," said Zeb, the voice of reason. He sounded calm, yet in control. He was the leader we needed right now.

"We can't go home. All we have is what's on us and what we can find in this truck."

Gideon left his seat, coming up behind. "At least they don't seem to be following us."

Sully wasn't doing a good job of pretending things were fine: I could feel the tension pouring off him in waves. The air inside the truck was thick with unspoken emotion, and each passing moment only seemed to exacerbate the stifling atmosphere. Several moments passed with only the sound of the road beneath our tires filling the space. When he finally spoke, it was with quiet resignation.

"Somehow, I don't think that's the last we'll see of them."

His words hung heavy in the air.

10

THE CLEANER

Black smoke billowed from the burning trucks, mixing with the heat of the flames. Their acrid dryness scratched at the back of his throat, making him thirst for water.

Having eaten through the fuel that had leaked from the trucks, the fire was finally beginning to die down. Trucks lay in ruins, their twisted metal frames still glowing from the intense heat that had engulfed them only moments earlier. Charred bodies littered the ground, some so badly burned that they were no longer recognizable.

His men — or what remained of them.

Some had been with him through hell and back. They'd met serving in the military, risking life and limb as they battled hostiles in foreign lands. What they'd shared hadn't been just friendship, but a sacred bond. A brotherhood that was sealed with their own blood.

Now his brothers lay in pieces.

He forced the rising grief away, knowing there wasn't time for that now. There was much cleaning to do, and it had to be done *fast*.

He made the call, hating the silence that came down the line when he was forced to request an additional crew to help with the mess. But, with time of the essence, it couldn't be helped.

Milton hunched over the still body, his six-four frame awkward with the strain of an injured right arm, sustained during the pursuit when an explosion had flung him out of a vehicle. Only his sheer size had saved him when he'd landed in a ditch. Though The Cleaner knew it to be pointless, he watched as Milton pressed his fingers to the body's neck.

The man was gone.

"We need to move the bodies out of sight," he instructed Milton and his other surviving man, Bond. "Help is on the way, but we can't take the chance of someone driving past, spotting them and asking questions."

Bond nodded, face and beard crusted with dirt, making it seem as if he had turned gray early. In his late forties, he might be the oldest, but a lifetime of working out meant he was the epitome of health. His body was a well-oiled machine, one the Cleaner knew he could count on.

The three got to their macabre work, carrying or dragging their former colleagues away, hiding them in the fields of corn that flanked the road. The blood stains they could do nothing about, and the trucks would have to be left as they were for now.

When the road was as clear as they could make it, the three sat and waited.

When the job had come down the line initially, he had studied the notes with the meticulous attention to detail that he used for everything. Didn't matter if he was at home, surrounded by three noisy children, cooking a simple meal in the apartment he stayed at whenever he was on a job, or fixing whatever needed fixing for his bosses, John Smith — as he was known — was a stickler for details, planning everything within an inch of its life.

Take the raid at the Montpelier ranch.

He had scouted the operation himself. During his recon, disguised as an electrician from the local utility company, working alone — which is how he preferred it — he had been parked in his van, logging the family's comings and goings for several weeks.

Ever since his discovery of Xavier's experiments.

Every morning, the boy would pick up fresh donuts and pastries from the local grocery store though the sheriff never had much time for breakfast. The girl would play some game on her phone with the dog, usually with the vet and old man joining in. It all seemed so wholesome. Just your typical American family with their genetically modified, unnatural experiment of a pet. They were as predictable as the sun rising at dawn.

Or so he'd thought.

The paperwork that lined the walls at the abandoned school was unsalvageable, destroyed by the sprinklers, as were the computers with nearly two decades worth of Xavier's research. If not for that single strand of blonde hair he had found, attached to that ominous-looking tank in the basement, Smith wouldn't have had much to report.

But in that single strand of hair lay an enormous threat to the future of mankind.

And that there was the problem.

It should have been a straightforward operation, but he'd never bargained on the arsenal of weapons inside the house or the family's relentless will to survive. Left with no choice, they'd had to return fire.

His thoughts were interrupted by a car appearing on the horizon. Peering through his binoculars, Smith could see there was only the one driver. He felt a pang of relief.

One person could be easily dealt with.

His nightmare scenario would be a family… *with children.* Though he didn't want to think about it, he knew that no matter what his feelings were, he would have to do his job.

When the driver finally pulled over, hurrying out of his car to assist them, Bond handled the matter in the way he would have done himself. He knocked the driver out with a simple blow to the back of the head. He'd been so efficient, Smith doubted the man would ever know what had happened.

Hiding his car behind the wreckage of the trucks, they continued to wait.

Two hours later, they were rewarded by the sight of what looked to be a first response unit for a natural disaster. There were several fire trucks, ambulances, and police vans among the procession. Only the police vans darkened windows hinted that they might not have been the real deal.

Smith got to his feet to greet them. He had only to give the briefest of instruction. The men — and they were all men — got to work setting up cones and road signs, implying a burst gas main had caused an explosion.

The bodies were quickly sealed into bags, then taken away by ambulance for disposal at a nearby hospital. Their families would be fed a story of their heroic deaths and receive more money than they could ever use under the guise of insurance policies.

Back at the ranch, the area was going through a similar process where all trace of the warfare would be erased. Not a single bullet hole or shell casing would be left. He wasn't sure what cover story would be created — there was a separate PR department to handle that — but it would have to be strong enough for the locals to believe.

Leaving the crew to finish up the task, Smith was examined by a doctor, deemed fit if bruised and battered, and left at a nearby motel. Milton had been whisked away for his arm shattered arm to be replaced, leaving him with only Bond in the next room.

He showered, washing away the grime of the attack. Later, Bond brought over food from the place next door. The burgers were greasy, the fries, limp, but Smith inhaled them as if it was his last meal.

He'd spent several hours on his satellite phone, answering questions about the day's travesty that had cost his department six figures to handle. His bosses were not happy and needed assurances that the job would be completed.

He swore that it would.

When the light started to fade, Smith called home, his lips curling into a big smile when his three young kids answered, clamoring over each other to talk to him.

He answered their questions as truthfully as he could — it was much easier to bend the truth rather than outright lie. They and everyone else, including his wife, thought he was a consultant for an oil company. The cover gave him the freedom to take off at a moment's notice. It also paid well, helping him to look after his family.

"When are you coming home?" His youngest asked.

"Hopefully soon. I don't think this job will take that much longer to finish."

"Don't forget my present, Daddy."

Smith laughed, picturing the pout on his four-year-old's face. "As if I ever would."

"I brushed my teeth by myself," he boasted, so proud of himself.

"Wow. What a good boy you are. If you put yourself to bed, Mommy will come and kiss you goodnight soon."

"'K. Byeeee!" Smith heard him yelling as he started running to his room. A moment later, his wife's concerned voice came over the line.

"Did you hear about that explosion? Something about a gas main. I saw it on the news. It's not far from where you are is it?"

No, honey. Not far at all.

"I heard, but I wasn't near it. Don't worry."

He heard her exhale, relieved.

They chatted about her day, what the kids had gotten up to, how the house down the street had finally sold. Inane, boring conversation. It was music to his ears.

All too soon, it was time to go. After promising he would be home soon, Smith hung up the phone, then went to sit by the desk. Opening his laptop, he hit the power button, but instead of coming on, the screen filled with static before blinking out entirely.

Smith rubbed his forehead, fighting the urge to toss the useless thing at the wall. Truth be told, he should have checked earlier that it was in working order, but with one thing after another, it had slipped his mind.

And now he would pay the price.

Sighing, he picked up the phone again, keying in the number for his boss.

11

SULLY

All around us the landscape was flat, with the occasional clump of trees and a clear stretch of road before us, lined with endless rows of corn. A sea of yellow stretching as far as the eye could see that we could have been in the plains of Iowa instead of a hundred or so miles west of Montpelier.

Ordinarily, this would have been of some comfort, but today, the openness, the wideness of the expanse, made me antsy. We were exposed to every passerby. It made us sitting ducks, though if those men were to turn up again, the one positive was we'd be able to spot them coming from a distance.

The road remained mostly empty, with only an occasional car motoring past. If more men were coming, they wouldn't catch up to us for a while — and that's even if they knew what direction we had traveled. Even I didn't know where we were, or where we were heading. It was disorienting. I felt like I had no control over anything.

I had to hope the uncertainty would buy us time to plan our next move.

As I drove, I found my eyes glancing over at the artillery strapped to the walls of the truck. I quickly scanned the ammunition, pushing away any memories of the men and their guns targeting my family. My gaze moved to that high-tech laptop that had been returned to the upright table (somewhere, in the midst of all the chaos, it had been thrown clear across the cab), but there wasn't a dent on it. With its gleaming metallic lid and one-inch thick molded casing, it looked like it had landed straight out of a sci-fi flick. I wondered if we could make use of it somehow.

Zeb, however, had his mind on matters other than our weaponry. Reaching into his pocket, he retrieved his wallet. "How much cash do you have?"

We pooled our resources, Chase laying everything out onto the seat beside me.

Sam had her purse, but mine was back in our truck, along with our suitcases. We hadn't managed to bring them inside the house before all hell had kicked off.

Chase threw down a twenty-dollar bill she found in a back pocket. But other than that, there was only Zeb's wallet, which contained mostly cards rather than cash. When she turned to Emma, Emma clutched her bag tighter to her chest.

"I don't have any money. Can't you just leave me alone?"

Her misery tugged at my heart as an overwhelming urge to protect her came over me. I had to stop myself from launching across the truck to gather her into my arms. Of course, that immediately led to a crushing wave of guilt. As if my mind was cheating on my new wife with my old one.

Chase backed away from her. Since we had checked the contents earlier and knew what was — and wasn't — in there, we left her alone, neither one of us comfortable enough to approach her.

Taking out the cash from the wallets, Chase counted out our funds, which came to a measly hundred bucks.

"We're not going far on this," Zeb finally said, wishing desperately that the opposite was true.

Silence fell like a cloud. Still on high alert, her body tensed for any sign of danger, Sam's voice cut through our rising panic. "We should sweep the truck for bugs, cameras, and trackers."

She crossed to the table and felt beneath the underside of it while the others fanned out and began their search. When she couldn't find anything, she ducked her head under it only to surface moments later empty-handed. Gideon squatted down to examine the wheel-wells while I poured over the cab, keeping one hand on the steering wheel.

Chase didn't move, her slender frame perched beside me. "Um. What exactly am I looking for? Like, is it really going to have a flashing red light or beep like they do in the movies?"

"Just see if you can spot anything suspicious or out of place," Sam answered.

In lieu of responding, Chase's rolled her eyes, waving her hands around. Her meaning was clear to us all: *everything was suspicious and out of place.*

"I've only ever seen the ones Xavier used, which I swear he picked up at Radio Shack," Gideon replied. "Doesn't seem like these guys would have shopped in the same place."

"Would do you suggest?" I asked.

"Gideon, take over for Sully a moment. We need to work over this truck."

After checking the way was clear, I stopped the truck. We swapped places, though Chase shot me a momentary look of outrage until I raised a brow at her. "You really want the responsibility of driving this thing again?"

"No," she answered with only a hint of sulkiness. "Just figured you could at least ask, since I did such a great job."

"Woof!"

Ever her biggest cheerleader, Bandit made his opinion clear. I crossed over to the table and picked up the laptop.

Encased in steel, possibly even titanium, the laptop was small but looked indestructible. On the screen, a detailed 3D map of the surrounding area was shown. The map revealed not only road names but also nearby terrain. There were also indications of other elements of the landscape that would probably be helpful if only we had any idea what they meant.

A blinking green dot represented our current position. I pressed down on a few keys, but nothing happened.

I moved my fingers to the screen, wanting to see if it was touch-screen. Unfortunately, it responded to my touch by shutting down and a window popped up, requesting a fingerprint ID or user code to unlock it.

I uttered a curse under my breath.

Of course, the thing would be security protected. We'd be getting no further use out of it. "Other than our own phones, our biggest threat is that laptop," Sam said. "If it's showing our location to us, presumably it could do the same for them."

Beside the laptop, there were flashlights that looked as if they doubled as UV lights. Chase rummaged through the glove compartment to see what she could dig up, but the thing was empty. Not even a stick of gum.

"I've got nothing."

She checked the sun visors next, flicking them down, hoping to find paperwork or something tucked up in there, but, again, she came up empty.

The truck was conspicuously absent of any identifying information, and that filled me with no end of dread.

Only people that didn't want to be found, who had experience of staying invisible, could hide their tracks so well.

"You think these guys are related to Forbes? Or Xavier?" Chase asked.

"I don't think Xavier's involved with them. He was a two-man band. They do seem to be more Forbes' type of accomplice, but he's dead," I mused out loud.

"Not that it seems much of a problem these days," Gideon said, low enough that Emma wouldn't have heard him from the back of the cab.

"Gid, stop the truck for a sec. Park it off the road. I want to talk outside." Sam instructed.

Finding a spot he favored, Gideon killed the engine. We piled out of the truck — Gideon and I helping my dad out — though Emma stayed huddled inside, refusing to have anything to do with us.

"Leave her be. She just needs time to come around," Zeb seemed sure, though I didn't know where his newfound faith had come from, particularly given that he'd never met Emma before she had died. When we were a small distance away, Sam stretched out her hand to us.

"Give me your phones."

The adults passed their phones to her without hesitation, but Chase and Gideon's faces were identical in their displeasure.

"Seriously?" Chase moaned.

"Yes. You know they can track us on these," she replied.

"Can't we just take out the sim cards or turn them off?" Gideon asked.

"Even if we turn them off, devices can still be tracked nowa-days," Sam answered, killing the hope in their eyes.

Reluctantly, the kids handed over their phones. Taking out the sims, I crushed them in my hands, then tossed the phones to the ground, trampling on them with the heel of my boot until they were well and truly beyond repair.

"That hurt more than I thought it would," Gideon said.

"We'll get new ones when we come upon some cash. In the interim, you should think of the bright side," I offered.

"And that is?" Gideon asked.

"Since neither of you have any friends, anyone you would have called is already here." I was trying for a bit of lightheartedness, but it sank like a pound of rocks.

"So now I'm a loser with no friends *and* I'm being hunted by an army of killers? Great. Thanks."

I probably needed to practice my cheerleading skills and take a few lessons from Bandit.

"Now, the laptop."

Bandit bounded into the truck obediently, returning seconds later with it in his mouth, though he clearly struggled with the weight of the thing. Sam took it from him, ruffling his fur.

"Thanks, boy."

She threw it onto the ground. I stamped on it, hard as I could, digging in my heel, but I barely made a dent.

"Must be made of the same material as the truck," Gideon's mouth twitched, though he knew better than to outright laugh at me.

Moving to the truck, I positioned the laptop directly in front of one wheel and backed clear out of the way. On my signal, Gideon revved the engine and ran over it with the truck.

There was a popping sound as the laptop flattened into a thin disc. "Good luck tracing us with that," Chase commented.

"We need a place to stay, and supplies," Sam said. "And we need to get a move on. I'm not happy with us just being out in the open like this."

"I might know a place. Remember my friend Mark? He has a cabin on a lake in the middle of nowhere. He doesn't get out there very often and since he's got more money than sense, he refuses to rent it out, so it should be empty. He should be able to help us with money, too."

"Well, you can't call him with our phones," Gideon remarked unhelpfully, apparently still smarting.

"I wouldn't have used them, anyway. We need a public payphone."

We stared up and down the barren road. The only visible sign of human presence were the two sets of tire tracks that snaked down the center of the road from where we had come. Forget phones. There wasn't even a telephone pole in sight.

"What are we going to do until we find one?" Chase asked.

"The only thing we can do. Drive."

12

____

CHASE

With Sully now back in the driver's seat, he drove us onward. We kept our eyes peeled for anything to use to our advantage.

The fields of yellow were broken up by a house here or there, but with only a few sparse rows of trees popping up, it didn't seem like there was any place we could safely make camp. Nowhere we wouldn't be seen from the road.

Though the picturesque countryside rolled past our windows, we were still on edge from our narrow escape. With no idea where we were heading, we were just ambling along, hoping to find somewhere we could park for the night until Sully could make that call.

But, as if we didn't have enough to contend with, we had another problem within our ranks.

It had started innocently enough.

Shortly after we escaped, Emma had apparently gotten over her need for solace and had started hovering near Sully. Though it was Sam's natural place to be beside him, Emma stuck close to Sully, seeking the comfort she only found in his presence. He, in turn, seemed unable to ask her to leave.

And the thing was, he might not even want her to.

At times, I would catch him staring at Emma with this awed expression, like the one parents had for their newborn babies. When he realized I had noticed this, he'd hide it by coughing or turning away. But, if I had caught him doing it, I was sure Sam would too, which might go some way to explaining her rigid back. So straight and unyielding that it seemed like it might snap.

The result of all this was that Sam hadn't talked to her new husband since Emma's reappearance. While Zeb was zen-like about the whole thing, convinced that the situation would resolve itself given time, Gideon was doing his level best to avoid Emma. It was surprisingly easy since she ignored him completely.

Picking up on all the tension, Bandit tried to console Sam by placing his iPad into her lap, offering a quiz game for the two of them to play. Sam had tried, but her mind just wasn't on it. She gave up after only a few questions, pretending to have a headache. I couldn't stomach the disappointed sigh he gave, so we went a few rounds. He won every one, of course.

Having grown tired of watching Emma cling onto her man, Sam finally approached them, a determined expression across her face.

"Do you mind if I sit with Sully now?" Sam had asked, pointedly yet politely.

Apparently not valuing her newly granted lease of life, Emma responded, "You're not happy with taking my husband. You want this seat too?"

Sam's eyes had flashed dangerously, but she kept her voice even. "I just want to talk to him. We've had little opportunity."

"Still more than me, though, right? Since I've been dead for almost two years."

Not even Sam knew how to argue with that. "I'll check in with you later," Sully had pleaded with Sam then. Although I was pretty sure he would have preferred Sam's company, letting Emma sit with him seemed to keep her quiet. Since peace seemed as if it was going to be lacking in our near future, it was smart of him to take what he could.

This meant Sam was sitting with us. During the short time we had been traveling, she grew increasingly convinced that Emma was connected with those men.

"They only appeared when she did. We don't actually know if she's working for them."

"Maybe… but it doesn't make sense why she would lead them to us. She seemed genuinely shocked by it all." I was trying to see all sides, play Devil's advocate. Clearly, I must have hit my head during all the explosions. It was the only logical reason as to why I wasn't keeping my mouth shut.

"She might not have known that was what she was doing. I just think we need to be cautious around her."

"I've told you a million times already — I'm not working with them! Why won't you believe me?"

Emma's piping voice cut in behind us. We had been so lost in our conversation that we hadn't heard her approach.

Bandit shot me a woeful look, knowing he should have heard her first since dogs had much better hearing. I guess he must have been as caught up in the conversation as the rest of us.

Suffice to say, things had now soured between them to where they weren't speaking — to each other or anyone else.

I would catch Sam sending a hostile look Emma's way now and then, while Emma did her best to ignore her. It didn't help matters that Emma had those pictures of Sully in her lap and wouldn't quit studying them.

The tension in the truck was palpable, like a tangible force was keeping them apart. Every time Sam caught Emma looking at Sully — which in fairness was a lot — her fingers would curl a little tighter in her lap. Her hands resembled claws now she had been doing it for so long. I wanted to force them to relax.

But I wasn't stupid enough to get in their way. I hadn't survived this long without knowing which battles to avoid.

The rhythmic rocking of the truck soon lulled Zeb to sleep. His head relaxed against the back of his chair as a peaceful expression came over his face. He often napped in the afternoon, and even our current predicament couldn't stop the siren call of tiredness when it hit.

We'd been silent for a while when I soon felt a familiar rumble in my stomach, so loud it seemed to reverberate in the cab. My cheeks turned hot.

"We're way past our normal mealtime," was my only response.

Suddenly, Emma put down the photographs she had been studying intensely. Rummaging inside her bag, she retrieved an energy bar. She unwrapped it and immediately started eating it in front of my eyes. I was a little taken aback by the lack of consideration and could tell the others were, too. Sam's eyes burned a path toward her, but either Emma didn't notice or she genuinely didn't care.

Within three or four bites, she had almost eaten the whole thing.

"Aren't you going to share that with the rest of us?" Sam asked, sounding as incredulous as she looked.

"Why would I do that?" Emma replied, completely confused by the question. "I'm hungry too."

"But so is Chase — you just heard so yourself — and probably the rest of us by now. How can you hear her say she's hungry, then sit there eating that bar by yourself?"

Emma held onto the last bite of her bar, her voice surging into a plaintive wail.

"But it's my food. It was in my bag and I'm starving."

"So are the rest of us," was Sam's response.

The air was so thick with tension, you could have cut it with a knife. Not wanting this to become yet another thing between them, Sully finally spoke up. "It's all right. She can have it. We'll work out the food thing later."

Barely had the words left his mouth, then Emma shoved the remaining bite into her own, chewing so fast that I thought she'd choke. The fact that Sully was letting Emma get away with bad behavior *and* that he wasn't backing her up, didn't sit well with Sam. She sent a scathing look his way.

Sully was in for an uncomfortable conversation tonight. Of that I had no doubt.

Wondering if I should say something to break the tension, I was given the opportunity when a large shape outside caught my attention.

"Sully! Take us over there!"

My suggestion confused him, and he didn't initially see what I had seen until the barn came into clearer view.

A large hole had eaten away a third of the roof and it was over-grown with ivy and weeds. The place was unused and unloved, but what had gotten me excited was the sheer size of it: it looked big enough to hide our truck inside.

Sully beamed at me.

"Good spot, Chase. We'll camp here and move on tomorrow."

Swinging the truck off the road, we headed to inspect our home for the night.

13

SULLY

The ancient double-height barn had walls that might originally have been a rosy red, but time and weather had bleached the paneling dirty pink.

Where windows had once wrapped around the top level, only splintered holes remained. Wind whistled through the holes, growing gradually more intense as the sun began its descent in the mottled crimson sky.

I knew that we didn't have much time before darkness fell. If this was to be our camp, we needed to make it suitable as quickly as possible.

Behind the barn stood a few smaller buildings in even worse condition. One, a single storey residence, looked to have been a farmhouse once. Ghosts of its previous life were everywhere.

A wheelbarrow lay on its side in a ditch. A tractor missing its steering wheel and seat. A rusty weathervane — long fallen off its original perch — now lay half buried beneath layers of grass.

Another outbuilding contained piles of oily metal and machinery. I wasn't sure what any of it was for, only that they had to do with the large overgrown fields of wheat and barley that surrounded us.

I approached what was left of the farmhouse first, hoping to find something we could use. The front door was closed but when I twisted the door handle, it turned, if reluctantly. Stepping inside, I was immediately hit with a cloying, musty smell that scratched the back of my throat.

Coughing, I reeled back, needing a moment. I gestured to the others. "Stay back. There's mold. Let me check it out by myself."

"Be careful, son," Zeb instructed. He had woken from his nap and was now scoping out the area, his dark eyes taking stock of the place.

I stepped carefully inside, cupping a hand over my nose.

Dust and chaff danced in the half-light that barely passed through the dirt encrusted windows. Though its owners had long abandoned the house, some furniture remained.

A round wooden table and two chairs, both missing several legs. An oversized cupboard took up one wall. I approached the cupboard hopefully, opening its doors.

Inside, aged newspaper covered the bottom of the shelves, where a few chipped mugs and plates sat discarded. Unless we wanted to risk slicing open our mouths every time we took a drink, there was nothing we could use.

Moving to the kitchen, the source of the mold became clear. A sizeable area of black covered the ceiling. What wasn't black was brown with water stains, though there was no sign of the leak that had caused all the issues. Turning away, I scanned the rest of the room. Only the odd pot remained. There was no canned food. No hidden treasure.

I went through the rest of the house, but it was clear within moments of exploring that my search wouldn't reap any rewards.

I inhaled deeply as I stepped out of the house, relieved to no longer be breathing in the toxic fumes.

"I'm going to check over there." I pointed to a building containing the machinery.

Inside, it seemed in a better state than the house had been. My gaze went straight to a bucket containing a few discarded gardening tools. There was a trowel with a handle that had rotted away, but I struck gold with a pair of pruning shears that hadn't fallen apart. Picking them up, I rejoined the others by the barn.

"The good news *is* the barn is big enough for the truck," Gideon said. "But the bad news is we'll have to clear that vegetation growing over the doors before we can get inside."

I showed them the shears. "It's lucky I found these then."

"You think they'll do the job? They look in pretty bad shape." Chase eyed the shears in my hand, openly doubtful.

I ran my eyes over the weeds, relieved to see that they weren't too thick. "The worst of the culprits I can attack with the shears. You guys can probably get the rest off with just your hands. I don't see any thorns, so you should be fine. There are five of us, not including Bandit. I think we'll be able to clear most of it away before it gets dark if we get going now."

"I need to rest," said Emma from somewhere behind the group. "I've had a really trying day."

A bolt of guilt shot through me: I had actually forgotten she was here. I'd been so focused on the task at hand that she had gone clear out of my mind.

But with only the sound of her voice, everything came rushing back.

My thoughts were the only thing that was rushing, however, as Emma found a patch on the ground and went to sit on it. She curled up on the ground and closed her eyes, apparently going to sleep right there.

I was torn between two conflicting mindsets. On the one hand, I wanted to grab her and force her to stand up and help us, but on the other, I wanted to be understanding and give her anything she asked for. That devilish inner voice of mine reminded me that this wasn't something that ever happened — dead people did not come back — and that I should be thankful for every moment I got with her.

"Let's continue without her. No point forcing her to do anything. She'll likely be of little use to us," Zeb murmured.

He had been staring at me as if he knew exactly what I had been thinking. I shot him a grateful nod, happy not to have to consider Emma for the immediate future.

I made my way to the doors and started hacking away at the overgrown weeds with the shears, relieved when they started coming away from the doors. The kids went to work on my left, Sam and my dad on my right. Even Bandit tried to help, gathering what he could in his mouth, then backing away, swinging his head from side to side to tug it loose.

We went hard and fast, working up a quick sweat, though I didn't mind, finding the manual, thoughtless labor easier to deal with than the swirling mass of confusion that swam through my mind.

Sam hacked away at the weeds beside me but didn't say a word. That's not to say I couldn't feel her bristling. Her energy was wired like electricity and an explosion felt imminent.

All I could do for now was focus on clearing the weeds away so we could get inside. If I spent one second to consider all the things that happened since the morning, my brain would meltdown.

14

CHASE

We were in a race against the declining light.

The sun was almost on the horizon, a visual ticking clock representing how much time we had before we'd have to use the truck's lights — defeating the purpose of hiding away out here in the first place.

Bandit ran between us, helping when he could. He had stopped trying to pull the ivy off by himself as he'd ended up tangled up with it, and was now picking up whatever we had freed, dragging it to a pile off-side.

Zeb hadn't said much since we'd gotten here. His silence unnerved me and I found myself keeping an eye on him… just in case something else was going on with him.

He never acted his age, though I wasn't actually sure how old he was — whenever I asked, he just replied that he was several hundred years old. I was acutely aware of not only the terror we'd just experienced, but that he had only come out of a coma a few weeks ago.

I was worried this would be too much for him.

His color seemed good though, and outside of being quiet, he looked okay. Then again, I had always looked pretty okay too when I had been on the streets, even when I was so weak with hunger that I could barely see straight. Back then, faking strength had been part of my strategy to stay alive. I knew that if I showed no weakness, I just might last another night. Shooting a sidelong glance at him, I moved closer.

"So, this is all pretty terrifying," I began.

He looked at me and nodded. "Have to say I didn't see any of this coming. I had thought my final act would consist of sitting on the porch and watching the sun go down, not running for my life."

I flinched inwardly. "I'm so sorry Zeb. I feel so guilty about making you lose your home. Especially as I'd already done that to Sully. I can't believe it's happened again."

His eyes turned hooded. "Dear girl, you weren't the one who attacked us. I don't hold you responsible for any of your actions. That was a gutsy move, what you did. And it saved us. Anyhow, a house doesn't make a home, Chase. You of all people know that. Family, loved ones, that's what makes a home. The rest of it is immaterial."

Despite his words, I knew he was just trying to put a brave face on it all. Noticing my lack of conviction, he took my hand and squeezed it.

We went back to working side-by-side in silence. Sam had moved away from us. She hadn't spoken to anyone, but now and then I could hear her mumble angrily to herself as she tugged hard at the ivy. I couldn't hear what she was saying, only picking up a word or two. Enough to know she wasn't happy that Sully had let Emma off the hook so easily. It was seriously eating her up.

Not wanting to stare, or get caught staring only to suffer her wrath, I turned and found myself looking at Gideon.

He tore at the ivy, the muscles in his arms flexing in a way that had me staring. Sweat glistened on his brow but instead of being grossed out, I found myself thinking how *hot* he looked. Catching me staring, Zeb smiled.

"He's the most loyal person I've ever known, you know." He stopped working, his eyes taking on a faraway look. "Did I ever tell you how we met?"

I shook my head — I didn't know this story.

"I found him in my stable one morning. He was fast asleep in an empty stall with only the hay to keep him warm. I had heard noises coming from there in the night, but had put it down to raccoons — they love to pillage my vegetable garden, so I assumed they were spreading their net further afield. I was tired that night and didn't bother to investigate."

His lips curled into a smile at the memory.

"When I woke in the morning, I brought my shotgun down with me only to find this skinny kid sleeping like a babe. He had little on him and his clothes were dirty. It was likely he hadn't washed in a while. I didn't have the heart to wake him, so I went back to the house and rustled up a large breakfast. Took it out there for him, half expecting him to have woken up by then, but he was still out to the world. He later revealed that he had traveled quite far on foot and was exhausted by the time he had turned up on my property. I set the plate of food and a jug of water and juice on the barrel next to him, and left him to it."

Oblivious to the two of us watching him, Gideon carried on working.

"I went about my day not hearing a peep from him. Just when I was beginning to think that he had probably eaten, then done a runner, there came a knock on the door. Gideon stood on my porch, my plate in his hands. He had eaten the food, but had also washed the plate and the cutlery outside before handing it back to me. It was that minor detail that told me everything I needed to know about him. He was a good kid who had hit on hard times, but his heart was solid."

I would have gasped, but I didn't want to break the spell. Our stories were so familiar, both of us living rough on the streets, then being rescued and cared for by two generations of the same family.

Zeb continued. "I told him right then and there that he could stay if he helped around the ranch. I would give him a roof over his head and feed him if he helped with the odd job around the place. He proved so useful that I started paying him. That was two years ago and the rest, as you know, is history."

Gideon and I had spent a lot of time together, but we had an unspoken agreement to never discuss our past lives, making all of this unfamiliar to me.

"Has he ever told you about his family?" I asked.

"A little," Zeb answered. "He has two older brothers, never got on with either of them or his parents. By the sounds of it, they weren't very good people. His parents made them all quit school as soon as possible, insisting that they get jobs — any job — and pay them for the roof over their heads. Gideon wanted a better life. He wanted to make something of himself, but they wouldn't even consider letting him continue school. He was the only smart one in the family, and they resented him for it, treating him like dirt.

When he tried to stick up for himself, they said he was too big for his boots and threw him out. It may well be that they didn't actually mean for him to go: they could have been trying to teach him a lesson, but you know Gideon. He left and never looked back. You and he both have that in common."

The world was such a strange place.

You had people out there so desperate to have kids they would go into debt and risk everything in order just to try. And then there were our parents, who gave birth to us but couldn't wait to toss us away.

My thoughts came to rest on Sully and his relationship with Zeb. Although I didn't want to stir up any painful memories, I wanted to know more about them, more about their life before I had met them.

"What about you and Sully's mom? I know nothing about her. Neither of you talk about her much."

Zeb smiled a bittersweet smile. He must have formed a picture of her in his mind as his eyes turned bright with emotion.

"It's cliche I know, but I believe that when you meet the person who is right for you, you know it. You feel it in your heart and your gut, but it's nothing like how it's represented in the movies. There's no explosion. No world spinning out of control. It's actually the opposite. It's feeling like you've come home, that this is where you are supposed to be. If the person that you are with makes you feel like home, then that's the one you should be with. That's how it was with us."

A whole host of emotions flew across his face. He missed her with an ache that was palpable, but there was also a great love radiating from him. Even now, so many years later, Zeb was still madly in love with his wife.

I looked back at Gideon helping Sully with that door, confused thoughts swirling through my mind. I felt at home with Gideon, but wasn't that because we lived together as a family? Wasn't he already part of my home?

Thankfully, a loud creak interrupted my tangled thoughts.

Sully, Gideon, and Sam had cleared enough of the vegetation away that they were now opening the door. The door protested loudly since it hadn't been opened in such a long time, but they were able to work it free with a carefully timed pull.

Dust particles floated, creating a hazy filter through which I took in the sights. Beams of light fell in through the holes in the roof. Giant cobwebs hung from the rafters, making me suppress a shudder at what might also lurk up there with them. I knew I should be more concerned about men with guns, but at least they would make some kind of noise before they attacked. Spiders were deadly, silent, and just plain gross.

Hay bales were scattered around. Empty food troughs sat in rows along the walls, remnants of half-rotten grain still lining them. An earthy smell came from those troughs, but nothing too unbearable. If we cleared them up, pushed them to one side and swept the floor a bit, we would confine most of the smell to the one area.

"This will be fine for tonight," said Sully. "We'll pile the bales around us to keep out the cold. They can also offer some protection if those men do find us."

Emma stirred, waking from her nap (how anyone could have gone to sleep like that was beyond me). She yawned, stretching like a cat, and went to stand beside Sully. As soon as she looked inside the barn, she shook her head.

"It's so dirty. I can't sleep in there."

"You just slept on the ground," Sam pointed out immediately.

"That was different. That was outside. This is dirty *inside*."

Though she answered Sam, she addressed all of her responses to Sully, as if he was the one who had made the point.

"Emma's always been a bit OCD about cleanliness," he said without thinking, only to be immediately hit by the full force of Sam's hurt. She dropped her gaze, not wanting him to see it, but I caught it. It made me feel terrible for her. Not only had Sully inadvertently taken Emma's side again, but his comment made it seem as if it was he and Emma who were the couple.

"That's no skin off my nose. If it were up to me, she would sleep outside on her own where anyone can see her for miles around." Sam styled it out smoothly, like she hadn't just been stabbed in the heart.

Suddenly, Emma didn't seem so sure of herself. Glancing around at the open expanse, she must have realized how vulnerable she would be out here. Hugging her bag to her chest as if she were afraid we would steal it from her, she went inside.

"Since you all already smell, I guess it doesn't matter if I get dirty too," she said.

The others followed her inside, though it was a while longer before Sam would join us.

15
____

CHASE

The atmosphere was getting suffocatingly intense.

It felt like we'd been in the barn for hours already, though according to my watch it had only been minutes.

We cleaned out the mess until the back of the barn was relatively decent — about as decent as a crumbling barn could be, anyway. Still, some people couldn't be pleased.

Using a few of the hay bales, Sully had created a corner for Emma, laying out a tarp that he'd found so that the hay wouldn't itch her skin. The second she had inspected her bed for the night, though, Emma complained, declaring she wasn't an animal, so how could they treat her like one?

Bandit, my lovable Muttface, attempted to ease the awkwardness by bounding onto the "bed" he had already circled several times. He gave a cute "woof" to let her know that it was plenty nice enough for him, and therefore should be good enough for her too.

Emma was completely unaware of what he was trying to communicate and distorted the entire story to make it seem like Bandit was on her side.

Words were spoken, from Sam mostly. By the time they had

finished, Emma had retreated to her corner, but only after shooing Bandit away like he was nothing but a nuisance.

Sully attempted to make another corner for himself and Sam, but she stopped him with a death glare before snapping that she was quite capable of creating her own bunk for the night.

After that, Sully was completely lost.

He kept tossing looks between Sam and Emma, wondering who he should speak to. He would start walking to one, stop, turn around then head to the other, only to stop again. It was painful to watch.

Finally, realizing that whatever he did would be wrong, he mumbled something under his breath and went out to the truck.

16

SULLY

The night air wrapped around me, carrying the earthy aroma of the surrounding fields. The silence was broken only by the occasional chirping of crickets and the gentle rustle of leaves in the breeze.

Above, the stars twinkled against the fast-approaching night sky. As the barn faded into a black silhouette, I soaked up the momentary calm. Out here, I could pretend that all was well with the world. That the relentless onslaught of wonder, confusion, and fear wasn't waiting for me inside.

Reluctantly, I tore my gaze from the sky and retraced my steps to the barn. A movement caught my attention even before I heard the sounds of my dad's wheelchair scraping across the dirt floor. Random strands of hay were caught in the wheels, creating a rhythmic whipping sound as he approached.

"I'm just taking a breather before I start on your bunk for the night."

"I can wait, son. I actually wanted to talk to you. See how you are. Hasn't been much time for that."

My gaze swept the room, automatically stopping at Emma's corner only to find it empty. A bolt of panic tore through me, shocking me with its intensity.

"She's only taking a restroom break. She's fine, son." His voice cut through my alarm as his cool eyes assessed me. "I imagine this has all been hard to handle."

"You always seem to understate the moment."

"Never seen the point of working myself into a frenzy. It's not exactly productive. Saying that, I wouldn't know how to feel in your shoes. Tell me what's been going through your mind."

I looked into his concerned eyes. "I guess I don't know how to feel. The honeymoon was about as perfect as it could be. Sam and I were so happy, but ever since Emma showed up, my head hasn't been on straight. I can't understand how she's here, how any of this is happening."

"None of us can. It defies all logic."

"But that's not even the worst of it. The worst was how, once the shock had faded some, I'd catch myself feeling thrilled." I lowered my gaze to the ground, ashamed of myself. "I'd be excited that she's back, but then I'll turn and see Sam and it feels like I'm cheating on her. I'm a wreck."

Zeb smiled sadly. "You need to give yourself a break. This only just happened. Your mind needs time to get over the shock before you can even begin to fathom how to feel."

"But that's just it. We don't know how much time we have. We're out here, being hunted, yet I can't get my head around my relationship issues. What kind of man lets that happen?

Zeb laid his hand on my shoulder. "The kind who cares about his family and puts them above his own feelings and fears. Trust yourself, Jake. You're a good man. You'll do the right thing."

He sounded so sure of himself that for a moment, I actually believed him.

The sound of footsteps crunching over the ground interrupted our conversation.

Chase, Bandit, Sam, and Gideon headed toward us in a group. "What're you two gossiping about?" Gideon asked.

"We were just discussing our strange predicament."

"You're talking about Emma, right? Thank God. My brain is about to implode if we don't figure out what she is." Chase plopped herself beside me, folding her legs beneath her. "I have several theories already."

Forgetting in that moment that she was angry at me, Sam sent an amused look my way. Chase's theories were usually pretty entertaining.

"First off, and least most likely to be honest, we have alien."

Gideon cocked a brow at her. "Why would an alien disguise themselves as Sully's dead wife? What purpose would that serve except to drive him crazy?"

"Exactly, which is why that was the *least* likely option. Next, I'm thinking she could be someone else, someone who's had tons of surgery to make her look like Emma."

"You mean like the real life, Barbie?" Gideon asked.

"Yep. Just like her."

"What on Earth is a real-life Barbie?" Zeb asked.

"Exactly what it sounds like: someone who has gone crazy with the plastic surgery to look like a human doll. When we get our phones back, we'll show you." Gideon promised.

"Say that were possible. It would cost an absolute fortune, not to mention how painful numerous surgeries would be. Why would someone go to all that effort?" Sam asked, putting a dampener on our discussion.

We were all stumped there.

"Moving on then. What about... robot? That might explain why she doesn't react the way we expect her to, why she has no memory before waking up. Maybe "waking up" is actually code for "turning on?"

"It's not actually that crazy. They've been making robots for years in Japan, creating not only household helpers but also sex bots," Gideon volunteered.

Sam shot him a level stare. "And you know this, how?"

A blush tinged his cheeks. "Reddit."

Sam's only response was to stare at him until he withered under her gaze.

"But what's the point of sending a robot only to attack us immediately after?" Zeb queried, not buying it.

"I don't know. But you've got to admit it would explain some of her quirks."

"Or perhaps somehow, Xavier really did bring her back from the dead." At this, all the air was sucked out of the place. As unlikely as it seemed, Gideon's point wasn't one any of us wanted to entertain.

"We can discuss this all we want but the fact of the matter is, we don't really know," Zeb commented. "When you get to my age, you learn that asking questions that you have no possible answer for, is a fruitless task. Better to put your energy elsewhere, into something practical like helping me to get a bed ready. I need to stretch and get out of this chair."

A flicker of exhaustion flashed over his face. His mouth was pressed into a thin line, his expression weary.

It suddenly dawned on me what a toll this must be taking on him, and guilt quickly overcame me. Here I was, consumed by my relationship problems, when my father was barely keeping it together.

"Sure. Let me get something sorted for you quick." Chase jumped up and started grabbing armfuls of hay, spreading it around, layering it until there was an inch of straw covering the ground.

Gideon and I helped lay Zeb onto his "bed" but I could see he wasn't comfortable: his head was bent at an awkward angle.

Chase removed her cardigan — leaving her with a long-sleeved

T-shirt —and folded it into a makeshift pillow which she placed under his head. His grateful eyes traveled over to hers.

"Thank you."

Not for the first time, I marveled at how sweet a kid she was.

17

CHASE

After making sure Zeb was settled, I went about creating a little section for Bandit and me, using whatever I could salvage. After I was satisfied, I laid down on our bed to test it... and immediately wished I could get back up.

Despite the layers between my bones and the ground, the cold seeped through, turning my blood to ice. Knowing it would only get worse throughout the night, I gritted my teeth and gestured for Bandit.

"Come closer, boy."

Padding to me, he circled the ground, kneading it with his paws before laying down, setting his head onto my thigh with an enormous sigh.

His warm body pressed against me, taking away some of the chill. I stroked his head, running my fingers through his silky fur. The ordinary act of petting my dog calmed me, slowing down my spinning thoughts until my head felt clear enough to think again. Stroking him, I could almost forget that we were being hunted —
again.

Almost.

Bandit whined, blowing out a puff of breath. He could feel my tension. Could probably even smell it on me. Not wanting to move away from me, he pawed at the iPad around his neck. I obliged his unspoken request, taking it out and setting it on my lap just in front of his face.

His long pink tongue snaked out, licking my hand in thanks as he picked up the stylus-pen. I watched as he typed, reading the words before his iPad could speak his question.

"Why doesn't Emma like Sam?"

"I don't think she likes anyone too much."

"But Sam is nice."

I stole a quick glance at Sam, who was clearly having some kind of standoff with Sully and didn't seem quite as nice in this current moment. "Yeah. Then again, she doesn't seem to like you either."

"That is unfortunate."

"Right? Who doesn't like you?"

"The Bad Men," Bandit answered, managing to make the iPad sound solemn despite the naturally cheerful, youthful voice we had selected for him. *"They are back again. Why won't they leave us alone?"*

"I don't know." I wanted to say more, but my voice cracked. My eyes had begun to mist up which only made me angry on top of the fear. What would tears do for us? They wouldn't help us, they certainly wouldn't help Bandit. I had to be strong, especially with Sully's world spinning so far out of control that he couldn't see land. My family needed me to be brave.

Squeezing my eyes closed, I lowered my head, letting my hair hide my face as I fought to regain my emotions. Taking a few breaths, I didn't look up again until I was sure I had it together. I should have known that I couldn't fool him. Bandit stared at me with those beautiful, soulful eyes.

"Don't worry. It will be OK."

He woofed to let me know he really meant it. I didn't want to question his faith, but I had to ask.

"How do you know that? How are you so sure?"

"Because we are together. As long as we are all together, all will be OK."

I didn't answer him. I couldn't.

I didn't want to point out that the last time we had fought back together like this, Bandit had ended up on an operating table with his head open.

An icy shiver went up my spine as the horror of that memory refused to go away. Pushing it aside, I hugged Bandit, squeezing him with all of my might, when his head suddenly shot into the air. I froze instantly, tension flooding my body. Had they found us *already?*

"What is it?"

He typed quickly, making errors in his haste, though I could read his chilling message all too well.

"I cn snell blood."

"Whose blood?"

Instead of answering, he bounded to the far corner of the barn. I raced after him, senses firing.

"Bandit wait!"

My shout alerted the others. Out of the corner of my eyes I saw Sully's head pop up, but I didn't stop to explain. If there was blood, then I didn't want my dog anywhere near it, but Bandit kept on running, swerving around a wall of hay bales until he skidded to an abrupt stop, barking sharply.

I ran ahead of him, shielding him with my body. It was instinctual, and I had no real control of myself. If someone was going to get shot, it would be me first.

Instead of the bad guys I expected to see, however, there was only Emma.

She huddled on the ground, her back to us. When she heard our approach, she turned. I immediately saw how white her face was. She looked wan and scared. The patch of straw by her feet was dark and glistening wet. *Had she wet herself?* It wasn't until I took a step closer that I realized the hay was soaked in *blood*.

"Oh no." The metallic smell of the blood filled my nose, making my empty stomach flip-flop.

Emma turned toward me, leaving me with a clear view of her left arm which lay limply by her side. I could now see the deep and jagged cut running along it. The flesh was raw and the blood was still seeping from the wound, pooling onto the straw by her feet.

"I knew I wasn't a robot! See!" She showed me her arm, though her jubilation at proving us wrong lasted all but a second. Staring at her blood, her face grew even paler, if that was even possible.

"I didn't know there would be so much blood. I don't feel so good…"

She swayed and would have fallen if Sully hadn't leaped forward and caught her.

"For God's sake, what has she done now?" Sam gasped, rounding the corner with Gideon pushing Zeb in his wheelchair.

Emma flashed her an injured look beneath her lashes, but stubbornly refused to answer.

"She must have heard me talking. She was trying to prove she wasn't a robot," I explained, remembering all the things I'd said that were now making me feel very guilty.

Sam scanned the scene of the crime, taking in the jagged cut, then the rusty, blood-tipped nail that lay by Emma's feet.

"So you cut yourself open with a rusty nail? Of all the stupid…"

She stopped herself from whatever it was she wanted to say next. Taking a sharp breath, she commanded, "Stick your left hand in the air above your head and put pressure on the wound."

"Why?" Emma looked utterly baffled by this suggestion, as if Sam had just asked her to perform an Irish jig.

"It'll stop the bleeding until I can put something on it."

When Emma didn't move, Sully grabbed her arm and held it

above her head while Sam looked for something she could use to dress the wound. Spotting Emma's bag, she opened it.

"That's mine!" Emma protested weakly, sagging against Sully.

Flashing her an incredulous look, Sam rifled in her bag until she found a small bottle of water. Unscrewing the cap, she lowered Emma's arm back down, pouring water over it.

"Ouch, that stings," Emma flinched, but Sam held onto her.

Gideon tore a strip from the denim over-shirt he wore. Sam wrapped the strip around Emma's arm securely. When she was done, she looked Emma in her face.

"Don't ever do anything that stupid again. You could have hit an artery, or that arm could become infected. You could have given yourself tetanus for all we know."

"What's that?"

"It's a serious disease that's caused by cuts or punctures from a contaminated object."

"Like the nail?"

"Yes. If that nail is infected, you could become sick."

Emma's eyes had become very wide. "How sick?"

"Very sick."

Her eyes grew even wider.

"We'll know if you suddenly start getting muscle contractions and can't breathe."

Suddenly, Emma starting hyperventilating, flailing her hands around. "But I can't breathe! I must have it!"

Sam shot her a level look. "It doesn't happen that fast. What you are experiencing, is a panic attack."

Taking pity on her, Zeb smiled gently. "I'm sure you don't have tetanus. It's very rare in the US."

"Almost as rare as coming back from the dead," Gideon quipped before he could stop himself.

"Let's leave her alone so she can get some rest. There's been quite enough excitement," Zeb commented firmly as Gideon wheeled him away. Giving Emma one last look, Sam followed after them.

"Was the old man telling the truth? Is it rare?" She'd addressed the question to Sully, but he didn't answer.

"I think so," I responded, since Sully had yet to say a word. He busied himself replacing the bloody straw with a fresh layer as Emma peered into his face, something other than her arm bothering her.

"Aren't you going to say something? I thought you'd be happy that I'm not a robot?"

But happy was the last thing Sully seemed to be feeling. If anything, he looked stricken.

"Try to get some sleep."

Then, instead of returning to Sam as I expected, Sully started for the front of the barn.

"Where are you going?" I asked.

"Someone needs to keep watch. I'm taking the first shift. Sam, the next. Then Gideon."

"Bandit and I can do one," I volunteered.

"We've got it covered. Go to sleep."

Without another word, he retreated to his post, leaving Emma staring after him like a lost puppy.

18

CHASE

The night enveloped us, pitch black, without a single star in the sky to illuminate the way.

Thigh high grass whipped against my legs as I ran, lashing against my bare flesh. The pain was biting, yet I knew what would become of us would be ten times worse if we were caught.

The night air whipped at my face as I ran faster than I ever had before. Bandit raced alongside, but try as I might, I couldn't see him. I couldn't see anything ahead of me, only the faintest outline of the distant horizon that I was using as a guide.

The footsteps thundered behind us, increasing in volume and speed. I glanced back and could just make out the silhouettes of several hulking figures. In the darkness, they seemed impossibly large and though their faces were indistinguishable, somehow, I knew exactly who they were.

They were catching up.

I wanted to scream at Bandit to hurry, but a cloying fog stopped me from forming the words. Though I was screaming, though I was raging inside, only the thinnest sound emerged.

My fear had reached a fever pitch. Forcing my feet to go faster, my breath was coming in short, sharp bursts. My pulse racing, I ran so fast that I couldn't even feel the ground beneath my feet anymore. Suddenly, I went flying as something tackled me.

I hit the ground with a thud; the air knocked out of me. I heard Bandit whining, but I couldn't focus on anything other than that great weight that had fallen on top of me. My heart, my airways were being crushed — and there was nothing I could do.

I was going to die.

Despite not being able to see anything, a giant shape blurred toward my face. I was hit by the smell next. But it wasn't the acrid smell of poison or death I expected. The scent that filled my nostrils was familiar. *Loved even.*

The whining came again, this time right in my ears. So loud that it made me flinch. Something soft rubbed against my face, starting on my chin, then moving up to my cheek. I was becoming aware of my aching body next. Of the cold, rigid hardness beneath my back. And that heavy, crushing weight on my chest.

My eyes flew open.

The black spots took a few moments to recede, and when they did, I found myself staring up at Bandit's concerned face, now only inches from my own. And that heavy, crushing weight was just his body lying on top of mine.

I blinked, relief washing over me, as I tried to force the nightmare away. My eyes rose past Bandit's head and I noticed the ceiling was much higher than I expected it to be. This ceiling wasn't my ceiling from home. This wasn't my ceiling from the ranch.

Suspended from *my* ceiling was a cute mobile that Gideon had made for me during the two months he had fancied himself a metal worker. The sun glinted off the tarnished steel in the morning, as the portrait of the dancing girl and her dog twirled round and around. It was a sight that I loved dearly, but with a crushing ache in my heart, it slowly dawned on me that I would never see again.

Where I was now, no mobile girl danced. And the early morning light that streamed in came not through the window, but a gaping hole in the roof.

And suddenly, everything that had come to pass in the last twenty-four hours came crashing into my mind.

Bandit, who must have sensed my distress while I was sleeping, chuffed a greeting at me. His breath warmed my face as the familiar weight of him kept the mounting panic at bay.

For a moment, I thought of how dogs are often suggested as emotional support companions. They can sense distress from their owners without any type of teaching; they usually know to pin them down if they were having a panic attack. This was similar to the effects of an weighted blanket: providing comfort and security to its user. It's one of the many reasons why dogs are advised for people with PTSD. After everything I had gone through, even before I met Bandit or Sully, I wouldn't be surprised if I suffered from it myself.

Intruding on that thought, Bandit's words from the night before echoed in my mind, and I was suddenly struck by their relevance.

He had been right.

As long as we were all together, we would weather whatever storm that came.

I turned my head to find Zeb sleeping soundly beside me. A shaft of the pre-dawn light spilled over his face and illuminated the myriad of lines that carved their way across his features. I was struck by how old he suddenly seemed. How frail and withered. Had he somehow shrunk in the night?

Bizarrely, I knew the reverse of this to be true. At school, I remembered reading a textbook that explained how people actually began the day an inch taller. It had something to do with how gravity would compress the cartilage in our spine when we stand, walk, or sit during the day. When we sleep, the spine lengthens, making us just that little taller in the morning. Looking at Zeb though, it seemed the opposite, and I didn't like how anxious that made me feel.

I propped myself up onto my elbow to see the area littered with sleeping bodies.

Sam still slept in her corner, while, curled in a fetal position across the room, Emma looked strikingly young and vulnerable.

When she was silent like this, when she wasn't moving, I felt almost protective of her. She was so childlike and simple in so many ways that even though she irritated the heck out of me, I also felt kind of sorry for her.

Bandit chuffed softly at my face, wondering where my mind had gone. I moved a hand up to scratch his nose.

"Hey, boy"

He chuffed again, quietly, so as not to wake the others. Though he seemed in a relatively good mood — did dogs have any other? — his movements were sluggish this morning: I knew I wasn't the only one who'd had a tough time sleeping through the night.

Glancing up through the hole in the barn, I saw the purple-pink sky outside. Thin clouds crawled slowly across the horizon, as if they had only just woken too. In the distance, there was the sound of birdsong, but it wasn't the rousing chorus that signified the break of a new day. It was one or two birds singing an early morning tune. Their sleepy voices were the only disruption to the serene silence…

Until I heard a sound from outside the barn and moved Bandit's head from my chest so I could sit up. Through a thin gap in the wall, I glimpsed Sully pacing outside.

We got up, moving carefully around Gideon, who lay protectively on Zeb's other side. As soon as I emerged from the barn I was hit by the brisk morning air. It sent such a chill straight into my chest that I had to stifle the urge to cough. Rubbing my hands together, I looked at Sully. "Did you manage to get any peace last night?"

Sully raised red-rimmed eyes toward me, shaking his head. He looked bad, like he hadn't slept at all. "If you mean, did Emma and Sam finally resolve their issues so that we could all move on, then the answer is no."

I wish I could have Bandit's positive attitude and reassure him that things would work out, but the words died in my throat. Over and over, the question ran through my mind: how was Emma here?

What even *was* she?

Every movement Sully made was agitated; I could almost see the tension roll off him like a wave. He had been such a shell of a man after Emma had died. It had actually taken losing everything he had been clinging onto to finally move on with his life, though it seemed life wasn't quite done toying with him yet.

The world could be so cruel.

"One good thing that comes from not sleeping, is that I was able to come up with a plan of sorts," Sully interrupted my thoughts.

A tiny glimmer of hope rose in my chest. "Oh yeah, what is it?"

"We need help to get away from these guys so I'm going back to the gas station we passed yesterday. They must have a phone there. I'll call Mark and pick up basic supplies while I'm there."

I didn't want to knock his plan, but I had been hoping for something bigger and grander. Still, it was practical and didn't sound like it would be too difficult or risky to execute.

"Let us visit the restroom, then we'll be ready." I was already turning away when he stopped me.

"No. It'll be less conspicuous if I'm alone. Now that my leg's better, I can run again. Maybe not as fast as before, but I can make decent time."

When I had met him, Sully could not sleep without his wife beside him. His only recourse were the punishing late night runs he ran to physically exhaust himself, though after he had been shot in the leg during our escape from Forbes' lab, we weren't sure if

he'd ever run again. Sully had surprised us with his determination. The bullet had gone straight through leaving a clean wound.
After months of rehab, he graduated from walking to a slow jog,
but he had kept at it, determined that Forbes wouldn't take this
from him.

The last time I saw Sully running, he had managed to out-pace
me, which, technically wasn't a big deal since I wasn't ever going to
win any race. But, he'd been able to keep going while I was
wheezing and gasping for air after only a few minutes. I had faith
he would be able to do this, though I didn't have to like it.

Sully must have felt my objections, as he gave me a small smile.

"I'll be fine. If anything happens, if I see any sign of those men,
I can just disappear into the cornfields. You know it'll be easier to
do that on my own. As much as I'd love for the two of you to go
with me, I would have so much more to worry about. Alone, I can
be in and out before anyone notices me."

"You're just going straight there. You're calling Mark, grabbing
some food and then coming straight back?" I asked, reiterating the
plan, hating how needy I sounded yet kind of not caring either.
Sully nodded.

He looked past me, into the barn. I couldn't see where his eyes
landed, but I had a pretty good guess what — or who — he was
staring at. "Honestly… I could do with some alone time."

The weight of the world pressed onto his shoulders. He sagged
in front of me, becoming smaller until he suddenly shook himself,
straightening back to full height. "Let them sleep longer, but if
they're not awake by the time the sun is up, get them ready in case
we need to make a fast exit."

"Okay."

I wasn't able to say much else. Bandit pawed the ground, as
alarmed by our imminent separation as much as I was. Sully
wrapped me in a sudden, tight hug and stroked Bandit on the
head.

"Don't you two worry about a thing. I'll be right back."

He took off at a slow pace, trying to shake his muscles awake. I twisted my fingers into Bandit's fur, watching as he grew smaller and smaller, until his figure was a black speck in the distance, desperate to ignore the hollow feeling in my stomach.

19

SULLY

D on't look back.

Forcing myself to place one foot after another, and despite my senses shrieking at me otherwise, I jogged away from my family.

Away from my loved ones.

I was acutely aware that Chase and Bandit hadn't moved. I could feel their eyes boring into my back. Though my stomach churned like a river, it took every inch of willpower not to sprint back to them.

I knew what suffering was. I knew what it was to have loved and lost, to have your family ripped away from you, their lives hanging in the balance on the whim of a madman. So, their presence in my life wasn't something I ever took for granted.

I had made that particular mistake once, and it had almost cost us our lives. Nothing put things into perspective more than a near-miss with death.

It was for this very reason I had to do this alone.

I hadn't been lying when I'd said we'd draw too much attention if Chase and Bandit had come with me, but there was a darker thinking to my logic that I hadn't wanted to express.

If I ran into those men again, I didn't like my chances. Better that my family were hidden away with transport close to hand. If they needed to make a quick getaway, they could do so. I was learning the hard way that this is what fathers did.

They protected their kids against threats, and threw themselves into danger if that was what was required of them. Good fathers would at least not the garbage Chase and Gideon had the misfortune of growing up with.

Although, not all matters were so black and white.

Take my relationship with my father. There were years when we had never exchanged a single word. I was too busy feeling the righteous justice of my anger, while he had become so disappointed that I would never follow in his wife's footsteps — footsteps which he himself had never been able to fulfill — that he'd willingly cut himself out of our lives. Was there anything as dangerous or as self-serving as a parent who imposed their unfulfilled desires onto their child?

I was grateful we'd repaired our relationship now, though it had come at no small cost. If the stubborn fool had told me about the accident that had ultimately crippled him, I would have come home sooner, but pride had proven stronger than the fall.

I loved him, but I prayed I wouldn't make the same mistakes with my kids.

Unable to help myself, I tossed a quick look over my shoulder — and immediately wished I hadn't. As I had suspected, Chase hadn't moved an inch. Even with the distance beginning to separate us, I could see the miserable expression that clouded her features.

And I knew exactly what she was thinking.

There was still a large part of her that questioned if I was really going to return. She had learned growing up that nothing in life was ever certain, and it had become clear that this fear would persist even when we were together. Even if everything continued to go smoothly, there would always be that lingering doubt that our happy life together wouldn't last. But with the emergence of these men who were so intent on killing us, her worries proved true.

Have faith, Chase. I will be back and we'll climb our way out of this hellhole together.

My feet pounded the tarmac, the cramped tendons beginning to loosen up. My breath was beginning to catch as my pulse sped up. The crisp morning air swam into my lungs, shocking my system.

All night, my head had been filled with a manic clutter of questions, cycling from fears about the men and why they had shown up now, to Emma, sleeping less than fifty feet away from me.

Deep down, I knew it couldn't be my wife.

I knew she was dead.

But if you had asked me a year ago, I would have said dogs couldn't use iPads. The woman who had appeared in our house looked and sounded just like Emma, though the lack of memory was convenient. Chase was right: it wasn't beyond the realm of possibility that she was another woman who'd received extreme plastic surgery to look like my wife.

I had seen images of people who wanted to look like a movie star. No matter how many thousands of dollars they spent, the end result could never look quite like their idol; some features were too exaggerated, such as a nose or an eyebrow line that was slightly too perfect.

This Emma, however, was the spitting image of my own.

And that wasn't all.

I'd catch her with the same mannerisms as my late wife. It was never anything obvious, or something anyone else would notice, but I had lived with and loved her, and I knew her inside out. I knew how, whenever she was troubled, she tended to chew on the corner of her lip — just as this Emma did.

In the early hours of last night, I had found myself passing her corner more than once. Each time, she had been sleeping on her stomach, one hand beneath her face in exactly the way my Emma had always slept.

And when she had cut her arm yesterday, she had almost fainted from the sight of her own blood. It had been a running joke between us about how my Emma could work in a veterinary clinic yet be so irrationally scared of blood.

Each time I considered the possibilities, her frightened face would appear and my body would react. A protective surge would come over me, leading to a heavy sense of guilt that would leave me almost breathless.

It was enough to make a man's head explode.

Deciding it was safer to steer clear of those waters, I flipped my thoughts to the matter at hand. It wasn't safe to stay on the roads. I would feel much happier once we could ditch the truck for a different ride, even if those bullet-proof walls would be missed.

Picking up the pace, I pushed forward, the uncertainty and fear driving me toward the gas station we had passed yesterday, not long before we had found the barn.

Birds flew overhead while a light breeze rustled the stalks of corn on either side. As the sun crested over the horizon and painted the sky in wispy shades of blue, the turmoil brewing inside lent me the strength to keep going.

Eventually, I arrived at my destination and was relieved to see that my recollection of the place had been correct — the gas station was in an extremely isolated spot.

What I hadn't factored on was, given how off the beaten path it was, how popular the place would be, especially when the day had barely begun.

Five cars sat waiting beside a gleaming motorcycle, their owners inside grabbing gas or taking a leak. I spotted a pay phone but hesitated. From the direction I had come from, I could only see one side of the gas station. I would feel safer having scoped it out from all angles before using it.

With that in mind, I slowed my jog to a walk, crossing to the other side when my heart seized in my chest and I stopped dead.

Two large white trucks were parked in front of me.

I about had a seizure when I noticed the logo of a well-known oil company plastered to the side of one truck. Dried mud had baked onto the wheels of the other truck, which had no identifying features other than the two furry dice that hung off the rearview mirror. When I caught the California license plates, I felt my tension lessen.

The armored trucks that had come for us had been identical in their anonymity, but they were also brand new and so spotless that you could have eaten off them. It seemed unlikely that these trucks were owned by the same men who were after us.

Still, I felt uneasy. Keeping my eyes glued to the vehicles, I made my way to the phone. Rummaging in my pockets, I fished out a couple of coins, hoping they would be enough to cover it. I had no idea what it cost to make a phone call these days.

Holding my breath, I dialed Mark's number.

20

———

SULLY

Other than Sam, Dad, and the kids, Mark was the closest thing I had to family, even sticking with me during my year of bereavement when I'd acted like a clown.

A wave of shame came over me when I thought about how I'd behaved the time Mark had brought me a home-made lasagna that had been painstakingly prepared by his bedmate of the moment. We had a disagreement which culminated in my hurling it out of the window where it had shattered onto the sidewalk below.

Thankfully, we made our peace after that. He was even at the wedding, marveling at how the universe had let a schmuck like me get so lucky a second time.

Well, buddy, have I got news for you.

Mark worked on Wall Street, dealing with high-end accounts, making the kind of figures that made my eyes water. Irritatingly, he only worked a few days a week, spending the rest of his time golfing or entertaining his latest model conquest.

Despite how little he actually worked, Mark was the opposite of lazy and kept an early morning routine. Rising at five AM, he would hit his home gym so I knew he would be awake.

The phone started ringing. I held my breath in anticipation of him answering it on the other end. The phone rang once, twice, three times…

With each unanswered ring, my heart pounded faster.

I considered that Mark might be away on another one of his "work" trips, which seemed to consist of nothing more than going out with his firm's wealthiest clients for several days of debauchery, only to return nursing a hangover and an empty wallet. On one occasion, he'd returned looking like he'd been hit by a truck though he'd swore he'd had the wildest time of his life.

We both had a very different understanding of the word.

The phone continued to ring. I counted up to the seventh ring and was sure his voicemail would kick in when his pain laden voice finally sounded over the line, husky from sleep.

"Who in God's name is calling me so early?"

Hearing his familiar voice, my chest tightened with emotion. Uttering a quick prayer of thanks, I started talking. "Mark, it's me."

I made sure not to say my name. While I didn't know who these people were, I had already seen the kind of artillery they commanded. If they were anything like the mercenaries Forbes' had recruited, they likely had all kinds of gadgets at their disposal, so a trace on his phone didn't seem all that unlikely.

Mark gasped, his voice becoming quickly awake. "I've been trying to reach you! Where are you?"

The question seemed a bit much as he coughed, dry heaving coughs into the handset.

"I can't say. I'll explain in a minute, but… what's wrong? You sound like you're in pain."

Mark coughed again, a racking sound that rattled my own ribcage. "That's because I am. Hold on."

I heard him reach for a bottle of pills. He swallowed a couple, chasing them down with a mouthful of water. "That's better," he said.

"What happened?"

"I'm not sure where to begin."

"The beginning's usually a good place."

"I would if I could remember it. Thing is, I apparently had an accident."

Concern made me grip the telephone tighter. "An accident?"

"Well, they tell me it was an accident — but, I can't actually remember."

I tried to make sense of his words, but my brain was not yet firing on all cylinders. "I don't understand."

"I woke up in a ditch with two cracked ribs, a black eye, and a nasty concussion. My wallet and keys were gone, so they think I was mugged. Everything hurt like a bitch."

"Jesus. When did this happen?"

Mark didn't answer straight away. I heard him move, probably trying to get into a more comfortable position. When he came back, he sounded stressed.

"Yesterday. I knew I had been at work because my assistant confirmed that, but after I had a few drinks with a client, I was attacked and found in the park by my place."

Although the idea arose that this could be related to us, I said nothing of it — best not to tip off the bad guys if they were in fact, listening in on the call.

"That really stinks. I hope they catch the guy." My words sounded lame and would do little to console him though Mark didn't seem to mind. I said a lot about the guy but as a friend, he was as solid as they came, so solid that he didn't even notice I wasn't quite behaving as a caring friend should.

"Listen, I have more bad news. It's why I've been trying to reach you," he continued. "You need to steel yourself."

His tone had taken on a graveness I had only heard once before.

When the end was near, Mark had been waiting in the corridor outside Emma's hospital room. I had been holding onto her hand when she finally succumbed to the cancer she had valiantly fought for two years. I had been by her side every step of the way, encouraging her when she felt weak, and comforting her when she'd been afraid. But in the end, the cancer had taken its toll, slowly draining her life until she was nothing but a husk of her former self.

When her chest stopped moving, I had uttered a wail so full of despair that Mark had rushed into the room and held me like I was a baby. Over and over, he had said how sorry he was.

To hear that tone in his voice again, I knew that whatever was coming was going to be bad. Considering all that had happened recently, I squared my shoulders, preparing myself for the worst.

"It's Florence. She passed away. I'm sorry Sully, there was nothing anyone could do."

Of all the things I had expected, that hadn't been it. His words slammed into me with the finality of a ton of bricks. Only my hands gripping onto the phone stopped me from being leveled.

Florence.

Her lined face came into my mind. Since the opening of the clinic, she had seen me through the best and worst years of my life. In the absence of my mother, she had been, for all intents and purposes, my substitute one. She had been there to lend her shoulder after Emma had passed. She had been the one to plan and execute the funeral. In that initial, bleak week after my loss, when I couldn't move because of the grief, she had taken care of me.

But now she was gone and I would never speak to her again. Tears misted my eyes, despair welling up a storm inside. I felt myself crumpling, my body leaning against the walls of the phone box until it bore my full weight and was the only thing keeping me upright.

"How did she die?"

"She had a date to play bridge with a friend, but Florence never turned up or called. Her friend was concerned, so she went to her home. Florence had given her a set of keys on the rare occasion that she wasn't home and needed someone to feed her cat. She found Florence slumped in her favorite armchair. Her TV was on and there was a microwave meal on her lap. If it's any consolation, they don't think she suffered."

An icy cold stole over me.

Mark didn't know Florence like I did. He was unaware of her strange quirks, including her irrational fear of ballerinas. She believed they were emotionless and deliberately mangled their feet to balance in a way that was never meant for humans. Needless to say, she avoided ballet performances at all costs.

Mark didn't know that.

He also didn't know how much Florence abhorred microwaves.

She didn't believe in them and only had one in the house as it was gifted from her brother. She could not bear to part with it and disappoint him, so instead, the machine had sat on her side table, unplugged and unused because she could never accept that they used radiation to heat up food.

And it wasn't only her own use she was concerned with, frequently voicing her displeasure at me just for microwaving a burrito. Hell, the woman was such a purist, she wouldn't touch any food that couldn't be grown.

There was no way in hell that Florence would eat a microwave meal.

A lead weight dropped in the pit of my stomach as my thoughts took a darker turn. Had those same men gone after her? Had they killed her and tried to pass it off as a natural death?

It felt insane to even pose the question, yet I had already experienced what they were capable of.

"When did she die?" I asked, keeping my macabre thoughts to myself. I shouldn't say anything unless I had proof, and even then, I wasn't sure it would be a good idea. The less Mark knew, the safer he would be.

Except Florence hadn't known a thing, and she was dead now.

"Well, that's another bizarre coincidence," Mark continued. "It must have happened the same day that someone mugged me, if you can believe that."

My stomach sank all the way to the ground. I could believe it, and unfortunately, I now knew my suspicions were justified.

The men who had come after us had killed Florence and attacked Mark.

It took every inch of willpower not to blurt out the truth. What was the point in endangering him further? If I didn't reveal any of my predicament, maybe, just maybe, they would leave him alone. After all, if they had already gone after him once but left him alive, surely they must have concluded that he did not know anything.

"Anyway, you didn't know about any of this, so why are you calling so early?" Mark asked, suddenly concerned.

"I was actually calling for a favor. I figured your cabin would be empty this time of the year and wanted to ask if you'd mind us borrowing it. I was thinking of taking the family for a vacation, but it doesn't seem the right thing to do now, so scratch that idea."

I could almost hear him frowning down the phone line. I silently willed him to buy my excuse.

"Obviously, it's yours if you want it. There's nothing you can do to turn back time, so you shouldn't let what's happened spoil your time with the family. The keys are hidden in the flowerpot with a rose painted on it. The place is stocked with food too, so yeah, be my guest."

It sounded like the answer to our prayers so having to reject it felt like a physical blow.

"No," I answered, trying to keep my voice natural. "I'll figure something else out. Maybe we'll head back to Montreal. Sam and I just had a blast there for our honeymoon."

Mark went silent, and I felt myself grow wary. I was never able to hide anything from him and I worried he wouldn't buy my story. When he spoke again, a new awareness had crept in.

"What's going on? Is there something you need to tell me?"

It was on the tip of my tongue to spill my guts and receive his help, but I knew I couldn't risk it. He wasn't a part of this and he never could be. "I'm about as fine as I can be under the circumstances. Don't worry about me. I've got my family to pull me through. You just heal up."

I could hear the gears turning in his mind, but something in my voice must have told him to drop it.

"You know I'm here anytime you need me?"

"Yeah." I had to get off this call or I would blow it. "I'll call back in a few days to find out about the funeral. I assume her niece is organizing it?"

"Yeah, Paula's been a trooper. Even adopted the cat. That thing's going to be spoiled rotten."

Heavy silence came down the line. I cleared my throat, forcing my voice to sound neutral.

"I need to go. Take care of yourself, bud. Stay away from those parks and ditches."

Without waiting for a response, I hung up.

21

SULLY

Though the conversation with Mark had left me shaken, I couldn't allow myself the luxury of breaking down. I was only halfway through my task, and even then, I had struck out.

My head was spinning.

If they could kill an innocent elderly woman and leave a man half dead in a ditch, there would be no reasoning with them.

Faced with a relentless enemy, the stakes had never been higher. Their intentions were crystal clear — total elimination. It was a chilling reality, one that set this conflict apart from anything we had encountered before. With Forbes' men — in the initial stages at least — there had been a glimmer of hope amidst the darkness: the enemy's desire to keep Bandit alive. It was a slender lifeline in the midst of chaos. Yet, as the battle raged on, even that flicker of hope faded. Now, the transition from wanting Bandit alive to the ruthless pursuit of total annihilation marked a turning point, forcing us to confront an enemy devoid of mercy.

I had to grab provisions and hurry back to the others to relay my discovery. We needed to formulate a new plan.

Crossing the threshold into the gas station, my senses heightened, acutely aware of the stakes that rested upon my shoulders. The hum of fluorescent lights above echoed in the sterile atmosphere. My gaze darted, scanning for any telltale signs of surveillance. There, behind the cashier's counter, I spotted the glint of a lens – a silent sentinel capturing the movements of unsuspecting customers. Another camera, strategically positioned, kept a watchful eye on the gas pumps, its unblinking gaze tracking every vehicle that pulled in.

With a calculated calmness that I didn't feel, I took swift action. My hand reached out, fingers grazing the fabric of a baseball cap displayed on a nearby stand. It was a stroke of luck, a conveniently placed accessory that now became my disguise. Pulling it from the rack, I slipped it onto my head, feeling the reassuring touch of the worn fabric against my skin. In one fluid motion, I tugged the cap low, its brim casting a shadow over my eyes, obscuring my features from prying lenses.

As I adjusted the cap, I made sure to fold and tuck the price tag beneath the fabric, erasing any trace of my impromptu disguise. I was uneasy with the act of stealing, but there was no other way. I had to stay incognito. My family's safety depended on it.

The cashier, a young guy in his twenties, nodded at me. I nodded back a greeting but didn't say a word. Turning my head from the cameras, I moved toward a refrigerated unit. The chilled air wrapped around me as I swiftly selected an array of sandwiches, bananas, candy bars, nuts, and as many bottles of water as I could carry.

My arms already half full, I stopped a shelf of dog food and loaded up on the cans. Balancing everything carefully, I made my way to the waiting line when Florence's face flew into my mind with a forcefulness that left me breathless. It was impossible to grasp that she was dead because of us.

Because of me.

I'm so sorry, Florence. This wasn't the ending you deserved.

"You ready?" The cashier asked, interrupting my guilt trip.

Jolted back to reality, I jumped. "Yeah, sorry."

Dumping the food onto the counter so he could reach them easier, I watched, a boot tapping an impatient beat on the floor as I waited for him to ring them up. With every chime of the till, my money seemed to diminish faster than I could count. I forked over the bills reluctantly. When the cashier handed me my change, I had to suppress a laugh — was it really worth the effort of giving me back two dimes?

Unbeknownst to the diligent cashier, my nerves were stretched thin, every muscle in my body wound tight with tension. He worked with methodical precision, bagging up the goods carefully, heaviest items first. Under ordinary circumstances, I might have appreciated his precision, but why did it have to be this, of all mornings, for me to meet the world's most conscientious — and slowest — cashier? As I silently urged him along, a flash of metal caught my eye.

I glanced over at the coffee machine, which looked to have been buffed within an inch of its life — from this same guy, no doubt. What was he going for? Employee of the year? When, suddenly, reflected in the shiny metal, I saw a truck approaching.

And it was *identical* to the one we had stolen.

My stomach lurched at the sight. My senses were on high alert as adrenaline coursed through my veins. They were here! How had they found me so quickly? Could they have traced the call *that* fast? It didn't seem possible.

I only had seconds, a minute at most, to make a getaway without them seeing me. Scooping up the bag of groceries, I raced out of there. There was no attempt to stay undercover this time.

Trying to stop the panic from taking hold, I scanned the area to see if there was anything I could use since jogging back would be out of the question.

I needed a ride.

Glancing across the lot, I assessed my options. One car had its driver already inside, while another's tyres were being checked over. The other two vehicles were nowhere to be seen, having presumably left already.

Spinning around, I searched for something, anything I could use when my gaze landed on the motorcycle I had seen on my way in. It was a nice-looking bike. A Harley Davidson with the American flag airbrushed onto its leather seat, but what I noticed more than its atheistic appeal, was the absence of its owner. Hopefully, he was in the john.

Hurrying to the bike, I dumped the bag into the luggage rack at the back of the bike and climbed on. To my enormous relief, the keys were still in the ignition.

Shooting a prayer to the heavens, I turned the key. The engine roared to life startling its owner who — it turned out — wasn't in the john at all, but hidden from my view behind a gas pump on a mobile call. The biker, a stocky guy with a large tattoo of an octopus wrapped around his neck, yelled over.

"What the… That's my bike!"

As multiple faces turned toward me, I gunned the engine and peeled off, leaving a cloud of smoke in my wake.

22

CHASE

Watching Sully take off like that was a little like I had agreed for him to walk out of my life forever, as if my lack of action could be taken as silent consent.

Technically, I know that's not what actually happened, but I still couldn't shake that nagging doubt that wrapped its dark fingers around my heart. That absolute fear shocked me to my core, but also made me feel furious with myself.

Throughout my childhood, I had looked after myself. When my mom wasn't locking me in our trailer so she could abandon me to her ongoing hunt for a man, she would drown her sorrows or veg out in front of the TV for days on end. Forget her being the parent, I was the one who took care of us.

I was the one who did the dishes and cooked boxed mac and cheese in the microwave. I washed the laundry in the tub whenever we were low on cash — which was basically all the time. I even had to get up throughout the night to check that her cigarette butts were actually out, as she had a habit of dozing off while smoking on the sofa.

Yet despite everything I did for her, I know she never loved me.

I was never more than a slave she could boss around, her little caretaker. When Tubs came into the picture, things had grown ten times worse. Now she had a partner who drank even more than she did. Every one of their binge-drinking sessions ended in a violent fight with me somehow, always catching the worst of it.

But when Tubs started viewing me as more than just his punching bag, I knew I had to get out of there, but I didn't have a clue what I was really setting myself up for.

Living on the streets was a constant fight for survival, one you never got a break from. Finding food wasn't the only struggle — an empty stomach you quickly grew used to. The lethargy and weakness could be combated by carefully timed nibbles of an energy bar. No. The worst thing was never knowing where you were going to sleep that night… *and if you would ever wake again.*

The doorways and alleyways that were a typical homeless person's bedroom provided next to no security. Drunks and druggies often wandered too close for comfort. And sometimes, just the random creepy opportunist looking for a "good" time. I don't think I actually slept through an entire night while I was homeless. To think I only used to worry about my mom's cigarette butts; those had been the good old days.

Which is why, standing here now, I couldn't understand why I felt so helpless. I had been through hell and back, all on my own. It made no sense at all for me to feel like this.

A cold, wet nose nudged the back of my hand. In the depths of his green-eyed gaze, I saw a reflection of my own concerns mirrored back at me. Bandit's unspoken understanding bridged the gap between man and beast, a silent pact of loyalty and love that went beyond words. With a gentle touch, I scratched the top of his nose, his fur soft beneath my fingers, grounding me in the reality of his presence.

He nudged the iPad on the ground with his snout, a gesture both endearing and astute, and typed.

"Sully will be back."

Great. Now my dog was having to reassure me of my insecurities. Good job being the strong one, Chase.

"I know," I answered. "I just wish we could have gone with him. It doesn't feel right to have him out there alone without even a weapon or a way to reach us if something goes wrong."

Bandit lowered his head to the digital keyboard again.

"Sully is smart. He is our pack leader. He will be back soon and then we can leave together."

A sound came from behind us, the creek of the barn doors opening as someone stepped through. We looked over to find Emma staring at us in annoyance, running her fingers through her hair in an attempt to unravel the knots that tangled her blonde locks.

"It is too early for you to be making so much commotion," she said grumpily as she gave up on her hair, wrapping her arms around herself to ward off the chill.

We were barely a sound. I was just speaking to Bandit."

Her lips turned down with disapproval.

"The two of you don't know how noisy you are. You woke me from clear across the barn. It's not like I had much rest either, not with my arm hurting so much and all the snoring you did."

Was she on crack? I was incredulous and unable to hide it. "I don't snore!"

"Then what was that loud rumbling sound that came out of your mouth the whole night long. Him to." She pointed a skinny finger at Bandit, who shot me such a comical look of shock that a laugh almost burst out of me.

"For someone who has no idea what they're talking about, you sure do a lot of it," I shot back before I could stop myself. Her eyebrows rose a notch. I could feel my anger bubbling up.

"Well, you are a horrible little girl," she retorted.

I stared at her. "Seriously? That's all you've got?"

She glared at me then, stamping her foot. "And you smell! Both of you!"

With that, she turned around. With her nose in the air, she stormed back inside. Stomping every step of the way, she made as much noise as her ballet pumps would allow her.

"That's one way to wake up the rest of the clan, I guess."

"*Woof,*" came the answer by my side.

23

CHASE

U ntil Sully returned, breakfast was a pathetic affair.

All I had was some gum, warm from being in the back of my jeans. Sam fared a little better — she found a bag of peanut M&M's in her bag, which she divided between us. Well, between the rest of us, excluding Emma. She had retreated back into her corner, apparently not interested in anything to do with us now that Sully wasn't here.

The rest of us ate our candy quickly, eager for what little energy it would provide. Bandit had none since chocolate was poisonous to dogs. He said he was fine to wait for Sully, but Sam stopped herself from eating, staring at the meagre portion in her hand.

Observing Emma from across the room, a flicker of irritation marred her usually composed expression. She mumbled something; the words lost under her breath, but her tone was laced with frustration.

With a determined stride, Sam closed the distance between them. I watched as she split the meager portion, extending a peace offering toward the other woman. It was a testament to her kindness that she was willing to share, even in the face of her obvious annoyance. However, her attempt at goodwill was met with an unexpected reaction. Emma's eyes widened, a horrified gasp escaping her lips as if Sam had offered her something unimaginable.

"Are you kidding me right now?"

Sam's voice was hard and her eyes had turned flat. She snatched her hand back, withdrawing her offer of food. I moved towards them, unsure of what Emma had done that caused Sam to react in such a fashion. When I got there, however, I instantly saw what had drawn Sam's ire: Emma was halfway through another energy bar while an empty bottle of water lay between her feet.

"You drank the water too?"

She jumped guilty. "I only had the one bottle. My throat was feeling tight. I was worried I might have caught the Tetanus and wanted to make sure I could still drink…" she began, only for Sam to cut her off.

"You heard us over there. You know we barely have anything between us, yet here you are, hiding in this corner, so you still don't have to share your food with us. I can't believe how selfish you are!"

Shockingly, Emma's eyes brimmed with tears. "You're always yelling at me."

The tears took Sam by surprise, their sudden appearance like a crack in a dam that had been holding back a torrent of emotion. It was a vulnerability she hadn't expected, and she must have felt a pang of sympathy as she paused, softening her tone. "You need to think, Emma. We're all in this together. Everyone's hungry and thirsty, not only you. If you want us to treat you better, you need to think a little less about yourself and more about others. It's the only way we're going to get through this."

Emma fell silent. I actually thought Sam might get through to her for once.

"What does Sully say?"

Sam blinked, startled by the question. "What does it matter what he has to say?"

"He's my husband…"

"So you're only interested in what *he* thinks? Unbelievable!"

Emma didn't answer, looking trapped. Her lower lip trembled. I felt more tears might be coming. A low, drawn-out whistle emitted from Gideon's lips as he approached. I could tell he had woken recently as his clothes were rumpled and there was a smudge of dirt on his cheek. As tired as he looked, he had already helped Zeb into his wheelchair and was now pushing him toward the source of all the commotion. He ran a hand through his disheveled hair. "At least she's honest, right?"

A look of gratefulness came over Emma. "Thank you," she answered, as if Gideon had meant it as a compliment. "At least *he's* being nice to me."

Gideon's face turned surprised. "Just to clarify, I was being sarcastic."

Emma bit her lip, those tears finally spilling over. "So you're being mean, too. Yet somehow you're all shocked that I won't share my food with you. Why should I when none of you like me?"

"That hasn't got anything to do with this!" I burst out, unable to keep it together anymore.

"We're here as a team because someone is after us! We have to work together, and that means sharing what resources we have if we're going to have any chance of staying alive. You can't just do your own thing when you're with us. It doesn't work like that."

"We share whatever we have, Emma. It's what families do," Zeb agreed gently, but we may well have spoken to a brick wall for all the good it did. She retreated into a ball, hugging her bag to her chest.

"You can say whatever you want, but I know the truth. None of you are my friends. Only Sully cares about me."

I had half a mind to set her straight since I wasn't totally sure that was true. She made me so angry, especially when you factored in that she could be the very reason our lives were in danger. After all, we had been fine. Happily living our lives when she plowed into our home and ruined our lives.

What a selfish little—

Whatever curse word I was about to think was wiped clean from my mind at the sound of a motorcycle roaring toward us. Icy fingers of fear raced down my spine. My heart rate spiked, my stomach plummeted as I imagined those men to be back.

Sam waved at us frantically. "Back! Hide!"

I didn't need another warning.

Bandit and I sprinted behind a stack of hay bales while Gideon steered Zeb into a dark corner. Emma hadn't moved, her face white as a sheet. Like a rabbit in the headlights, she stood there until Sam pulled her down.

"Get down, idiot!" she hissed through her teeth.

For the first time since I'd known her, Emma didn't answer back. Cowering into a ball, Sam kept her hand pushed down against the back of her head, afraid that Emma would give us all away.

I stole a furtive glance at one of the many gaps that lay within the walls of the barn, but couldn't see the motorcycle or its rider outside. Bandit's nose twitched, trying to pick up a scent. I'd been with him long enough to recognize his warnings, so I steeled myself for his reaction.

He whined, a happy whine, then let out a bark. The tension that had flooded my body immediately left.

"It's Sully," I called out to the others.

Their faces came back into the light, reflecting the relief I was feeling. The bike was kept running though Sully appeared in the doorway, clutching a bag of what had to be food. Instead of the welcoming smile I was expected, his face was pale. The fear that was in his eyes was tangible.

"We need to get out of here. Now!"

We hurried over to him, talking over each other in our haste.

"What's going on?"

"Did they find us?"

Sully gestured for us to simmer down. "They're right behind me. I saw one of the armored trucks as I was coming out of the gas station. We need to leave."

Gideon's hands tightened into fists, unable to take in the news. "But we got rid of all electronic devices. Nobody has one they can trace, do they?"

A chorus of head shakes was his answer. Sam had already explained how they could be easily tracked. I hadn't known until she explained that if a cell phone that was turned on, even for a few seconds, it could give an indication of its location. It's how law enforcement officers caught criminals all the time, but we were smart enough to know better.

Well, except for one person, maybe.

Without meaning to, we all turned to Emma.

"You don't have anything in that bag that could have led them to us, do you?" Sam asked Emma in the voice she used at work, the one that reeked of authority and had lesser men quaking in their boots.

Not Emma, though, who wasn't smart enough to know better. "We already went through this! You saw what was in my bag. All I had were pictures and food. Why are you trying to blame this on me?"

"It's not about blame. It's about finding out how they got to us," Sam explained carefully.

Picking up on her tone, Emma glared. "You don't have to talk to me like that. I'm not an idiot."

The two women faced off against each other as the air grew heavy. From the corner of my eye, I saw Gideon move toward the truck we had stolen. Without warning, he suddenly dove beneath it. I wasn't sure what he was hoping to find, but within seconds, he emerged with a flashing, coin-sized device.

"They have been tracking us this whole time," Gideon explained, a sick look on his face.

Sully turned an even paler shade of white.

"I should have known. I can't believe I didn't check under the truck." He looked so mad at himself that Sam entwined her fingers with his. The simple gesture caused Emma to give them the side-eye.

"None of us thought to look there. Don't be so hard on yourself. Let's just get out of here before they arrive. We could just leave the tracker here to buy us time?" she mused.

"No," Sully responded. "The gas station is too close. It wouldn't be a long enough distraction."

I looked at him, mirroring the concern I saw in Sam's eyes. Some kind of plan was forming in his mind, yet I knew instinctively that I wouldn't like it. "What are you thinking?"

"I'm going to take the tracker with me on that motorcycle. We'll both take off at the same time, but I'll go in the opposite direction. I'll lead them away."

A frown creased Sam's forehead, ageing her by several years. "No. We shouldn't split up again. It's too risky."

Sully stared into her face, wavering. He didn't want to leave us either, but he pushed her toward the truck.

"We haven't got time to discuss this. Get in the truck, then take off down the road. We'll regroup after I've gotten rid of the tracker and lead them astray. I think that's our best bet."

I clung to the expectation that her sharp mind, the one we had come to rely on in our worst moments, would conjure an alternate plan. But as I scanned her expression, a sinking feeling settled in the pit of my stomach.

Sam's face, usually a study of determination, was now marred by a profound sense of defeat. I could see the gears turning in her mind in its desperate search to keep Sully with us, but the gutted expression that clouded her features told me she was coming up empty-handed.

"I don't like it, but I can't think of a better idea right now," she began hesitantly. Sully took that as the confirmation he needed. He kissed her quickly and steered her to the other side of the barn. He took out the map we had found with the truck.

"There," he pointed at a location on the map. "See this town up here. We'll meet there. It's several towns away, so in the event that they do find us, at least we won't be open targets. There will be civilians and witnesses. If the situation calls for it, we should be able to escape.

We nodded our agreement.

"Chase, you have the route memorized?" he asked me. "Because I don't have a photographic memory, I'm taking this map with me."

I tapped the side of my head, nodding. Sam went to hug her husband one last time when, with a speed that surprised everyone, Emma threw herself at him, jostling Sam out of the way. Her arms wrapped around Sully as if she believed she could physically anchor him in place.

"You can't leave me with them. You're the only one who likes me." Sully pulled her awkwardly off him, shooting Sam an apologetic look.

"That's not true. The others will look after you as well as I can. You all need to go now."

"But..."

Sully held up a hand to her face, stopping her protest. He dumped the bag of provisions on the floor of the truck and jumped back onto the bike — which I suddenly realized I had no idea how he had gotten it — and sped off down the road leaving us feeling hollow, overwhelmed with devastation.

24

SULLY

The Harley roared beneath me, vibrating through my entire being as I gripped the handles, my fingers white with tension. The powerful engine drowned out the world blurring past in streaks of yellow as I went at a breakneck speed.

Considering my limited experience with motorcycles, it was astonishing that I managed to keep the Harley upright. Until now, my interactions with bikes had been confined to the occasional joyride on the ones from Mark's extensive collection. I used to tease him relentlessly about his mid-life crisis machines, never truly understanding the allure of the open road and the freedom they offered.

However, in this moment of chaos and desperation, my perspective had shifted drastically. The skills I had learned, albeit begrudgingly, during those weekends, had become my lifeline. I clung to the handlebars, my knuckles aching, drawing on every bit of knowledge I had absorbed from those rides. Without the protection of a helmet, the wind howled in my ears.

As I sped away, the vivid, nightmarish images of the men attacking us back at the ranch replayed in my mind like a horror film, causing my chest to tighten with a mix of fear and anger. Each detail, every menacing face and hostile gesture, was etched into my memory, fueling my determination to escape their clutches. My grip on the bike's handles tightened involuntarily, my fingers pressing into the grips.

I stole a glance into the rearview mirrors, my eyes scanning the road behind me for what felt like the hundredth time since I had pulled away from the barn. Every nerve in my body was on edge, expecting to see those menacing trucks barreling down on me. Yet, for reasons unknown, there was no sign of them. Although it seemed impossible, my anxiety rose another notch as the thought that they could have seen through my plan and found my family already, snaked into my mind. I dug my fingers into the handles until I thought they would bleed.

I would know if something had happened to them. Somehow, I was sure I'd feel it in my gut.

The tracker was now securely tucked inside the luggage rack. I remembered the way it had blinked insistently when I closed the lid, a beacon of hope in the darkness.

Despite the adrenaline that pumped through my veins, an empty ache formed in the pit of my stomach. I wished desperately that I had had more time with them, that we hadn't been torn apart so abruptly. But in that split second when I had fled, with the threat closing in around us, this was all I could think to do. With the map tucked into my shirt, I focused my thoughts and energy on rallying with them at the designated meeting point.

I rode in silence, with nothing but the never-changing scenery to keep me company. The sun shone down, bathing the world in such glorious light that our desperate fight seemed almost like a dream. But whenever I tried to picture Sam behind the wheel and my family riding in the bed of the truck, a lone grenade would blast into the windshield.

Shaking my head, I fought the nightmare away. If I kept entertaining these worst-case scenarios, all that would happen is I'd crash this bike and be of no use to anyone.

Determined to draw the men away, I pushed on until some twenty minutes later, a large sign greeted me. It was another truck stop, this one much bigger than the last. I scanned the surroundings, taking in the gas station and a busy diner, advertising a $4.99 deal for breakfast that must have been popular judging by the cars that packed the parking lot. An idea came to mind, causing me to take better stock of the place. I slid the bike into a tiny space at the front.

Spotting a trashcan, I thought about simply dumping the tracker there, but I wasn't sure that a static signal would be the optimum option. Ideally, I needed to lead them as far out of the way as possible, and since I couldn't do it all by myself — not if I was going to meet back up with them again soon — my best bet would be to attach it to one of the vehicles that were already here.

Without warning, I felt the hairs on the back of my neck rise and turned to find a man openly staring at me. My first thought was that it was one of the bad guys.

My hand was reaching to turn the key in the ignition when I noticed that he was adorned with vivid tattoos that snaked across his arms and neck. His weathered face bore the marks of countless battles, with a rough beard framing a set of lips that seemed permanently etched in a scowl. His eyes, deep and cold, were like two smoldering embers, emanating a fierce intensity that seemed to challenge those who dared to meet his gaze.

Clad in worn leather, patches and insignias adorned his jacket, marking him as a person who thrived on rebellion and independence. The sound of heavy boots echoed with each step he took.

Those facts gave me pause.

Then I noticed the other tattooed guys surrounding him, sporting bald heads and beards, and oil-stained jeans, looking like they had all stepped out of a TV show. They either sat astride or stood beside various makes of Harleys. And as I took in that bit of information, my stomach sank.

They were all riding Harleys.

The biker who had been staring at me shouted over. "That's a nice bike."

I hoped we were just shooting the breeze, though I suspected we weren't.

"Yeah, I think so too," I answered, hoping that would be the last of our conversation. Of course, I wasn't so lucky.

"I'd be interested in knowing where you got that seat from. Haven't seen any of those around these parts."

Sensing trouble, his friends were starting to look my way. I tried to keep my voice natural under the increasing scrutiny, wondering about my bad luck. A confrontation with these wannabe Hells Angels was the last thing I needed.

Despite knowing his question could be a trap, I couldn't see a smart way to extract myself. Besides, I had an inkling he knew damn well where I had gotten the bike from or he wouldn't be asking.

"It's amazing what you can get on eBay these days," I replied as my eyes slid away from him, still looking for that suitable place for my tracker.

I didn't hear another question out of him, which I took as a hopeful sign. Climbing off the bike, I took a step toward the cars in front of the diner when I felt a tap on my shoulder. It was the tattooed biker. He had crossed the distance between us and was now standing right behind me.

"The thing is, friend," he said in the unfriendliest voice I'd ever heard. "That's not something you can buy off eBay. In fact, that particular seat is an original and handmade by my buddy Mike Sheldon. That there bike you're riding belongs to him, and since he is my friend, I know how much this baby means to him. I know he would sell his wife before he got rid of that bike. So, for you to be riding it means only one thing: you stole it."

I would have thought it admirable how he was sticking up for his friend, except there was a nasty air about him. Every word he spoke was laced with malice and came with a sneer. He was spoiling for a fight. This wasn't about being a Good Samaritan.

I sized him up. Beneath his shirt, his muscles rippled. He had bulging biceps that spoke of countless hours spent in the gym — and possibly steroids. He reeked of menace that was impossible to ignore.

I knew without a doubt my morning was about to take an even darker turn.

"This is not what you think," I began, trying to buy time. He cut me off with a wave of his abnormally large hand. What kind of protein shake was this guy on?

"Oh, this is exactly what I think," he said. "Which is why you're going to give the bike to me."

I took a step away from him, my muscles coiling with tension. The air crackled, heavy with the weight of anticipation. Every nerve in my body screamed caution, urging me to be vigilant, to watch for the subtlest of movements, the tiniest shifts in his expression that could betray his intentions.

His eyes, dark and inscrutable, bore into mine, holding my gaze with an intensity that sent a shiver down my spine. I felt like a cornered animal, aware of the danger but uncertain of how to escape. I clenched my fists, my palms moist with sweat, and tried to steady my breathing.

"Thing is, I would love to, but I actually can't."

"Well, that's a shame. And here I was thinking you were smart," he said, lying through his teeth.

Suddenly, he came at me — all two hundred pounds of him. Reeking of cigarettes and gasoline, he smashed a fist into my face. I saw it coming from a mile away, as though he was strong, he was also slow, signaling his intent clearly. I dodged, ducking my head to one side. But he knew the move was coming and adjusted himself accordingly.

His fist connected with my cheek as pain shot through my skull. I felt my teeth rattle and the bitter taste of blood flooded my mouth. My head snapped back as the world danced rings around me.

I barely had a second to breathe when the guy came barreling toward me again. I knew I couldn't outfight him — he was too strong. I would only get out of this with all my limbs intact if I used my head.

Knowing he had the advantage, he was expecting me to defend myself when I struck out, aiming a kick to the back of his knees that he wasn't prepared for. Losing his balance, he toppled to the ground, hard. Trunk-like arms flailing like a windmill. I even thought I heard something snap.

I felt a rush of euphoria, but that quickly subsided when his buddies started our way. My hand palmed the tracker and I feigned a stumble as I tossed the thing into the saddlebag on my opponent's bike. Feeling a grim sense of satisfaction, I shot him a look as I gunned the engine on my bike.

"Have fun, jerk."

Before his buddies could come after me, I peeled off, leaving a cloud of dust in my wake.

25

CHASE

We piled into the truck as fast as we could. Sam ran around to the driver's seat, climbing in.

"Do you want me to drive?" I heard Gideon ask as I bent down from the interior of the cab to help lift Zeb into the truck.

"No. I've got it," Sam replied.

Gideon grabbed hold of the wheelchair, then shot me a look. "Ready?"

Preparing myself, I planted my feet and nodded.

"Lift!"

I pulled with all my might, while Gideon groaned from the strain. He was doing most of the lifting since my muscles weren't exactly known for being strong.

"Bend your knees, son. Careful," came Zeb's urgent voice. He braced his hands on either side of his wheelchair, but could do nothing to help us other than to stay as still as possible.

Gideon's muscles strained as he hoisted Zeb's wheelchair up high enough to set it down inside the truck. After double-checking that Emma and Bandit were with us, I slammed the gate shut. Sam revved the engine and shot a glance in the rearview mirror as Gideon clambered into the passenger seat.

"Everyone belted in?"

There was a quick chorus of yes's, then we were off, bumping along the farmland until we swerved onto the road where the ride turned smoother.

I sat with my arms around Bandit, my face in his soft fur, though who was comforting who, I couldn't say. Thoughts flew through my mind. Terrible, dark thoughts that I didn't want to give any power to, but it was impossible not to worry about Sully.

Not that I didn't have faith in him — if anyone could do it, it would be him — but those men were armed to the gills. There were so many of them and they were trained. We'd defended ourselves against the first wave that had attacked us. I knew we'd caused some casualties, maybe even fatalities, but not even twenty-four hours later, they were back. Even if Sully could take care of a second group, wouldn't that just delay them? Wouldn't they just send more men after us?

I glanced over at Gideon, wishing I was sitting next to him so we could talk. We'd gotten pretty close lately, and even though we argued about stuff constantly — stupid stuff like who lost the remote this time — when it came to anything serious, we always had each other's backs. We weren't just family now. We were fast becoming best friends.

And maybe even something more.

He sat straight, his spine rigid as his eyes scanned first one direction, then the next, constantly keeping watch for danger.

I felt Sam's gaze on me. Her eyes, usually warm and lively were now hooded with concern, though she tried to hide her fear with the quick, small smile she flashed my way.

"Chase, you're on food duty. Why don't you see what Sully brought us?"

"I'm not really hungry," I said, realizing it was true the second the statement left my mouth.

Gideon spun around with absolute disbelief in his eyes. "Did you hit your head?"

Sam's smile turned understanding as she continued. "Sully went to all that trouble for us. It won't do him any good if we collapse from hunger, Chase. It's OK to eat something. We need to keep our strength up."

Bandit laid his head on my knee and woofed. I realized he must be starving, since he had missed at least two of his own meals. Feeling like the worst owner in the history of pet owners, I opened up the bag Sully had left for us.

There were enough sandwiches that we could have one each. I tossed them to the others, hesitating only when there were two left. One had obviously been meant for Sully, and the other, Emma. Sensing my hesitation, she stared at me with those unfathomable blue eyes. After the way she had behaved, she didn't deserve any charity or kindness, especially since she had already eaten.

I was expecting Emma to say something as she usually couldn't help herself, but she surprised me with her silence. Her eyes eating up the sight of the sandwich in my hands, however, communicated a world of longing. Gritting my teeth so I wouldn't say anything, I tossed the sandwich over to her.

Finding several cans of dog food in the bag, I took one out, then stopped, having hit a snag. Watching me, Gideon pulled a face as he realized my predicament. "Don't suppose anyone has a can opener by any chance?"

Of course, no one did. "I don't need a can opener," I informed him. "I can get it open with a knife or a spoon, even a fork."

Gideon grinned suddenly, taking out a folding knife from his pocket. He often carried it around on his key chain in case of an emergency. He hopped over his seat, brandishing the knife as he came closer.

"You sure this is safe?"

"I've done it a million times. No one owns a can opener when they're living on the streets. You make do with whatever's around."

His eyes went a darker shade of green and seemed to hold a myriad of emotions. I felt a subtle shift in the air, as if the energy around us had changed. Gazing at me intently, he didn't speak, but his look made me self-conscious.

"Hand it over then," I said, reaching over and taking the knife from him. Setting the can vertically on the floor, I flicked the knife open.

"OK, stand back a bit, just in case. While I've done this before, I haven't actually opened a can in a moving vehicle. Best if we keep our fingers and paws a safe distance away."

Bandit and Gideon obediently shrunk away, giving me the space I needed. Lowering the point to the inner rim of the can, I wrapped one hand securely around the metal handle of the knife. The knife wasn't exactly easy to hold, especially while the floor kept shifting beneath my feet — but I had no other choice. My Muttface needed to eat. My right hand balled up into a tight fist

Keeping my body as still as possible, I brought my fist down onto the top of the knife handle, just above where my fingers gripped it. The point of the blade bit into the can, puncturing a tiny hole into the surface. Positioning the knife so that as much of its point sat in that hole, I repeated the same move, resulting in a slightly larger hole.

Behind me, Gideon gave me a supportive whoop. "Hey. That's pretty neat."

"Yeah, but now we've come to the hard part." This was where it could go horribly wrong.

I slid as much of the knife into the hole as I could, then angled the blade so that its sharpest edge aligned with the unopened part of the can. Taking hold of the can with my left hand, I gripped it tightly and starting working the blade in a forward-back motion, sawing at the can.

The metal started giving way, but not without a lot of pressure from me. I blew out a breath of effort that lifted the hair out of my eyes before it fell down around me again. I found myself wishing I had something to tie it back with.

Gideon must have sensed my frustration as he leaned toward me and took up my hair in his hands. He was so close I could feel his breath on my face, warm puffs of air tinged with the familiar earthy scent that clung to him. It was a smell he always seemed to have, the one that came from his time spent working in Warrey's garage or tending to Zeb's vegetable garden. A subtle blend of motor oil and soil, the aroma wrapped around me. His very proximity made me lose myself momentarily. I had to stop sawing or risk losing the use of my hands completely.

"What's wrong?" he asked.

I searched my brain frantically for an answer that wouldn't reveal how mixed-up I was feeling. Why were my hormones going crazy? What terrible timing was this?

"Nothing. Just waiting for the truck to smooth out," I lied. We hadn't actually been hitting any bumps, so the fact he didn't question this was a minor miracle.

I went at the can, working the knife first one way, then another, twisting the can to follow my progression until I had finally cut away enough of the end. Still using the knife, I slid it beneath the opening then, flattening the blade against the lid, I bent the lid back.

I got a big whiff of meaty dog food for my efforts.

"Woof!" Bandit said happily. He did a happy little dance, four paws doing some version of a jig as his butt shock with excitement. Without meaning to, his tail whipped painfully against my arm as he typed into his iPad, impatient for his food to be served up. *"I'm so hungry, Chase. Hurry please!"*

Even starving, my dog had better manners than me.

"You did it!" Gideon congratulated me, letting go of my hair. I felt a moment of disappointment that he didn't seem as affected as I had been by his closeness but I shoved the thought aside. Bandit needed to eat. I'd have to deal with my weirdness later.

"What're we going to dish it up with? I know he's super smart, but he still can't use a fork to eat out of a can."

"No. I haven't figured out how to do that yet," Bandit agreed.

Since none of us had the forethought to bring plates with us, I rummaged inside the plastic bag to see if there was something I could use. Other than the one uneaten sandwich — which I was determined to save for Sully — I found a bunch of bananas, bottles of water, a few bags of nuts, some more cans of dog food, and six bars of candy.

None of which was particularly helpful to us at this moment.

I turned my head from the floor, staring around the truck, but all I saw was ammo and more ammo until the bag under my fingers struck me with inspiration. I emptied it, turned it inside out, then smoothed it along the floor of the truck. Grabbing the can, I tipped it upside down, watching as the dog chow landed on the bag in one big plop.

"I know this isn't perfect, but it's the best I can do in a pinch," I apologized to Bandit. "You'll have to be careful that you don't bite through the plastic since it won't taste great and is probably really bad for you. I've heard plastic does terrible things to animals when it's ingested."

He nodded, his eyes shining at me with gratefulness. Then, with an enormous sigh, he dived into his food, eating it as daintily as I had warned him to. I swear his teeth never even touched the plastic: he used his tongue to flick the food into his mouth.

"That's disgusting."

It was Emma, of course. Hearing her voice, I was reminded how she was like an unwanted guest. One who would never go away.

"Do you have a better idea?"

"Just give him the other sandwich so he won't make such a mess. That stuff stinks."

"That's human food. Besides, it's also Sully's. We're saving it for him. He'll be hungry when we meet up with him."

"If we meet up with him," Emma grumbled.

I think it was meant to be under her breath, but she was like a child who didn't realize their whispering was as loud as their normal volume. We all heard her, even Sam. I saw her shoulders tense and her fingers grip the wheel more tightly. Her jaw clenched tightly. I think it took everything she had not to snap back a retort. Trying to smooth over the moment, it was Zeb who spoke.

"Sully will be there."

His voice had a finality to it that brokered no argument. Hearing the warning in his voice, Emma bit back whatever response she may have had. Not wanting to engage with the worrying thought that flitted in the corners of my mind, I waited for Bandit to finish.

When there was nothing left, and he had licked every inch of the gravy from the bag, I took it away from him, and hung it over the edge of the table, weighing it down with the other cans.

I wasn't sure of anything right now, but we could need the bag again, so it paid to be diligent.

As the miles flew by, we were left alone with our troubled thoughts, the rhythmic hum of the road beneath us, a steady reminder of our relentless drive forward. I gazed blindly out the window, watching the fields blur past in a hazy green and gold mosaic as the landscape transformed with every passing moment. The sky above was a canvas of shifting colors, from the soft pastel hues of dawn to the mid morning glare.

Despite the beauty that surrounded us, all I could do was to count the minutes since Sully had left us behind. I prayed desperately that we wouldn't run out of time.

26

CHASE

I don't know how long we had been driving, maybe a few hours, when a strange spluttering sound emitted from the truck's engine, startling Gideon awake.

It seemed strange that he could sleep at a time like this, but I remembered reading how stress could bring out different reactions in people. Some became hyper like they had drunk a gallon of caffeine, while others simply crashed out.

A curse shot out of Sam's lips as her eyes jerked to the dashboard meters — specifically at a needle that had slid past the letter E. Gideon blinked at her with groggy eyes.

"Is that saying what I think it's saying?"

Sam's lips were a thin, white line. "Yes."

Zeb called over to them. "What is it? Is something wrong with the truck?"

Sam looked over her shoulder at him. For someone who was usually so expressive, her face was strangely emotionless.

"We're out of gas."

As if to emphasize her point, the engine stuttered, then went out completely. The sudden silence was a shock to the system. We sat around, our faces looking equally stunned, when Sam suddenly punched the steering wheel.

"How could I have been so stupid?!"

I didn't want to say anything, but I actually agreed. The second the thought went through my mind, though, I felt a hot flush of shame. Sam was under a lot of pressure. She had made a mistake.

But this mistake could cost Sully his life.

Bandit whined at me, sensing my distress and feeling his own. Surprising me, he picked up one of the candy bars and left me to run over to Sam, where he laid the bar on her lap as an offering of comfort.

Sam reached up to pat him on his head. "Thank you, boy, but I'm good for now."

Bandit stayed with her, pushing his body against her as overcome by emotion, Sam's eyes began to glisten with tears. Her shoulders shook. I could see her fighting to gain control of herself.

Gideon smiled supportively. "Don't blame yourself. It could have happened to any of us."

"Of all people, I should have known better. I'm a Sheriff, for crying out loud!"

"Whose husband is off alone to deal with an army of dangerous men while his dead ex-wife sits not ten feet away. I think you've earned the right to slip up."

This had come from Zeb. Having detached himself from the seatbelt, he moved over to her. "Sully, wouldn't want you to feel this way."

"No one blames you, Sam." I felt like such a jerk for saying it, when in fact I had been blaming her only a few seconds ago. But, she needed my support, and I was fast getting over my disloyalty.

"Why doesn't she get told off when she makes a mistake?" piped up *that* voice from the corner. Three guesses who.

"Because it was an actual mistake, while yours wasn't," Gideon responded.

"But we're completely stuck. What are we supposed to do now?"

"Now we get out and walk," Sam said. She jumped out of the truck, slamming the door behind her.

"Not me. I'm staying right here until Sully finds me." Emma folded her arms across her chest.

I couldn't help the exasperated look I gave her. "The rest of us are leaving. You can't stay here alone."

"Yes, I can," Emma answered without even looking at me: her were eyes fixed at a point past my head.

"What's going on here now?" Zeb wanted to know.

I nodded my head at Emma, replying in a scathing voice. "*She* says she's not leaving. *She* thinks Sully's going to come and rescue her."

"Let's try to make this easier for everyone, shall we?" Zeb suggested in a gentle tone, far too kind for my liking. I wanted him to be more confrontational, but he was taking the part of mediator. "If you stay here, you risk being found by those men. Even if Sully could come back to you, what good do you think he could do against them all? If we stay together, we can keep each other safe."

Emma fixed her gaze on him, her eyes partially veiled by her long lashes as she carefully weighed his words. The air seemed to thicken with anticipation, the silence stretching as she pondered the implications of what he had said. Finally, after what felt like an eternity, she let out a sigh, a sound heavy with the burden of her thoughts. In a sudden burst of energy, she sprang up from her seat.

"Alright, I'm coming, but only because you're begging me to." Without a further glance at us, she marched out of the truck.

Zeb looked at me, one gray brow arched high. "Spirited, isn't she?"

"Not the word I would use," I said. We helped him off the truck and took stock of our surroundings.

The sun hung low in the sky, casting a warm golden glow across the vast fields of corn that flanked the empty road where we stood.

The air was still, filled with the faint rustle of leaves and the distant calls of unseen birds.

With a sense of growing unease, I cupped a hand over my eyes, shielding them from the glare, and scanned the horizon. I strained my eyes, hoping to catch a glimpse of something — anything — that could provide a glimmer of hope or direction.

My gaze traveled along a distant tree line, followed the curve of the road ahead, and traced the outline of the sky, but there was nothing. No distant silhouette of a building, no hint of civilization on the horizon. Just an endless expanse of nature, untouched and undisturbed.

"You guys have everything you need?" Sam checked with us before we set off.

Gideon tossed a look inside the truck, his eyes straying to the ammo. "It feels wrong to leave all of that there, but since we don't have the right guns…"

"They would only weigh us down," Sam decided for him. "Come on. We've got a long way to go. I don't want us still out here when it starts getting dark."

We set off, leaving the truck where it stood. God knows what someone who came upon the bullet-dented vehicle was going to make of it.

We started walking along the country road. I offered to push Zeb, but Gideon wouldn't hear of it. Flexing his muscles at me, he assured me he was fine, though it wasn't long before his breathing became more labored. Not wanting to embarrass him, I decided it was best not to make a thing of it, trusting that he would let me know when he needed a break.

Bandit kept up with my pace, walking alongside. Every so often, his ears would perk up as if he heard something, and I'd feel a wave of anxiety until a rabbit or fox darted out of the cornfields.

The once-bright morning sun had disappeared behind thick gray clouds, leaving a chill in the air. I tightened my cardigan around me, knowing the others were feeling it too. Gideon had tucked his hands inside the sleeves of his jacket; he used one sleeve to grip Zeb's wheelchair handlebars so that not even metal could touch Zeb's skin. The blanket he had been using before we were forced to leave the ranch covered his legs, or else he would have suffered much more than he currently was.

As fast as we were going, our progress was slow, hindered by the wheelchair. When Gideon started stumbling, Sam swapped with him. And when her pace slowed, I took over.

Emma never volunteered to help.

She kept to herself at the back of the line. Occasionally, I could hear her muttering — it seemed a personal hobby of hers — but I could never make out what it was she was trying to say. Which was lucky, really, as I was pretty sure I wouldn't like it.

We'd been going less than an hour when Emma's mumbling grew progressively louder until Sam finally couldn't take it anymore. Turning, she shot her a glare that could have cut ice.

"Just spit it out! This incessant mumbling is driving me nuts!"

Emma seemed taken aback. She stuttered an unintelligible answer and had to try again. "We can't get anywhere like this, not when we're going so slowly."

"What would you suggest we do otherwise, genius?" Sam stopped walking, placing a hand on either hip.

"We're not going as fast as we can because of him." Her finger pointed at Zeb. "He's slowing us down. We should leave him and come back later. Without him slowing us down, we'd get to Sully much faster."

She finally stopped talking as the rest of us were looking at her in horror. Bandit broke the silence first, placing his paws on Zeb's knees and barking twice.

NO!

"Do you even hear how crazy you sound when you speak?" Gideon was seething, filled with disgust — mirroring how the rest of us felt. Bizarrely, instead of being ashamed of her suggestion, a look of utter confusion came over Emma's face.

"Why are you all looking at me like that? This is the only thing that makes sense. We can't get to Sully quickly with that wheelchair, slowing us down. I'm not saying we kill the old man or anything. I'm saying we just leave him here for now. How is that crazy?"

"His name is Zeb," Gideon replied, a chill in his voice.

"You're a monster, you know that?" Sam spat out the words, letting each one have full effect. "He's family. We don't leave family, so you need to shut up." A sudden surge of red-hot rage erupted from Sam. The sheer force of her anger hung in the air, so palpable and raw that it sent shivers down my spine.

Emma, caught in the torrent of Sam's fury, stood frozen, her eyes wide with shock and fear. The words she had been about to utter died on her lips, replaced by a stunned silence. It was as if the sheer intensity of Sam's rage had stolen her voice, leaving her unable to respond. I could see the confusion etched on her face, the innocence of her intentions clashing with the unforeseen ferocity of Sam's reaction.

In that moment, I knew that Emma truly did not understand the magnitude of what she had said, the impact of her words were lost on her. Her face was a mask of bewilderment. Her body language mirrored her confusion, her shoulders hunched, and her hands trembling.

Which really made me wonder.

What kind of person would not know how awful a suggestion that was? The answer would elude me for a while to come.

27

THE CLEANER

The cleaner, Smith, wasn't having a good week.

Ten hours had passed since anyone had laid eyes on Sullivan and his family. After a restless night on a mattress that seemed to defy the definition of comfort, Smith was relieved when his new crew had arrived. Their entrance brought not only some welcome fresh faces, but a shiny replacement laptop. By the time the signal from the tracker had flashed up, they were packed and preparing to leave the motel behind.

As Smith pushed forward on the road, his eyes caught a glint of metal up ahead. The source of the glimmer soon revealed itself: a speeding motorcycle, its exhaust pipe trailing a smoky haze in its wake. Out here, in the middle of nowhere, Smith felt his skin crawl. He much preferred the high rises and bustling anonymity of city life. The thought of residing in a close-knit community, where not only your name but also your secrets were common knowledge, petrified him.

Of course, maybe his line of work made him see things differently.

Smith's life was a delicate balancing act. His job, shrouded in secrecy and reliant on the cover of darkness, forced him to navigate the blurry lines of morality. Yet, he was a soldier, unswervingly loyal to his commanding officers. To him, their actions, no matter how dubious, were justified in the name of the greater good and the safety of his country. Following orders without questions had become an ingrained part of his existence. It was a mantra that allowed him to find peace amid the chaos.

This cloak of secrecy, however, while essential, cast a heavy veil over his existence. Smith's world was a grayscale, devoid of the vibrant hues of ordinary life. Few knew of his existence, and even fewer understood the weight he carried on his shoulders. Yet, it was precisely this anonymity that propelled him forward, shielding his family from the dangerous world he inhabited.

In the quiet moments between missions, when he could finally be the father his children needed, Smith found solace. Tucking his kids into bed was a scared ritual and a reminder of the life he was fighting to preserve.

Inside the van he had chosen for this mission, he and his crew remained hidden, faces obscured from prying eyes. Smith had learned to evade attention, realizing that the gleaming armored trucks he usually favored would stand out too conspicuously. They screamed of newness, drawing eyes and questions he preferred to avoid.

Adapting to his environment, Smith constantly switched vehicles, never opting for the same one twice if he could help it. A precautionary measure, this meticulous attention to detail was his way of ensuring that he and his crew remained ghosts in the shadows. It was a survival tactic that had kept him one step ahead for years.

Smith understood the messiness of humanity all too well. Even his highly trained men, skilled in the art of disappearing, left traces of their existence. A DNA sample here, a strand of hair there, remnants of their presence were scattered like breadcrumbs, potential hazards waiting to be discovered. In their line of work, invisibility was paramount, and any trace, no matter how minuscule, could compromise their mission.

"We're all set up," came Jackson's voice, breaking the tense silence inside the van.

With his nondescript appearance and forgettable face, Jackson was relatively new to him, having only served with him one time before. If Smith had his way, Jackson wouldn't even be on the mission, but their horrific disaster yesterday had cost him dearly, to the tune of eight men.

Smith's eyes flickered over the monitors, calculating their ETA.

"If we stay at this speed, our ETA is in three minutes," he announced, his voice firm and steady, betraying none of the lingering unease he had felt ever since he first discovered Xavier's perverse experiments.

Cracking his knuckles, Smith tried to quell the surge of adrenaline that started coursing in his veins. It wasn't the thrill of violence that fueled him, but the anticipation of closure. The knowledge that another mission was reaching its climax. Unlike some of his colleagues, Smith did not relish the act of taking a life. The aftermath weighed heavily on him, haunting his thoughts long after the job was done.

After each assignment, he retreated into seclusion, seeking refuge in the sanctuary of his apartment. Days were spent cocooned away, the outside world reduced to digital transactions and food deliveries. His connection to reality became tenuous, a deliberate act to shield himself from the memories of his victims.

The faces of those he had erased persisted in his mind, their silent specters haunting his every waking moment. Only when their ghostly presence faded could he muster the strength to return to his children, to don the mask of a loving father and shelter them from the darkness that defined his existence.

It was this streak of humanity that made him the best at what he did.

He was a master profiler, a cunning detective who could slip into the minds of his targets, anticipating their thoughts and predicting their next moves with unnerving accuracy. His ability to understand the psyche of his adversaries was uncanny; it was as if he could see the world through their eyes, mapping out their intentions and unraveling their secrets. Once he had a scent, a mere hint of his target, it was only a matter of time before they were ensnared, trapped by the web of his expertise and the relentless pursuit of his team.

In his two decades on the job, Smith had made remarkably few mistakes, a testament to his skill and experience. Yet, Sullivan's friend, Florence, had been an exception, a stain on his otherwise impeccable record.

A few nights ago, his team had descended upon her house under the cover of darkness, following orders to extract information about the elusive dog. They had applied their specialized concoction, a blend designed to loosen her tongue and wipe her memory clean of the night's events. It was a formula crafted by brilliant chemists, a tool in their arsenal meant to ensure their operations remained undetected.

But fate had other plans.

Florence's heart had given out unexpectedly, an outcome that no one, especially not Smith, had anticipated. She hadn't been on their list for elimination; her death was an unfortunate consequence of their well-practiced techniques gone awry.

Smith had been absent during the incident, engrossed in interrogating Sullivan's other associate, Mr. Wall Street. When news of Florence's untimely demise reached him, he had acted swiftly, issuing orders to his team to stage her death as natural. It was a desperate attempt to cover their tracks, to minimize the fallout from their unintended actions.

His phone buzzed, signaling the arrival of a message. The sender was simply named "Employer." Even if Smith had known his bosses' real names — and there were several, though he tended to have only the one point person — they were careful never to use any names in their exchanges.

Have you found them?

Smith typed into the phone quickly, his fingers flying over the keys.

Negative. Should have news by the end of the day.

The response was instant.

See that you do.

Smith put away his phone, knowing it was the end of their exchange. Glancing ahead, he saw the top of Sullivan's head, hidden beneath a helmet spray painted with the image of a sultry woman in a red dress. She pouted at him, blowing a kiss in an exaggerated sexual manner that reminded him of Marilyn Monroe.

Smith waited, biding his time until their van was only inches away.

"Now!" he shouted, bracing himself.

The screeching of tires filled the air as Jackson slammed his foot on the gas, propelling the van forward with a sudden burst of speed. The vehicle surged ahead and cut off Sullivan's path unexpectedly. Caught off guard, Sullivan lost control of his motorcycle, falling to the tarmac with the weight of his bike pinning his legs to the ground.

As the van came to a halt, Jackson killed the engine, plunging the scene into an eerie silence broken only by Sullivan's moans of pain. Smith sprang into action, bounding toward his target, a gun gripped firmly in his hands. He signaled his men, a silent command for them to cover the area, to keep their weapons ready but their trigger fingers disciplined.

"Where are the rest of them?" Smith demanded, cutting through his moans.

The helmet turned toward him, but the man didn't respond. Thinking he might be in shock, Smith nudged him with a boot.

"Your family, Sullivan. Where are they?"

Slowly, Sullivan raised his hand, a deliberate movement meant to show he was unarmed, and flipped up his visor. The eyes that stared up at him weren't the ones he was expecting. In fact, they were the eyes of a complete stranger.

Smith's gaze shifted from the unfamiliar eyes to the rest of the man's form. He took in the bald head, the tattoo creeping up his neck and disappearing beneath the collar of his leather jacket. Now that more of him was in view, Smith could see he was bigger than Sullivan, with a stockier build and an attitude to match.

"I don't know who this Sullivan is, but he isn't me," the biker growled, his words tinged with both pain and frustration. He spat out a mouthful of blood, defiance etched on his bruised face. "You've got the wrong guy."

And just like that, Smith's week had become ten times worse.

28

SULLY

G lendale was a little town off the highway.

Our chosen meeting point, I didn't know anything about the place — hadn't heard of it even — but it looked like the typical small-town you'd find dotted around the US. I knew the type, though I had never had much cause to visit, having stayed in Connecticut before I'd been forced to leave.

I tossed another look behind me, but the road was clear: the trucks were nowhere in sight. Unbelievably, I'd made it here in one piece.

The afternoon sun cast a warm glow over the quaint little town, making the green and white Welcome sign appear even more inviting. It was a typical American small town, the kind you see in movies and read about in books. The kind of place where life moved at a slower pace.

The population here was small — under five hundred — but as I crossed into it, I could see that what it lacked in people power, it more than made up for in businesses.

Main Street stretched out before me, lined with shops and eateries, each one telling a story of the town's history and character. The colonial-style buildings stood tall and proud, their painted shingles adding a touch of cheerfulness to the atmosphere.

My eyes were drawn to a charming restaurant that stood at the heart of the town. Its red and white striped awning and vibrant flower baskets gave it a welcoming feel. I could see families gathering inside, enjoying hearty meals and sharing laughter. It was a place that seemed to have a soul, a place where memories were made.

Beside the restaurant, a smaller ice-cream and dessert parlor beckoned to passersby. Though not as grand as its neighboring eatery, it had its own charm. The scent of freshly baked waffle cones wafted through the air, enticing anyone who walked by. Despite its size, the parlor seemed to hold a special place in the town's heart, offering sweet treats to both locals and visitors alike.

A few doors down was a brightly branded pizza joint. Then came several bars. Their windows were adorned with daily specials with the kind of prices that wouldn't have bought a coffee back home. Speaking of the devil, I suddenly caught the tantalising aroma of a rich, dark brew. My mouth watered, my cravings take over.

It had only been a day since I had my last cup of coffee, but it felt like a century. A grumbling sound emitting from my stomach reminded me that I hadn't eaten in a while, either. A car pulled up behind and honked at me, startling me out of my thoughts. I needed to get out of the middle of the street or I'd start annoying other drivers and causing more attention to be thrown my way. Spotting a parking lot outside a grocery store, I headed there when I stopped in my tracks.

If those other bikers came to this town, they'd spot the bike and would know I was here. It was too risky to leave it out in the open like this. Checking that no one was nearby, I maneuvered the bike to the alleyway behind a grocery store. The smell of days-old urine and rotten food filled my nose, reminding me that even in Niceville, people still treated alleyways like they were their personal public restroom.

Wheeling the bike behind a dumpster, I dug out a few flattened boxes from inside, arranging them over the bike, covering it the best I could. I was about to head back into the town when the ground suddenly shifted beneath my feet. I caught my breath until I realized it was just a sign of low blood sugar.

Having lived with Chase and her high metabolism long enough, I knew I needed energy or there would be a crash coming. I checked what money I had left — less than eighty bucks. I hesitated, not wanting to spend a dime of it, but I was struck by another wave of dizziness that left me nauseous.

I had to eat something or I wouldn't be of any use to anyone.

Scanning my options, my eyes lingered on the pizza place. Loaded pies with long strings of mozzarella cheese and glistening slices of pepperoni that would have given my favorite joint back home a run for its money. If only they sold by the slice.

Dragging my eyes away, I shuffled into the grocery store where I picked up another cheap sandwich and a candy bar. Not wanting to pay for water, I stopped by the drinks station, sighing with relief when I saw the jug of tap water provided for customers.

Filling a large paper cup, I gulped it down, then knocked back several more, stopping only when my stomach felt bloated.

I paid, headed back outside and took a walk around town while I ate my food, keeping my eyes peeled for any sign of the other truck. All things being equal, my family shouldn't be too far behind so I wouldn't venture far. Keeping my eyes down, I tried not to draw attention to myself.

As I passed the less frequented parts of town, the once-charming atmosphere began to fade away. The buildings lost their cheerful facade, replaced by a worn-out appearance. The motel on the Southside came into view, a stark contrast to the cozy businesses I had seen earlier. Its deteriorating siding whispered stories of neglect, and the creaky wooden sign, barely hanging on its rusty chains, seemed to groan in the wind.

The fading sign had almost completely scraped away the word "Glendale," so that all that remained was "lend al" from "Glendale Motel." The rundown motel consisted of two floors that housed twelve rooms if that. Each window looked like a blank stare, devoid of life and warmth.

My footsteps echoed on the sidewalk as I continued my vigil. I couldn't afford to let my guard down. The hollow feeling in my stomach persisted, intensifying with each passing moment. Despite my efforts to fill the void with food and water, the gnawing worry for my family overshadowed any physical discomfort.

I glanced back at the motel, a passing thought crossing my mind. It might have been a place to lay low, to regroup and plan my next move. But something about it felt off, the aura of neglect making it an unappealing option. Then there was that issue of cost...

I decided to press on.

After I had gone up and down the length of Main Street, I knew I had to find a better way to kill time or that unwanted attention would surely be heading my way.

Pushing open a door, I stepped into a bar. The dimness inside matched the heavy stench of cheap beer. The place was practically empty. A wino slumped over a pint in one corner looking as if he hadn't washed in a week. He probably smelled the same too, as the bartender — a guy who looked to be in his twenties, wearing hipster pants that sagged at his butt but clung to his skinny legs — was giving him a wide berth.

A girl in a miniskirt batted her eyelids at the bartender. The pimply-faced guy looked like he thought it was his lucky day. The two were so involved with each other, they didn't even look my way.

A glowing neon sign pointed the way to the men's room. As I stepped inside, darkness enveloped me momentarily until my fingers found the light switch.

The ceiling light flickered on, casting the room in a dingy yellow pallor. Dust covered the rim of the light, not having been cleaned this side of the century. Luckily, the stalls looked decent enough: I was glad I couldn't smell anything other than the cheap floral dish soap in the dispenser by the sinks.

I crossed to the mirror where my wan face stared back at me.

The biker had done a real number on me. I had a cut above my right eye where the blood had now congealed. My cheek felt tender. Though the skin held only a hint of red now, I was sure it would turn a wicked purple by tomorrow.

I splashed cold water onto my face, gingerly washing around the swelling. Pumping a few pumps of that soap into my palm, I washed the back of my neck and under my arms. The cold water felt good against my tired body, and even though I wasn't able to get a proper scrub-down, I still felt better. Tearing off a few squares from the paper roll fixed to the wall, I dabbed myself dry, then gave myself a final once over.

It was still me who stared back from the mirror but at least I didn't look as haggard as when I had first arrived.

I headed to the bar, and waited for the barman to stop talking to Ms. Miniskirt long enough to serve me, but after a full minute, he hadn't even turned my way. I tapped my fingers impatiently on the bar top, the sound growing louder with each tap until he couldn't ignore me anymore.

Fixing me with a look that somehow seemed to convey he was more annoyed than I was, he asked, "What'll it be?"

"Coffee. Black."

The words were barely out of my mouth before the bartender gave me a look.

"Sorry. Kitchen's closed." Turning to his friend, he laughed, feigning a wide-eyed look. "Wait, what am I saying? We don't even have a kitchen."

On cue, the woman burst into giggles. Now that I could see her up close, I realized my mistake. She wasn't a woman at all, but a girl who couldn't have been more than eighteen, with a face that was plastered with make-up and thick, tarantula-like fake lashes.

I couldn't see what was so funny.

"I'll have a can of whatever is cheapest."

If the look he gave me before was bad, this made me feel like I was something he had to scrape off his shoe. Reaching under the bar, he retrieved a can of off-brand cola from a mini fridge, slamming it down onto the counter. The girl all but dismissed me with a fleeting glance.

"Do you need a glass with that too?" his tone dared me to answer.

"I think I can manage." There was a hint of danger in my reply. The punk was testing my last nerve and he needed to know it.

He looked me up and down, though he was shorter than me. The air turned heavy with tension before he came to his senses and shifted his focus back to the girl. His posture had changed in the last few seconds, his shoulders braced for impact. Knowing he had caught my drift was enough for me. Taking my drink and what was left of my ego, I sat down at a table with a decent view of the town.

Popping open the can, I took a small sip. Normally, I shied away from sugary drinks, so the intense sweetness hit me by surprise and made me long for water to wash it down. Trying for optimism, I comforted myself with the fact that it wouldn't be diffi-cult to make the drink last. I would have at least an hour before that barman finally got bored with the girl and kicked me out.

Tossing another quick look at them, I mentally adjusted the time by another hour. They were giving off some serious heat. Hope-fully, they would keep each other distracted for a good while. Shifting my attention back outside, I anxiously waited for my family to appear.

29

CHASE

You know when you're stuck doing something you don't want to? Well, that was me right now, down to a T.

Caught in a hard place between two women with some major issues with each other while a sinister SWAT team came after us. And then there was Sully, off playing chicken with the bad guys. I felt like I was suffocating under the weight of our predicament.

The more we had to walk, the more I could feel the resentment pouring off of Emma. One second she was a child, all vulnerable and wounded, and needing our protection, then the next, she was a powder keg ready to explode at a moment's notice. Her mumbling became a constant background drone with the only recognizable word being "Sully." Her fixation on him only added fuel to the already blazing fire, intensifying the strained atmosphere that surrounded us.

Despite harboring negative feelings toward her, I couldn't deny she had a real connection to him, though my mind refused to believe that she was actually his wife. I mean, it just wasn't possible. Even Bandit kept his distance from Emma, a feat made easy by her apparent dislike for him. Other than all the bad guys we'd ever come across, she was the only person in the world who didn't like him.

And you know what they say about people who don't like animals…

Sam had been leading the way for the last hour or so, Gideon and Zeb bringing up the rear. Emma was somewhere between us, but I hadn't bothered to check on her in a while. Where she was concerned, no news was good news.

After walking for so long, I could feel the cold seeping through the soles of my sneakers. It made me worry about Bandit's paws. If my feet, wrapped up in socks and cushioned by my shoes, felt like they were turning into blocks of ice, how were his paws doing? Staring down at him, I asked, "Are you okay? Is the road too cold for your paws?"

He nuzzled my hand as if to say he was grateful for my concern, then barked twice for no. He was a lot sturdier than me, it seemed, even with all my training on the streets. I've always suffered from cold feet, even as a kid. It was actually the one thing I inherited from my mom.

Thinking about her now, I recalled her face, but it was like reopening an old wound. Whenever her image came into my mind, it was accompanied by a pang in my chest, a visceral reminder of the complex feelings I harbored. Since she had taken off, I avoided thinking about what she had done. How she had betrayed me and sold me out. It just brought too many complicated emotions to the surface.

Emma's relentless mumbling jolted me from my thoughts. Tossing her an irritated look that she didn't catch, I sped up my pace — Bandit matching me stride for stride — until we caught up to Sam. She gave us a small smile that didn't quite reach her tired eyes.

"How are you guys doing?"

The normally cheerful demeanor, which had always been her trademark, was nowhere to be found. Lines of stress etched her face, replacing the usual softness with a weariness — and hurt — that was alien to me.

"Oh, you know. Tired, hungry, worried about Sully, but what else is new?"

Sam didn't answer, choosing to cast a glance at Emma instead. She opened her mouth as if to say something, but decided against it. I guess she didn't want to open up that can of worms, not that I could blame her.

"The town sure looked closer on the map," I said.

"You're telling me." Reaching up, she massaged the back of her neck, attempting to rub the day's tension away. "Isn't that always the way? Just when you think you've gone far enough, along comes something that makes you realize you haven't even scratched the surface."

I knew exactly what she was alluding to, though only a fool would continue down that treacherous path. Instead, I changed the subject and focused on the most pressing thing on our minds. "You think he's okay?"

"Look at everything that's happened to him. All that he's gone through and is *still* going through. If I'm sure of one thing, it's that Sully can take care of himself, even if he has a hard time believing it. We just have to stick with the plan and keep going."

Footsteps approached from behind. I hoped it was Gideon, but the steps were lighter than his usual graceless thump. Instinctively, I felt my stomach clench.

"This is stupid. You should stay with the wheelchair man while the rest of us go on ahead to meet Sully," Emma volunteered unhelpfully.

Sam squeezed her eyes closed for a moment and went completely still. I think she must have been counting in her head or something. Maybe praying for strength. "I told you before. We move as a group. We're not splitting up and were not leaving anyone behind, and that's the end of it."

Unfortunately, Emma wasn't done. Reaching across, she tapped Sam on the shoulder as if she were a stranger of no consequence.

"But I don't understand why we have to listen to you. Sully didn't say anything about leaving you in charge when he left."

Her tone wasn't the least bit insolent. She honestly seemed to think it was Sully's decision to make. An irritated sigh hissed out of Sam, but her only response was to take another deep breath.

"I'm just saying we should consider other options, since Sully is waiting for us and we shouldn't keep him waiting."

It was, apparently, the final straw. Sam's eyes turned flat as all the fear and rage she had bottled up inside suddenly erupted. "I'm well aware that my husband is out there on his own! I don't need you to tell me that."

"But if you cared about him, you'd be trying to get to him as fast as possible." Emma twisted her fingers together, fully convinced of the truth in her words.

"I've tried to be patient, but you are testing my last nerve. Let me say this plainly in a way that even you can understand: while you might have bulldozed your way back into our lives, you are not part of our family, so you don't get a vote. You do as I say until we meet up with Sully again and you become his problem."

"I am part of Sully's family too," Emma corrected sulkily.

Sam's face went as red as the shirt she wore. "He's not your husband anymore! Stop acting as if you have any kind of claim over him!"

Bandit pressed into me, his whines a mixture of confusion and unhappiness. I wanted to comfort him, to offer a reassuring stroke, but I didn't dare make a move. I was worried that they were about to tear each other apart, in which case, I would need both of my hands. My eyes slid over to Gideon as I silently pleaded for him to help defuse the situation.

"Technically, she kind of is his wife," Gideon began, but it was absolutely the wrong thing to say. Both Emma and Sam glared at him, yelling simultaneously, "Shut up!"

"Oh boy," Zeb murmured, steering himself well clear.

Shaking my head at Gideon, I picked up the pace, hoping to put as much distance between Sam and Emma as possible.

30

THE CLEANER

Smith stared down at the biker, a vein popping on his forehead.

"My legs…" the biker moaned, face pale as moonlight. "Jesus, they hurt."

"I'm so sorry, sir. This is our mistake," Smith apologized, signaling for his men to move the bike off him. They lifted the bike as if it weighed no more than feathers as Smith ran his eyes over the man's legs.

The worn denim of the biker's jeans was now streaked with a dark, viscous oil. Relief washed over him as he noted the absence of blood, a small mercy in the chaos that had unfolded. In Smith's line of work, the spill of innocent blood was not only a tragedy, but a disaster for his secretive department. They preferred to settle matters discreetly, compensating victims generously under the condition of a strict non-disclosure agreement. The value of silence always outweighed the cost of a financial settlement. However, while Smith's mission was to eliminate his targets, depending on how risky his employer considered this man, it was possible this particular slate would have to be wiped clean, too.

He hoped that wouldn't be the case.

The biker attempted to shift his weight, testing his injured limbs. A sharp intake of breath escaped him as searing pain shot through his body. Still, he continued, testing the other leg only for a curse to spit out from his lips.

"Cops are gonna have a field day with you," he threatened.

Jackson leaned down to examine the biker's legs when the man waved him away. "Get away from me. Haven't you done enough?"

Jackson raised both of his hands, but glanced at Smith for his directive. Smith issued a barely perceptible shake of his head, to which Jackson backed off to await further instructions.

"We don't mean you any harm, sir. You have nothing to fear from us other than this unfortunate incident."

Smith flashed him an FBI badge, one of the many fake credentials he had in his armory. "We're from the Federal Bureau of Investigations. Unfortunately, you matched the description of the suspect we were looking for."

The biker squinted his eyes, studying Smith with a mix of skepticism and suspicion. The lines on his weathered face deepened as his frown etched itself into his features. Doubt hung heavy in the air as he wrestled with his story, trying to discern the truth. "And your man just happened to be riding a bike like mine, wearing the exact same helmet?"

His question was laced with sarcasm that he didn't bother to disguise. Smith adopted a contrite tone. The man may not know it, but his very life depended on how well and fast Smith could settle this matter.

"No. But the tracker we had placed with him lead us to you," Smith explained. It was the truth too, though a slightly distorted version of it. The biker's eyes turned dark with confusion before they cleared.

"Tracker? Your man put a tracker on my bike? But when would he have gotten the chance to…"

He trailed off, as a culprit emerged in his mind. "That jerkoff! The man you're looking for… is he a slim guy, in his mid/late thirties. Looks like city scum?"

Instead of opting for a vague reply, he delved into his pocket and retrieved a photograph. It was a picture of Sullivan, captured in a moment of relative tranquility before the chaos had broken out. In the image, Sullivan's features were frozen in a half-smile, his eyes reflecting a glimmer of mischief that hinted at the adventurous spirit within him. This was the image that was prominently displayed at the veterinary clinic during his time there.

Wordlessly, Smith extended the photograph toward the biker. The biker's eyes flicked from the image to Smith and back again, recognition dawning in their depths.

"That's him! That's the punk who stole my buddy's bike."

Smith felt a wave of relief pass through him as the biker confirmed his story. It was important not only for the man's future, but also their mission. The injured biker couldn't stop talking now, detailing each part of his encounter with Sullivan. Smith paid close attention, evaluating what he heard and asking questions where necessary. He soon had an accurate description of the illegally obtained vehicle.

Smith sent his men to contact local authorities about the stolen vehicle, and asked Jackson to take care of the biker until they could fly him to a hospital where "FBI" representatives would take over the legal proceedings. Smith knew that the man would be rewarded generously for his injuries and silence.

Having put the call out to the local boys in blue — or brown, as was more likely the case around these parts — Smith waited to be notified of any sightings of Sullivan or his family.

31

SULLY

What a difference two hours could make.

The bar had been transformed, having gone from empty to half-filled as a flood of mid-afternoon drinkers appeared.

With it, the noise had risen tenfold, leaving me more conscious of my solitary stay. The other side of my table was still unoccupied, though it was unlikely to remain that way for long. The empty cola can — which I had long finished — played between my fingers as I spun it first one way, then another, filled with a tension that was overflowing. I knew I should grab another drink, just so I wouldn't be encouraged to leave, but I was going to wait this out as long as I could.

Having made plans to meet up with Hipster-Pants later, the flirty girl at the bar had gone, and was now replaced by a group of men wearing ill-fitting suits and carrying fake leather briefcases. Cups of coffee clutched in their hands, they attempted to speak and joke together, yet what words I could pick out seemed forced. Their desperation clung like a cloud exposing them for what they were: salesmen, touting for business of some kind — my money was on insurance.

My eyes zeroed in on their coffees, feeling a wave of resentment toward the barman who had served them. Apparently, there was a dress code for certain beverages that I hadn't met. Any any other day and I would march right up to the punk to let him know exactly what I thought.

Instead, I stared back at the same spot in the distance that had held my focus since my arrival.

The clock above the door loomed large, its hands moving steadily, measuring the passage of time in relentless ticks. Each second seemed to echo, resonating in the corners of my mind like a drumbeat of impending doom.

They should have been here by now.

They should have gotten here only moments after my arrival.

The salesmen, the noisy crowd, and the increasingly-busy bartender all faded into the background as unwanted images crashed through my mind in vivid detail. I saw my family heading toward me in the truck when, with a screech of tires and a sickening crunch of metal, a grenade detonated, engulfing the truck in flames that swallowed my family whole. When the fire died out, I saw the road littered with the charred remains of my loved ones.

My eyes welled with tears as I imagined their smiling faces, their voices fading into the recesses of my memory. The weight of grief pressed down on my chest, making it hard to breathe.

The horrific nightmare rolled into another.

My heart leaped with joy as I saw my family arriving in the town, relief flooding through me like a warm embrace. Sam, my beautiful wife, led the way, her eyes scanning the streets until they met mine, locked in the window of the bar. A smile, full of love and happiness, illuminated her face as she lifted her hand in a wave. My chest swelled with love and gratitude; the sight of her able to dispel any fear that dared to linger.

Behind her, the familiar figures of Chase, Gideon, and my dad came into view, their faces mirroring the same happiness that radiated from Sam. But before I could fully comprehend the scene unfolding before me, chaos erupted. Bandit, sprinted toward them, barking furiously, a desperate warning that I could feel in the depths of my soul.

Chase, her eyes wide with terror, looked up at me, her mouth opening to shout a warning. Just as she was about to speak, the world imploded. Bullets tore through her body in a hail of deadly projectiles, stealing her life away in an instant. I watched in horror as she fell, her body crumpling to the ground, the light in her eyes extinguished forever.

A scream ripped itself from my throat as Sam dropped to her knees beside Chase, her hands trembling as she cradled our daughter when another bullet found its mark *and ate a path through her head*. She slumped over Chase, their blood mingling on the pavement.

Gideon and my dad, my pillars of strength, met the same fate, their lives taken from them in the blink of an eye. The world seemed to spin, the sounds of gunfire and anguish mingling into a cacophony of despair. I was frozen, my mind unable to comprehend the nightmare unfolding before me.

Only Bandit remained, his mournful howls cutting through the air, echoing the grief that gripped my soul. His cries reached a crescendo, a heartbreaking melody of loss and pain, before he too was silenced.

The can shot from my fingers, hitting the floor of the bar with a bang.

Tears fogged my vision. I fought to keep it together, knowing I had to preserve my sanity to save my family from whatever was delaying them. And it had to be a delay.

Anything else was unthinkable.

Wiping the tears away and steeled myself, my jaw clenched in resolve. *Come on, Sully. There's a normal explanation for why they weren't here yet.*

The thought of them just being lost flickered through my mind, but the devil on my shoulder chimed in, reminding me that Chase's memory was infallible and that her getting lost wasn't a likely scenario.

Well, maybe there was a problem with the truck then.

Right… The unwelcome voice in my head answered. *Because the truck was so rundown and on its last legs.*

Well, maybe the men managed to disable it remotely. In which case, they would all be dead by now.

I dug my fingers into my hands until the pain was sharp and immediate.

Pain was good.

Pain reminded me that I was alive, that I still had a purpose. I needed to focus and be rational. I had to be clear-minded enough to know what to do when they did finally arrive.

Grateful that the voice had been silenced, I toyed with the idea of buying another cola when a shadow loomed over me. The barman. And he didn't look too pleased to have to deal with me again.

"Unless you're going to be buying several more and *expensive* drinks, I'm going to have to ask you to leave since I need that table."

He gestured to the group of salesmen who stood sheepishly behind him, cups of coffee in hand. I hesitated, debating between accepting the offer and knowing I couldn't afford it. I slid my hand into my pocket and fingered some change, wishing I had the coin pouch Sam had given me as a gift.

I wasn't very disciplined at using the thing the way it was intended, stuffing as many bills inside as actual coins. Consequently, there was quite a bit of cash in there. Sadly, the pouch was sitting on top of the dresser at home where I had left it.

"I'm going to need an answer from you," the barman pressed.

It was on the tip of my tongue to tell him where he could shove his answers when a weary group of familiar faces appeared down the street. My heart soared. I shot to my feet.

"My family just got here!"

The barman's face twisted with confusion. "How nice for you."

So much joy rose up inside me that I couldn't be bothered to tango with this waste of space any longer. Slapping him on the shoulder — a little harder than was necessary — I grinned.

"Yes it is."

I rushed outside. Bandit noticed me first. Picking up my scent, he barked and sprinted for me at a breath-taking pace. I caught him just as he was about to knock me to the ground.

"Am I happy to see you, boy!"

Bandit's pink tongue slobbered over my face, catching me from chin to cheek. Planting a big kiss on his snout, I looked over to the others.

"Did they find you? Is that why it took you so long to get here?" I asked, unable to stop myself. Walking toward me, Sam had a giant smile on her beautiful face when someone crossed rudely in front of her path.

Emma.

I blinked, startled, having forgotten for the moment that she was even back. Then I caught myself, as my body flooded with the shame and guilt that momentary lapse in my memory caused.

"Have you any idea what I just went through?" she demanded. "None of them would listen to me. I kept making suggestions, but they kept ignoring me. If they had taken me seriously, we would have gotten here so much sooner."

Behind her, Sam glowered with an irritation I had never witnessed before. Side-stepping neatly around Emma, she wedged herself between the two of us.

"What happened to your face? Her hand went up gently to explore my injuries.

"I bumped into a friend of the guy whose bike I stole. We got into it but I managed to get away before too much damage could be done. What about you? What took you so long?"

"We were out of gas, if you can believe that," Gideon supplied.

"*Somebody* let it run dry, so we had to walk half the way here.

Slowly," Emma said resentfully, shooting Sam a dagger-filled look. A nervous twitch tugged at my face. *Had the two fought the entire way here?*

"I didn't know what was taking so long. I was getting pretty worried."

"Well, we're here now. Have you gotten rid of the bike? It's the first thing they can ID and could lead them straight to us," Sam asked, stepping into her sheriff shoes.

"I ditched it in an alley and covered it with boxes. I don't think anyone will find it. Not for a while, anyway."

While we were speaking, Chase was staring at me strangely, mentally evaluating my injuries and possibly calculating the likelihood of my death.

She must have decided that the odds were looking pretty good, as the tension eventually left her shoulders. I threw my arms around her and gave her a tight squeeze. She leaned into me as Bandit flanked my other side.

"Do we have a plan for how we're getting to your friend's cabin?" Zeb asked.

"No…" I fell silent, his question suddenly reminding me of my conversation with Mark — and the bad news that had come with it. "We can't go there, unfortunately."

"Why?" Chase asked, her face twisted with confusion. "Couldn't you get in touch with him?"

I didn't answer right away. The hollow feeling that had been in my stomach worked its way up to my chest until it felt like a great weight was pressing down onto it.

"I could, but… Florence is dead. Mark told me when I spoke to him." The others gasped, the shock in their faces reflected in my own.

"How?" Sam asked. Her quiet, one-word question made my heart lurch. Until this moment, I hadn't been able to feel the impact of Florence's death. But now that words were being spoken, the truth was undeniable.

"She was found dead in her armchair. They're saying it was a heart attack, but I know better. Florence may have died, but it wasn't by any natural causes."

"What makes you say that?" Sam asked carefully. I explained about her abhorrence for modern conveniences, how she hated microwaves most of all, and how her friend had been the one to find her. "Her killers have ensured that no one will pry into her death."

Sam's eyes were troubled. She didn't comment, her mind working through the details of my revelation as if it was one of her cases. The kids didn't know what to say and stood around awkwardly, while Emma's expression barely changed. I could have been discussing the weather for all the effect it had on her.

"Who is this Florence? Was she another wife of yours?"

She asked the question without any hint of spite.

"No. She was a dear friend of ours." The word *"ours"* slipped out before I could stop it. I felt, rather than saw, Sam tense.

"I'm sorry, son," Zeb uttered his condolences. "I know how much she meant to you." He patted me on the arm as he couldn't stand to hug me.

"The people who are after us killed her. I'm sure of it. They went after Mark, too. He'd been out jogging, but then somehow blacked out. They found him in a ditch without any memory of how he had gotten there."

A gasp left Emma's lips. "Just like me."

"Not exactly," I corrected. "Mark can remember nearly everything, but there is a gap in his memory from the time he started jogging to when he woke up. Both incidents happened on the same day. It's too much to be a coincidence."

"I agree," Sam answered. Several strands of her blonde hair had fallen across her eyes. I reached up and brushed them away as Emma's eyes bored into my back.

"But Mark had a place for us. And money!" Gideon blurted.

"We can't get help from anyone?" Chase asked, a horrified look on her face.

"Not from anyone they can trace us to," I answered reluctantly, the burden of my words heavy on my shoulders.

"We're on our own."

32

CHASE

"You can't be serious?"

Usually able to keep his emotions in check — particularly if they were a cause for alarm — Gideon was doing a pretty bad job of faking it this time. Not that I blamed him. His world had been uprooted and our one chance of survival had just been taken away with a throwaway comment from Sully.

"We can't risk calling anyone and putting them in danger. I can't have another death on my hands. Florence was alone when they got to her. Mark too. God knows who else they'll go after if we ask for their help."

Sully's expression hadn't changed though his tone softened in the way I had heard him use with Bandit, whenever he'd had to do something he didn't like — like bath time.

Sam moved forward, her expression turning darker. Before she even spoke, I felt a lurch of fear in my stomach. That knot that seemed permanently wedged there grew exponentially.

"What about the people who are already involved?" she asked, her voice all the more urgent for its quietness.

"We're already here," Zeb answered, unable to understand her point.

"Not all of us," Sully suddenly replied sounding frustrated at himself.

My mind raced, trying to piece it all together. Gideon, Bandit, and I exchanged puzzled glances, our brows furrowing in confusion. Then, like a bolt from the blue, realization struck like lightning.

"Oh Jeez, you mean Doc Robins, don't you?"

Sam nodded reluctantly, her blonde curls bobbing around her face.

"Is Doc Robins another friend of ours?" Emma asked Sully.

"She's a friend of the family," Zeb corrected gently. "You haven't met her."

Sam continued, "It's possible that they haven't made the connection, and I know we haven't told anyone about her involvement with us, but what about the adopted families of all those dogs she saved? Do we really think that none of them would have said something? That there isn't a Facebook post up where she is being thanked for all that she has done for their family?"

"You honestly think they would target her?" Sully asked.

"I would if I was them," Sam replied. "She knows far too much. And she visited us at the ranch when she came for Pixie. If they know that, they would consider her a liability."

Chills raced down my spine.

"But if we call her, they might be able to trace it," Sully mused, his face growing paler by the second. He didn't have anything to do with the situation, but I knew he would take it personally. That's just how he was - always looking out for everyone, and not just humans. It's why he was Sully.

Sam knotted her fingers together. When she spoke again, it was hesitant, as if she couldn't believe what she was going to say. "That's why we'll have to go to her instead."

Zeb had been listening to us working through our options but he interjected. "In Arizona? That's a long way and we don't have the transport or the means."

He cast his eyes downward to his legs, his frustration palpable. The challenge of reaching this town had been so arduous, the question seemed to hang unspoken in the air: *what were the chances of successfully making it all the way to Arizona with him?* His frown silently conveyed this doubt.

Sully's gaze shifted to his dad. "I guess we'll figure that out. Let's just move away from here. I don't feel safe, not with all the ways we can be spotted."

Standing on the edge of the group with her arms folded across her chest, Emma voiced her concerns.

"You all keep talking about going somewhere but have you considered how? What are we going to do, steal a car? Even I know that's wrong."

Gideon shot me a look that I knew would get us in trouble.

I knew exactly what was coming next and braced myself for Sam's inevitable reaction.

CHASE

We sat on a metal bench around the corner from a parking lot where Sully, Gideon, and Bandit had taken off to, the latter acting as a watchdog — in all senses of the word.

After Gideon had broached his plan to steal a vehicle from the lot, as I had expected, Sam expressed some serious objections to the criminal act. Especially as it wasn't the first time he had stolen a car while being with Sully.

Not even the second, actually.

Nope, the third time was not the charm and Sam was taking real issue with this nasty little habit Gideon seemed to have developed while living under Sully's roof. Still, after her initial objections, she eventually arrived at the same conclusion as the rest of us. It wasn't as if we had much choice in the matter. Lives were at stake and not only our own.

My stomach rumbled. I crossed my hands over it, hoping to dull the sound. Food would have to wait until we were out of this town.

As if waiting for Gideon to steal a car while Sully and Bandit kept watch, and not being able to do a single thing to assist wasn't nerve-wracking enough, we kept finding curious stares tossed our way.

While the folk here seemed friendly enough, they were obviously used to a certain crowd and I guess our ragtag family loitering around was causing quite the stir.

"Why are they taking so long?"

Emma's voice cut through my nerves, making me jump. For someone who had shown such incredulity when the idea was first introduced, she had come round faster than a fish took to water.

Her piercing blue eyes darted toward the parking lot as she paced back and forth. With each restless step she took, her shoes clicked against the tarmac.

"They're going as fast as they can. Best we be calm, and perhaps lower our voices so we draw no more attention to ourselves," came Zeb's sensible suggestion.

As if she hadn't heard him, Emma glanced at Sam, addressing no one in particular. "Didn't *she* say she's a sheriff? You'd think she'd have a bigger problem with this, but no. It's only when I do something. It's only me who gets told off."

I could see Sam's shoulders tighten. She took in a long breath, then let it out slowly, refusing to take the bait.

"Can we just concentrate on Gideon and Sully? If there's trouble, we might need to jump in. Maybe we could just focus," I pleaded.

Emma's mouth snapped closed. Thankfully, it seemed she would accept my suggestion, as her only reply was to stare across the lot where Gideon had stopped by a three-rowed saloon.

I couldn't see too much from my position, only that it was an older make which Gideon had previously admitted were the best for stealing as new cars can't be hot-wired. Newer cars also had some kind of computer system, which meant it could be easily traced.

He explained how many of the electronic devices used in cars relied on satellites to pinpoint their location in order to give directions on a GPS. That same technology could be easily reversed, causing the car to emit a trackable signal. All of this just meant that every time we were forced to steal a car, it would never be a new one.

So we could forget onboard Wi-Fi, TV screens on the backs of the headrests or even a charging dock for the phones we didn't have anymore.

It was old school all the way.

Gideon glanced behind him a few rows, at another car that he seemed to consider. This was a beaten up number with a rusty rim job and plates that were barely hanging on. I knew looks didn't count for much, but I doubted the thing would even start, much less get us across the country. Gideon must have thought the same as he turned his attention back to the saloon.

I watched, holding my breath as Gideon stooped down as if he was unlocking the door. His body barely moved, only his hands that skillfully hid the lock picks he was using. After all the tight spots we'd been in before, he carried them on him at all times, something I'm sure we were all grateful for now.

The door sprang open.

Quick as a flash, Sully and Bandit dove inside. Sully slid behind the wheel while Gideon opened the back door for Bandit. When all three were inside, they pulled out of the lot and drove to us.

They helped maneuver Zeb into the car while I folded up the wheelchair. As soon as Zeb was settled in the backseat, Sully ran back round to the driver's seat and popped open the trunk. I struggled to lift the wheelchair inside when Gideon came over and took it out of my hands. Grateful for his help, I nodded my thanks and hurried to the car to find Emma already ensconced in the middle row. Sam had taken the passenger seat beside Sully, leaving a space by Zeb or Emma.

It was immediately apparent that the curvature of the back seat would make it impossible for me and Bandit to both sit next to Zeb.

It was sit with Bandit and Emma or with Zeb on my own.

Much as I loved Zeb, I couldn't bear to be parted from my Muttface, even in a car, so there was no real choice. Sully twisted in his seat, casting a look at all of us as Gideon slammed the trunk closed and climbed in beside Zeb.

"Buckle up," Sam instructed, ever the safety girl.

And we were off.

I had one arm around Bandit — who thankfully, acted as a physical barrier between Emma and me — while Emma braced herself against the armrest. Tension hung heavy in the air, and no one spoke. We were wracked with nerves that wouldn't abate until we were out of this town and safely on our way to Arizona.

The vehicle was in much better condition than I had given it credit for, its engine surprisingly powerful beneath the worn exterior. Despite the unexpected reliability, I couldn't shake the feeling of unease that gripped me, my senses on high alert, waiting for the telltale signs of law enforcement.

I kept my eyes fixed on the rearview mirror, half-expecting to see flashing red and blue lights, and hear the shrill sirens that might pierce the air, signaling the authorities in hot pursuit of us for the stolen car. Each passing moment felt like an eternity, my nerves on edge, anticipating the inevitable confrontation with the law.

Outside the window, the vibrant shop fronts blurred into streaks of color, a surreal tableau that contrasted sharply with the tension inside the car. The world outside moved at a frenetic pace, oblivious to the adrenaline-fueled drama unfolding within the confines of the stolen vehicle. As we approached the back of the Welcome sign, a landmark that marked the edge of town, I couldn't help but hold my breath, the tension in my chest reaching its peak.

When we passed the sign, my breath finally hissed out of my lungs like a released valve, a sound that seemed to startle Emma, who shot me a look as if to ask what was wrong with me. Outside the window, the landscape changed, the urban scenery giving way to open roads and vast expanses. The town we had left behind became smaller and smaller, shrinking into a mere speck on the horizon.

"Good job," Sam finally said to Gideon, her eyes finding his in the rearview mirror. "But don't ever do that again."

"Why?" Gideon asked. "I'm getting really good at it."

She fixed him with such a baleful stare that he slid down into his seat. Sully's lips twitched but then the grin faded from his face when she fixed her attention to him.

"This is only a short-term solution. We're in a stolen vehicle, so even if those men can't find us, highway patrol soon will."

"But you just said we can't steal another car?" Gideon looked confused, his tousled hair tumbled over his eyes in a disheveled mess.

"Once we get to the city, I have an idea of how we can arrange for something more suitable."

I couldn't wait to hear how she figured that would happen.

34

——————

CHASE

W e hurtled down I-35S, the asphalt beneath us a blur as we embarked on our epic journey to Arizona. According to Sully's calculations, a trip that stretched over twenty-four hours loomed ahead, provided we drove without interruption, with three drivers tirelessly working in shifts. I wasn't part of the designated driving trio, a fact I didn't contest. If it were up to me, it would be bicycles for the win.

The rhythmic hum of the road reverberated through the car, lulling most of us into a drowsy stupor. Bandit, lay draped across my lap, emanating a comforting warmth like a living, breathing, hot water bottle. Emma had succumbed to sleep, her head resting awkwardly against the window. I was convinced she'd wake with a crick in her neck, which seemed like poetic justice since she was such a pain in ours.

In the backseat, there was a stillness broken only by the regular cadence of Zeb's heavy breathing as he, too, succumbed to a much-needed nap. I remained wide awake, however, unable to sleep. Despite the distance we had traveled, I couldn't shake the feeling that I needed to keep a watchful eye out for danger. I had to protect my family. Even when the scenery unfolded before me, an ever-changing tapestry of landscapes, and the amber fields transformed into a sprawling cityscape, I couldn't bring myself to close my eyes.

Skyscrapers reached for the heavens, their steel and glass mirroring the setting sun and casting a warm, golden glow over Kansas City. Although I had limited knowledge of the place, I knew the city sat on the western edge of Missouri and had a rich cultural heritage, steeped in jazz music and barbecue cuisine.

That last part was really all that mattered to me — I was pretty gutted we wouldn't be here long enough to sample any of it. Just once, I'd love to visit a place when we weren't on the run.

Sully navigated the roads and slowed the car to a halt in a shadowy side street, in a spot hidden from prying eyes, between two flickering streetlights that barely pierced the approaching gloom.

My stomach churned. Sitting up in my seat, I leaned closer to him. "This is it?"

My voice was a hoarse rasp that felt foreign, as if I were the eighty-year-old version of myself. Emma blinked awake, eyes growing increasingly wide with alarm as she quickly took in our new — and dubious — surroundings. Her confusion hung in the air like a storm cloud .

"Why have we stopped?" Hugging her knees to her chest, she looked like a scared child.

Sam turned to face us. I heard Zeb and Gideon stir as they stretched tired and cramped muscles. "We're here. This is where I'm going to get us a new vehicle. From the police impound."

My eyes widened, the disbelief etched on my face, as I stared at her, slightly bug-eyed. "Sorry. I must have blanked. For a second there, I thought you said you were going *to* the police?"

Sam nodded, her eyes dark with a seriousness that sent shivers down my spine. "That's right." Her voice carried a steely resolve that seemed to defy the gravity of our situation.

"I hate to state the obvious but we're in a stolen vehicle right now," Gideon chimed in, his tone echoing my own shock. She nodded again. I kept waiting for the other shoe to drop but it didn't seem to be coming.

"That's why you're all staying here, out of sight, while I go talk to them alone. Sheriff to cop."

"Do you have any jurisdiction here?" Gideon continued, unable to make head nor tails of this plan.

"No, but I think this will work. Just give me an hour. I'll either be successful or I'll come back empty-handed." She unclipped her seatbelt as if what she had just suggested wasn't the riskiest idea on the planet.

Sully stopped her with a firm hand on her arm. "I'm coming with you."

"You can't. If I'm on official sheriff business, why would my husband be with me?" Sam's response seemed completely reasonable which made it all the harder to dispute her point.

"Then I'm not your husband. I'm your deputy, your driver. Hell, I'll be your dancing monkey so long as I can come with you," Sully pleaded, a note of desperation creeping into his voice. Sam smiled, a tender expression on her face, as she cupped his face in her hands.

"Honey, they're not after me. We haven't been caught with the stolen car, and even if there was an APB out for us, it would be for two women, two teenagers, a man, a dog, and an elderly man in a wheelchair, not for Montpelier's sheriff. I'll be fine, I promise. If there's any sign of trouble, I'll come straight back."

Sully's eyes burned with intensity, his concern etched deep into his features. "I'm not happy about this," he admitted, his voice low and strained with worry.

Sam arched a blonde brow. "Then that makes two of us."

Without waiting for Sully or the rest of us to voice any more objections, she slid out of her seat and gracefully exited the car, her silhouette stark against the fading light.

"There are no CCTV cameras around here, I made sure of that.

Still, you all need to keep your eyes peeled. Any sign of weirdness, any tingling in your gut and you just get out of here and head on."

"But how will you find us?" My voice trembled, reverting to the tone of a whiny, worried kid.

Sam winked, flashing a grin. "I have Robins' address. If it all blows up, I can get myself there."

A collective unease spread through the ranks, the impending separation weighing in our hearts. Sam flashed a big, determined smile, attempting to ease our fears.

"Don't worry. I won't be long."

And with those six words, she vanished into the fast-encroaching night.

35

———

CHASE

S am had gone, and she seemed to have taken all the air out of the car with her.

Without her, Sully couldn't relax. His fingers drummed a nervous, irrational beat on the dashboard that set my teeth on edge. I wanted to ask him to stop, but couldn't find the words. Unable to bear the tension any longer, I made my way out of the car, craving the refuge of open space and the chance to stretch my stiff muscles.

Gideon joined me as we stood half-hidden in the shadows, our eyes glued to the twinkling lights of downtown. The cityscape glowed like a constellation of stars. "I wonder what she'll say to them," he said without shifting his gaze away from the skyline.

"Whatever it takes, I guess."

We remained side by side as night descended and the temperatures dropped. Goosebumps prickled my skin and I shivered until Gideon wrapped his arm around me. His warmth enveloped me like a protective shield and I sank into him, much like how Bandit pressed against me, enjoying both the physical and emotional support that exuded from him.

Through my concern for Sam and the immediate threat to our safety, there was a new awareness dawning inside me, a realization of something unspoken yet palpable. Something was changing between us, a shift in the dynamic we had always known. Our relationship was evolving, morphing from the familiar brother and sister dynamic into something deeper, something… more.

My eyes lingered on the profile of his face, taking in his strong jawline and the familiar ridge of his nose. Feeling my stare, he turned to me, his gaze burning with their intensity, electrifying us both. The hairs on the back of my neck tingled. The air between us seemed to crackle with an unspoken tension, and the world around us blurred into insignificance until there was only the two of us.

But before the moment could fully envelop us, Bandit barked suddenly, his warning tone slicing through the charged atmosphere, and jolting us both out of whatever-this-was.

We both jumped away from each other, the spell broken, and our heads snapped around to see Bandit staring intently at a spot a few cars down. Black figures approached — three of them. Hulking figures who seemed larger than life. Was it my imagination or were they deliberately avoiding the pockets of light thrown down by the streetlights?

My body tensed, fear eating away at me. Gideon reacted swiftly, tapping a warning on the glass of Zeb's window. I sensed rather than saw Sully and Zeb's attention shifting towards the front of the car. Bandit ran ahead of me, positioning himself between me and the approaching figures. His keen senses were on high alert, sniffing the air, searching for any sign that the approaching group might be unfriendly.

"Get back into the car," Gideon instructed us quietly. Normally I would have argued, not one to take orders without question, but there was something about those ominous black shapes that had me gritting my teeth.

I climbed back into the safety of the car, gesturing for Bandit to follow. The men were now just two cars away from us, yet their features remained obscured, their faces as dark as the jackets they wore.

Sully moved his hand to the ignition. He waited until the group moved closer, then suddenly, he gunned the engine, turning on the high-beams. Light shone out, blinding the three men. Startled by the glare, they shielded their eyes with their arms.

I finally got the chance to get a proper look at them.

They were older than me and Gideon, but younger than Sully. Their jackets, which had seemed black before, were actually a deep blue and had a logo of two entwined red letters, K and C sewn onto the chest. I snapped my gaze to their hands, terrified that I'd find weapons aimed at us. Instead, they were holding half-eaten burgers, still in their wrappers.

They were nothing more than three sports fans on their way to a game.

Bandit whined an apology for spooking us like that. Gideon lowered a hand to stroke him, but kept his eyes on the guys. The one in the middle, the largest of the trio, called out to Sully, gesturing at the lights.

"Hey, you mind?"

Sully flicked them back to normal, winding down his window. "Sorry, guys," he called out of it. "This is the wife's car. Still getting used to it."

The lie was quick and convincing. The tension that had ramped up dissolved immediately.

"No problem," the guy replied as he took another bite of his burger. They continued past, chatting about their upcoming game, their excitement palpable.

I breathed a sigh of relief as Gideon made it back to the car. Even Sully's loud drumming didn't faze me now.

"I'm so hungry," Emma suddenly announced. "And their food smelled really good."

"Eat another one of your energy bars then," I answered, trying not to sound like a brat but failing miserably.

"There's none left. Where's that other sandwich?"

My gaze rested on her face, looking for any sign of awareness about how unreasonable she was being, but there was no hidden agenda or shame in her expression. "Sully ate it earlier."

"While I was sleeping? He should have waited to share it with me." Her lower lip jutted out in a pout.

"I think we have some nuts left," Zeb offered with apparently endless patience.

"Well, I'm not a dog."

Her answer had us stumped for a second. It was Bandit who finally answered.

"Do you mean squirrel? They eat nuts."

Emma shrugged her thin shoulders. "Whatever. One animal's the same as the next."

Sully stared at her through the rearview mirror as if he couldn't recognize her. When he spoke, his voice was deceptively soft.

"When Sam gets back and we're away from Kansas City, we'll make a stop for more provisions."

"But that's still *hours* away!"

"Yes."

The wind was cut from Emma's sails. She settled back, sulking silently at the injustice of it all.

Time seemed to stretch endlessly as we continued our vigil, our eyes scanning the dark horizon for any sign of Sam's return. Every approaching beam of headlights sparked a glimmer of hope, only to be extinguished when the passing cars carried on

After God knows how long, my mind was beginning to crack from both boredom and pressure, and I was giving serious consideration to playing a game on Bandit's iPad. Just as I was reaching for the device, a distant rumble pierced the stillness of the night.

My head snapped up, my senses on high alert. The approaching lights, unlike the low headlights of previous passing cars, were positioned higher, casting an eerie glow in the darkness. The ground trembled beneath the weight of whatever was approaching, and a wave of dread washed over me when I realized those lights didn't belong to any car.

They belonged to something much bigger... like a truck.

Sully reached the same conclusion, his instincts kicking in as he flicked on our high-beams, momentarily blinding the approaching driver. I held my breath, expecting the inevitable crash of metal meeting metal. Instead, the massive truck skidded to a stop, its tires screeching against the asphalt.

"Little hostile for a welcoming committee," Sam's amused voice called out from the 'truck.'

Sully leaped out of the car, a broad grin stretching across his face, as the rest of us followed suit. When I was within a few feet of the vehicle, I realized it wasn't a truck Sam had brought back at all... but an RV!

She beamed at us like she'd won the lottery, her pearly whites flashing in the dark.

"Are you kidding me right now?" Gideon was practically giddy with happiness.

Sam nodded. "Welcome to our new home. I've christened her: Buffy. She may not look like much, but she packs a mean punch."

"I don't get why everyone's so excited. If the new truck stopped working, won't this old thing do the same? As usual, Emma didn't share the same level of excitement as the rest of us.

"I think we'll be alright," Sully answered. "We're in a much better shape than we were five minutes ago."

We took turns to explore Buffy and survey her condition up close.

She wasn't brand new, but there was plenty of room inside for all of us and she didn't need an additional car to tow it. Despite a few dents, the RV appeared to be in good condition for its age.

"How?" Sully was so impressed he could not formulate a complete sentence.

"Police station's impound vehicles all the time, from drivers who fail to pay their parking fines to those running criminal activity inside them. This baby was involved with the latter, but since her owners are currently serving twenty to life, they're not coming back for it anytime soon," Sam explained.

"They don't just hand these away, though?" Sully asked, straightening up from examining the tires though what he could see of it in this light, I had no idea.

"I flashed them my sheriff's badge and asked if we could come to a deal. The vehicle would only go off to auction once the requisite time has passed. I have it on good authority that there are too many issues with it for it to sell for much. I made an offer, large enough to cover the towing and storage fees, and they accepted."

"But we don't have any money?" Call it habit, but the thought was always at the forefront of my mind.

"And we don't need any. They're billing it to my work. By the time anyone realizes we were here, we'll be long gone. And this kind of paperwork takes days to get through. My deputy will try to reach me and when he can't, it'll just delay the entire process. We're pretty much good to go."

Sully shook his head in admiration. "This is exactly what we needed. Exactly what we needed." He kissed her passionately, dipping her into a dramatic pose and making her laugh.

Having experienced nothing but terror and trouble in the last two days, we desperately needed this moment of lightness, this win for the good guys. I couldn't stop my instinct to look at Emma to see her reaction. Instead of the jealousy or anger I expected, she pulled a face as if their affection disgusted her.

I don't think I would ever understand her.

Tail wagging in excitement, Bandit bounded ahead of me into the RV, his enthusiasm infectious. Following him, I climbed up the steps and crossed the threshold into our new home — and was immediately assaulted by a mix of odors. The predominant scent was that of dusty vinyl flooring. Cheap pine-scented air freshener hung on every window. I found myself standing in the central area of the RV, dominated by a u-shaped fabric sofa curving around a table. This formed the main living space, modest yet functional. Behind the seating area, there was a compact kitchenette, complete with a tiny sink and a two-ring electric stove. A mini fridge and some wooden cupboards completed the culinary setup. It was a space that seemed designed for efficiency rather than luxury, every inch utilized to its fullest extent.

As I moved toward the back of the RV, the vinyl flooring gave way to a stained carpet that looked as though it had seen better days. There were no bloodstains on it, however, which was my bar for what I could live with, so there was that I suppose.

I passed by a shower head that was mounted over the toilet and saw how the floor of the "shower room" curved upward. The entire setup made me do a double-take.

Apparently, to shower, you were supposed to stand over the toilet. Gross.

Still, beggars couldn't be choosers. If hot water could come out of that thing, I would be singing for joy. Beyond the shower room, there were two large spaces where I assumed the washer and dryer would have been if there was one. A double bed surrounded by built-in cabinets took up the rear of the place. There wasn't any bedding on the battered-looking mattress that dipped in several places. Not even a sheet.

Heading back into the main area, I checked out each of the cupboards, but only came up with a pair of plastic tumblers and four plates. No cutlery, but I there was a pan with a half-melted handle.

I flashed Sam a broad grin. "It's perfect!"

"We need to air the thing out and clean it up a bit, but it'll do," Sam replied. She crossed to the windows and snatched up the air fresheners, shoving them into a bag she had found and tossed the lot into a trashcan outside.

Of course, our enthusiasm hadn't made its way to Emma. "How are we all going to sleep in here?"

"The women can take the bedroom. Gid and Dad can use the room here — those seats look like they convert into a double bed. And if I'm not mistaken, there's another double hidden above the driver's seat."

Sam nodded and pulled down the bed when a cloud of dust fell, making us all choke.

"Sorry," Sam apologized. "Should've known that would happen."

Back at the sink, I turned on the faucet. Water came out though there was a murky tinge to it. "That's coming out of storage tanks, Chase. I'm not sure how much is left in there. Maybe you could turn it off?"

Feeling chastised, I immediately did as she suggested.

"That water is only to be used for cleaning. It goes without saying that no one drinks from it. Bandit, that especially goes for you." Sam gave him a pointed stare. I swear Bandit's cheeks flushed. He woofed, managing to make it sound like it was ridiculous for her to even consider such a thing — though we all knew he would.

He might be the cleverest dog in the world, but he was still a dog.

No one else seemed as excited as I was by the running water, but that was the thing about me: I didn't take anything for granted. Life came with unexpected disappointments, so we had to roll with the punches or we'd all be in a heap on the floor.

Take me.

When I was a kid, during one of those periods where my mom was in-between men, so it had been just the two of us, she had wanted to do something nice for me. She hadn't always been so bad. I think people have way more shades of gray about them: we're not all black and white.

I remember being on her for this dollhouse that all the other kids were getting, even the ones in the trailer park. Owning one had been my reason for living. I know now that's pathetic and materialistic, but I was too young then to know any better.

The two of us had gone to Walmart to pick up the dollhouse for my sixth birthday. The pictures on the box looked amazing, with all the dainty furniture that even included window boxes full of plastic flowers and gadgets for the kitchen. I'd watched the commercial on television for months, so I knew everything about the house.

I knew it came with a bed and an adorable vanity table that had a real mirror in it where you could see your own reflection. The bathroom had a toilet, sink, and tub that was big enough for your doll to fit inside. The kitchen/diner housed a table and chairs and these tiny dish clothes you could hang off the sink. It was as real a house as my six-year-old mind could have dreamed up.

Mom had counted out the money she had saved up, working at a local diner, trying not to wince as she forked over the bills, sharing an excited smile with me. Two bus rides and a ten-minute walk that seemed to have lasted much longer in my tired kid mind later, we finally made it home.

She had pre-warned me that the house didn't come assembled, that we'd have to put it together ourselves, but she was sure we could do it. Opening the box, she took out the instructions and all the pieces.

Which was when we realized there was a problem.

All those cute pieces of furniture we'd been seeing on the ads and even on the box itself? None of them actually came with the house.

We'd have to pay for them all separately.

My mom became so mad that she couldn't put the house together. Her hands were shaking too much. The next day, I woke to find all the pieces of the house in the trash, having been smashed to bits.

We never spoke about it again, but I learned a hard lesson that day. It was why I had to check every nook and cranny in the RV.
I had to make sure it wasn't another empty dollhouse.
When I was convinced it wasn't, I flew at Sam and hugged her, thankful that we had a roof over our heads again.
She hugged me right back, her eyes unusually bright.

36

SULLY

The night sky unfolded above, an expansive canvas painted in deep hues of navy blue, adorned with a multitude of stars that flickered like distant beacons. I kept our RV to a steady speed, ensuring we'd go unnoticed as the lights of Kansas City gradually dimmed in the review mirror, and the towering buildings that inhabited the skyline were now reduced to small stories.

I drove solo for the time being. Sam and Chase had gone into the bedroom after the first half hour together. Ever since Chase had toured the RV, something unspoken had passed between them. Call it gut instinct, but whatever it was, I didn't want to intrude.

Emma sat at the table, not saying a word, though I would catch her staring at me every now and then. When I looked at her, my heart would surge with joy… until apprehension and guilt took its place.

I couldn't get my feelings straight about her. The whole thing was impossible.

I pushed my feelings aside and focused on the highway, hoping that she would eventually tire of boring her gaze into the back of my head.

Gideon bustled about in the kitchenette, cleaning up dishes with damp napkins. Retrieving a can of dog food, he opened it with his penknife, using the technique Chase had demonstrated earlier. I knew I was long past a meal of my own when the smell of dog food made my mouth water.

Only two days on the road and I was already giving real consideration to dog food.

Unbelievable.

"Bandit, come get some chow," Gideon called to him. Bandit jumped off the sofa beside Zeb, padding to him. I fought to contain my envy when he dived snout first into the food.

Fishing out our remaining provisions, Gideon counted out three candy bars and one last bag of nuts. He split everything into six portions including a few nuts that he passed to Zeb, who accepted the offering with a nod of thanks. His next stop was Emma, who wasn't quite as gracious, taking the meager offering with a look of disbelief.

"When I asked earlier, you said we only had nuts left?"

"No, Zeb offered you nuts, which you declined. No one said anything about candy bars."

"But you knew what I meant," she murmured. "I just so hungry my stomach hurts." Her eyes grew large and luminous. She seemed even more of a child at that moment.

"Ours too," Zeb responded. "Hang on in there. We'll get a real meal soon."

I took the food Gideon offered, nodding my thanks as he headed to the back with the remaining portions. I reached for the radio, tuning it to a country station. The music sounded tinny and emerged from only one speaker, but it was better than having to listen to Emma's continuous suffering. The male singer crooned about lost love with a haunting refrain of what could have been. The words struck a melancholy chord in me as I found myself wondering the same.

With several windows wound down, the once oppressive artificial scent of pine, gave way to the freshness of clean air. Most of the dust had been wiped away, leaving a semblance of cleanliness and order. I could hear a chorus of crickets outside, their intermittent chirps weaved into the mournful melody of the country song, providing an additional soundtrack to the unfolding journey. I hadn't felt safe enough to try any of the shops back in the city, busy as they were even during this late hour. Following my intuition, I continued driving until the moment felt right.

We cruised by numerous rest stops along the highway, each beckoning as a potential refuge. However, as we approached them, a quick assessment revealed that they were either teeming with fellow travelers, their parking lots overflowing with vehicles, or they exuded a modernity which likely meant cameras or CCTV were in play. What we needed was some hole in the ground that wasn't part of a chain, and was likely to have only the one owner.

I almost missed the gas station when it first appeared. The neon sign that would have announced its presence was dark or more likely, broken. Only the lights inside notified me of its presence. I pulled off the highway.

Sam and Chase emerged from the bedroom as soon as the RV came to a stop. I could tell by their red-rimmed eyes that they hadn't slept much, if at all.

"We're stopping here quick."

Sam leaned down, casting her eyes over the joint. "Looks kind of neglected. Good choice."

I rummaged inside my pocket and took out what little remained. Handing it to Zeb, I said, "You're in charge of the money. I want to check over the motor home quickly before we leave again; can't afford any technical hitches."

"I have to use the restroom," Zeb mentioned quietly. The admission carried a tinge of frustration, acknowledging the need for assistance that irked him.

"I'm not entirely sure the one onboard is working," Sam replied.

"Let's try the one in the gas station and grab what we need while we're there," Gideon answered.

Between us, we got my dad outside, but it was tougher than it had been going in. This motorhome didn't have any concessions for disabled users, something we'd need to address in the future if we were going to use it for any length of time.

Gideon's gaze lingered on the restrooms situated on the exterior of the building, his eyes narrowing as he focused on a poorly written sign that hung precariously on one of the doors. The haphazard placement of the sign mirrored the overall state of neglect that seemed to permeate the surroundings. "Looks like the disabled restroom isn't working. We'll have to try the regular one."

Zeb's only response was a terse nod of his head.

The two of them headed inside.

37

CHASE

No sooner had I set foot in the gas station then a gruff voice barked over, sounding annoyed as heck.

"No dogs allowed."

I looked for a sign that would back up this outrageous claim. Sure enough, there was a faded red warning stuck to the door that I'd walked obliviously past. I'd gotten so used to our friendly stores around Montpelier, where the shopkeepers knew and loved Bandit, I'd totally forgotten to prepare for this outcome.

I looked down at his trusting face as the two of us contemplated our options. It wouldn't take me a few moments to grab the food we needed. Bandit could wait outside until I was done. Still, a wave of unease swept through me at the thought of leaving him outside. I hated being separated from him, no matter how short the time.

He seemed to sense my reluctance and chuffed at me, reassuring me that he would be just fine. His jaws parted into what I knew was a smile then he sat outside, just by the doors where I had a clear view of him. Feeling a little reassured by this, I went inside.

Heat blasted out of an ancient air con unit that sat above the door, making sweat gather at the base of my neck. While it wasn't quite the height of summer anymore, that kind of heat wasn't necessary and did nothing for the tense knot of anxiety I already felt.

Trying to ignore my discomfort, I tackled the shelves, scanning through each row, mentally calculating the energy each item would give versus the cost. I didn't need to think too hard since I had already done most of my calculations on the streets of Greenwich.

My eyes roamed over a bags of chips as I felt the corresponding pull in my stomach, but chips were one of the worst things I could spend our dwindling funds on. Yeah, they tasted amazing, but the salt would make us thirsty, while the empty carbs would be burned in no time.

Reluctantly I turned away from them. I passed refrigerated units with a rainbow of sodas on display, but all that processed sugar would only provide a passing boost of energy, followed by the inevitable crash.

What we needed was protein and lots of it.

Finding the ready to eat meat snacks, I grabbed as much as I figured we could afford, dumping them into a basket. I picked up a few more cans of dog food and a small bag of dog biscuits, a brand of which, ordinarily, Sully wouldn't have allowed. Apparently, there was more bad than good in them. Still, Bandit loved the stuff, and it was cheap, so into the basket it went.

I carried on shopping until I began to sag under the weight of the basket. I'd been mentally tallying up the total as I went along, so we shouldn't have hit our budget yet. When Zeb finally emerged from the restroom alone, he came to my side, eyes wide and impressed.

"You've been busy."

"I thought I would get enough supplies here so that we don't need to stop again; that way, there's less chance that someone will spot us."

"Good thinking."

Seeing my struggle to move with the weight of the basket, Zeb took it off my hands and set it onto his lap.

"Thanks."

"You looked like you needed help," he winked.

"Is Gideon going to join us at some point?" I asked, only a little bit peeved that he wasn't helping with the heavy lifting.

"Guess he needed extra time in the restroom," Zeb replied.

I was about to respond with something smart when a movement outside caught my eye. A couple around Sully's age were bee-lining their way toward Bandit.

Dressed in typical jeans and boots, they bore a striking resemblance to us. They looked like they were on a similar pit stop, but I *really* didn't like it when strangers went anywhere near my dog — especially if I wasn't right there with him.

Craning my neck, I scanned the area for our troops, but Sam and Sully must have been on the other side of the RV as I couldn't see them. Fingers of apprehension ran down my spine. Catching my unease, Zeb followed my gaze.

"I've got this," he said quietly. "Go."

My sneakers squeaked on the linoleum floor as I hurried outside. Hearing the couple's approach, Bandit stood to attention, strategically positioning himself by the doorway so if they tried anything, we would have the best chance of reaching him.

"Who's a good boy?" The woman cooed in a friendly voice. Bandit's tail stayed still as a rock, ears pricked forward, listening for any sign of danger. It took everything I had in me not to bolt to his side, knowing the attention that would draw. Closing the distance in a few quick steps, I placed my hand territorially on the back of Bandit's neck.

"Is this your dog?" The man asked. I studied them discreetly, taking in the matching wedding bands and friendly expressions, trying to see if there was that telltale bulge of a weapon tucked under their checked flannel shirts.

"Yes, why?" I tried to keep my voice natural. It was a normal question to ask after all.

"We had one just like him," the woman explained, her eyes misting up. "He was seven when we found out he had a heart defect. He died only weeks after he was diagnosed."

My heart gave an involuntary lurch, their shared pain resonating with me as if it were my own. However, I resisted the pull of empathy that threatened to overshadow my caution. This could be a ploy, a meticulously orchestrated distraction to manipulate my sympathies. I motioned for Bandit to remain close, just beyond their reach. He pressed against my side, senses on full alert.

"That's horrible. I'm sorry."

"Yeah, it's tough. Been six months now but still hurts like it was yesterday." The man said, smiling down at Bandit. "You mind if I pet him?"

I froze, unsure how to answer.

38

ZEB

The basket, laden with groceries, pressed firmly against Zeb's numb legs as he navigated the crowded aisles of the gas store.

Despite the lack of sensation in his limbs, he could still perceive the weight of it, pushing down on him. Hurrying to the checkout, Zeb hoisted the basket onto the counter, hoping the attendant would sense his urgency and get to the job quickly. It seemed his luck was in as the attendant efficiently scanned the items. The scanner beeped and the numbers on the display climbed higher, but Zeb turned away from the balance. His gaze fixated on the scene unfolding outside the store.

Chase was engaged in conversation with the couple, her hand resting on the back of Bandit's neck. Neither seemed in imminent danger, but the undertones in Chase's body language revealed a wealth of caution. Bandit too, displayed an unusual stillness. Zeb couldn't remember a time when his tail hadn't wagged. This was as abnormal a sight as the sun not rising, creating a knot of concern in his stomach.

His eyes darted across the aisles to the restroom, mentally

urging Gideon to hurry. What could be keeping the boy so long? Though Sully and Sam were somewhere nearby, their invisibility added to Zeb's growing unease.

He felt a tightness in his chest and anxiety washed over him.

Struggling to catch snippets of the conversation, Zeb's mind raced with wild possibilities, conjuring vivid scenarios of potential threats or complications. Every passing moment seemed to stretch, each second laden with suspense as his gaze darted anxiously between Chase, Bandit, and the couple. The inability to hear what was being exchanged heightened Zeb's sense of vulnerability. Fear of the unknown took a firm hold, casting a shadow over his thoughts and leaving him even more on edge.

When the register finally showed the total, Zeb handed over the money that was gripped in his fist. The attendant accepted the payment with a hint of annoyance at Zeb's apparent distraction, but Zeb paid him no mind, his gaze focused outside.

"This isn't enough."

The attendant's voice jolted Zeb from his scrutiny. He glanced at the bagged items before quickly returning his attention to Chase and Bandit. "I don't have time to go through and fish things out."

"Do you have another form of payment?"

The cashier's question hung in the air, prompting Zeb to act swiftly. Without a second thought, he handed over his debit card, his eyes momentarily shifting towards Bandit, who had gravitated closer to Chase. It looked like the couple had asked a question she wasn't sure how to answer.

He saw Chase shake her head.

Anticipating trouble, Zeb had seen enough. Grabbing the provisions, he briskly made his way toward them. When the couple saw his arrival, they showed no outward sign of guilt or alarm. Instead, they only smiled, a palpable fog of sadness enveloping them like a shroud

"Sorry. You probably don't want strangers talking to your granddaughter, but we just wanted to pet your dog." The man explained, attempting to diffuse any concern. "We lost ours and haven't quite gotten over it yet."

"I told them about Fido's problem," Chase interjected quickly, filling him in with whatever story she had concocted for them. "How he can't stop himself from snapping at strangers on account of how he was abused before."

"We've been working on that for a while but haven't cured him of that bad habit yet," Zeb continued smoothly.

"I know we shouldn't bother every dog we see, but we can't seem to help ourselves," the man's wife finished, her tone apologetic. "I'm sorry, Fido. We'll leave you alone now. Enjoy your evening."

They smiled sincerely, expressing regret for the intrusion, and retreated into the store. Chase and Bandit visibly relaxed, their shoulders dropping with relief now that the tense encounter had passed without incident.

The cashier's irritated voice pierced the moment, calling out, "Hey, mister, you left your card."

Chase stopped in her tracks, the blood draining from her face as she looked at Zeb.

"You used your card?"

The words slipped out of her mouth like an icy whisper, sending a chill down Zeb's spine. He stared at her in shock, realizing the gravity of his oversight.

"We didn't have enough. I didn't even think about it."

Chase's eyes grew haunted, her fear transferring to Zeb. "Wait here."

She sprinted back into the store, reaching the checkout counter just in time to see the attendant holding Zeb's card. However, the attendant refused to hand it to her until Zeb confirmed she was his granddaughter.

Snatching the card from the cashier, Chase raced back to Zeb's side just as Gideon finally emerged from the restroom. Sensing their panic, his expression turned guarded. Chase didn't waste anytime explaining. Grabbing Gideon's arm, she practically dragged him out of the store, hissing, "We've got to go… now!"

Hearing her urgent command, Sully emerged from behind the RV, closely followed by Sam, both wearing startled expressions.

"Get in! There's no time to explain. We just have to go!"

Chase jumped into the RV with Bandit, gesturing for the rest of them to hurry. In a daze, Zeb allowed himself to be hoisted inside, all while the sickening knot in his stomach grew.

39

SULLY

I stalked a tense circuit within the cramped confines of the motorhome as Sam expertly navigated our escape route, her face etched with worry.

"I'm sorry, son. I don't know how I could have put us all in danger like this," my dad apologized for the third time, but his remorse offered little solace on our shaky ground. His hands were a wringing mess in his lap, his gaze fixed on the floor, his complexion as pale as a sheet.

"It was a mistake." Bandit, ever the comforter, attempted to console him.

"You all seem to make a lot of those," Emma commented, her usual lack of tact not harboring malice, only keen observation.

"It's not like we have a lot of experience with this," Gideon retorted, a defensive edge in his tone that only deepened Zeb's sense of guilt. Emma, her eyes wide like saucers, turned to me, expecting me to defend her viewpoint. But, I averted my gaze, unwilling to exacerbate my dad's distress any further.

"Never mind." Emma's response hung in the air as I continued to pace, my mind haunted by the impending arrival of those men.

Would they sneak up on us in stealth helicopters like Forbes' men had, on that first ranch attack? Or would we see a fleet of those armored trucks? Picturing the artillery that had lined the shelves I caught myself assessing the frame of our motorhome, hating how much more fragile our vehicle seemed by comparison.

What chance would we stand if we were attacked?

"Let's not panic yet," Sam cut into my spiraling thoughts. "It's possible that they might not be waiting for us to use our cards, and even if they were, they would only know that we were there thirty minutes ago, not where we are now."

She was trying to keep us calm but her logic didn't hold, something even Emma noticed.

"But aren't these roads straight? Wouldn't it be obvious where we were going?"

And just like that, with her usual lack of a filter, the tension skyrocketed. Sam continued in a measured tone that belied her own concern.

"Not necessarily. We've already passed by one junction. We'll reach another in a few hours. There are still any number of ways we could have gone. We just need to keep going."

"But..." Emma started again, only for Sam to cut her off with a withering look.

"A wise person once said, there's no point worrying over things that haven't happened yet."

Emma studied her intently, trying to process what she had said.

"Who?"

"Who what?"

"Who was the wise person?"

Sam froze, momentarily caught out. "I can't remember. It was just someone."

"Then why would we listen to the words of a person we don't even know?"

"It's a saying, Emma. Haven't you heard one before?"

"None that I can remember."

And there was that uncanny ability to derail a conversation again. Sam wisely decided it would be better to drop the conversation before it went further downhill and focused on the road ahead. The air inside the motorhome felt heavy with dread. I tried not to stare at the sweat that beaded on my dad's forehead; he was taking his mistake, hard.

"Dad… It could have happened to any of us. We're tired, hungry, and scared. Don't beat yourself up about it. What's done is done. We need to stay upbeat, focus on what we can do, not what's already past."

He nodded, acknowledging the truth of my words even if he didn't exactly subscribe to the theory. Bandit padded to the bag of food we'd picked up at the gas station, nosing through the plastic bag until he surfaced with a bottle of water that he held gently between his teeth.

He set the bottle in Zeb's lap, nudging it with a dogged purpose. A glimmer of hope returned to my dad's eyes, and some of the despair he was feeling began to fade away.

"Thank you."

But as he reached for the bottle, it slipped through his fingers.

A cruel twist of fate sent it careening across the floor, just out of reach of his wheelchair. A hiss of frustration escaped in response to the relentless betrayal of his uncooperative body.

Gideon shot after the elusive bottle and handed it back to him though my dad's aggravation was palpable.

40

SULLY

The night flew past as I kept my eyes peeled for any sign of activity.

Every speck in the sky that appeared to be moving, every vehicle that approached, the air would grow steadily heavier until it passed by without incident.

Eventually, we relaxed enough to share a small meal, though none of us had much appetite. We ate mechanically, forcing dry sandwiches down our throats. As I choked down the stale bread — one of the disadvantages of shopping at a quiet and out-there gas station, it seemed — a beloved memory flashed into my mind.

As the family gathered around the kitchen table, a breathtaking sunset painted the sky in hues of pink, orange, and gold, casting a warm and vibrant glow that streamed through the windows. The flickering candles on the table danced in harmony, creating an enchanting ambiance. The room was bathed in a soft, golden light that accentuated the elegant details of the embroidered tablecloth carefully chosen for this special occasion.

Sam and I, a team in orchestrating this surprise celebration, became silhouettes against the backdrop of the enchanting sunset.

The air was infused with the tantalizing aromas of the dishes we presented to each family member. While the exact details of the menu had blurred with time, I distinctly remember the heart-warming sight of Bandit, chomping down with gusto on the grass-fed marrow bones I'd ordered from a local farm.

We'd been so happy then. So filled with the excitement that our announcement and upcoming wedding would bring.

It all seemed like a distant chapter from a lifetime ago.

We sat in silence until I caught Sam shooting a sidelong glance at me. Her lips had shifted to one side, a telltale sign that she wanted to talk, but was having a hard time figuring out how to start the conversation.

Having no energy for guessing games, I decided to bite the bullet.

"What's on your mind?"

A startled look came over her face. She laughed, though there wasn't any mirth in the sound. She seemed on the verge of denying any concerns but opted for honesty. She shook her head, a rueful smile now on her lips.

"You know me that well, huh?" She paused, pausing to choose her words carefully. "I was wondering if you've thought about what we're going to do when we get there?"

"I've thought of nothing else, actually. I've run every possible scenario I can think of through my mind, but I've come up with zilch. I'm counting on Elora being able to assist us. At the very least, she has access to resources that can provide us with some answers."

"You mean, how Emma could possibly be back?"

My eyes slid to her still figure where she napped on the sofa, her hands tucked under her head like a pillow.

"Yeah."

"Chase's theories were actually pretty sound last night, though I'm no closer to forming an opinion either way." Sam's gaze followed mine to dwell on Emma.

"I don't know what she is. I just know that I'm responsible for her."

"Because she's your first wife?" There was a tone in her voice. Not exactly harsh, but something lingered. I knew I was treading on thin ice.

"No. It's almost like she doesn't think like an adult. Even Bandit knows better than her. She's more like a child who needs to be taken care of."

"I've never seen any kid who behaves like her."

Sam's attempt at lightness fell flat. There were too many unknowns to laugh about. It was all too fresh and raw.

"You don't have to worry. If that's what's on your mind."

Sam flashed me a small smile, but remained silent. Didn't speak again for a while, in fact. I could tell from her body language that she wanted to drop the conversation and I was more than happy to oblige.

By my estimate, we were about four hours away from the gas station when fatigue crept in. I felt myself sinking into exhaustion when Sam's voice jolted me.

"What is that?"

She stared ahead at a black object in the distance, sitting at the road's edge. As we approached, I noticed it wasn't moving.

I sat up straighter in my seat, my tiredness dissipating immediately.

"Should we carry on?" Sam asked quietly, not wanting to alert the others unless necessary.

"Let's get a little closer until we can actually see what it is. We're still a ways away; if it's a problem, there's still time to turn around."

She kept going at the same pace, her tensed shoulders the only visible sign of her concern. The black object grew larger on our approach until we finally identified it as a sedan with its hood propped open. Spotting us, a lone driver got up from the ground where he had been sitting, signaling for our attention.

"Who is that?" came Chase's voice over my shoulder.

She must have woken in the last few moments. She was such a light sleeper that the slightest sound would wake her, something which had probably kept her alive when she had been homeless.

She rubbed at her sleep-filled eyes as movement stirred in the back, indicating the others were waking. Bandit padded up beside me, his nails clicking on the cheap vinyl floor.

"Just someone whose car's broken down."

"Tough to have that happen in the middle of nowhere," Gideon commented by Zeb's side. He had been half dozing with his head on the dining table. A tuft of his blond hair stuck up like a baby mohawk.

I looked around. Nothing but dry, black land stretched as far as I could see. No lights behind or in front of us. No vehicles would be coming down this highway for a while. It wasn't this guy's day.

"We could stop, let Gideon have a look at his car?" Zeb volunteered.

"I don't think that's a good idea," Gideon disagreed. "Let's just carry on."

"But what if he just woke up with no memory, too? What if he's like me?" Emma asked in a plaintive voice. That she even thought it could be an option tugged at my heart.

"He's not like you," Chase was certain. "His car broke down is all. He can wait until the next person comes along."

"But that could be hours, days even." Emma looked aghast. I wasn't sure why the idea of this guy being stranded affected her so strongly.

"We don't have to stay long. Gideon can just pop out to see if there's anything he can do to fix it." Having lived in a small town for the last decade or so, my dad had grown used to being a helpful neighbor. The idea of lending a helping hand was second nature to him, a reflection of the close-knit community values ingrained during his time in Montpelier.

"We need to come to a decision quickly. We're almost on him,"

Sam interjected. She had slowed the RV right down so we could get a look at the stranded driver.

He was around my age and height, though it was clear that even under the denim jacket and black jeans he wore, his body was athletic: there couldn't have been an inch of fat on him. He smiled at us, white teeth glinting in the headlights, relieved by our appearance. We were almost with him when the RV continued rolling past.

"What are you doing? Stop! He needs our help!" Emma said, looking out the window, one hand pressed against the glass. But, behind the wheel, Sam's face was clouded with indecision.

"I don't know. Something is off..." Sam stared back at him, uncertain how to proceed. Suddenly, she did a double-take and cursed loudly.

"He's not a stranded driver. He's a scout! Hold on to something!"

In an instant, Sam slammed on the gas, causing the wheels to shriek as the motorhome lurched. Chase stumbled beside me and would have fallen if I hadn't grabbed her arm. The vehicle jolted backward as I got a brief look at the driver's face.

My stomach plummeted when I saw that he wasn't shocked so much as he was irritated.

Seeing the hurtling vehicle coming for him, he darted to one side, but Sam clipped the edge of his car, sending it fishtailing his way. He dove out of danger with an effortless agility that I knew no regular person would have been able to execute.

I went ice cold.

"Sam's right. We need to stop him before he signals someone!"

Like he had read my mind, he reached into his jacket, revealing not a phone but a gun — a gun that he aimed dead at us. As if in fast-forward, he jogged backwards like some superhero straight from an action movie.

"Duck!" I yelled, forcing Chase's head down and pulling on Sam's arm so hard that I almost dragged her out of her seat. Her foot slipped off the gas pedal and the motorhome came to a sudden halt.

Bullets pierced the night air. The metallic tang of fear gripped my throat, and my pulse quickened with each gunshot that echoed in the dark. The very air I breathed became charged with tension as I braced for impact, but the shots veered off target as the stranger struggled to aim while on the move.

"Give me your gun!" Gideon yelled at Sam. Stuck behind the wheel, and aware that Gideon had the best marksmanship among us, Sam slid it across the floor to him.

Gideon seized the gun, taking cover behind a window as the man continued firing shots in our direction.

"He's almost out," Gideon called to us.

Three more shots blasted into the night before an eerie silence descended. Without missing a beat, fueled by a potent mix of adrenaline and determination, Gideon sprang into action. He ran for the door, flinging it open with purpose as he bolted outside.

"Gideon, wait!" I called after him.

But he was already gone.

41

CHASE

I lay sprawled on the floor, Sully's hand still pressing against my head, when his cry shattered the air, snapping me out of my panic-induced stupor. Wrenching my head from under his grasp, I turned to see the door wide open.

A lead weight dropped in the pit of my stomach. Gideon had bolted outside in pursuit of the man.

Panic surged within me, my heart pounding violently. Rising unsteadily, I staggered toward the door just as Sully shot through it. Sam, still struggling with her seatbelt, fumbled with it until the restraint finally gave way.

I think her fingers were as numb as I was. She cursed loudly.

"Stay here," she commanded, as she too ran outside.

Bandit whined somewhere behind me, but I didn't turn to look at him, too scared of what might be happening outside. What might be happening to Gideon. Even though Sam had given strict orders, I knew I couldn't obey them.

I stepped out of the RV and into the open space.

The man with the gun was attempting to run away, but Gideon was hot on his heels. He had been right. The guy must have been out of bullets, as he wasn't firing at us anymore. Gideon could have shot at him, but, despite the truck full of ammo we had stolen, none had fitted Sam's gun, which meant we had precious little bullets ourselves.

Instead of wasting them, Gideon tore after him, Sully and Sam close behind.

The man limped as he ran, obviously in pain: Sam must have caught him with the RV when she rammed into his car. It was this limp that Gideon used to his advantage. As his eyes narrowed with purpose, he closed in with a calculated swiftness. With a yell that I could hear from here, he took a flying leap at the guy and tackled him to the ground.

They both fell with such a heavy thud that I thought for sure, bones would be broken. Gideon's eyes were like black pits, fixed grimly on the man beneath him. As the man started to buck him off, Gideon pressed Sam's gun firmly against his head.

The man stopped struggling.

Gideon waited until Sully and Sam arrived, winded and out of breath. The two of them restrained him before Gideon would climb off him. In a slick move that spoke of her years on the job, Sam handcuffed his arms behind him and shoved him toward the RV.

"Move."

As Sully, Gideon, and Sam returned to my side, relief washed over me. The relentless rush of blood that had pounded in my ears began to subside, and my heart, which had been racing like a runaway train, gradually slowed to a more manageable pace.

However, this was all shattered by Bandit's high-pitched whine, a sound that seemed to cut through the air like a knife and raised the hairs on the back of my neck.

It finally registered that he had been doing that the entire time we had all run outside. I had thought he was just as worried as the rest of us, but now that the immediate danger had passed, I sensed something else in his voice.

A desperate tone that I couldn't mistake.

Something was wrong.

Like really, *really* wrong.

And this wasn't about the guy who had just fired at us.

I ran back into the RV to find Emma hunched over Zeb, her left arm raised above her head while the other pressed against his stomach. Seeing my arrival Bandit — lying beside Zeb — suddenly howled.

I skidded to a stop as Emma's panicked eyes flashed up at me.

"It's not working! Why isn't it working?" She babbled. "Why can't I stop the bleeding?!"

And with that, the whole world fell apart.

42

———

SULLY

Blood glistened on my hands.

Warm and sticky, pooling from *a hole in his body*. Throughout my time at the clinic, I'd seen my fair share of blood, but it had always belonged to a patient.

Never had it belonged to a loved one.

"Oh, God."

Sam drew in a shocked breath behind me. Her feet, rooted to the spot. She and Gideon had escorted the man into the RV, but I had no idea what they had done with him — and I didn't care. My attention was focused solely on my dad.

On his blood that seeped out, soaking my hands that pressed desperately against his open wound.

Emma, sat back on her heels, and relented only after Chase emphatically explained that lowering her left arm wouldn't offer any assistance. It was a minute before either of us realized that she had taken Sam's instruction from the day before quite literally.

Stick your left hand above your head and put pressure on the wound.

Those had been Sam's exact words when she had found Emma cowering in the corner of the barn and had tended to Emma's own bleeding arm. And now, Emma was applying that same logic to my dad.

What a bittersweet moment for her to have finally discovered her humanity.

My dad's forehead was clammy with sweat. Deep lines furrowed across his brow, but it was the pain reflected in his eyes that was difficult to bear. Tendrils of terror gripped me, accentuated by the realization that I had never dealt with the intricacies of the human anatomy before. Regardless, a gunshot wound was a gunshot wound. And this needed immediate, lifesaving, first aid.

Frantically, I ran over what should be done in my head, but instead of the clear points of action I needed, my thoughts were a jumble of manic noise, racing from one unrelated thing to another. I couldn't get my act together…

And my father was dying because of it.

A familiar, taunting voice slithered into the recesses of my mind — a sinister echo I believed I'd locked away for good. The voice, a relentless phantom from the past, resurfaced with cruel precision, each word a venomous reminder of years spent branding me as a disappointment. It tried to undermine my resolve, replaying a litany of past failures, each crescendo culminating in the haunting refrain that if I'd only become the surgeon they had always wanted, I'd have some idea what to do now. At the very least, I could ease some of his pain.

Dad looked at me, the fog in his eyes clearing for a moment as he reached for my hand. But then he froze, flinching, as pain lanced his side. I caught his hand in my own.

"It's not… your fault…" He wheezed at me.

Darkness filled his mouth, and I recoiled at the sight of red staining his teeth — more blood. A ribbon of it trickled out of the corner of his mouth. I brushed my thumb over it, needing to wipe the sight of it away, to erase it from all existence, but all I managed was to smear it over his pale cheek.

"I know what… you're thinking. I don't blame you." He

stopped, gulping in air. Talking was too much of a strain for him. I had to get him to stop.

"Save your energy, Dad. We're getting you help." I felt a hand squeeze my shoulder and knew it was Sam. Her voice sounded in my ear, soft yet supportive.

"I'll take over here." She covered my hand with her own, gently prying away my cold fingers. When my hand was free, she held onto Zeb for moral support while keeping her other hand pressed tightly against his wound.

Staggering into the living area, I found Chase and Gideon waiting with Bandit and Emma. Gideon still had Sam's gun pointed at the shooter. The two had secured him to the table that was fastened to the floor of the motorhome. Grimly, the thought flashed across my mind that he wouldn't be getting out any time soon — if, at all — if I had any say on the matter.

As I materialized, Gideon charged towards me, eyes wide with a primal fear that appeared to have sheared years off his life.

"He needs medical help."

"I know. But we'd be walking into the lion's den. We'd never be able to avoid being seen."

Gideon turned to me, fury flaring in his eyes. "But they're the only ones who can save him!"

"The second we step foot in a hospital, his men will have us. We can't risk that." I glanced at our hunter to see if my assumption was true. His silence gave me the confirmation I was searching for.

"Not even for your own father?" Gideon's eyes flashed with accusation.

Emma stood up suddenly, rushing to my side. "I agree with Sully. There's no point in us all dying."

Her voice, earnest and well-intentioned, sought to appeal to their common sense. She believed she was helping, but her words only managed to draw a sharp gasp from Chase and fueled Gideon's rage another notch.

"I'm only saying what you already know. Why are you all

looking at me like that? Why do you act like I'm a monster?" Her blue eyes usually so clear, suddenly brimmed over with tears. "I was trying to help! I did what she said I should do!"

I could never bear Emma's tears. She never had any real reason to cry, except during those heavy moments when there was nothing more to be done for an animal, and even then, there was an understanding, an awareness, beneath those eyes. But not this Emma. Despite being the spitting image of my wife, she had none of the personality. This Emma lacked comprehension of the world around her.

Ordinarily, I would have comforted her, as I would anyone who was in distress. But time was a luxury we couldn't afford. I had to decide whether it was worth the risk of going to a hospital.

And I knew I couldn't.

As much as I had come to love my father, the risk to all our lives was too great. And I knew he wouldn't want me to jeopardize the family for his sake.

"The only thing we can do is hurry to Elora. She'll be able to help him, and no one will have to find out."

Gideon's frown deepened, conveying his mounting desperation.

"You're really going to make him wait? Can't you see how much pain he's in? How do you even know he'll survive the journey?"

"I'm well aware of the dangers, but this is the best we can do. This is hard for us all, Gid, not just you. Please remember that."

I hurried to the driver's seat.

Moments later, we sped away as I prayed to the heavens that I wasn't making a catastrophic mistake.

43

CHASE

Sam and Sully traded shifts behind the wheel, their determined
eyes reflecting the gravity of our situation. Two of us were
always stationed at Zeb's side, as we tried to keep him calm and
distracted.

Trying to keep him alive.

Gideon and I hovered over him, making him as comfortable as
possible, though it seemed not only a losing battle but a ridiculous
one. No matter how soft a mattress was, or however much we
could elevate his head, it wasn't going to do anything about that
gaping hole in his stomach.

Or the unrelenting torrent of blood that continued to seep
through our makeshift bandages, no matter how frequently we
added another layer to them.

Just as I'd think it could be clotting (which would be a good
sign), more of that crimson would blossom through. With a heavy
heart, I turned away, unable to take another moment of the agony
that was etched all over his face.

Bandit stood off to the side, panting with distress. Now and
then, a warning growl would sound from his throat and I'd find

him facing off against the man who had shot Zeb with a fierce protectiveness that mirrored our rage and desperation.

I glared at him, hoping he could feel every inch of my hate. Sam's gun sat a few inches from my hand, far enough away from him that he wouldn't be able to snatch it up, even if he wasn't bound to the table. My fingers itched to grab it. The cold metal of the barrel seemed to mock me, daring me to try and make a move.

It took every inch of willpower not to pump a bullet straight into his head.

In the thick of the silent standoff, Sully broke through the tension with a shout that cut through the air like a knife. "Did you call anyone?"

The man, however, met Sully's question with a chilling indifference, as if he had only enquired about the time.

"I said, did you call anyone?!"

When the man didn't answer for the second time, Gideon's face contorted into a fierce snarl, his hand moving faster than I could comprehend. In a swift motion, he grabbed the gun and swung it with brutal force at the man's face that he would have been knocked down if it wasn't for his restrained hands holding him upright.

The man spat onto the floor, a glob of blood mixed with saliva, testing his jaw gingerly to see if it was broken. Despite the violence, there was no anger in his tone when he spoke.

"He's going to die if you don't get him to a hospital," he stated matter-of-factly, shooting a pointed look at Zeb.

"Shut up! The last thing we need is your advice," Gideon erupted, his hand moving toward him again with the gun. But I intervened, catching his arm before he could land another punch.

"He's more useful to us alive."

The minute the words had come out of my mouth, I knew they were true. "He's the only link we have to them. If we kill him, we'll have nothing."

Gideon's tortured eyes met mine. That familiar green of his

irises now glistening over with tears. Zeb's moans of pain cut through the moment. Gideon immediately rushed back to his side, leaving the gun by me.

"If you release me, I can get him the help he needs," the shooter offered calmly, as if it was he who held all the cards.

But before Sully could even answer, Sam spoke up, her voice loaded with cold determination. "We don't negotiate with killers."

"Then I hope you have a nice plot ready for him."

Sam marched towards him like a predator, her steps heavy with intent as she closed in until she was mere inches from him. Quick as a flash, her foot lashed out with a powerful kick to his stomach that sent him doubling over in pain. Snatching up a fistful of his hair, she jerked his head back and held it there in a vice-like grip until his pain-glazed eyes met hers.

"Chase is right. We need you alive. But that doesn't mean we can't make your every surviving minute a misery." She leaned in closer, her breath hot against his face. "You say anything else about Zeb — and I mean, anything — and you will live to regret it. Do you get my drift?"

He nodded, wariness flickering over his features before he schooled his expression into one of neutrality. She released him abruptly, like she couldn't bear to keep touching him. I had never seen Sam like that before — sparks had literally flown from her eyes.

Still giving him the evil eye, she searched him thoroughly for weapons or trackers, finding nothing except for his wallet. She rifled through its contents, spreading them out on the table for us all to see — a handful of debit and credit cards under the name John Smith, two hundred dollars in cash, a loyalty card to Subway and a photograph of him with his arms wrapped around a picture-perfect wife and three young children.

"John Smith?" She sounded every bit as skeptical as I felt.

"Like anyone believes that." I blurted out.

He shrugged nonchalantly, as if to say, 'suit yourself.'

I couldn't believe it. This cold-hearted killer, with his startlingly plain face and disarming smile, had a family. Three children with hazel eyes and glossy chestnut hair, looking every bit the perfect American family in the photograph he showed us. My mind couldn't reconcile the image of this man with his innocent-looking kids and the brutal murders he was responsible for.

"Are those really your family?" I asked incredulously.

"Yes."

I hadn't expected the truth. I had expected lies, fabrications, anything other than that straight forward answer unless this was all an elaborate plan to unnerve us. Maybe he was trying to get under my skin, disarm me so that I'd reveal some secret he wanted.

Well, I wasn't that dumb.

"You're telling me these are your kids? That you go around killing people but you keep a picture of your family in your wallet?"

His eyes held mine in a level gaze. There was no animosity there that I could see. None of that desperate madness that had been in Forbes or the fervent narcissism that had driven Xavier. In this man's eyes, all I saw was him.

"Correct."

"Why would you risk having a picture of them on you?"

"We never get caught, so it isn't usually a concern of ours," he said, almost casually, as if murder was just another part of his everyday life. He shifted positions, settling himself more comfortably while Bandit bared his wickedly sharp teeth, warning him not to try anything. Smith gave him a leery look.

"I'm just changing positions, that's all."

Bandit's responding "woof" was a guttural growl full of ferocity and primal instinct. No hint of my Muttface remained. In his place, this dog was ready to attack the man who had caused us so much pain.

"You don't look like a sadistic killer." And I meant it. He seemed more like one of my high school teachers than a ruthless murderer.

"That's because I'm not," he replied evenly, not a hint of irony in his voice. "I know what you think, but you're wrong. I don't get any enjoyment out of this, but it is my job. I am a cleaner. I clean whatever needs to be cleaned. The orders come from above and I carry them out. I do it for my country."

His words were rolling into one. I had no idea what he was talking about. What orders? Who were his bosses?

"Your country?" Sully said from the driver's seat. His eyes locked with Smith's, turning bright with shock. "You work for the government?"

Smith's silence confirmed our worst fears.

"That's insane. What branch of the government would allow the murder of innocent people, of kids?!"

"The kind that works to keep the country safe."

"But that doesn't make any sense? We're not a danger to anyone. You're the ones trying to kill us," I cried.

Bandit barked yes, typing into his iPad. *"You are one of the bad men."*

Considering that Smith hadn't witnessed Bandit speaking before, his reaction wasn't what I expected. Usually people were filled with awe and delight, but Smith just looked spooked, making me wonder what kind of terrible lies his bosses had filled his head with.

"I wasn't actually trying to kill you at first. If you recall, my men and I turned up at your ranch when you started firing at us. It was self defense."

I snorted, not caring how unladylike I sounded. "Yeah, with snipers! You shot at us with snipers!"

"They were equipped with tranqs. They wouldn't have killed you. Our orders weren't to kill you all."

There was something in his voice, something he wasn't quite

telling us. I ran through his words in my head, remembering his reaction to Bandit.

"*All?*"

His eyes slid over to Bandit…then Emma. "Our orders are only for the dog and the woman. The rest of you can still live. I can wipe your memory so you won't remember any of this. You won't even remember the dog. You'll be able to go on with your lives as if none of this ever happened. It's your choice."

I backed away from him, horrified by his suggestion. Forget my Muttface? Over my dead body!

"Why are you talking like you have any option here? You're in no position to make demands." Sully challenged.

Smith licked his lips, his eyes growing dark with intensity. "Because I know how this ends. If you get rid of me, I will only be replaced by another. I don't think you realize quite how far this goes. You cannot win."

Each word struck like a hammer, driving home the chilling truth of his words.

"Is that why you're telling us this, because you know you can wipe our minds after?"

Smith nodded. "You know I'm telling the truth. Just think about your friend, Mr. Wall Street." He addressed Sully. "We did it with him. Now he's free to live his life, none the wiser."

"After you brutalized him," Sully snapped, not giving an inch.

"That's incorrect. He was only hurt as he came at us and suffered a few blows in the process. If we had managed to take him the way we had planned, he wouldn't have been hurt at all."

"Then explain Florence because she sure as hell didn't die of natural causes."

A flicker of remorse passed over Smith's bland expression, startling me.

"That was an unfortunate consequence. Her heart couldn't handle the shock. There was nothing we could do for her. I am sorry about that. Killing her was never our intention."

"But why are you targeting Bandit? What has he done to you?"

"It's not what he has done, but what he represents. What they both represent." At the word "they" his gaze shifted to Emma.

"We don't have anything in common," she cried. "He's an animal and I've already proven to them that I'm human. Why would anyone want me dead? This doesn't make any sense."

"No it doesn't," Sully agreed.

Smith looked at Emma, his stare piercing through her with an unreadable intensity.

"I don't get paid to ask questions. But like the dog, she is a freak of nature. She's a threat and must be eliminated."

44

SULLY

Thirty minutes later, Sam switched with me so I could spend more time with Dad.

His face was unearthly pale, his skin stretched tightly against the bones like a paper-thin veil potentially moments away from being ripped apart. His eyes were mere slits, barely opening to acknowledge my presence. He tried to form a smile on his lips, but it quickly dissipated.

I was shocked by how he had deteriorated in such a short space of time.

I had wanted to tell him what we had learned from Smith, but none of that seemed to matter now. Hearing my approach, his eyes fluttered open weakly. His mouth twitched as he tried, but failed to make a smile.

"We're a few hours away from Arizona, but you can make it," I said in desperation while grabbing onto his hands as if they were my last hope. My old man looked at me, a clear understanding in his eyes.

"We both know that's not true."

"Maybe I can drop you off in a hospital. We'll drive near to one. I'll take you inside—"

He cut me off with a weak shake of his head.

"Son… that won't work. Besides, you can't risk… your lives for me. I won't allow it. I've been a burden… to you. Emma was right about that."

The way he said her name was a dagger stabbing straight through my heart. It took a moment before I had the clarity of why that was.

"I wish you'd met my Emma. The real one. You would have loved her."

Zeb's chest heaved with each breath, feeling like it was slowly cracking as sorrow bled from every pore. He bowed his head, unable to bear the intense pain that gripped him.

"It is my biggest regret… that I didn't go… to your wedding. I'm sorry… I was a fool… and will carry… that… to my grave."

The gaps between his words were growing longer as he fought to catch his breath.

"Save your strength. You don't need to talk like this." And I meant it. Those years spent resenting his treatment of me melted away into nothingness. All of our arguments seemed insignificant now. Nothing really mattered other than staying alive.

His breath came again, a thin, raspy sound that whistled between clenched teeth. His fingers squeezed mine with an iron grip, giving me a false sense of hope that he'd pull through. But then, as swiftly as the glimmer of optimism had surfaced, his fingers relinquished their grip, and I heard the deafening silence. Time itself felt suspended, as if the universe paused to bear witness to the silence.

No breathing. No more raspy whistles.

Only the hollow echo of the road rolling beneath us.

"Dad?"

I whispered his name, terror flooding my body, constricting my throat so that I could barely make a sound. Praying for his wheezing breath to come again, my eyes scanned over his face, desperately searching for any sign of life.

But there was none.

His chest was as still as stone.

"DAD!"

I screamed his name. Grabbing his shoulders, I shook him violently, forgetting everything else around me. Forgetting that it would cause him immense pain. All I knew was that I needed him to move.

I needed him alive.

Only silence greeted me, and that rumble of the tarmac beneath the wheels of the motorhome. A heavy shroud of grief draped over my shoulders, and the weight of loss pressed down on me with a physical force.

"DAD!"

My voice wailed his name as the enormity of his death hit me like a freight train. My fingers turned numb and icy cold from the horror as the world fractured apart in an instant.

An unbearable void opened up where I should have been and I felt myself slowly dissolving away into nothingness.

I couldn't think, couldn't feel.

Could not speak.

Someone thundered into the room. Gideon. Beyond my stupor I caught his stricken face taking in the scene before me. He said something to me, but I couldn't hear it over the wrathful cacophony that had taken up residence in my head. A relentless buzzing ringing in my ears until it blotted out all other noise. I couldn't be in here anymore.

I had to get out of this room.

Shuffling to the living area, I stumbled past Chase and Bandit, both looking at me in utter horror as they darted past me to the bedroom. The buzz was getting louder now, drowning out everything but the one thought.

Moonlight glinted off the cold metal object on the table and drew me in like a magnet. With robotic precision, I snatched it up and pressed the gun against Smith's temple. The noise in my head grew to a crescendo, but it couldn't mask the simple fact.

He was the reason for all of this.

He was the reason my father was lying dead not ten feet from me. The ache of grief, the weight of loss, and the flames of anger coalesced into a singular purpose — avenge my father's death. Emma sprang up fearfully, hands trembling as she stepped back towards Sam.

"Sully? What are you doing?"

I heard her question, though she might as well have been speaking Chinese for all the sense it made. She tried again.

"I don't think you should be doing that."

The floor shifted beneath my feet. I felt the RV lurch to one side and the smoothness of the road vanished, replaced by the rough-ness of an unpaved surface as we took an abrupt detour. My finger wrapped around the trigger. The biting cold sent shivers down my spine, cutting into the fog that had wrapped itself around my head.

Everything stopped until I heard footsteps approaching. Through my daze, I caught a glimpse of blonde curls and that familiar face I loved.

"Honey… you don't want to do that. Listen to my voice, babe. Hand me the gun."

She spoke in a reassuring voice. Her calmness had an imme-diate effect on me, though I still wasn't able to do as she asked. I wanted him to suffer, just like Dad had, and if he died, there would be one less person coming after us.

"Sully. Please. Don't do that. You're in shock, but this isn't what you should do; we need him alive in order to have any chance of surviving them. But if you kill him, we'll be left with nothing. We need you with us, Sully. We need you so that we can fight them. I know you're hurting, baby. I know you're sad and filled with rage, but if you kill him, you'll only make things worse. You have to trust me. Please. Hand me the gun."

Smith stared up at me without any fear, only a deep resignation, as though he had always expected death to come to him like this. How could he stay so calm knowing that his life was so close to ending? His wife and children's faces flashed before me, cutting through all the noise and making me pause. A bead of sweat formed on my brow, dripping down my face, though I felt anything but warm. Sam moved closer to me, her hand outstretched, waiting for me to do as she asked.

"Baby?" She asked softly, her voice heavy with the weight of the world.

Slowly, I moved the gun away from Smith's head, unhooked my finger from the trigger, and gave her the gun. Sam took it carefully, tucking it into the back of her jeans. Then she wrapped her arms around me, squeezing me as hard as she could. Suddenly, I broke down into sobs as tears flooded from my eyes.

No one said a word.

The kids were crying in the bedroom. Bandit howled his sorrow into the night. I felt Sam's tears mingle with my own.

Only Emma stood still and silent, seemingly unmoved by our growing anguish.

I held onto Sam like she was my lifeline.

45

SULLY

I couldn't say how long we stayed like that, how long I clung to my wife as if she were the only thing anchoring me to reality.

She sat me down — sat us all down — and went to cover Dad's body with his blanket. Bandit squeezed himself between Chase and Gideon, a paw on each of their knees, consoling them the best way he knew how.

Sam made us take sips from a bottle of water, before quietly returning to the driver's seat, and setting off again. Our shock would take a while to fade, she explained, but we weren't safe out here on the highway. We had to get to Elora — and we were close, within a few hours of reaching her.

So the RV continued as if our world hadn't just shattered into pieces. The air was heavy with grief and our usual camaraderie replaced by an uneasy silence, broken only by a stifled sob as each of us grappled with our own emotions.

While Sam had cared for us, Emma had watched her intensely like a child might study an adult. Her blue eyes opened wide, taking in every one of her actions. With Sam back in the driver's seat, Emma approached me hesitantly with the bag of food we had picked up from the gas station.

"Do you want something to eat?"

I shook my head stiffly, the simple act of it sending me into a tailspin. The very thought of food caused my stomach to lurch, and it was all I could do not to throw up. She looked at the kids, offering the bag, but they turned her away too. She focused her attention back on me.

"I can get you another drink?" She asked hopefully, like that would solve all my problems. Frankly, I wanted her to leave me the hell alone, but apparently, she wasn't getting the memo. My throat felt constricted, words caught in a tangle of emotion. I wanted to scream, to release the pent-up frustration that threatened to consume me. Instead, I forced myself to meet her eyes. I shook my head again, unable to get my mouth to formulate any words.

Her fingers were tightly intertwined, and a furrow appeared on her brow. She looked lost and unsure of what to do. Eventually, unable to elicit a response from any of us, she turned to Smith.

"Would you like a drink, then?"

Chase gasped with horror, and Gideon's eye's turned flat with hate. At Smith's grateful nod, Emma carefully — so carefully — raised the bottle of water to his lips. In a sudden outburst, Gideon lunged across the short distance and slapped the bottle out of her hands, sending it flying across the room where it bounced against the window and burst, raining water over the dirt-encrusted glass.

"What do you think you're doing?!" He screamed, an unhinged man.

Emma stared at him in shock. "I was just trying to help…"

Gideon glared at her with all the fury in the world. "He is the reason that Zeb is lying dead in that room, but you're going to *reward* him?"

Confusion clouded Emma's face as she stammered out, "No… that's not what I was doing." She was completely thrown by his anger.

"Then why, after everything they've done, would you even consider helping him?"

Emma blinked at him, startled, and turned to me, as if I would defend her. "That's what *she* did. I was just trying to be like her because you all seemed to appreciate it."

Sam glanced at us from the driver's seat. Though she kept her opinions to herself, her mouth was a thin and terse line.

"Sam was trying to comfort us…" Gideon stopped, choking on his words. I knew immediately he was picturing my father with that gaping wound in his stomach. The details of his death replayed in vivid, excruciating detail. Over and over. Haunting our very breath.

Swallowing, he tried again. "She wasn't helping the man who wants to destroy our family. She's not helping the man trying to kill us."

"I… didn't know…" Emma stuttered, her voice trailing off.

"What? You don't know the difference?" Gideon spat out the question. "I mean, how could you not? Only a monster would be this clueless. The hell is wrong with you?!"

"Nothing! There's nothing wrong with me!" Emma snapped in response, suddenly angered. Throwing the bag of food onto the floor, she stormed off to the only place she could get away from them — the bedroom.

Tossing them a hateful look, she slammed the door, causing the entire RV to shake.

                                    46
                                  ─────

                                CHASE

The RV reverberated with the sound of the slamming the
door.

My chest was so tight I struggled to breathe. So much was
happening, but I wasn't prepared for any of it. How could you
ever steel yourself for something like this?

Silence hung heavily in the room, thick with unspoken sorrow
and the aftermath of a confrontation that had left us all feeling raw.
Gideon stewed beside me, his anger a palpable force, a shield
against the overwhelming pain that threatened to crush all of our
hearts. He kept tossing looks toward the bedroom door, glaring at it
as if that was the source of his grief. If his rage could manifest as a
physical energy, that door would have burst into flames.

Smith spoke up suddenly, his voice cutting through the thick
tension that had settled like a storm cloud. His voice sounded
insultingly normal.

As if the world hadn't just ended.

"She was only trying to help."

A strangled sound came out of Gideon as he leaped toward
him. Sully jumped up too, his eyes relaying a deep concern that

Gideon would pummel Smith to death. Part of me secretly wished he would kill him, yet deep down, I knew it would only satisfy his temporarily unchecked fury. Eventually, he would come to his senses and the weight of what he had done would consume him, leaving no trace of the Gideon we all loved behind. He must have realized this too, as instead of completely destroying him, Gideon tore a strip from his shirt and tied it around Smith's mouth so we wouldn't have to listen to him.

I wasn't sure why none of us had considered that option before. It seemed so obvious now, after the fact. Knowing that we had a brief time out from either Smith or Emma speaking for a while, a little of the tension lifted. It wasn't much of a relief, but at least I could finally breathe again.

I gulped in large mouthfuls of air, filling my lungs until my heart stopped racing and I started to feel a little more like myself — as much as I could under the circumstances , anyway.

Sully held his head in his heads, overcome not only with grief but the heavy burden of guilt. It was ultimately his decision, his choice, not to go the hospital. I emphasized with him and understood his reasoning. I probably would have done the same thing in his place, but it didn't make the truth any easier to bear.

We sat in silence, each of us wrapped up in our misery until Gideon started pacing the length of the room. At the end of each circuit, he would glare back in the direction of the bedroom. My eyes followed his every stomping stride until the muscles in the back of my neck began to spasm.

I finally mustered up the courage to ask, "What is it? What're you thinking?"

Gideon's green eyes flicked onto me. Those golden flecks seemed to glow with feeling.

"Emma."

"I know. She's difficult to understand sometimes."

"You mean all the time. Everything she says or does is wrong. She drives me crazy. I wish she'd shut up and disappear. We were fine until she came into our lives. We were happy. She's made everything so much worse."

His words made me flinch.

I knew he was right: Emma was incredibly frustrating and annoying. But she was also new to everything. She was scared and confused and trying to make sense of a world she didn't fit into. Each time I found myself getting angry at her, I would have to consciously remind myself that she wasn't being malicious; she just didn't know any better.

I looked at Sully, but the only outward sign that he had heard Gideon was a tightening of his shoulders. His eyes stayed glued to the floor, where I was unable to read them.

"She's not doing it on purpose. As annoying as she can be, she doesn't mean to upset us."

He didn't answer me. Troubled, he stared at the closed door again as if he was hoping to be able to see inside.

"Better or worse, it is her, right?" Gideon directed the question at Sully. He finally raised his head.

"That's Emma, isn't it?" Gideon pushed.

Sully didn't immediately respond. "I don't know. I guess."

"Well, if they brought her back from the dead, can't they do the same for Zeb?"

Sully's mouth fell open. I felt the ground shift beneath my feet and had to brace myself with my hands, even though I was still sitting on the sofa.

"You can't mean that?" I gasped, shock sending me immobile. The very idea of manipulating life and death, even in the face of grief, was a shocking violation of the laws of nature.

"Why not?" He snapped, daggers flashing from his eyes. "They brought her back, so they can him too!"

"Son…" Sully began in a voice deeply laden with regret, "Even if that's what's happened here, you can see she isn't right. She isn't the Emma I loved."

"I don't care how they bring him back as long as he comes back with a pulse!" Gideon roared, eyes glistening with tears. "He can't be dead, Sully! He just can't!"

His voice broke, and the emotional intensity that had fueled him moments ago dissipated, leaving him visibly diminished. Sully reached across and pulled him into his arms, holding him tight.

"It's not natural, Gid. You know that. Even if it were possible, even if we could find the people who could do that, it wouldn't be him… and that would hurt even more. It wouldn't fill the hole within you. Trust me, I know what I'm talking about."

Gideon didn't respond, but he held onto Sully, their bodies joined together in shared sorrow.

Bandit let out a long, mournful whine that somehow managed to convey how we were all feeling.

47

CHASE

Endless night passed by, a black gaping hole of nothing that seemed to have engulfed the world, emphasizing the darkness within our hearts.

Sully had moved beside Sam now, the two of them sitting close together as she steered the RV through the night, holding his hand in her lap. Though they said nothing, I could see that Sully was leaning heavily on her support. Every now and then, she squeezed his hand just to let him know she was still with him. They had a silent understanding that transcended words. She was his rock, saving Sully from the despair that threatened to devour him.

By comparison, it was like a wall had come up between Gideon and me.

We hadn't spoken since his outburst. Each time I tried, he would offer only the barest grunt as a response — that or he would simply wave me away. I wanted so desperately to talk to him, to share how we were feeling together, but instead of moving closer, he just pulled away.

He now sat as far from me as was possible in the small space. Unable to process his grief, he had shut down, creating an emotional distance that seemed insurmountable. Even though I knew it wasn't personal, his withdrawal still felt that way. My heart, which had already been broken once tonight, now felt as if he had taken a sledgehammer to it. What remained lay in pieces, scattered over the cold vinyl floor.

What had happened to our earlier closeness? Had I imagined it all? Or did he not feel the same way about me that I felt for him?

The doubts swirled relentlessly in my mind, creating a dense fog that clouded my thoughts and emotions, amplifying the uncertainty that lingered in the silence between us.

Sensing what was troubling me, Bandit tilted his head at me and emitted a soft whine. His big, soft tongue snaked out and gave my cheek a quick lick, his breath warm, comforting and familiar.

"Don't worry Chase. He is upset."

"I know, buddy. We all are."

I smiled, though I wasn't sure who it was meant to convince. Besides, Bandit could see straight through me — he always had.

He whined again, and scooted even closer to me, his tail thumping in emphasis, *"You are my best friend and I love you."*

Those earnest words, spoken in the simple love language of my dog, cut straight to my heart. Tears misted my eyes again. I wiped them away with an irritated hand and stared at the space we had initially kept Smith. The space beneath the table was empty now, thankfully. He had been moved to the back room and now sat securely bound beside Zeb's body. None of us wanted him to glean more information than he already possessed. The fear of him using our mistakes against us had propelled us to shift him out of earshot.

Emma had seemed unnerved at first when we'd moved him into the room, but she had decided to stay in there rather than face the rest of us.

Knowing what we knew his orders were, I suggested that maybe she wouldn't want to be left alone with him… just in case. But she had shaken her head, her blonde hair flying, stubbornly insisting that she would be fine. She was so hurt over our perceived slights that she was willing to take the risk though the raw pain and visible confusion etched across her face had struck a chord in me, causing me to question my earlier judgement. Maybe she really didn't know how tactless she was coming across. What if she really was trying?

What if this was the best she could do?

I pulled my knees up, resting my chin on them, and stared outside, waiting for a light that I was afraid would never come.

48

SULLY

At the crack of dawn, our weary journey finally brought us to the quiet enclave of Elora's neighborhood — Sunnybrook.

It was a suburb filled with near-identical ranch houses, each adorned with perfectly manicured yards. Exuding an air of tranquility, it was the kind of place where people sat on their front porches, sipping iced tea while observing the joyful chaos of children playing outside.

Sunnybrook felt like a page torn from my memories of Ellington, my hometown in Connecticut, where Emma and I had once created a haven and set up the clinic. The neighborhood resonated with familiar sights — meticulously landscaped front yards, houses receiving annual paint touch-ups, and immaculate, wide streets free of any litter. Rows of expensive cars graced the driveways, an indication that the affluent homeowners had yet to leave for work due to the earliness of the hour.

This was a community saturated with class and privilege, a place where affluence was as conspicuous as the well-tended lawns.

Where, if something bad happened, the owners would be out in force to protect what they owned. This was, in a word, the epitome of safety. Nothing would be a better deterrent to Smith's men than the curtain-twitching, security camera recording, rich folk that called Sunnybrook their home.

Knowing that it would blow their cover if they attacked us here, I felt a degree of safety parking the RV by a man-made park. Still, it took some convincing for the others to let me continue on my own, even if we knew it made the most sense.

Leaving the others, trying not to let Chase and Sam's uneasy faces haunt my mind, I set off at a brisk pace toward Elora's residence, hoping to reach her house before my seemingly inconspicuous morning jog drew unwanted attention.

At a passing glance, I would be mistaken for an early morning jogger, but if they stared longer, or came up closer and saw the boots I wore in place of running shoes, raised eyebrows could be thrown my way.

I was hoping to make it to her house before that happened.

The pink-tinged sky cast a cheerfulness over the area that was in stark contrast to my heavy heart. Normally, I would find enjoyment running in the fresh air at the dawn of another day, with the springy grass beneath my feet.

Today, it only made me want to claw my eyes out.

Driving had provided some escape from the grief. The mundane task had given me something else to focus on. With each passing minute, as the sky grew lighter, a fraction of the weight in my heart lifted, only for it to plummet again in the next moment, a crushing pain that turned my heart to stone.

Shaking my head to dispel the encroaching despair, I forced myself to continue, putting one foot in front of the other. Succumbing to my emotions was not an option; the well-being of my family depended on my ability to keep it together. The burden of saving them fell squarely on my shoulders, a responsibility I carried with grim determination.

A man wearing a cozy bathrobe took small sips from his coffee, still adjusting to the early morning. He stood in front of his house, watching over his white poodle as it relieved itself. I jogged past, quick on the offensive, shooting him a smile in the hope that he would be disarmed by my gesture.

"Morning," he called out, friendly if tired.

"Looks like another beautiful day." Trying not to choke on the lie, I gave him a quick wave and continued on my way.

The tidy streets twisted through more pastel-hued houses. I ran past so many picket fences that I lost count. My feet finally came to a stop in front of a house with a red letterbox bearing a stylish cursive font and a name I recognized.

Heart hammering in my chest, I sprinted up the stone path to the matching red door. Stabbing the bell, I craned my head, anxiously peeking through the glass panels on either side of the door.

Please be home…

The words reverberated in my head, a mantra or prayer I couldn't tell. A dog began yapping, high-pitched and frantic, growing increasingly louder. Suddenly a blur of brown streaked toward the door followed by the appearance of Elora, wearing a set of pinstripe pajamas. Her usually long and dark almost-black hair — now with a new blunt fringe — was tied into a neat ponytail, her feet encased in furry slippers. She peered over her rimless glasses at me, her eyes growing round.

Seeing her, a smile, my first genuine smile, burst out from me.

Staring from the other side of the glass, she blinked, not able to believe I wasn't a mirage. It was only when I beckoned to her that she jumped out of her daze and hurried to the door.

"Sully?" She gaped, opening the door, taking in my haggard appearance. "What are you doing here?"

She trailed off, her quick eyes noticing the flecks of blood that had gotten onto my clothes but could only be seen up close. Her alabaster skin turned impossibly whiter. The door opened wide as she moved aside.

"Come inside."

I stepped past to find a familiar dog looking timidly up at me.

At the sight of me, her small body began to shake, not out of fear but in anticipation. Her tail wagged hesitantly as if she was waiting for my reaction before committing to her own.

"Pixie?" I asked, shocked to see her here.

"Woof," she answered, surprising me with her response.

She had the face of a German Shepherd, though her small size and short legs seemed more suited to a Corgi. I was fairly certain she was a mix of both of those breeds.

Although her coat had been thin and unkempt before, it was now lustrous and healthy. However, there was a small shaved patch on her head where fur had recently started to grow back. Pixie swirled around, dancing playfully on her paws. As she turned, I caught sight of a bold vertical scar with neatly sewn stitches that appeared to be healing well. It was clear that Pixie had undergone surgery not long after Elora brought her back with her.

Behind me, Elora shut the door, drawing the chain across it as a second thought. She motioned for me to follow her into the front room, where two leather sofas were positioned across from each other by a roaring fireplace. A large coffee table made of walnut wood separated the sofas, adorned with several oversized gardening books. I sat down on one sofa while Elora took a seat across from me, studying my face with a puzzled look.

"What's going on?"

I blurted out every awful thing that had happened in the last few days, skimming through the details so I could get the gist of it over quickly, conscious that every second it took for me to explain was another away from my family. I wanted them off the streets and out of danger as soon as possible.

Elora absorbed every word with unwavering attention, her focus unbroken as I recounted the events that had unfolded. She interjected only when clarification was needed, otherwise main-taining a respectful silence that allowed me to articulate the horror of what we had faced. When I was finished, her response was immediate. She grabbed hold of my hands, sympathy shining from her eyes.

"I'm so sorry about Zeb, Sully."

I couldn't do anything but nod, not trusting myself to speak.

She intertwined her fingers together, desperately searching for comforting words to ease the pain I was feeling. In the end, all she could offer was a sympathetic smile.

"I didn't want to come here, but there was no one else I could think of. I don't want to put you in any danger—"

Elora held her hand up, stopping me mid-sentence. "Of course I'll help. You'll all stay here until we figure this thing out."

Her offer came so easily that I wondered if she truly knew what she was getting into. Maybe I hadn't stressed the danger enough.

"You understand that you'll be at risk? These people shot up our home. They attacked Mark, killed Florence and… my dad… They're not kidding around."

"I understand the dangers and I'm willing to accept them."

The burden that rested on my shoulders lifted, although a small shred of uncertainty still lingered. "I'm more grateful than you know… but why? As much as I don't want to ask, I have to. Why would you risk your life to help us?"

Elora's eyes dimmed with shame. "Because I had an enormous hand in this. I was there, helping Forbes to create this mess. I should have been stronger and stopped him, but I wasn't. As a direct consequence of that, Bandit has suffered his entire life, and even now, when he finally has a life and family of his own, he is still being pursued. Still being hunted. I owe him, Sully. I owe him and by extension, all of you, and I am finally willing to put my life where my mouth is."

My gaze lowered to Pixie, who sat beside Elora's feet, her dark eyes focused intensely on me. "Is that why you kept Pixie? I thought you were going to find her a home."

Elora turned her attention to the small dog, instinctively

reaching out to pet her. Pixie leaned into her hand, her expression turning blissful as her tongue slipped out at one side.

"That had been my intention, yes. When I took her from you, I had all these ideas about how I could undo the damage Xavier had caused and find her a loving family. But when I got into her head, and saw the extent of the damage he had inflicted… I had flashbacks of Bandit. It hit me then how much pain and suffering my actions had caused, even though it was unintentional."

Her lips quivered as she stifled a sob. Taking a deep breath, she fought to gain control.

"The operation with Pixie was a success. I managed to remove the multiple tumors Xavier had placed inside her. She isn't the same dog she once was. She's still smart, smarter than most dogs, but she's not at Bandit's level. All the aggression he had engineered in her. That's all gone now. She's a lovely little thing, so appreciative of every little gesture. When she came out of the op, I knew that one of the ways I could help was to adopt her myself. By helping her through her rehabilitation, and caring for her, it was my intention that she could finally experience a happy and fulfilling life."

Pixie listened to Elora with a rapturous expression on her furry face. There was no hint of the maliciousness I had seen before. Nothing of the calculating, twisted mind that had targeted Bandit. She really was just a normal dog now, one who had been given a second chance.

"I know my part in this, Sully, and I'm more sorry for it than you will ever know. I will help however I can."

I squeezed her hand in mine, relaying my thanks.

49

CHASE

An hour after Sully had left to find Doc, we gathered around her living room, choking down cups of coffee and as much toast, eggs, and ham as we could. The coffee was bitter, and the toast was burnt, but we ate because we were starving and needed sustenance. Yet, none of us took any pleasure in our meal.

We ate, all of us, except for Gideon.

He couldn't bring himself to and despite a combination of threats and pleas, he refused to eat. It wasn't until I looked deep into his eyes and made it clear that starving himself would not bring Zeb back, that he finally caved.

However, he wasn't the only one feeling on edge.

Ever since we'd walked in and Bandit had caught a whiff of Pixie, he had been leery of the dog. Waiting for the moment she would revert to her psychotic self again. He kept his eyes on her at all times, unable to relax.

Pixie appeared to remember how she used to act around him — how she had been with all of us — and seemed determined to make amends, particularly with Bandit who'd had the most issues with her. She kept approaching him, whimpering for forgiveness. She'd lower onto the floor and roll over to reveal her stomach which, for a dog, was the most vulnerable thing they could do.

But Bandit wasn't buying any of it.

He kept close to my side, baring his teeth if she came too close though he did manage to refrain from snarling, which was something. Having seen what she was capable of, I wasn't ready to jump onto the forgiveness train either, so the two of us kept our distance.

The RV was now parked in Doc's private driveway, which was flanked by some very tall, very bushy Cypress trees that hid it from view, unless the bad guys came from above, at which point, there would be no disguising its presence.

Working in shifts, making sure that someone was guarding him at all times, Sam took food and water out to Smith. Sully gave him a bucket and a toilet roll so he could relieve himself even while handcuffed. He had just the right amount of leeway to use the bucket, but there wasn't enough to tear off the tape that was now stuck over his mouth.

The hum of the refrigerator and the occasional creak of the wooden floor were the only audible sounds in the room, accentuating the tension that enveloped us. We sat around the kitchen island, Sam warming her fingers around a mug of coffee though I hadn't seen her take any sips yet. Emma perched at the end on her own, looking very much out of place despite not doing anything outwardly weird.

Doc tried but failed in her attempt not to study her. Not a minute went by when her eyes didn't stray to Emma, who must have been the greatest scientific mystery she had ever come across. Her curiosity about her was tangible. Her fingers would point toward her as if they couldn't wait to get their hands on her, but she kept those urges to herself, showing the kind of restraint I knew most people in her line of work wouldn't possess.

Gathering our empty plates, Doc carried them to the sink just as my stomach rumbled again. Her eyebrows shot up so high they disappeared beneath her fringe.

"Sorry," I mumbled. "High metabolism."

"So I hear," Doc smiled, opening her cupboards. But all she came back with was a half-empty bag of something dark and murky.

"Don't suppose you'd like some sugar free, gluten-free, nut-free Swiss muesli?"

Looking inside the box, she pulled a face. "Actually, scratch that. I think we're well past the use by date. You've eaten me out of house and home. I'll have to swing by the grocery store."

"You don't have work today?" Sam asked, swiveling that mug between her fingers.

"It's Saturday," Doc reminded her gently.

"Oh," Sam replied, looking surprised that she would forget such a thing. In that precise moment, she didn't look like the Sam I knew her to be. In that precise moment, the familiar contours of Sam's demeanor shifted.

This version of Sam was unlike the one I knew. She seemed less sure of herself, revealing a vulnerability that was usually concealed under her self-assured façade. It was as if all the burdens and challenges had chipped away at the tough exterior she typically presented, leaving behind this scared and uncertain version of herself.

As if he knew how she was feeling, Sully chose that moment to return.

"My shift's up," Sam murmured. Giving him a small smile, she headed back outside. The thought crossed my mind that she actually looked relieved to be leaving, although I wasn't sure why. Seemingly not picking up on any of the strange vibes, Doc found a box of organic cookies and handed them to me.

"I don't have anything with much sugar or chocolate in it, sorry."

I took it with a grateful smile. "When you've had to live off whatever you can find in dumpsters, you stop becoming so fussy."

Doc's smile wavered, and I had to remind myself that my mouth didn't need to blurt things *all the things*. Some people weren't prepared to hear about the harsh realities of life, and it wasn't like we hadn't thrown her for a loop already this morning. I could probably pipe down on my jaunts down memory lane unless I wanted us all on suicide watch.

"We need to discuss our next move." Sully gently steered the conversation to more pressing matters.

Doc pushed her glasses up the bridge of her nose and came to attention, suddenly all business.

"I don't think these people will tie you to me too quickly — if at all — and judging by what you've already explained, they seem to only come after you when you are isolated from the public.

Based on the description of their weapons, they could have attacked you again by now. The fact that they haven't suggests they are following orders from someone who doesn't want to be associated with this situation."

Sully nodded, having come to the same conclusion previously.

"This Smith is our best lead in finding out who's targeting you and why. My suggestion is that you all stay here, rest, clean up. I'll go back to my lab and mix up a little something that will loosen his tongue — much like whatever he used on your friend Mark. On my way back, I'll grab some food and withdraw as much money as I can. I already have some upstairs, but I'll take out the maximum amount I'm allowed, in case we need to make a quick escape."

"You can make a truth serum just like that?" I asked, impressed, and a little intimidated by her skills.

Doc tilted her head to one side. "It shouldn't be too difficult. I have some prior… experience in this area." Her cheeks flushed, and she looked away guiltily. The confession hadn't come easily to her.

Putting the remaining dirty dishes into the sink, she dried her hands. "Let me get dressed and I'll be on my way."

"I want to come with you," Emma announced suddenly, causing several heads to turn her way.

"To my lab?"

"They keep saying I'm not normal, but I'm trying the best I can. I want to find out what I really am." Emma wrung her hands, filled with a desperate need to know as I felt the shame of a hundred people descend on me.

"As much as I'd love to, I can't take you there. Not when these men are likely to be looking for you."

Emma's sapphire eyes flashed with sudden heat.

"You're just like them. No one wants to help me!"

"That's not what I said," Doc answered calmly, as if she were talking to a child or one of her terrified canine patients. "Tell you what, why don't I bring a testing kit home? I can do some basic tests here, then run the results back at the lab tomorrow. It's the best I can do for now. Does that sound alright?"

Relief surged out of Emma. Her body relaxed and a genuine smile spread across her face. For a moment, I caught a glimpse of the woman Sully must have loved once. When Emma smiled like that, she wasn't only beautiful, she was radiant.

"I like you. You're the only one who's been nice to me."

And just like that, I felt myself becoming irritated again.

50

CHASE

A few minutes later, Doc had gone, leaving Pixie alone with us. The little dog had been shaken when it was clear that Doc wouldn't be taking her with her. Tossing us a look as if to ask if she was really going to leave her behind with us, Pixie whined anxiously by the door and had to be comforted by Doc until she finally stopped crying.

Watching how scared and timid Pixie seemed, I felt an inkling of sympathy, though that didn't stop us being cautious, having been duped by her previously. Picking up on our feelings or maybe having her own residual ones toward us, Pixie stayed away. Lying in her doggy bed in the far corner of the room, she studied us, an unfathomable expression on her face.

Having not seen any clean water in days we took turns to shower even though Doc had two bathrooms. Should the bad guys come calling, we didn't want to be caught with our pants, quite literally, down.

When it took Doc longer to arrive home than we expected, Sam had rummaged through her kitchen, throwing together a pretty decent pasta dish using creamed soup as a sauce base while Gideon and Emma flicked mindlessly through the television.

At one point, I heard Sully and Sam discussing what to do with Zeb's body, though from what I could gather, neither of them could come to any conclusions, not any they could stomach, anyway. When they left out of earshot, nothing had been decided.

I spent my time on the internet — in Incognito mode of course — I wasn't that removed from reality that I had forgotten the basic rules of the web. I looked up the Montpelier News website which was our local newspaper, wondering if anyone had reported the battle that had taken place on our ranch, when an article flashed up with a picture of our home.

Instead of the war zone I was expecting to see, the ranch had turned into a building site. I couldn't even see the house covered as it was by a giant blue and yellow striped tent. I spotted what looked like a logo of an insect on the bottom corner of it.

I read over the accompanying description.

Termite infestation. That's the story they had gone with to hide all the destruction. A snort shot out of me resulting in a questioning chuff as Bandit read the article over my shoulder.

"Those were some high-velocity termites that ate our house huh, boy?"

"*Woof.*"

It warned that people should keep away or risk spreading the infestation and mentioned that our family was happily relaxing on an insurance paid vacation while the works took place.

I turned away from the computer, a sick feeling in my stomach. Not only did these people have endless clout and resources, but they also weren't afraid to go big with their stories. If they could cover up something as huge as our home being destroyed and our entire family having disappeared with it, I didn't want to know what else they would be capable of getting away with.

When Pixie asked for a toilet break, Sully took her outside. As the one who'd been closest to her at the time, he'd asked Gideon if he wanted to do the honors, hoping to draw him out of his funk, but he'd only shaken his head, sinking further into the sofa.

When the two returned, Pixie must have decided we wouldn't hurt her after all as she went to her bed and picked up an old rabbit toy. Very deliberately, she placed it by Bandit's feet, whined then backed away, waiting for his reaction. He gave it a cautious sniff that turned into a happy bark.

"It's the one I gave her," he said.

One ear was beginning to fall off from being loved on a bit too much, while the eyes had kind of sunken in from being picked up by two rows of sharp teeth all the time, but there was no denying that this was the toy he had given her to comfort her when Doc was taking her away. It was her one reminder of us and Bandit and had been his gift to her so she wouldn't feel completely alone.

And now she was saying thank you.

Bandit barked then typed his response very carefully. *"You are welcome."*

Pixie yapped, dancing a happy little dance then settled by his side.

Just like that, they were buddies in a way they had never been before.

The sky was almost dark by the time Doc finally returned.

Sully greeted her at the door, his relief palpable. She breezed through equally relieved, arms loaded with bags.

"That took a lot longer than I thought it would."

In addition to her oversized purse, she carried several Whole Foods bags filled to the brim with groceries, and a metal briefcase. Sully took the bags off from her and headed into the kitchen as the rest of us followed.

"I wanted to call and let you guys know what the delay was, but thought better of it, in case they are listening in somehow. You never know how these things work, but I've seen enough Netflix shows to know it wasn't worth the risk."

Sam started unpacking an array of colorful vegetables and protein. She fished out cans of dog food and high energy snacks for us that I was relieved to see contained all the aforementioned sugar and chocolate she normally abhorred.

Doc set the briefcase onto the counter.

It wasn't very big, slightly larger than an A4 sheet of paper with a criss-cross pattern embedded in the metal. It looked pretty innocuous considering the kind of dangerous drug I knew was contained inside.

"Was everything OK?" Sully asked in a voice filled with trepidation.

"There was an accident in town that caused a jam everywhere. Nothing to do with you guys, I promise. That wasn't the only problem I ran into though. Considering I had told Sam what day it was, I totally forgot once I was out there and with the banks closing early, I had to drive to several places in order to take out this little lot."

From her bag, she pulled out several wads of notes. Without counting, I figured there must have been several grand there at least.

"*How much do you make?*" I asked without thinking.

Doc flushed guiltily. "More than I should."

"It's in there?" Sam asked, nodding toward the briefcase.

"Yes. I managed to work up a similar solution to what's used in the military. At a push, it should do what we need it to."

"How is it administered?"

"With a simple injection. Once it gets into his body, the results should be pretty instant."

Sully and Sam swapped looks, an unspoken message going between them. When Sully spoke again, it was to Doc.

"So we do this now?"

"No time like the present." Her words were breezy though the feeling behind them wasn't. Sully had a grave look on his face, after all, once we found out who Smith's bosses were, there would be no turning back. If he wanted to back out, this would be the time to do it.

I held my breath.

"Let's go," Sully finally said.

Taking hold of the briefcase, we trooped outside.

51

SULLY

S mith's intense gaze followed my every move as I entered the RV, clutching the ominous briefcase tightly in my hands. The rest of the group maintained a cautious distance, their eyes reflecting a mixture of anticipation and apprehension.

Now that we were free from the confines of the motorhome, we had relocated Smith to the main living area. The windows had been hastily covered with newspaper, shielding him from prying eyes, but this also cast the area in an oppressive half-light that mirrored the shadows inside my soul. Seeing the briefcase, Smith's expression turned wary.

I set the case onto the small, round table as a palpable tension filled the air. With deliberate precision, I opened the case revealing two wickedly long syringes nestled inside. One syringe was filled with a vivid blue liquid, while the other ran clear like water. Smith's eyes flickered between the syringes, uncertainty etched across his face.

Looking over my shoulder, Elora reached for the blue syringe, explaining, "The other syringe will render him unconscious for a few hours in case he tries to overpower us."

I felt a rush of approval: I liked a woman who prepared for all possibilities.

"So how do we do this?"

Elora turned her focus to Smith, seemingly unaffected by his presence. "I need you to restrain him so I can have a clear shot at his arm. We just need to roll up his sleeve."

"Does it hurt?" Gideon asked. He had barely spoken since we'd arrived at Elora's so this was clearly important to him. His haunted eyes darted to the closed bedroom door, thinking of the motionless figure beyond it. It must have taken every ounce of self-control for him to be so close to Smith without being able to exact any kind of revenge.

"I don't think so," Elora responded carefully.

Disappointment oozed out of him.

"I have a question too. How do we know if it's working?" Chase asked.

"When he stops struggling and starts answering our questions. I'm no expert at this, however. I have only seen this done."

We fell silent, the weighty ramifications of her words sinking in.

Approaching Smith, I considered the best way to restrain him. He was already handcuffed to a table leg that was bolted to the floor, so I wasn't worried he about him getting away. But, it didn't leave much room for maneuvering around him.

I'd have to approach from the front.

But as soon as I got within a foot of him, he lashed out at me with his feet. I jumped back, but he still caught me on the leg hard enough that I knew it would bruise.

Circling around, I lunged at him again, but he shuffled away, twisting left and right, making it next to impossible for Elora to get a clear shot at his limbs.

I pulled back, searching for another option when Sam suddenly jumped onto the couch that formed a U around the table. Quick as anything, she bent down, hooking her arm under his chin, putting him in a chokehold. Smith started bucking wildly, but my wife, my lady, stayed firm.

"I can't hold him forever," she warned.

Gideon and I sprang into action. "The left arm. Grab his left arm!"

We tackled him together as he kicked and bucked in an attempt to escape. But there were just too many of us.

Finally finding a clear spot, Elora swiftly jabbed the needle in and pressed down on the plunger with an expertise that sent a chill racing down my back. I watched with a kind of twisted enjoyment as the contents entered his body.

At a nod from Sam, we let go of him, quickly moving clear out of his way. He still had tape covering his mouth which I ripped off from him now. He stared at me, a sick defeat in his eyes, knowing the inevitable would happen.

We waited for the drug to take effect.

I stared down at him, watching for any sign that he was ready for questioning when I noticed a change in his demeanor. His expression became pinched, the blood draining from his face, and his chest started heaving at an unnaturally fast pace. Then he fell to the floor gasping for breath, and with a look of utter pain in his eyes.

"He's faking," Gideon sneered, dismissing it as a fake performance, but I wasn't so sure.

My expertise as a trained veterinarian had primarily been dedicated to the well-being of animals, yet in that critical moment, I recognized pain and suffering as a universal language that transcended species. As I studied Smith, it became evident that this language had etched its narrative across his face in stark and undeniable strokes.

His features contorted with agony, his eyes reflecting an intensity of pain that resonated with a depth of suffering. His head snapped away from me in a violent jolt, as his body began thrashing and convulsing uncontrollably.

"Sully…" Sam murmured.

From the corner of my eye, I saw Chase backing away, a look of complete fright on her face. She had seen seizures before, when Bandit had been wracked with them, and this must have brought several terrifying memories to surface.

"Out of the way!" I reached for the keys to the handcuffs in my pocket.

"Don't be dumb," Gideon snapped. "The second you unlock those cuffs, we've had it. He's a trained killer!"

"The man is going into cardiac arrest!"

"Are you sure?" Elora hissed, unable to believe what was happening.

"I need to lay him down. Move his arms out of the way."

Without waiting for their help or permission, I slid the key into the cuffs and unlocked them. Smith's arms flopped down to his sides as I carefully positioned him onto his back. Opening one of his eyelids, I noticed his eyes rolling into his head. Interlocking my hands, I laid them over his chest and began CPR, pressing down hard and fast, while keeping track of the depressions in my head.

"How is this happening?" I heard Chase ask.

"He must be having a reaction of some sort," Elora responded, her voice tinged with guilt and confusion. I knew her well enough to know that she couldn't have meant for this to happen.

"Good," Gideon spat, a far cry from his usual self. Gone was his youthful and wry exuberance; instead, there was only bitterness and resentment. "Stop helping him. If he dies, that's one less enemy to worry about."

"You can't mean that," Chase gasped, clearly shocked by his callous statement.

"Of course I do! The question is why aren't the rest of you with me on this? He's the reason Zeb is dead! You're honestly going to save the man who killed him?"

My eyes flickered towards him but I couldn't answer, not without losing count. Thankfully, Sam's voice broke through the tense atmosphere, attempting to bring calm and reason to the situation.

"That doesn't mean we should let him die. They're the monsters here, Gid. Not us. If we don't try to help, then we're no better than them. Besides, while we have him, we still have a bargaining chip."

"All I'm hearing are the words of a coward."

He was taking Dad's death much harder than even I had expected. I knew I needed to talk to him, help him through his grief.

But first, I needed to keep Smith alive.

My arms were cramping, feeling the strain but I couldn't stop. Not until his breathing regulated and his heart started back on its own accord. I wished I had a defibrillator to shock his heart, but we were all out of luck there.

My hands would have to do.

The seconds felt like an eternity. Beads of sweat formed on my forehead. Finally, just as I was summoning up the courage to call it quits, a breath hissed out of Smith's lips. It was so slight, that I mistook it for my own. But when another came, followed by another, I knew I could stop.

He was unconscious, but he was alive.

And that would have to do for now.

52

CHASE

We took turns keeping watch on Smith for the next few hours, making sure he wouldn't die even and that he couldn't escape. Everybody but Gideon had paired off to keep an eye on Smith. It was a silent agreement that we would never leave him alone with Gideon until his anger subsided, and for once, Gideon didn't argue.

Smith's near meeting with the Reaper had shaken me much more than I realized it would. I knew he was the enemy, that he had caused Zeb's death, but it still didn't mean I wanted him dead. I had seen so much pain and death in the last two years that it wasn't something I ever craved, not even from my worst enemies.

While we waited for him to come around, Doc performed a few tests on Emma. She swabbed her cheek, took blood, hair, and nail samples, weighed and measured her, and created a DNA profile. All the while, Emma let Doc work on her patiently. She wasn't ever this agreeable normally, which only showed just how much she wanted to know what she was. When Doc was finished collecting her samples, she couriered everything to her lab before taking a shift outside with Smith leaving Sully and Sam to cook for us.

Sully heated up the griddle on the stove while Sam tossed in some oil and butter and seasoned some steaks. Sully crossed the kitchen for a pair of tongs, simultaneously rinsing some of the vegetables Doc had brought back as he was closer to the sink. After handing off the colander of chopped vegetables to Sam, he returned to manning the griddle.

Their movements flowed together like a well-choreographed dance. I wasn't even sure if the two of them were aware of how much of a team they were, but Emma definitely did. She watched them intently, studying their every move.

"I can help," she volunteered out of the blue, surprising us all.

Sam was the first to respond with a smile. "That would be great. Can you do the carrots?"

Emma nodded eagerly, pleased to have been included with a task. Moving to the sink where the mound of carrots were waiting, she suddenly froze, staring down at them. "What do you mean by 'do'?"

Sam pointed to the peeler on the counter, miming the motion. "Peel them with that."

Picking it up, Emma attempted to peel the carrots but her fingers were as clumsy as a child's and she kept fumbling. When she wasn't dropping the carrots into the sink, she was dropping the peeler, so progress was painfully slow, but none of us wanted to take over since it was the first time she'd wanted to make herself useful. It also gave us time to consider our options. Which wasn't much in the grand scheme of things.

With Smith out for the count, we would have to wait for him to regain consciousness before trying to get information from him again.

"I hear waterboarding works well." Gideon said it in such a blithe manner that it actually sounded like he meant it.

Red from the heat of the stove, Sully raised a disapproving brow until Gideon shrugged.

"That was a joke."

I forced a laugh, trying to infuse lightness into the heavy atmosphere when Bandit piped up, *"What is waterboarding?"*

Sully shot Gideon another pointed look. "See what you did there?"

Stroking Bandit, I answered, "Something you don't want to know. It's not a nice thing to do to someone."

"Does it hurt?"

"Yes. It's a form of torture."

Bandit's eyes grew wide. *"Like being locked in a cage?"*

He was referring to the experiments conducted at Platinum Industries. Although Bandit had never personally experienced any torture himself, he had witnessed the other dogs being terrorized on a daily basis, until they were a shell of themselves, too broken and too scared to even turn around to look at me when they were being rescued. I still caught him whimpering in his sleep at night sometimes, paws paddling the air in a desperate bid to keep the "Bad Men" away.

I said a silent prayer of thanks that Doc had missed this conversation: she would have been crushed if she had heard him.

We ate our steaks although I still couldn't taste or appreciate any of the food being served my way. I was in a weird half daze, swinging from moments of okay-ness, to being hit by a wave of grief so strong that it left me breathless. Part of me wanted to shout and yell at the world, at the others even. Zeb was gone but here we were, eating and talking around a dining table. Acting as if his body wasn't outside in the RV — decaying.

Anytime I tried to talk to Sully about what I was feeling, he looked away from me. I think he knew what I wanted, he just wasn't able to deal with it yet. Not when it was all so fresh.

When we were done eating, and the food sat uncomfortably in my stomach, I stepped out into the back yard. Stars twinkled down at me, crickets chirping a happy song. I took in the fresh air, breathing deeply in an attempt to diffuse my pain when Gideon's voice snapped at me from the darkness.

"I don't need a babysitter."

He emerged from the shadows, staring at me with a hard expression in his eyes that I had never seen before. My heart skipped a beat.

"I didn't even know you were here."

I didn't bother to hide the edge in my voice. He wasn't the only one in pain, and I was starting to get a little tired of his attitude. I wanted us to support each other through all of this instead of him cutting me out. This wasn't how we behaved. This wasn't what we were to each other.

"We all miss him you know," I began but I stopped myself, knowing I had started on the wrong foot.

"No, you don't understand. No one does." His lips pressed into a thin line. He was wound up so tightly it was a miracle he didn't leap out of his skin.

"I know you were close to him, that he was like your father, but he actually is Sully's dad so think how he must be feeling."

"He didn't seem too concerned when he refused to get him help."

I threw up my hands, exasperated.

"You know damn well that was a tough decision for him, but he had more than just Zeb's life to consider. And it wasn't like he wasn't trying — he was hoping Doc would be able to save him. We just ran out of time. Are you really going to hold that against him?"

A sound came out of him, a mixture of disgust and anger.

"Of course you would stick up for Sully! Just because the two of you have a special little relationship, no one else gets a say about anything! It's just you and him, all the time. And if it's not you and him, then it's you and Bandit! I don't even get a look in over a stupid *dog*."

I reeled back as if I'd been slapped. Was this how he really felt or was this the grief talking? I couldn't tell but I knew he'd crossed a line when Bandit stopped in his tracks, on his way to us. He stopped a few feet away, his tail dipping between his legs in misery.

My heart broke at the hurt expression on his furry face. Hurrying to him, I wrapped my arms around him.

"He didn't mean it, boy. He's just upset. Don't listen to him."

Gideon flinched, and I knew I'd cut him to the quick. I opened my mouth to apologize, but he spun on his heels and stalked away.

I sank my face into Bandit's fur wondering how my world had imploded by quite so much.

53

CHASE

When it was approaching midnight and Smith still hadn't woken up (though he was in a stable condition), Doc appeared, arms laden with blankets that she set onto one of several sofas in the room.

"I only have the one spare room which I think Sully and Sam should take. The rest of you can camp in the living room here."

"Thanks, Elora," Sam responded, looking ready to crash.

Bandit and I made our way to one of the sofas, claiming it for our own. I was pretty exhausted from everything and wanted nothing more than to curl up somewhere warm and dry, with four solid walls around me.

I should have known that Gideon wasn't ready to do the same. He stood in the middle of the room, making no move to settle himself.

"I'm not leaving Zeb out there with *him*. I'll take the night watch and sleep in the RV so I can keep an eye on them both."

As much as I thought I knew Gideon, he had been acting like a stranger all day so I didn't feel as if he could be trusted with Smith on his own. Sully must have had the same thought as he replied, "I'll stay out there with you."

"I can handle it by myself," Gideon protested, a stubborn glint to his eyes. "I'd prefer to be alone."

"I want a lot of things, doesn't mean it's going to happen." Sully's tone brokered no argument though I half expected Gideon to challenge him.

"Fine," Gideon snapped back. Not gonna lie, I was pretty surprised at how quickly he had caved. Underneath all the bravado, he must have been just as exhausted as the rest of us were. Sam offered a supportive smile, and nodded her agreement.

"I hate to bring this up… but we do need to have a discussion about the body. There are certain procedures we should follow—" Elora started but was instantly interrupted.

"Tomorrow, okay? Can I just have tonight to say goodbye?" Gideon pleaded. His voice cracked at the end of the sentence and I felt my heart ache for him.

Seeing how he was barely holding it together, Doc nodded quickly. "Of course."

"I want to sleep out there too since I can't get any around here. Due to all the snoring," Emma chimed in earning a glare from me. "I'll take the bedroom."

"You understand you'll be sharing it?" Sully asked.

"With you? OK."

"No, not with me," Sully sounded flustered and I couldn't blame him. He seemed determined not to meet Sam's eyes when he spoke. "Dad is still there."

"Oh. Can't we move him then?"

She spoke as if she were talking about a piece of furniture, not a person we desperately loved.

Gideon's face hardened. "You either stay with him or it's here with the others. Those are your choices."

"I'll stay out there," Emma replied quickly. "I'll share with the dead old man even though he doesn't need a bed anymore."

All but Emma drew in their breaths. The seconds ticked away until Doc was the first to become unfrozen.

"Right," she said, looking at us all with an unnaturally bright smile. "Everyone good?"

Sully nodded, ruffled Bandit's head, hugged me, then gave Sam a goodnight kiss before escorting Gideon and Emma out the door.

"Sully… one moment," Doc said, just as he was about to step out of the house.

"Go on," he said to Gideon and Emma.

I tried not to flinch when Gideon left without even giving me a single glance.

Doc handed him her cell. "In case we need to reach you or vice versa. The phone's unlocked. I've programmed my number under "Home.""

He took it from her, sliding it into a pocket. "Thanks."

Shooting us one last look, Sully left.

My stomach clenched uneasily. He wasn't going to be far, only a few feet away. He also had Doc's phone now and could call at the first sign of trouble.

Why then did I feel like all the air had been sucked out of me?

That we were standing on the edge of a cliff face, moments from pitching forward?

Trying to keep my worries to myself, I lay down onto the sofa and waited for sleep to come.

54

ELORA

With her guests left to sleep downstairs, Elora lay in her bed, hoping for restful oblivion but the day had proven too much for her.

Although she had only met him once, Zeb had been a kind man and his death was a terrible tragedy. She couldn't help but feel the cloud of sorrow that clung to her friends — even the perpetually cheerful Bandit, who was only a shadow of his former self.

She wished she could do something to alleviate their grief though the only thing that would help now, was time.

While she could do nothing about that, there was something she hoped she could assist with.

Too wired for sleep, Elora slid out of bed and made her way to her dresser. She powered on the laptop that sat among her hairbrushes and cosmetics items. She kept several computers around her home, all were synced to her work server so she could look things up at a moment's notice or communicate with her team if an idea were to strike, whatever the time.

Opening her email account, she sifted through the day's correspondance, hoping to find a specific subject heading. When her eyes alighted on the topic she was looking for, she clicked on the email with a growing sense of excitement. She read through the message quickly, opening the myriad of attached files.

Information flooded her screen, of scans, charts, and impossible calculations.

The results for Emma's tests were starting to come in and they were startling. She wasn't sure how this could even be possible…

She had half a mind to rush outside and tell Sully the truth, but discovered that while she had been poring over the documents, more time had elapsed than she had expected. She had been so consumed with the findings that it was almost two in the morning. He would be fast asleep now, as would the rest of them.

She felt a rush of impatience but had to force it back down. They had waited so long already. One more night wasn't going to change anything.

Closing her laptop, Elora climbed into bed, turned off the lights and fell asleep dreaming of DNA helixes.

55

CHASE

I woke early having only had a few hours of sleep.

It wasn't the sofa's fault — in fact, it was probably the most comfortable sofa I had ever been on — but I had tossed and turned all night, plagued with dreams of Gideon slipping away from me.

I knew we had both suffered a terrible shock. We were being hunted by killers, with no real idea of how we were going to get out of this. With so much on his mind, Gideon had no time for me. But it seemed so unfair when all I wanted was to talk to him, and all he could do was pull away from me.

The babble of early morning television drifted over. Bandit sat in the middle of the floor, watching Good Morning America. The volume was low enough so as not to wake me, but was probably a little too low to actually understand, hence the subtitles on the bottom of the screen.

My Muttface was the most considerate dog in the world.

Even more surprising than the sight of my dog watching television was the fact he wasn't alone: Pixie sat close by. If I'd had a phone, that picture would have gotten a gazillion hits on Instagram. Probably would've gotten me a spot on Hellen — one of the most popular talk shows — too.

I squinted at the television, searching for the time only to see it wasn't even six yet. The door to Sam's room was still closed, I couldn't hear any movement from her. Judging by Pixie's lack of excitement I could tell Doc was sleeping too. In all likelihood, so were Sully and Gideon, but I was feeling uneasy about our fight yesterday and how we had left things.

I wanted to make sure Gideon was okay.

I slipped on my sneakers, the only thing I had taken off to sleep — when your life was in danger, it was better to have your shoes close to you and to be fully dressed so you could make a quick getaway. Rule Number 1 of Living on the Streets.

Bandit chuffed a greeting at me. "Let's go check on Gideon."

He nodding, not wanting to bark, and followed me to the door as we let ourselves out quietly. Pixie followed us then stopped, turning back to glance up the stairs, torn. She whined, wanting to follow yet not wanting to leave Elora.

"We won't be long," I reassured her. "You can wait here."

Satisfied with my answer, she went back to the television. The brisk morning air chilled my lungs, shocking me awake. Wrapping my arms around myself, we headed for the RV, but as we drew closer, I saw that the driveway was empty.

I turned to Bandit. His eyes mirrored my own confusion.

"The RV should be right here, shouldn't it?"

He answered with a sharp bark that sent another shock to my system. My heart began to pound, filling with panic. I fought to bolt it down.

Maybe they'd had to move the vehicle somewhere. Maybe someone had come snooping in the middle of the night. Hurrying, I stood in the exact spot where the motorhome had been.

But there was no sign of it.

I couldn't move. Shocked to the core, one terrifying question buzzing through my mind: had Smith overcome them?

Bandit's head shot up into the air. He sniffed, then bounded behind one of the Cypress trees, barking like crazy. I ran to him but skidded to a stop when I saw a familiar brown boot poking out of the shrubs.

Sully's boot.

My eyes traveled up the length of the boot to find his leg still attached. Diving forward, I shoved away the branches that hid him from view, ignoring the shooting pain that lanced through my hands as the branches lashed out at them. I kept going, frantically moving them away until Sully's face finally came into view.

"Sully?"

I shook him, numb with the terror that he would not wake even as my eyes ran over his body, searching for wounds. I couldn't see any, but Sully wasn't waking up.

What was wrong with him?

Bandit pawed at something on the ground. A square of something yellow. It was a piece of paper… no, several Post-It's that had been stuck together to form a note.

I recognized Gideon's untidy scrawl immediately. Snatching it up with frozen fingers, my eyes raked over the tersely written words.

I'm sorry, but I can't let him die. If they could bring Emma back, they can do the same with Zeb. I'm going to offer them Emma and Smith. This new Emma doesn't belong in our lives.

She was destroying our family's happiness, what was left of it.

This is the best way.

You'll see.

I t was signed by Gideon.

I read the entire note several more times before its message finally sank in. Bandit hopped impatiently beside me, wanting to see the note for himself. He read it quickly, his tail sinking lower and lower until it disappeared from view.

I shook Sully again, harder.

"Sully! Why aren't you waking up?"

Sticking my hand beneath his nose, I could feel the warmth of his breath, and some of my numbness receded. Gideon wouldn't have done anything to harm Sully, but it was still a relief to know that he was alive.

I went behind him and slid my arms under him, intending to half drag, half carry him back to the house. Digging my heels into the ground, I pulled until my arms felt they would pop from their sockets.

We hadn't moved an inch

I wouldn't be able to get Sully to the house by myself, not with his dead weight.

"Hurry back. Get Sam. I'll stay with Sully."

Bandit woofed sharply at me and tore off.

56

CHASE

I kneeled behind Sully, cradling his head in my lap, trying not to worry over how his face seemed colder than the ground that bit at my knees.

How long had he been out here like this?

Cupping his face, I tried to warm it up when something glinted, half hidden in the grass beside me. I brushed the grass away to reveal a syringe, but the clear liquid that had been inside last night was now gone.

Recognition hit me like a freight train — Gideon had used Doc's knockout drug on Sully. The realization sent shivers down my spine as the pieces of the puzzle fell into place.

A thought niggled at the back of my mind, a memory from last night. Something that I had noticed but hadn't paid attention to at the time. If only I had given it more thought, I could have — *should have* — seen this coming.

When we were discussing sleeping arrangements last night, Gideon had given in to Sully far too easily. I had even thought it strange that he'd had no objection to Emma staying there, especially after she had spoken so poorly about Zeb.

But of course he didn't have a problem with that, not when it was his plan to exchange her for Zeb. I was floored by how easily he had fooled us all.

"Chase?! Where are you? Are you OK?!" Sam's worried voice called out.

"Over here!"

She bolted around the corner, her hair still tied in a long braid that flew behind her as she ran. Seeing Sully's condition, her panic grew more pronounced.

"God… Is he alive?"

"Yes. But Gideon's gone! He knocked out Sully with that other syringe. He's taken Emma and Smith. He means to trade them for Zeb!"

I knew I was babbling but I couldn't help it. My thoughts were a mad jumble like my emotions. My heart was in my throat and I could barely get the words out.

"For Zeb? I don't understand."

Even as she asked the question, she crouched down beside me, checking to see how Sully's eyes were, pressing a finger to his pulse.

"He thinks they can bring him back… that if they have Emma, they can use her to learn how to bring him back."

Horror flashed over her face. "But that's…"

"Impossible… I know."

"I was going to say barbaric and impossible. He can't just sacrifice her like that. Her life isn't his to give."

A gasp sounded behind her. Doc had arrived with Pixie at her heels, still in a striped robe and fluffy slippers, having only just woken up. Doc's eyes widened as she tried to take in the chaotic scene in front of her.

"What's going on?" She asked, her voice trembling with concern. "Where's the RV?" But Sam paid no attention to her questions, turning instead to address me.

"Did Gideon say anything to you about this?"

"Of course not!" I replied frantically. "He was acting weird all night. I should've guessed this was what he was going to do, but I didn't." Sam's face fell and she let out a heavy sigh. "Now it makes sense why he wanted to stay out in the RV… I didn't know Sam! I didn't!"

My voice caught in my throat as I choked on a sob. Sam's expression softened, and she placed a comforting hand on my shoulder.

"We'll get him back before anything happens to him, I promise. Help me get Sully inside first. We need to wake him."

Doc took one look at the empty syringe and immediately understood what had transpired.

"That reckless boy…" she said but never finished. Working in unison, the three of us carefully lifted Sully. Bandit and Pixie lead the way, dancing anxiously on their paws as they waited for us to carry him back into the house where we laid him onto the sofa.

"I'll be right back," Doc said, disappearing momentarily before returning with a small vial that she waved under his nose. The moment Sully breathed in the strong scent, he began coughing and slowly regained consciousness. His bewildered eyes stared at our faces.

"Why do I feel like I've been hit by a truck?"

By the time Sam had explained everything, Sully's face had grown tighter and tighter until it looked like it would crack at the slightest provocation. His anger simmered beneath the surface, threatening to erupt at any moment.

"I could kill him right now!" Sully growled. "Taking Emma like that, how could he do that to her?!" Sam looked at him, her expression not quite aligning with his outrage. Thick lines creased her forehead. She looked for all the world like a concerned mother. When she spoke, her words carried a tone of understanding that sought to temper Sully's anger.

"You're more worried about Emma than you are Gideon? He's in shock, Sully. He just lost the person he considered his father.

How can you be angry at him? Gideon is still a child, even if he doesn't look or act like it. He's still a teenager, no matter how hard he pretends otherwise."

"But he's a teenager who should have known better than to do something like this. Emma isn't smart like he is. She's not worldly. She needs to be protected, and he's betraying all of us with this. Even if you don't like Emma, it doesn't make this okay."

I knew the second the words were out of his mouth, he regretted them. That look of utter hurt and betrayal on Sam's face was something I wouldn't forget in a hurry. Stunned into silence, she snapped her mouth shut and dropped her gaze to the floor.

Interrupting the charged atmosphere, Doc interjected, her tone seemingly ordinary, though the gravity of her words sent a shiver down my spine. "I need to tell you something. Last night, after you all went to bed, I couldn't sleep, so I checked my emails. I received some of Emma's results and while more testing needs to be done, I feel fairly confident in saying that I think I know what she is."

Sully and Sam were taken aback, not anticipating this news to come at this specific moment. Sully's anger seemed to dissipate, replaced by a mixture of surprise and confusion. His brow furrowed, and the intensity in his eyes softened as he processed the unexpected revelation. Beside him, Sam, who had been grappling with the aftermath of Sully's harsh words, now wore an expression of disbelief, her distress momentarily eclipsed by the weight of Doc's announcement.

"What is she?" Sully pleaded, desperate to know, yet fearful of learning the truth at the same time.

"After comparing our results to your wife's — your previous wife's — existing medical records, we found that although her DNA is the same, there are enough small mutations to prove that genetically, although she is as close as she can be to the real Emma, she isn't actually her."

"So what are you saying?" Sam asked for clarification, as Sully didn't seem able to speak.

"This Emma must be a clone. Somehow, Xavier got hold of the real Emma's DNA, cloned her, and managed to accelerate her development into an adult woman."

My head was spinning with this revelation, so I had no idea how Sully must be feeling.

"A clone? But is that even possible?" He finally managed to ask.

"Until now, only animals have been successfully cloned. And many in the scientific community find it highly unethical to clone a human, so it isn't generally attempted."

I gasped as a sudden thought came to me. "Remember when you went to visit her grave, Sully, when we made that trip back east to your clinic? You said it had been disturbed, but we didn't believe you? That must have been when they found her DNA."

"That all makes sense now." Sam agreed. "I'm sorry we doubted you, Sully."

"But how do you explain her attachment to me?" Sully didn't seem ready to accept the diagnosis.

"She had all those pictures of the two of you that she must have studied before she even showed up on your door. And we don't know what messages they could have been feeding her while she was growing. She could simply be brainwashed."

Doc squeezed Sully's shoulder. "You knew deep down that she couldn't come back to life. At least you now know why she behaves the way she does. As much as she looks and sounds like her, she isn't your wife, Sully. She never was."

Sam's eyes brimmed over with tears while Sully just looked shell-shocked. I wasn't sure what he was making of the news.

"I wish you'd been able to tell us this last night." I wasn't trying to guilt her, but if Gideon had known then, we wouldn't be in our current predicament.

"I know. I'm so sorry. I wish I had woken all of you up to tell you, and now there's something else we have to consider. If

Gideon has Smith, if he really is making some sort of deal with him… then they're going to find out about me, aren't they?"

Sully had to fight not to hang his head. "I'm sorry. We shouldn't have come here."

"No, that's not what I'm concerned about," Doc replied. "The other dogs, the ones we saved. Could they and their new families be at risk?"

The world spun around me. I didn't want to think about all those poor dogs and their helpless, terrified faces when we had rescued them.

Had we saved them only to drag them into this… again?

Doc stood up straighter, pushing the glasses up her nose. "Don't apologize, Sully. This isn't your fault. You're just trying to protect your family. It's these villains coming after you. They're the ones who need to be stopped. I need a moment to think."

She fell silent. I could see her mind ticking over, working through the possible scenarios.

"Unless Gideon took off in the middle of the night, he doesn't have that much of a head start. You can take one of my cars and go after him… except we have no idea where he's gone? And we don't know where Smith's people are, either. They could be heading anywhere."

She paused before changing gears.

"Can I have my phone? I might be able to summon some assistance —" She stopped as Sully reached into his pocket, only to come up empty.

"I don't have it."

"Did Gideon take it from you?" Sam asked.

"No… not unless it was after I blacked out."

Doc reached for her iPad resting on the mahogany coffee table, her fingers dancing across the smooth screen. After a few swipes, she let out a joyous cry, her face lighting up with excitement and relief.

"He does have it! Look, there he is!"

She spun the device around so we could see the Find My Phone app she had opened up. Doc beamed at us. "We can track him with this."

"But he would know that, wouldn't he?" I interjected, frowning. "Gid isn't stupid."

Sam's brows rose a notch. "Maybe he didn't take the phone. Is it possible that it fell out of your pocket when you were struggling with him?"

Sully leaned back on the sofa, taking a moment to mull over Sam's question. "When he injected me?" Sully asked, giving it some consideration. "Yeah. Quite possibly," Sully nodded.

While they had been talking, I felt myself experiencing a heavy sense of déjà vu. It was as if we had been through this before, and not even once, but countless times. And I knew with a crystal clear clarity that we would never be free of them. Not of Forbes, Xavier or the Bad Men.

For whatever reason, they would always come for us.

"This is never going to end, is it?

The doomed tone in my voice sliced through their chatter. Sully looked as if I had struck him. He reached out to me, but I stepped back. I didn't want comfort right now.

I wanted a resolution.

"As long as Bandit's alive, and especially now that we know Emma is a scientific breakthrough, there'll always be someone after us, someone who wants to be able to create 'special' dogs or human clones."

"So we'll fight them every step of the way. Or we'll run. We're getting really good at it," Sully responded. But I shook my head.

"We'll make a mistake one day. Besides, we can't live the rest of our lives like this. I think we need to do something else."

An idea struck me like a bolt of lightning, sending electric pulses through my body and setting every hair on end. It was as if the answer had been staring me in the face the whole time. I could feel the chills of realization run down my spine. I knew I was onto something.

"I think the only way to protect us is to do the opposite of what we've been doing so far," I proclaimed, my voice trembling with both fear and excitement at the potential consequences of this bold plan. The words hung heavy in the air, each one carrying weight and importance. This was it, our only chance to turn things around and finally triumph against our enemies.

They stared at me, eyes clouded with confusion. Turning to the television where the morning show still played in the background, long forgotten now, I laid out my plan.

They listened. First with shock, then increasing horror, but I stood firm, knowing it was our only chance at survival.

But there was a caveat — a pretty big one.

My plan would either save us from the Bad Men forever.

Or it would get us all killed.

57

SULLY

An intense pressure clamped down on my head, making it feel like it was trapped in a vise.

The world hadn't stopped spinning. Every few moments, I found myself hit with a wave of dizziness that would stop me short, but at least I was conscious. Not that it would help our situation all that much.

Gideon's last words echoed through my head for what seemed like the millionth time since Chase had shown the note to me. Red-hot rage churned like a volcano, threatening to erupt.

Yet alongside that anger, fear lurked, a vast and all-consuming black hole waiting to swallow me whole. I should have been able to set my own emotions aside to talk to him. Instead, like a selfish fool, I had pushed him away and dismissed his feelings.

And now we had come to this.

It'd been a few moments since Chase had outlined her plan. We'd wasted precious minutes arguing to and fro on the sense of it, but at the end of the day, despite trying, no one else had come up with a better idea.

We had no choice now but to split up.

I took in the two cars parked in the garage. Elora's usual ride, a sleek, silver Lexus, gleamed under the dim lighting. Next to it, the SUV seemed a much less flashier — if roomier — cousin. The SUV was a recent purchase, bought to help her ferry the dogs we had rescued from Platinum Industries since the other car hadn't been as practical.

I stopped by the SUV.

"We'll take this."

"But the Lexus is faster. You'll need it to catch up to Gideon," Elora objected.

"Are you sure? I can't promise you'll get it back in the same condition."

"It's a car, Sully. I can always get another."

"When this is all over, we should have a conversation about your salary and what I have to do to be making it," Chase said to Elora. I was grateful that even in our darkest moments, she was able to make a quip — a self-preservation tool — even if her heart wasn't really in it.

I fumbled with the keys, my hands shaking as I unlocked the Lexus, ducking to climb into the driver's seat. The smell of leather and pine drifted towards me, mixed with the familiar scent of my own fear of confusion, when another wave of dizziness hit. It was only when I braced myself against the roof of the car that I was able to stop myself from falling.

"You can't drive, Sully."

Sam's voice was firm, brooking no argument. She stood beside me, her sapphire eyes flashing with determination.

"The effects of the drug should wear out within an hour or so, but she's right: you shouldn't be operating any kind of machinery, least of all a car," Elora chimed in, her brows knitting together apologetically.

"I'll be fine." My stubbornness flared up. I was a great driver and I knew there wouldn't be any trouble.

Sam turned her gaze to me, her eyes hard with feeling. "Said every person in the world who then crashed their car. You're in no condition to drive and we all know it. Either Elora or I will go with you, but since there's likely to be trouble when we eventually get to him, I think we know who the better option is."

"That's certainly not me. I've never even touched a gun. I guess this means Chase and Bandit will go with me. I promise to keep them safe," Elora answered. "You two focus on stopping Gideon before he does something he truly regrets."

She shot us a convincing smile, but the stress of all that had happened in the last twenty-four hours was finally taking its toll. My body began to shut down. I felt small and vulnerable in the face of it all.

The weight of responsibility weighed heavy on my shoulders. Memories of my mother's death resurfaced, and I felt myself withdrawing into a familiar darkness. I felt like I had when my mother had died and I had withdrawn into myself. But I was the head of the family now and it was my responsibility to fix everything. I had to put us back together again.

Shaking myself out of my stupor, I gripped Chase by the shoulders with a newfound determination.

"If you find yourself in any trouble at all you get out of there, understand? I don't want you being brave or foolish. I want you safe. If you and Bandit are at risk, then nothing else matters. So if you see danger heading your way, just get the hell out and we'll figure out the rest later."

She nodded, Bandit barking loudly in agreement beside her. Then she threw herself into my arms, her thin frame trembling slightly as she spoke into my chest.

"Bring him back safely, okay? Don't let anything happen to him."

I wanted more than anything to promise her that, but the words caught in my throat. I wouldn't lie to her. I refused to promise what I couldn't.

She released me only for Sam to squeeze her tight. We did the same with Bandit until we were a tangled mess of hugs and doggy licks.

"We won't be long. We'll find Gideon and catch up to you. You just get in position and wait for us."

Elora nodded, one arm around Chase while the other rested on Bandit's neck. Pixie sat perched beside Bandit, her head tilted to one side and her intelligent eyes taking in our every move. She seemed to understand the gist of what was going on, if not exactly everything that we were saying.

"Don't worry. I will protect Chase," Bandit said, thumping his tail in emphasis. The certainty and love shone from his eyes, and it was all I could do not to melt down into a flood of tears.

"I know you will, buddy. You just make sure you watch out for yourself, too."

It was time to leave, but I couldn't make my feet move. It was as if they were cemented to the floor. Without a word, Sam took me by the hand and gently started to pull me away.

"Come on. The faster we go, the quicker we can be back with them."

Tearing my gaze from my kids, I let Sam lead me in the opposite direction. As I got into the car, all I could think was how fragile and young Chase looked.

Yet all of our lives now rested on her.

58

CHASE

Before we could leave, Doc had to make a quick call on her landline since she had neither her cell nor iPad anymore.

I stood next to her, my hands clenched tightly as she spoke to the person on the other end of the line. Her words were rushed and urgent, explaining that they and their dog — one of the rescues from Platinum Industries — might not be in danger.

A barrage of questions came down the line, but Doc cut them off sharply. "I'm sorry, I really don't have time to explain everything. Just call the others, let all the families know. We have a plan to stop them in LA but I can't disclose what it is. Just keep an eye out. You'll know if we've been successful."

With that warning hanging in the air, we hurriedly took off.

The highway stretched out before us, a ribbon of concrete rushing past. We left the suburban peacefulness of Doc's neighborhood and were now tearing down the streets as fast as we could without breaking speed limits.

Bandit sat in the middle of the backseat, his keen eyes scanning ahead of us while Pixie curled up beside him in a small ball. Since we had gotten into the car, she had been eerily calm — she was probably the calmest one among us.

She had changed so much in just a few short weeks. Whatever magic Doc had worked on her must really have been something as she was nothing like her previous self.

Greedily, I took as much comfort from Bandit's presence as I could. As much as I trusted Doc, she wasn't part of our family and it was never far from my mind that I was heading in the opposite direction to all the people I loved.

The scenery outside blurred together as we continued on our journey at breakneck speed.

More pretty box-like houses lined the streets, their vibrant colors eventually fading into the dullness of retail stores. But as we continued on our journey, even these buildings disappeared, leaving us surrounded on all sides by an acrid, yellow desert. The sharp scent of sand and dust filled my nostrils, making it difficult to take anything in.

If you had asked me what I had seen only a second ago, I wouldn't have been able to tell you. My thoughts were stuck on Gideon and what might be happening to him. Feeling my anxiety, Bandit laid a paw on my shoulder and whined into my ear.

Doc looked at me with concern, trying to assuage some of my fears. "It's a smart plan, Chase. A clever one. It's our best chance of surviving this insanity."

Bandit barked loudly in agreement, my ever present cheerleader. I guess she didn't know what else to say or how to make small talk, even as she turned on the radio soon after. "Let's listen to some music. It will relax us. This is Pixie's favorite station."

At the mention of her name, Pixie's ears swiveled to Doc, but she remained in her relaxed position. I tried not to envy her. A mellow song came through the high-tech speakers. Instead of listening, I stared blankly out at the sandy landscape. All I could see for miles was the blue sky meeting with that yellow sand and the odd human-like cactus. As the stress flooded my body, every nerve felt frayed and raw.

My hands were clenched tightly in my lap, fighting against the urge to scream. My heart pounded wildly in my chest, causing the world around me to spin despite sitting completely still.

It was the beginnings of a panic attack.

I bit my lip, trying to tell my heart to slow the heck down. Closing my eyes, my focus shifted to my breath, inhaling deeply and exhaling slowly in an attempt to steady myself. In then out. I counted my breath slowly, letting my mind go blank until all I heard was the sound of the road below the tires and Bandit's breath by my ear.

I don't remember falling asleep, but when I opened my eyes again, it was several hours later, and we were barreling down the I-10. The barren desert landscape had transformed into a bustling cityscape. Buildings stood tall and proud, their steel and glass structures glinting in the sunlight. Both dogs were asleep on the backseat, somehow curled together so that Bandit's chin rested on top of Pixie's head, proving what I had always known — even dogs needed comfort.

My lips felt dry and chapped. I ran my tongue over them only to feel a sharp pain as the movement cracked the skin. Doc caught my reaction and reached over to open the glove compartment. Inside were several small bottles of water and chocolate bars.

"My secret stash, in case I ever break down."

I shot her a small smile of gratitude and reached for the bottle, gulping down the cool liquid. A road sign flew past my head, but I missed the words by a split-second, though I didn't need to see it to recognize the city we were now approaching.

Palm trees towered above us as we entered the city, their fronds reaching towards the sky like giant green hands. Billboards adorned every building, advertising the latest movies and TV shows in flashy lights. Everywhere I looked, there were promises of love, beauty, and unimaginable wealth.

The energy of the city was palpable. Everything seemed larger than life and brimming with endless possibilities.

As we drove through the bustling city, towering glass buildings loomed over us in every corner. Each one seemed to house a luxurious hotel, with black stone fountains adorning their entrances and sharp-dressed valets bustling about. My eyes were drawn to the LAX airport in the distance, where giant gray jumbo jets waited patiently in lines for their turn to take off.

Bandit and I both got a kick out of seeing those. I have never been on a plane, never seen one this close either, but they were *enormous*. I was actually kind of grateful that I hadn't been on something that big. It didn't make sense how it could fly.

A retro looking diner passed by, chrome metal gleaming in the sun, which I swear I recognized as it'd been featured in several movies before. Then I saw a sign with the words Sunset Boulevard on it, just like the Broadway show. If we weren't in such dire straights, I might have enjoyed this little sight-seeing detour. As it was, I silently urged Doc to drive faster.

I wouldn't feel safe until we got to our destination and one way or another, all of this was over.

Despite how unspectacular the car looked, it came with all modern amenities, including a GPS system that also doubled as a TV. We were using the GPS to guide us. It had the little map thingy on right now with an arrow above an icon that represented our car. Jazz still played on the radio, which I suspected was one of the reasons I had fallen asleep in the first place. Like Gideon, it really wasn't my type of music.

The number was just finishing when the announcer suddenly cut in. The urgent voice of the news anchor crackled over the TV.

"We've just received reports of a possible terrorist cell working in the LA area. The extremist group is considered armed and very dangerous and should not be approached. If seen, please call this emergency report line."

A grainy black-and-white image appeared on the screen. Low

resolution, as if it had been captured from far away. There were several figures in the blurry frame — and a dog.

Blinking, I leaned in for a better look, trying to make out more details.

The dog had the same dark patches of color that I knew well. While I couldn't see all the figures clearly, I recognized the old man in the wheelchair, and the young girl standing beside him at a gas station.

"Oh Jesus, that's us."

Doc's eyes snapped to the screen. As she stared at the image in utter disbelief, a phone number flashed up on the bottom of the screen, followed by the words:

REWARD $500,000 if your tip results in their capture.

"How do they know we're here?" I tried to think about how they might have learned of our plan.

"I don't know." She paused, wracking her brain for a possible answer. "Oh no… What if I leaked it?"

"I don't understand?"

"There were almost a hundred dogs that we saved and had adopted. They're all calling each other now because I told them to. I was so scared that the families were at risk, I didn't even think that it could all get out."

My heart began thudding in my chest again. That panic attack I had managed to hold off was threatening to erupt this time. Doc gritted her teeth.

"Let's think about this. I only told them that we were heading to LA but not what we're going to do. They're looking for a large group of you. They don't know you've split up, or that both Pixie and I are now on the scene. To an outsider, you'd look like my kid, and since my face wasn't in that bulletin, I don't think anyone will recognize you, Chase. LA is so densely populated, they won't be able to pull you out of a crowd."

"You think so?" I asked hopefully.

Doc nodded, but there was a slight hesitation in her gesture that gave her away. Regardless of what she was saying, we both knew the truth.

We were in big, big trouble.

59

CHASE

The minutes ticked by, each one feeling longer than the last as we raced towards our destination. My nerves were on edge, waiting for the inevitable shoe to drop. It wasn't that I wanted to question Doc's logic, but I couldn't be as calm as she was.

The news had branded us terrorists!

Which ratcheted my nerves all the way up to the DANGER klaxon level.

Every fiber of my being screamed with fear and adrenaline at the thought of Smith and his men closing in on us. They had always operated under a cloak of secrecy and stealth, using truth serums and memory wipes to keep their actions hidden from the public eye. But now that our faces were plastered across the news, it could only mean one thing — Smith was back in control. He must have overpowered Gideon or tricked him into complacency, and Emma's life would be in grave danger.

As utterly terrifying as the thought of them being hurt — maybe even killed — was, I couldn't break down. I still had the rest of my family to save. And now that all bets were off, I wanted revenge, too.

I needed to stop these people from ever coming after us again.

Bandit lay low in the backseat, keeping out of sight, while I tried to hide as much of my face with my hair as possible. Throughout it all, the bright Californian sun shone down like a spotlight, seemingly determined to signpost our existence to the rest of the world.

I glanced at the car beside us, worried that the driver might turn to look and recognize me when something small flew past the car that created a whistling sound. The windows were up, so I wasn't entirely sure what I had heard, but then that same whistling sound came again… and was followed by another.

Then another.

I shot Doc a confused look when something thundered into the back of our car. I screamed, fear turning my blood to ice. Doc jumped in her seat, pressing on the gas pedal too hard in her panic.

The car jerked forward, sending the dogs flying before she could get it under control again. Bandit spun around and got up to peek out the windows when I suddenly understood what was happening.

"Those are silenced shots! They're firing at us! Everyone get down!"

Bandit hit the floor immediately, grabbing Pixie's collar as he went, dragging her with him into the footrest. The two of them huddled close, out of my line of sight, but hopefully also our mysterious attackers. Doc's knuckles were white on the steering wheel.

"Who would be firing at us? Surely not the police. That would be madness!"

Even as the words left her mouth, three police cars screeched around the corner toward us, sirens blaring. Faces appeared in the cars on either side of us, stunned with shock as they moved their cars as far away from us as they could, opening up a lane for the police.

Their passenger windows rolled down, and an officer took aim at us with his gun. It was a normal gun, though, not the silenced snipers I had heard.

Which meant the snipers were further away.

I stole a glance at the towering buildings that formed downtown LA, knowing that they could be literally anywhere. I was so mad at myself, I wanted to scream.

I knew we should have dumped the car and gotten off the highway as soon as we'd heard the news bulletin.

Instead, here we were out in the open, vulnerable and exposed. Sitting ducks. I waited for the police to say something, and insist we give up, but their only reply was to fire at us.

Bullets thundered overhead, exploding everything they touched. I ducked, covering my hands over my head. Doc couldn't do the same though. She had to keep driving, keep us moving, or we'd be dust for sure. Beads of sweat flew off her face as she hunched as low as she could while still driving.

The civilian car to one side of us screeched to a halt while the other car careened into a lamppost. Smoke billowed from the engine, filling the air. The driver looked out of his window, dazed and confused, a trickle of blood from a nasty gash on his face running down his cheek.

"They can't be real police," I said incredulously. "They wouldn't shoot first. They wouldn't risk civilian casualties."

"They think we're dangerous terrorists, so maybe they would. We've no real way of knowing. I need to get us out of here!"

Doc slammed her foot on the gas. The car shot forward so fast I snapped my head on the back of the headrest. We sped forward, weaving between the now stationary cars littering the street as terrified faces watched from the shadows of their cars.

I hung onto the door handle with all my strength, feeling the metal strain under my fingers as our car scraped against another. The deafening sound of metal on metal filled the air, sending sparks flying and causing my heart to race in fear.

"Bandit! You and Pixie hold on back there!"

I heard his whine of terror as the left side of our car struck a Toyota, snapping off the mirror which flew off behind us, landing on the ground below, where it was immediately crushed by one of the pursuing police cruisers.

I spared a glance at the men chasing us and was immediately struck by their lack of animation. All wore serious expressions, but none of them were speaking. Not even a word.

They weren't the real police: they couldn't be.

Real police would have been speaking into a radio, calling for more backup, describing the surrounding chaos. Their priorities would have been twofold: not only to capture us but to keep the public safe.

But not these guys.

These men had to be cleaners like Smith.

And they didn't care if they killed us in full view of the public. I suddenly understood the reason for the news bulletin now: it gave them the perfect excuse to shoot first. By the time the questions came, they would be long gone.

Doc floored it past several stopped cars when I saw an intersection fast approaching. Our lights were amber, but they were about to turn red.

And we were going way too fast to stop.

The blood drained from Doc's face. "Hold on, this is going to be rough."

Instead of slowing down, she slammed her foot on the gas all the way to the floor.

We shot forward so fast that everything became a blur. Just as on that first day when I had met Bandit when he had saved my life at the edge of the road, details suddenly came at me in slow motion.

Like how the family in a station wagon on one side of us had a young boy whose face was pressed up against the window as he watched us, wide-eyed. Our lights flashed to red as the other lanes began moving across. Either they hadn't seen us or they hadn't been paying attention, but when they started moving, we were already hurtling toward them.

Suddenly, a car shot ahead faster than the rest. It was another police cruiser. And they were coming straight for us.

"I can't get past them…"

I heard Doc say before our world exploded.

The other car smashed into our own, somehow ramping off us and flipping upside down, before exploding into a ball of fire. Our SUV slammed to a juddering halt. The impact jolted me forward and I would have hit my head on the dashboard if the airbag hadn't deployed.

My face slammed into it, burning from the contact.

It might have saved my life, but it didn't stop it from hurting like crazy. I think my tooth went through my lip as I tasted blood in my mouth. I tested my teeth with my tongue until I felt one of them move, loosened by the impact.

For a few moments, I couldn't do anything. There was only that burning pain on my face and the world spinning. I could hear screaming, the general confusion of a disaster, but it all swelled into one great noise.

I waited in terror, hoping for my senses to come back to me — and fast. We had to get away, as we weren't safe here. Lifting my head from the airbag, I attempted to turn my head. Pain hit, my muscles screaming at me, but that fact that I could turn it, I knew no bones were broken.

Not up top, anyway.

Turning all the way to my left, I saw Doc's own airbag had saved her life. She wasn't as out of it as I was, however, already reaching into the glove compartment for some kind of knife that she jabbed into her airbag, before turning it on her seatbelt, which was locked tight. Her hands sawed back and forth in a frantic motion as she started to cut through it.

"You okay?" she asked in a dazed tone.

"I think so."

"Bandit? Pixie? What about you guys?" she asked of the backseat.

We heard a low toned "WOOF!" followed by a higher pitched one. Their barks were shaky, but at least he and Pixie were safe.

"Can you get out of your seat?" Doc asked me.

Reaching over, pain shot up my side. I think I must have banged it pretty badly in the collision. Gingerly, I felt it with my fingers, but when I couldn't feel a wound or blood, I counted myself lucky. I found my seat belt and unclipped it. Bandit popped up in the space beside me and licked my face.

"I'm okay, buddy," I assured him. "But we need to get out of here."

There was utter chaos outside. We weren't the only cars who had crashed. Cars on either side and behind us had collided into each other. There must have been at least twelve vehicles affected. Maybe even more. The two cops inside the overturned car — whether they were real or not — were not moving. I was pretty sure both of them were dead.

I didn't have time to concern myself with that though: we still had four remaining cars after us. From the corners of my eyes, I saw the dark navy-clad figures climbing out of their cars, stone cold eyes fixed on us. They were coming toward us when they were suddenly swamped by terrified civilians, grabbing hold of them.

One woman asked, "What's happened?"

Another, "Is this a terrorist attack?"

Faced with a panicked public, the eight men — the fake police — didn't know what to do. They tried shaking them off only for more to take their place. They could not reach us through the throng of people that surrounded them.

"We need to go now!"

Opening my door, I slid out as Doc did the same. Reaching over, I opened the back door. Bandit and Pixie shot out. Together, the four of us bolted across the street.

60

CHASE

Casting a quick glance over my shoulder, I could see the determined fake officers still hot on our trail. They were struggling to navigate through the panicked and frazzled crowd in their efforts to catch up to us. But we were already several steps ahead, weaving through the chaos and gaining ground with each passing second.

We sprinted down the bustling street, our feet pounding against the pavement as we turned into a quaint business block. In the center, a charming courtyard greeted us with its lively atmosphere. The air was filled with the sweet scent of climbing roses, their vibrant blooms weaving around a white wooden gazebo that stood proudly in the middle. Several benches were scattered around the gazebo, positioned perfectly to offer a picturesque view of the surrounding area. On any other day, I would have taken a moment to admire the beauty of this place. Instead, we ran right past and kept going. Doc pointed to an opening on the left.

"This way."

We emerged from the block to be met with six lanes of traffic stretching endlessly in both directions. My heart sank as I frantically scanned for a pedestrian crossing. Didn't people walk in LA? How were you supposed to get to the other side?

The sound of approaching sirens spurred us on, knowing that at any moment the cops would be on us. Still, attempting to cross this street would definitely result in an injury, or even worse, death. For sure, we'd draw an awful lot of attention our way by trying to. Neither option was particularly wanted. With no transportation or taxis in sight, panic bubbled up inside me. Had we come this far only to lose out to *traffic*?

Was this really where our story was going to end?

Bandit limped to my side, favoring his right paw. His stride was slower than normal and a little hesitant, his normally wagging tail held low and still. I could see the worry and concern in his big green eyes as he looked up at me.

Meanwhile, Doc gingerly held her left arm, her face twisted in discomfort. She winced with every step, but refused to let go of her determined expression. Despite their injuries, they both seemed laser focused on finding a solution to our predicament. The mid-afternoon sun shone down on us, casting a warm, yellow glow over our tense group. Every honk of a car or rustle of a leaf made our hearts race as we searched desperately for a way out.

"We need transport," Doc said through gritted teeth.

I was about to suggest we continue on down the street when I caught sight of one of those Hollywood tour buses idling just a block away. A line of elderly Japanese tourists, their sun-kissed skin and vibrant outfits standing out against the muted buildings, were eagerly lining up to climb aboard the bus. Each carried a camera as if it were an extension of their arm.

"There! The tour bus! Hurry!"

We ran for it, moving as fast as we could. The dogs got there first — even with Bandit's limp — and stood, pawing the ground in agitation until Doc and I finally caught up.

A chorus of polite smiles greeted us as we hopped onto the crowded bus. They even nodding a greeting to the dogs. We searched for an empty seat and finally settled in, maneuvering ourselves away from the windows while the dogs hid themselves between our legs. A bell chimed and then we were off. I didn't let myself breathe until the bus started moving away.

"Are they coming?" Doc whispered to me.

I shot a quick glance behind us. "Not yet. I think we're okay."

The words were barely out of my mouth when a looming shadow fell over us. My shoulders tensed for the inevitable confrontation.

"Is there a problem here?" The question had come from the ticket collector. Half of his face was covered by a thick gray beard. His eyes, lined with wrinkles and twinkling with kindness, reminded me of Father Christmas somehow. Despite his elaborate uniform and the old-fashioned ticket machine strapped to his chest, he exuded an air of warmth and approachability.

"Er… yeah? Why?" I asked, adopting my most confused expression.

"You look like you've been through the wars," the conductor remarked, his kind gaze lingering over our disheveled appearance. I could feel my cheeks heating up as I shifted uncomfortably under his gaze. Before Doc could speak, I jumped in with a reply.

"We're fine. Our car broke down on the way here and we tried to fix it, but you know, we have no idea what we're doing. We just don't want to be late for the taping. We waited months for these tickets, so obviously everything that could go wrong today, has. We're just hoping we'll be able to get to the studio on time."

The conductor's brows furrowed, creating deep creases in his forehead as he stared at us with a puzzled expression. His eyes darted back and forth between us, clearly unsure whether to believe our story or not. The tension in the air was palpable as we waited for his response.

"We go past a few of them. It is LA after all."

"That's perfect," I said, hoping he would leave us alone. But he continued to stand there, staring at us, as if he were psychically trying to beam his thoughts into our heads. It took a few moments before I realized why he wasn't leaving. Turning to Doc, I nudged her gently.

"Hey Mom, we need to pay the guy."

Doc blinked, nodding in embarrassment, catching onto my lie, quickly.

"Of course. Sorry about that. Don't know where my head is these days."

She rummaged through her bag, which miraculously made it out of our crash with us, and paid for the tickets. Once the money changed hands, there was no reason for him to hang around any longer. Apparently buying our story, the conductor moved away as we sat back and allowed ourselves a moment to catch our breaths.

61

SULLY

The air was thick with tension, a blanket of unease that hung over us like a storm cloud. It wasn't all due to our concern for Gideon and Emma's safety — there was something between Sam and I that needed to be addressed.

We'd been going for an hour or so, yet Sam had barely said two words to me since we'd left the others. Her usually warm demeanor had been replaced by a cool, distant edge. I knew we needed to thrash out whatever was on her mind and it seemed like now was the time to do it, before all hell broke loose when we finally caught up to Gideon. I took a deep breath and spoke cautiously, hoping my approach would soften her defenses.

"I didn't say the right thing earlier," I started, choosing my words carefully.

"Oh? When you accused me of letting my emotions cloud my judgment about Emma?" Sam retorted with a raised eyebrow. "You know how I love being told how I feel by a man."

I sank further into my seat, immediately regretting that I'd brought anything up at all. We were on dangerous, dangerous territory here.

"That's not what I meant. I meant it in another way."

Her blonde brow arched even higher. "What other way is there?"

"Just that… It's obvious there has been tension between the two of you…"

"What I'd love to know," Sam interrupted me sharply, "is how you would feel if my ex, the love of my life who I had grieved for a solid year, returned out of the blue and you were forced to spend every waking hour with him? Would you still think I was overreacting then?"

I fell silent, knowing there wasn't much I could say in response. But before I could even attempt to offer an apology or explanation, Sam continued.

"Come on, Sully! Give me some credit. I'm not a jealous little girl who can't take the added competition. I am your *wife*, who you swore to love for the rest of your life. But now I'm starting to wonder if that's true, especially when you seem more concerned about Emma than Gideon."

"That's not true. I'm just worried about her in a different way. Gideon is more than able to handle himself."

"But he's out of his mind now, Sully! He's so lost, he's actually convinced himself that Zeb can be brought back to life. I know Emma needs help too — especially after what we've learned today — but she isn't as delicate as he is right now. Gideon is the one we need to be concerned with."

She stopped to catch her breath, hands gripping the wheel so tightly I thought it would break.

"I understand that, Sam, but Emma doesn't know about the world. She didn't even know how to peel a carrot for crying out loud! How do you think she'll cope going up against a team of Smith's men? She's completely vulnerable."

Sam squeezed her eyes shut for a moment, thinking long and hard before she spoke again.

"We're obviously not getting anywhere with this so just answer me this: if this Emma *had* been your Emma, if she wasn't a clone at all but the real thing, what would you do? Would you go back to her?"

It was such a loaded question that I didn't answer straight away. Images of the two fought for attention as a movie of our greatest hits played in my mind. I saw Emma's radiant smile on our wedding day, surrounded by family and friends. Even some of our dearest animal clients and their fur-parents had turned up to shower us with love, as rice rained down upon her, mingling with her happy tears. Florence, alive and thriving and wearing another one of those stiff cotton dresses she habitually wore, had stood next to Mark, beaming with joy.

The movie changed then, bringing me to the day I first met Sam, and she had given us a ride to my dad. I could still hear her singing with unabashed gusto, filling the truck with music and laughter. She was a breath of fresh air and a healing balm to the pain that had consumed me for an entire year. Both sets of memories flooded me with emotion, making it difficult to form words. I opened my mouth to answer when my eyes caught the familiar sight of our RV ahead of us.

My mind became a swirling collage of memories, each one fighting for attention like scenes from a movie playing in my mind. First, I saw Emma's beaming smile as she walked down the aisle on our wedding day, surrounded by our loved ones and showered with rice. The happiness radiating from her was almost blinding. Then, the movie shifted to Florence standing next to Mark, tears streaming down her face with pure joy. The love and support from our friends and family on that day was something I would never forget.

But then, just like a film reel changing scenes, I was transported to the day I first met Sam. She had given us a ride and her infectious laughter and singing had filled the truck with warmth and light. She was a breath of fresh air and a healing balm to the pain that had consumed me for an entire year. Both sets of memories flooded me with emotion, making it difficult to form words. I closed my eyes and took a deep breath, willing the confusing memories to fade away. After a moment, they began to dissipate, leaving behind only a lingering ache in my heart.

I opened my mouth to answer when my eyes caught the familiar sight of our RV ahead of us. "There they are!"

Relief surged through me, momentarily pushing aside our conversation. Sam sprang into action beside me, disregarding any potential onlookers as she frantically flashed the lights as we raced towards the RV.

As the motorhome came into view, I noticed it suddenly picking up speed. In that split second, I knew Gideon must be behind the wheel. Had it been the Cleaner driving, I was pretty certain we would have had a different outcome. I derived some small joy from this fact.

"Hold on tight," Sam warned me, but I had already braced myself against the car.

I said a quick prayer of thanks for the mostly empty road ahead of us as Sam jammed her foot on the gas and we shot forward like a rocket. The wind whipped through my hair and stung my cheeks as we barreled past the RV, Sam expertly yanking the wheel to cut him off. Her hand slammed down on the horn in a deafening blast, drowning out any other sound on the road. But in that moment, neither of us cared about being loud or causing a scene; all that mattered was stopping Gideon.

As our car now led the way, Sam started easing up on the gas. Either Gideon was going to slow his roll, or we were going to crash.

He played chicken with us, his pale face staring out at us grimly in the side mirrors. It broke my heart to see how young he suddenly looked, barely old enough to drive, let alone endure everything he had in the last twenty-four hours.

Sam's eyes flicked nervously to the speedometer, watching as the needle sank lower and lower. We were inching closer and closer to the back of the RV, but Gideon showed no signs of relenting. The tension in the car was palpable as we braced ourselves for impact, uncertain of what would happen next.

"I sure hope you know what you're doing," I said.

"You're not the only one."

I held on grimly, my knuckles turning white from the sheer force of my grip, desperately hoping that he would come to his senses and stop the RV before we all died, but Gideon seemed determined to continue driving the RV at breakneck speed. Finally, just as our bumper nudged into the front of the RV, Gideon slammed on the brakes. The RV came to a screeching halt, grazing the back of our car.

My body flung forward, but I managed to catch myself before I could be thrown out of the car. Heart racing, I leaped out of the car and ran towards the RV, adrenaline coursing through my veins. My hands shook as I tried to open the door, but it was locked tight. My foot lashed at it, unable to contain myself any longer.

"Open this door Gideon or I'll break it down!" I yelled. "So help me God, I absolutely will!"

Beside me, Sam unclipped her gun from her holster and held it at the ready.

"You have a count of three before I shoot the lock off this door, Gideon. It's up to you," Sam called out, cool as a cucumber. Despite the anger and frustration that had consumed her just moments ago, she remained calm and collected. The ensuing silence that greeted us was in stark contrast to the deafening noise we'd just experienced. Widening her stance, shoulder-width apart, prepared to make good on her promise, Sam began counting.

"One…"

There was no response.

"Two…"

Her voice grew louder, a hint of strain toward the end of the callout. Only the slightest wobble of her gun-wielding hands showed the toll this was taking. She opened her mouth to say 'three' when a familiar voice called from inside.

"I'm opening the door. Don't shoot!"

At last, the door finally swung open as Gideon's tear-streaked faced looked back at us. His panicked eyes darted between Sam's gun and Smith, who was still tied up and had been moved back by the table again, but he was clearly alive.

"You have to let me do this! It's the only way we can save him!"

I pushed past Gideon, entering the RV. The bedroom door was closed. All was unnaturally quiet within, which caused my heart to freeze in my chest.

I crossed the RV in four short strides, flinging open the bedroom door to find Emma on the bed, bound and gagged. I ripped the gag off her mouth as Emma shot up onto her knees, completely outraged.

"It's about time you got here! That boy tied me up and stopped me from speaking! He wanted to give me to the bad guys, can you believe that? He needs to be punished, Sully!"

As much as I shared Emma's anger at how she had been treated, I knew that wasn't the answer. I untied her bonds.

"I'm sorry," I said sincerely. "Just wait here. I'll handle this."

As soon as her hands were free, she squirmed away from me and rubbed her sore wrists.

"I've seen where your leadership, or whatever you call it, has gotten us," she spat out. "These kids don't respect you. Nobody listens to you, so why should I? I'm going to handle this myself," Emma pushed past me towards the door.

I stepped in her way, blocking her path.

"I understand your frustration, but punishment is the last thing he needs right now. Zeb took him in when Gideon's own family threw him out. It wasn't until he lived with Zeb that he learned what it feels like to have people who loved and cared about him. He just lost the one person in the world who he loves the most, and this is his way of trying to deal with it. It's not great, I know, but that's all he's doing. Let me talk to him. I think I can get through to him. Let me talk to him before you go charging out there."

My gentle but insistent plea had taken the wind right out of her sails. I knew it the moment her eyes softened. "Okay," she said quietly. "But if he doesn't appreciate that what he did was wrong, I get to punish him after."

I didn't respond, but instead turned and left the room, shutting the door behind me. As I walked down the hallway, I couldn't help but feel the weight of Emma's words and their implications for Gideon. Inside the living area, Sam put her gun away and bit her lip in her effort not to cry over how distraught Gideon was. She pulled him into a tight hug, offering comfort in any way she could.

I knew I couldn't wait any longer. It was time for the conversation that the rest of us had already had without him.

"Gid, I know how torn up you are over this. God knows we all loved him, but you need to realize that nothing can bring him back, and before you say anything, Elora has already confirmed that it isn't possible to bring someone back from the dead. That means no one can bring Dad back."

Gideon's gaze drifted past me to the bedroom door. "But Emma—"

"Elora received some results from her tests last night... We now know that Emma is a clone. We think she must have been the result of the experiment Xavier had bragged about to us."

I could see Gideon's eyes glaze over. I wasn't sure if he was taking any of this in.

"Do you understand, Gideon? Emma is not the real thing, no matter how close she may seem. There is nothing that can bring dead people back, and I need you to hear me right now. What you are doing here is incredibly dangerous and foolish."

Gideon's face began to crumple as the words started to sink in. The realization slowly grew until he broke down into tears. He dropped his eyes to the ground as shame washed over him. "Does she know? Have you told her?"

"I'm waiting until we get back to Elora. Emma might be a clone but she is still a human being with feelings, so this is going to come as a shock to her. We're going to need to do this the right way.,

His head nodded in a slow, tired movement as he wiped the tears from his face with the back of his hand. Gradually, it dawned on him that we were a few people short. "Where are Chase and Bandit? Are they still at the Doc's?"

Sam and I exchanged a glance, wondering how to break the news to him gently.

"The thing is," I began hesitantly, "when you took off like that, you left both Elora and all the dogs she had rehired, vulnerable, so they couldn't stay there anymore. It wasn't safe."

A pained expression crossed his face as he realized the consequences of his actions. My heart ached for him.

"But Chase came up with a plan," Sam interjected, trying to offer some semblance of hope. "We think it might be the only way to keep us from having to run ever again."

His eyes widened with apprehension as he stared at the two of us. "What plan?"

I opened Elora's iPad.

"It's probably easier if I show you." As I logged onto the news channel, my heart raced with anticipation and fear. I prayed that everything had gone according to schedule, but my hopes were crushed as the footage revealed a harrowing incident unfolding in LA. Police cars screeched through the city streets, their sirens wailing in a desperate attempt to catch the terrorists wreaking havoc. My finger trembled as it moved across the screen, trying to switch to another channel for some glimmer of good news. But my stomach dropped when the faces of the terrorists appeared on the screen. And then I saw our own faces staring back at us.

"That's us." Gideon grasped.

Sam leaned in to get a better look at the screen, her expression growing dark with concern as she processed the shocking news. "I think they're saying it was Chase who caused that accident."

My mind couldn't fully comprehend what was happening as I watched the devastation unfold before my eyes. It felt like an out-of-body experience, like I wasn't really part of it all.

People huddled on the sidewalk, blood pouring from their wounds. Smoke billowed from an overturned squad car. Emergency services rushed to help those injured, but it seemed like there were too many victims and not enough hands to save them all.

This was not part of the plan at all.

"Jesus, what the hell is going on?"

62

CHASE

One of the tourists looked our way. The fifth by my rapidly growing count.

If it wasn't for the admiring looks they sent Pixie and Bandit, I would be jumping out of the nearest exit.

They were just being polite. I could see it in the friendly smiles they gave us. Normally, I would have let Bandit charm them with a few simple tricks — nothing crazy, a simple high-five or a beg, the kind that the average dog would know — but since we couldn't afford to attract any more attention to ourselves, we'd have to do away with the niceties today.

I looked out the window, but instead of the view, all I could see was Doc's pale visage reflected in the glass. She cradled her left arm gingerly, wincing in pain every so often and supporting it with her other hand. I wasn't sure what was wrong with it, but the pain that flashed over her face was a cause of concern.

In an attempt to help, I unhooked the leather belt I wore with my jeans. I looped the end of it together and offered it to her. "It's not much, but the leather's soft. You can rest your arm in it."

A grateful smile lit up her face as she took the belt from me. "Thanks."

She struggled to pull the belt over her head, but a sharp breath of pain forced her to stop. I gently took the belt from her and arranged it so that the flat side lay against her neck. With careful movements, I helped her arm through the loop until it sat snugly against her body. It wasn't much of a sling, but it would do in a pinch.

"It might be broken," she explained, wincing in pain. "I have some painkillers in my bag. Can you help me with them?"

"Of course," I replied, searching through her neatly organized bag. Everything had its own place, making it easy to find the pills. Fishing them out, I handed them to her. She swallowed them dry, waiting for the effect to take hold when the sound of an approaching helicopter caused my blood to turn to ice.

Cupping a hand over my head as if to block out the sun (instead of obscuring my face), I searched the sky, only to locate the black and white helicopter almost immediately. It was close, maybe only a few blocks away.

"LAPD" was painted onto the side of the helicopter in bold black lettering, though from recent experience, I knew that didn't mean a thing. Further away, my gaze landed on another one, circling above a different part of town. My heart sank as I spotted more black specks in the distance.

Whether they were the real police or Smith's men, the air support was all for us. The deafening roar of the helicopters overhead drowned out any other sounds, causing my heart to race and my hands to tremble. I felt a clammy hand grab hold of mine. Doc's panic mirrored my own, and we both moved as far from the window as possible, fighting the irrational urge to flee. The only chance we had was if we were smart and didn't act on our instinct to run. We couldn't draw any more attention to ourselves.

Hunkering down, we sat, tense as all hell, hoping that a bullet wasn't going to come flying through the window at us.

Amidst the chaos, the bright and bubbly voice of our pre-recorded "tour guide" sounded over the speakers from every corner of the bus. As we passed famous landmarks, she regaled us with stories that were meant to be entertaining, though I found myself flinching from her fake cheerful air. Her facts were ridiculous too, amounting to no more than general gossip at times though I welcomed the inane chatter. At least it drowned out some of those helicopter blades which seemed to be getting closer and closer.

I was more than relieved when the ticket conductor finally called out, "Last stop, folks."

Exhausted and on edge, there were only a few of us left on the bus now, most of the tourists having left already.   I looked up at the giant sign that loomed above me with just two words and that iconic logo: UNIVERSAL CITY. A shiver of apprehension ran down my spine.

This was it.

For better or worse, this was where everything would change for the rest of our possibly very short lives.

Climbing off the bus, I could feel the ticket man's eyes on us. Although every instinct told me to avoid eye contact, I forced myself to smile at him. Even managing a wave with a sunny, "Have a good day."

If he did recognize us, I wanted to make it as difficult for him to report us to the cops as possible. We entered the theme park, blending in with the crowd of colorful tourists and enthusiastic families. The scent of popcorn and cotton candy filled the air, mixed with screams from roller coasters and the distant sound of carnival music. We headed towards one of many ticket booths, relieved to see that there wasn't much of a line at this time of day since most visitors would come earlier in order to get the most bang for their buck. There were actually more people peddling toys and souvenirs than there were paying customers at this point.

I stopped by one of them, picking up two baseball caps with the

Universal logo. Doc paid for them without question, instinctively knowing why I had wanted them. Once they were on, they shielded half of our faces and made us seem like every other thrill seeker.

We had paid for two tickets and were just passing through the barricade when the ticket seller, a pimply guy in his twenties with an earnest expression and a terrible man-bun, saw Bandit and Pixie by our feet.

"Dogs are only allowed in specific areas. Please familiarize yourself with those areas in the leaflet I've just given you."

Doc smiled at him. "Don't worry, we're not taking them anywhere they shouldn't be."

The seller looked down his long nose at us, lording his power. I would have loved to have put him in his place, but bit down on my lip instead. After some deliberation, the barricades rose, and we were in. Ignoring the colorful array of entertainment, I poured over the map.

"This way."

We hurried past numerous food stalls lining the street. Tantalizing aromas flew my way, causing my stomach to rumble, but to my credit, I didn't look at their wares, not even once. It was strange that even at this moment, with all the uncertainty and terror, my body could still crave food. Guess I must be what they call an emotional eater.

Excited children tore around the place, bouncing from one sight to another while their long-suffering parents followed behind, arms loaded with brightly colored balloons and soft toys.

Everywhere I looked, there were people. Above, glinting security cameras documented our every move, their presence making the hairs on the back of my neck permanently stand on end. We were like sheep walking into the lion's den, completely exposed and vulnerable. I thought for sure that at any moment an army of security guards would surround us, but somehow, we made it to our destination without drawing any attention to ourselves.

The rectangular beige building was only a few stories high, but what it lacked in height, it made up for in length, reaching several blocks long. Three colorful letters stood over the glass entry doors, "NBC", followed by the smaller worded "Studios."

Knowing what this represented, I felt the first flush of excitement, only for it to be immediately dampened when I saw the fortress of metal detectors and X-ray machines lined up before me. The guards standing diligently at their posts added to the air of security that surrounded the area. It was like a maze of safety precautions, designed to keep out any potential threats — including us.

"You don't have a weapon, do you?" I asked the Doc.

She shook her head. "Of course not... but I'm not liking the thought of going through all that security."

Bandit chuffed, letting us know he was in agreement. He pawed the ground, gesturing at a small sign for the parking lot.

"Good idea," I congratulated him.

The four of us hurried over to the parking lot, where we were met with two lanes of traffic entering and exiting the studio. Each lane was blocked off by sturdy barricades and manned by a guard inside a booth. The lane furthest from us was currently dealing with a group of rowdy college students, while the other lane's guard had a clear view of anyone approaching too closely.

Still, this was our best chance of getting inside. I turned to Bandit. "I need you to draw that guy's attention so the rest of us can sneak past him."

Bandit nodded, crouching low to wait for further instructions. I was suddenly hit by a burst of love so strong that it could have knocked me down.

Walking through the streets of New York on my own, struggling to find food and shelter every single day, I had written off the rest of my life. As far as I was concerned, I was destined to be on my own forever. I would never know what it felt like for someone to have my back, much less, love me. I fully expected to go to sleep one night in a disgusting, roach-infected alley, only for it to be my last.

Then Bandit had appeared in my life.

A skinny mutt who had been just as desperate and alone as I was.

We hadn't known then how much our lives would change or how we would need each other. Somehow, he, and the rest of the gang had become my family and if we were to have any chance of living the rest of our lives in safety, this had to be done, no matter how terrifying I found it.

With precision timing, we waited until no cars were coming down either lane before making our move. Bandit confidently strolled up to the guard's cubicle, his scrappy fur standing on end as he bravely faced the imposing figure behind the glass. My heart raced with fear as he approached.

The rest of us stole toward the building, hugging the shadows and keeping low until Bandit's arrival drew the guard's attention. He turned his back on the barricade as the three of us crept inside. We half ran, half crouched and hid behind a parked car.

"Hey fella, what are you doing here?"

Bandit whined convincingly, holding up a paw. The guard must have been an animal lover, as he understood what the deal was immediately. "Did you hurt yourself?"

Even though the guard didn't speak our shorthand, Bandit barked yes, then threw in another heart-wrenching whine. The guard's face softened. He reached down to stroke him earning a tail thump in response.

"You are the loveliest thing, aren't you? You stay right there and I'll get you help." Turning away from Bandit, he picked up a phone that hung on the wall of the booth and pushed a button. He spoke into the handset, just loud enough for me to hear.

"I've got an injured dog here. He seems friendly and possibly someone's pet. Can you send someone to collect him and check if any of our families are missing a dog?"

I had no idea what the other person said, but by the time the guard turned back to Bandit, he had already vanished back to my side.

63

CHASE

The sound of our footsteps reverberated off the concrete walls of the dimly lit parking lot. Despite the sun's brightness outside, it seemed to have no effect on this cavernous space. We walked within the shadows, making our way to the studio building only to reach another obstacle.

The doors that led inside could only be opened with the right pass and since we hadn't come via a car, we didn't have one. So, we hung around outside, pretending to be on a call (Doc was using her wallet since we didn't even have a cell phone on us), while I made a show of entertaining the dogs.

Just a forgetful mom trying to contact her husband to let her in.

Our luck changed when a family of six finally approached. They thought nothing of letting us inside, even holding the doors open for us. If I were criminally inclined, a mother, daughter and their dogs tag-team seemed like it could really do some damage.

No doubt Sam would have something to say about that.

The grand lobby welcomed us with long, regal corridors, each lined with elegant purple doors. These doors branched off into separate wings, leading to different stages that housed their own unique productions. The air was electric with excitement and anticipation as I scanned the walls, admiring the framed photographs of famous faces who had graced these halls over the years — actors, musicians, and celebrities all captured in moments of fame and glory.

When I passed by my mom's favorite actor, a rush of bittersweet emotions washed over me. She had always been addicted to daytime talk shows and soaps, and would have gotten such a kick out of being here.

Pushing her face from my mind, I ran through the plan one last time.

I had come up with the idea this morning when, in between the madness, I had noticed Good Morning America in the background. I knew that if we could just get Bandit onto one of those news shows, the world would have to listen to us. He would show everyone how special he was and what he could do. It would be undeniable and if everyone in the world knew our story, there would be no point in anyone coming after us.

The Smiths, Xaviers, and any others like them wouldn't be a threat anymore. As long as we could get in front of the cameras, we'd be able to convince the world that we deserved to be left alone. Maybe even protected.

That was my plan, anyway, and I was sticking with it.

One of the purple doors opened beside me as a harassed-looking production assistant burst out from behind it, almost crashing into us in his haste. His face was flushed, and he held a clipboard with well-thumbed through pages in one hand, while balancing a cup full of something hot in the other.

"Sorry!" He called over his shoulder at whoever was inside the room, then, activating the radio that sat in his shirt pocket, he talked, speaking faster than I'd ever heard someone speak.

"He wanted green tea, not black!" The urgency in his voice managed to make it sound life or death. Without another word, he hurried down the corridor, apparently to rectify the crime. I chased after him, tapping him on the shoulder, when he finally slowed down enough for me to catch up.

"Excuse me. Can you tell me which stage Good Morning America is being filmed on?" I asked, breathless from the unexpected sprint.

He turned to me, irritation evident in every line of his face. "Is that a joke?"

Confused by his hostile reaction, I blinked at him and shook my head. "No… I genuinely want to know."

He let out an exasperated sigh before replying. "The show's filmed in New York. Plus, it's already the middle of the afternoon. You'd be far too late for a recording even if they were filming here." With a final huff of annoyance, he spun on his heels, jogging away, not caring that he was spilling some of that black tea onto the polished floor. I stood there, rooted to the spot, feeling sick to my stomach.

"I should have checked where the show is made before rushing us out here. I can't believe we put our lives at so much risk for this!"

How could I have done this to us? You stupid, stupid girl! My thoughts berated me, each syllable a harsh lash against my conscience.

As if he knew what I was doing to myself, Bandit stepped over a puddle of tea and pressed against me to offer his comfort, putting a stop to my inner diatribe. Pixie raised her face upward to me and whined in support as Doc's calm eyes stared at me, cutting through my panic.

"It doesn't have to be that show, Chase. Any show will do so long as it's being broadcast live. That's what we've got to look for, a live broadcast."

Her words were like a lifeline, pulling me out from the depths of panic. My heart relaxed a beat, knowing she was right.

"Come on."

Giving me a gentle nudge, Doc took off at a fast pace. Following her lead, we moved quickly through the twisting beige corridors that matched its equally beige exterior. Signs flashed overhead with bright letters spelling out SILENCE, letting us know that a show was currently being recorded inside. Every door had a simple notice beside it, listing the production currently underway.

Each of the doors bore a small glass panel that I could look through. One stage contained the cozy interior of a popular coffee shop, complete with wooden tables, wide sofas, and steaming mugs of coffee. Another held an impressive replica of an apartment with a plant-filled outdoor balcony overlooking the bustling cityscape. But the most mesmerizing stage was the one that housed a snow-covered forest, its trees glistening with frost and icicles hanging from their branches.

It was wild how lifelike everything seemed, as if I could step through the door and be transported into a whole new world.

It was only when I passed by that the illusion was shattered when viewed from another angle — the seams and supports of the set were visible, but that was the magic of Hollywood I guess. Nothing was ever how it seemed.

As we continued on, my heart raced with excitement and fear. The names of several shows that Gideon and I enjoyed flickered past, but I had to push away the thought that I might never see his face again. Sully and Sam were on a mission to find us, and since they had no way of reaching us, I had to trust that they would be successful.

Any other outcome was unthinkable.

We were still searching for a suitable show when Doc stopped in front of a wall, her eyes sparkling with hope as she read the signage. She turned to me with a grin.

"Stage Eight," she said breathlessly. "That's where we're going!"

"What do they film there?"

"Entertainment Now News!"

I felt light-headed with relief. It was the perfect solution, one that I had been hoping for. EN News was always on and it had its own dedicated channel, making it the ideal place to broadcast our message.

Following the signs, we headed towards stage eight. The illuminated sign above the door read ON AIR. I swallowed my fear as I grasped the handle and turned it, half expecting it to be locked. To my surprise, the door swung open easily, and we hurried inside.

Compared to the other stages we had seen so far, this one was much smaller. In front of us were two EN anchors, a man in his late thirties with slicked black hair and designer stubble. His co-anchor was a blonde with impossibly glossy hair and a soft, appealing voice. Behind them, a large screen displayed a freeze frame of a famous actress from her latest monster movie that was currently taking the world by storm.

The set was buzzing with energy as three bulky cameras recorded the anchors' every move, each manned by a skilled cameraman. A few additional crew members scurried around frantically, checking equipment and gathering cables, while a makeup artist stood off to the side with brushes and tubes poking out from her utility belt.

Other than this handful of people, I was surprised that no one else was here. I had expected there to be far more people involved in producing a live news segment. Psyching myself up, I looked at the others.

"Are you guys ready for this?" I asked, my voice shaky with anticipation.

Bandit nodded confidently, while Pixie jumped up and down with excitement. In the back of my mind, I heard Sully comment that small dogs were always the bounciest. The flashback down memory lane felt like a knife in the heart when my twisted mind taunted me with the cruel thought that I might never hear his voice again. Doc shot me a tentative smile, cutting into my thoughts, looking just as apprehensive as I felt.

"Lead the way."

I swallowed the dry lump in my throat. Trying not to lose my nerve, I marched straight towards the EN anchors.

64

CHASE

As the male anchor, whose name was Marko, continued to deliver his lines with practiced ease, his bright smile faltered for just a second when he caught sight of me. His eyes widened before quickly returning to their professional gaze, never missing a beat. It wasn't until Bandit, Doc, and Pixie stepped directly into a spotlight that the rest of the crew even seemed to take notice.

Marko's voice cut off abruptly as he turned towards us, his attention now fully on our unexpected presence. "I'm sorry for the interruption, but we seem to have a situation here."

The crew turned toward us and I was met with a sea of blank faces. Nobody knew what to do. It was the perfect moment to seize the opportunity. I could feel all eyes on me as I stepped forward into the light. Keeping my voice calm and strong, I spoke.

"I need you all to listen to me. This is really important."

The two hosts exchanged a confused look, neither of them seeming too alarmed by our sudden appearance. I guess a girl, a woman, and their two dogs weren't particularly threatening. Ignoring me completely, Marko spoke over my head to someone in the blackness behind me.

"Is this some kind of joke or are we letting random people walk onto the set now?" His co-host, whose name I now remembered as Alicia, started to rise from her seat, clearly flustered by the unexpected turn of events.

"Where's Lucian? Cut the feed."

Here's a thing you should know about me. Aside from my mouth loving to shoot off without me thinking, there are few things I hate most in this world than to not being taken seriously. Whether it was because I was young or a girl, poor or from a trailer park, ignoring me was a surefire to earn my ire.

"Do not cut the feed! This is not a joke!" I demanded, my voice rising above the chatter in the studio. "Haven't you heard about the dangerous terrorist cell in LA? They're talking about us! Look at me. Turn the cameras on me."

I yanked off my hat with Doc following suit. Marko looked at me like I was insane, but his cohost's eyes suddenly turned wary. She pointed a finger at me, polished nails glinting in the light, and took cover behind Marko, using his body as a shield.

"She and that dog do match the description. Can anyone pull up the alert?"

An aide came running onto the set with their phone in hand, and I got a caught a glimpse of my own mug shot on the screen when they passed by. Alicia sat back down as Marko's face drained of all color.

"You heard what she said. Turn the cameras on her."

Staring into the giant black lens of the camera, I felt horribly vulnerable and had to lean into Bandit for strength. He nuzzled my hand, helping me to gain some command of myself.

"My name is Chase Ryder and I am not a terrorist. Neither are any of the people shown in those images. They are my family. We are innocent." I ran my tongue over my parched lips before speaking again.

"We are not terrorists, but there are people who are after my family right now. They are the ones who are feeding you the wrong information in the hope that you will hunt us down, or lead them to us. They are calling us terrorists to force you into helping them because they want us dead. And do you know why?"

My words came out in a rush now, my heart pounding against my ribcage.

"Because I stumbled upon some heinous illegal experiments that were being conducted. At first, they experimented on animals, but now they have moved onto humans. My dog here," I gestured towards Bandit, who let out a sympathetic whine, "is the result of one of their experiments. But they don't want you to know about him because they are worried about the consequences if the truth gets out."

Bandit licked my hand. Absently, I stroked his head as I continued.

"Apparently, the people who are after us believe that this kind of knowledge is dangerous, or maybe they just want to keep the science for themselves. I don't really know why, and I don't care. All I know is they are trying to kill us and we can't run anymore. They have already killed one member of my family. His name was Zebediah Sullivan. He was kind and wise and… he was like a grandfather to me. I'm not going to let another one of my family die, so I'm here to tell you our story. I'm here to tell you about Bandit."

Marko's gaze slid from me to Bandit. He knew the situation was serious — he wasn't looking at me in a way that showed he thought I was lying — though I could still see that he was struggling to comprehend it all.

"I don't understand," he finally said, breaking the silence. "Who are these people that are coming for you?"

"I don't know exactly," I admitted. "Just that they work for the government."

Marko's eyes narrowed skeptically, but before he could contradict me, Doc cut in. Her voice was calm and unwavering as she continued our story.

"She's telling the truth. My name is Elora Robins and I am a scientist. I used to work for Sebastien Forbes, who you will remember as the billionaire who died last year when he went mad and attacked an innocent family." She paused, her face contorting with guilt and sadness. "Chase and her family are the ones he attacked. He owned Platinum IIndustries, which was a cover for the illegal experiments he was conducting on animals. I know because I worked there. I… was one of those scientists conducting those unethical experiments."

Her eyes began to fill with tears.

"I knew it was wrong, but he was blackmailing me, threatening to kill my family, and I wasn't strong enough to fight him then. But I'm here now. I'm ready to tell you everything… and it all starts with Bandit."

"Okay," Marko said carefully. "You have the world listening. Can you tell us what's so special about your dog?"

Bandit barked once, though of course, the only ones in the room who knew what he meant was us. Now that Doc had laid the groundwork, however, I felt able to continue our story.

"Bandit was a lab dog," I said. "He was created and raised in Platinum Industries until he escaped, and I found him on the street. But it wasn't until he saved my life that I realized he was different from other dogs. Bandit is super intelligent and I don't just mean for a dog. He is as clever as you or I am. In fact, he is smarter than most people I know. Bandit can read and write and he can speak. "

I knew I'd lost them suddenly when a veil came down over their eyes. I could see them looking to call security. They had me pegged as a silly girl, one overly attached to her dog.

Little did they know I had a trump card up my sleeve.

"I know how this sounds, but I can prove it to you. Watch and you'll see." Turning to Bandit, I asked, "Can you say something to them?"

He barked once. "That was the first thing I taught him. One bark for yes, two for no."

Bandit set his sleek, silver iPad on the ground and picked up the stylus pen in his mouth. The crowd around him held their breath in anticipation as he began to type, each tap of his paw deliberate and precise. The camera beside me whirred out, zooming in to capture the words being formed on the screen.

"My name is Bandit and Chase is telling the truth."

Gasps sounded from all corners of the room. Alicia was the first to regain her senses. "That's amazing, but it's not really proof of anything," she said skeptically. "You could have trained him to do that. That doesn't really tell us anything."

Was she kidding? Had she been hit on the head when she was a kid?

"He just spoke to you using an iPad. I don't think there are any other dogs that can do that."

"I hate to burst your bubble, but news correspondents are taught to always be wary of things that seem too good to be true. Your dog could just be very well trained or this could all be a clever little trick."

I felt a surge of frustration building inside me as I tried to think of a way to prove Bandit's abilities when Doc spoke up.

"What about that game, Chase? The one he likes to play?"

"Jeopardy?"

"Yes," she said. "Maybe if he answers some Jeopardy questions, they will believe you."

I crouched down, getting ready to turn on the app, when there was a commotion off to the side. The aide was looking at her phone. Something was happening though I wasn't sure if it was good or bad. My stomach did a flip flop as I waited for her to relay the news.

"What's going on?"

She looked at me, hesitant to speak until Marko nodded his permission.

"The story has gotten out. Instagram, YouTube and Facebook are exploding right now. Millions of people are watching this feed."

The floor shifted beneath my feet. My knees felt weak, and I had to lean against the nearby table for support. "Millions of people are watching? And commenting? What are they saying?"

"They're saying that if your dog is so smart, prove it. Get him to play Jeopardy right now."

"That's what I'm doing. I've got the app right here."

Marko interrupted me. "I don't think they mean the app. I think they mean the actual quiz show. There's a special charity edition shooting right now."

His words were swimming inside my mind, but I couldn't quite make sense of them. Bandit too, was looking a little goofy. His tongue lolled out from his mouth and he had this bug-eyed look about him. "Wait, Jeopardy is filming here? Right now?"

Marko nodded. "Literally down the hall from us."

Before I could even turn to Bandit, I felt him somersault in the air. He typed again into the iPad, his happy voice peeling out across the room.

"Oh boy, oh boy, oh boy!"

65

CHASE

"They're filming it down the hall?" I parroted like an idiot, my mouth agape in shock.

But as soon as it sank in, a rush of excitement flooded through me, mirroring Bandit's. He spun around, tail in the air, dancing on his paws. Even the normally stoic Doc couldn't stop grinning, clearly thrilled by this turn of events.

Despite the history that was about to be made, Marko and Alicia stayed in their seats, seemingly unwilling to participate.

"I thought your jobs were to report big stories? You won't get a bigger scoop this year. I can promise you that," I exclaimed, trying to convince them to join in.

Marko finally got to his feet, shrugging with a 'what the hell' attitude as he gestured at the camera crew.

"Do we have any cameras that can follow them?" he asked. One of the cameramen, the oldest one there, nodded, picking up a much smaller camera than the massive, bolted down giants they had been steering. Setting it onto his shoulder, he turned to the man behind him. "Follow me with the cables," he instructed.

His assistant, a young man with wiry glasses and a box bristling with wires, gave a confident nod to signal they were ready.

The camera crew forged ahead, their equipment buzzing and clicking with anticipation as Marko and Alicia trailed closely behind, their voices a steady stream of excited chatter for the viewers at home.

"Good evening, ladies and gentlemen," Marko began, his voice projecting over the bustling atmosphere. "We interrupt your regularly scheduled programming for an extraordinary event. We have been graced by the unexpected appearance of this young girl and her dog. But what's truly astonishing is that she claims to be one of the most wanted terrorists in the country, with a bounty of half a million dollars on her head."

Alicia nodded in agreement before taking over from Marko. "That's right, folks. This is live on EN News and nothing about it is rehearsed or staged. According to this brave young girl, she and her family are not terrorists at all, but rather victims being hunted by the government because of her dog, Bandit. If you just tuned in this is the most astonishing story and it's all happening live right now. This is not staged in any way. I have no idea what's going to happen, but stick with us as we're about to experience what could be the most exciting edition of Jeopardy that has ever been filmed."

The maze of twisting corridors was never-ending. Our hurried footsteps echoed off the walls as we darted down one nondescript hallway after another, all of them blending into one. People tossed startled looks at us as we passed, wondering what kind of stunt this was, yet no one intruded. Not while that red light above the camera let the world know we were live on air.

Bandit trotted alongside, a pep in his step despite how precarious our situation was. Maybe he was able to compartmentalize better than me. Don't get me wrong, the closer we got to the show, the more my own excitement grew, but with it, there was also that underlying fear that it could all go wrong. That it could backfire and leave us exposed and vulnerable.

And if it did, there was no going back.

We had put ourselves out there for the entire world to see, our faces and our story now irrevocably intertwined. My stomach churned with nerves and I worried I might actually throw up.

I focused on Bandit's expression, desperate not to let the fear take over. This was such a big moment for him. For the first time in his life, he wouldn't have to pretend anymore. He would have the chance to let the entire world know who he was — and it was all happening on his favorite show, of all things.

The iconic Jeopardy logo appeared before us, its bold and curvy letters standing out against the stark white background. It was a simple laminated sign not much larger than an A4 page, encased in a plastic holder, but to Bandit, it might as well have been a flashing neon sign the size of a skyscraper. His excitement was palpable as he let out a howl and his tail whipped into a frenzy.

No one loved a pop quiz as much as my Muttface.

As we waited for the production assistant to open the door, I could feel my heart racing with anticipation. And then, finally, we caught our first glimpse of the awesomeness that was the Jeopardy set. The room was abuzz with activity and lights, and the first thing that caught my eye was the massive wrap-around blue screen that contained the actual questions. This room was unlike any other studio I had been in before — easily twenty times bigger than the one where EN News was filmed.

And then there were the people — a giant live audience filling every available seat, their excited chatter adding to the already electric atmosphere.

As we walked in, we were met with confused faces, even some hostile ones, irritated by the lights on the camera. Studio workers waved their hands in an attempt to stop us, wondering what the heck we were doing there.

The show was currently in process, but instead of its usual host, this live charity edition was being hosted by Hellen, a comedian who was now the most popular chat show host on television. She was known for her kindness — as well as her wit — and was often giving away great sums of money or cars to deserving people. She even gave away houses one time. Seeing that she was hosting today, some of my nervousness faded. If nothing else, I knew she would be kind to us, especially as she was a big animal lover with her own menagerie of pets.

Bandit's nose touched my hand. He was confused about seeing Hellen, but we'd watched her show many times together and were both fans.

Dressed in a smart pinstriped suit with her customary white sneakers, Hellen had just asked a question to the panel of celebrities who were the contestants today. I recognized all three of them: two were famous actresses, and the other, a wrestler-turned-actor, was now one of the highest paid movie stars in the world.

All four of them had stopped what they were doing to look at us. Hellen delicately touched her ear, waiting for instructions to come down the earpiece she wore.

The EN hosts took stock of the situation. Alicia, with her perfectly coiffed hair and dazzling smile, waved at the audience. "Folks, we apologize for the interruption, but this is important. Please remain in your seats."

Meanwhile, Marko addressed both the audience and the celebrities on stage, his tone serious as he explained why we were gathered there. As he reached the end of his explanation, bright spotlights suddenly flashed in my direction and I found myself frozen like a rabbit caught in the headlights.

"What's your dog's name again?" Marko asked, though his voice sounded distant, and I could barely see his face through the haze of white light that now flooded the immediate area.

All eyes were on me now. My palms grew clammy as stage fright threatened to consume me.

"Bandit," I answered, barely louder than a whisper. Clenching my fists tightly, I tried again, this time forcing my words out louder and clearer. "His name is Bandit."

"Right," Marko continued, undeterred by my nervousness. "Chase here claims that Bandit is a product of illegal experiments, giving him human-level intelligence, and we're about to prove whether her claims are true or not, right here and now. This has serious consequences — there's currently a manhunt going on for these individuals. The police may already be on their way, so if you're going to make your point, it needs to be now."

Doc's head bobbed in agreement. "Quickly Chase."

I made my way onto the center of the stage, Bandit bounding up beside me with eager excitement. But as I turned to address Hellen, my words caught in my throat. I wasn't in my own body.

This was my first celebrity meeting. Up close she was so much daintier than I thought she'd be, even smaller than me. Though she must have been so confused by it all, she sent a warm smile our way, and that gave me the strength I needed.

"Bandit loves Jeopardy," I explained. "It's his favorite show and we never miss an episode. We even play the game on our phones after breakfast. If you ask him the questions, he will answer. Then everyone will know I'm telling the truth."

Hellen's smile faltered a little, her eyes growing dark with confusion as she struggled to process my request.

"You want me to play Jeopardy *with the dog*?"

"Yes," I nodded. "Please hurry."

66

CHASE

Hellen's gaze drifted into the distance, settling on a small windowed box that I hadn't noticed before. It was tucked away behind the audience. Figures could be seen standing against the glass. From their posture, I guessed they were the people in charge. Suddenly, Hellen shrugged, flashing one of her famous grins at the audience.

"Well, it looks like we're really doing this."

There was a smattering of laughter from the crowd, but most of them seemed more bemused than amused. Hellen turned back to me, her eyes sparkling with mischief.

"So, any particular subject matter you want to focus on, or should we carry on with random questions?"

I took a deep breath, trying to quell the nerves bubbling up inside me. "Well, we haven't covered history or geography yet. But he's really into film and television, and he loves illustrated books even though he's not quite reading at an adult level yet. He's a huge fan of classic books, especially ones featuring animals, you know, like Charlotte's Web. And we watch a lot of Netflix."

There was a large rumble of laughter from the audience. I bit my lip nervously, knowing they were mocking me. One of my hands instinctively went to Bandit's head, though to comfort him or me, I wasn't sure. I only knew I felt better when we were physically in contact with each other.

Hellen glanced up at the giant wrap-around screen behind us, with several categories already displayed on it, but they abruptly reset until the categories morphed into: children's books, young adult books, Netflix, TV shows, and Movies.

I knew from experience that these weren't the usual catchy and cryptic categories the show usually featured, but we hadn't given them much time to prepare themselves, so I was grateful they were accommodating us in this way.

The studio fell silent as a tense energy filled the air. Bandit set his iPad onto the floor of the studio and gently gripped the pen-stylus in his mouth, preparing to play. Even if people thought this was the trick, they were clearly already impressed. Phones came out as pictures were being snapped and videos recorded.

I was filled with a jittery tension that wasn't solely due to the impending arrival of the police. I felt like a nervous mother, waiting for her child to perform in front of a hostile audience for the first time.

Bandit was my best friend, and he had just the sweetest nature. He had gone through so much adversity, but never felt sorry for himself. His heart overflowed with love for everyone he encountered, making it all the more heartbreaking if that love wasn't returned.

"Okay then, Bandit. Which one of those do you want to go for?" Hellen asked, her tone playful yet expectant. I had to give it to her, the woman was a pro. It was almost as if she was dealing with her usual contestant instead of this one of the four-legged kind.

Poised with the pen-stylus in his mouth, Bandit took in the categories on the screen then very carefully, he typed out the word *"Netflix."*

A collective gasp rumbled through the audience, their eyes wide with shock and disbelief. I felt a smug satisfaction wash over me, knowing that they had all doubted his abilities. *Just you wait.* The celebrities on stage, along with Marko, the host, all wore expressions of equal amazement. Even his usually composed mouth was hanging open in astonishment.

"For those of you at home who might not have a clear view, Bandit just typed 'Netflix' on his iPad. I promise you that this is live and not staged. This is actually happening. The dog just correctly answered the question by typing it into his iPad." He paused, overwhelmed by the moment. "I honestly don't know what to say right now. This is truly incredible."

Ever the professional, Hellen stepped in to keep the show moving. "Well, I guess there's no better time to begin. Bandit, are you ready?"

Bandit responded with a loud bark, earning cheers and applause from the audience.

"One bark means yes, two means no," I supplied, unable to hide my grin. It was pretty satisfying to see all these skeptics proven wrong.

"Of course it does," Hellen chuckled. "Good luck, Bandit, though I'm sure you won't need it."

"Woof woof!" Bandit barked again, exuding confidence. The audience erupted in laughter once more, louder this time.

"Now let's see those answers," Hellen gestured excitedly towards the screen, where a bunch of answers now appeared.

Instead of picking one, however, Bandit looked at me, tilting his head with a puzzled expression across his furry face. I bent down to him.

"What's up, buddy?"

"No money, just questions?"

"That's right, we're only playing with the questions today." I got back up to address Hellen, feeling amused by the awed silence that had suddenly fallen over the crowd.

"The app we play has different game types, one that's just like the show where you bet for money, though we usually just do the quick-fire round."

Hellen's face was a picture of astonishment. She shook her head as if to get her thoughts clear. "We can do that too if you'd like? Make it faster and simpler for you?"

Clearing her throat, she waited for a question to be fed to her through her earpiece. "Right folks. Let's rock and roll. First question. This mother can only protect her two children by losing one of her five senses."

Bandit's tail started swishing across the floor in excitement. He absolutely knew the answer to this as we'd watched the movie together, completely gripped all the way through. We'd even discussed which of our own senses we'd hate to lose the most. Bandit had chosen his sense of smell, something so crucial in the process of information gathering for dogs, while I had gone — rather predictably, Gideon had said at the time — for taste.

"What is Bird Box, Hellen," Bandit's youthful and joyful voice, and so like how I imagined he would sound if he could actually speak, answered from the iPad.

Hellen's head shook with disbelief, her eyes wide and stunned. "He even spelled my name the correct way."

Someone clapped in the audience, timidly at first, until they were joined by another pair of hands. Then more until the place erupted. People started cheering too, whooping as if their favorite sports team had just scored a homerun.

Tears misted my eyes as the fear that had me gripped started melting away. I beamed at Doc, who grinned right back at me. Pixie danced in a figure of eight around her, unable to contain her excitement. Hellen waved at the audience, asking for silence, then spoke again.

"Let's try another question."

As the cheers subsided, she continued. "When a young boy disappears, his mother, a police chief, and his friends must confront terrifying forces in order to get him back. Who is the special friend he makes?"

Bandit didn't even need to look at the answers, knowing this one by heart. Typing furiously, his tail thumped wildly, and he had trouble keeping his butt still.

"Who is Eleven from Stranger Things, Hellen! It's my favorite show!"

At his response, the place went absolutely *crazy*.

If there was any doubt in anyone's mind, he had just erased them. Hellen couldn't stop exclaiming over Bandit's genius, wondering how this could be happening, while Bandit tore around the stage, soaking up all the attention and barking with uncontrollable delight.

Then, in a moment of pure joy and spontaneity, Bandit leaped off the stage and into the front row of the audience.

People eagerly reached out to pet him, some nearly injuring themselves in their frantic attempts to touch him. Camera phones flashed and families jostled each other to pose for pictures with him. I watched the whole thing with happy tears in my eyes, finally believing that things might actually work out okay...

But the instant the thought came into my mind, the studio plunged into total blackness and the camera feed went dead.

67

CHASE

Sudden stillness descended upon the room, leaving an eerie silence as the cameras were turned off.

Gone was the hum of the electrical equipment, and the cheers of the audience ceased to exist, replaced by a sense of unease and confusion as people wondered what was happening. I came to my senses first, snapping my fingers at Bandit in the precise way we had trained during our safety drills. Sam had come up with this form of communication in the event that we were ever gagged or had our hands bound. I guess her time being Xavier's captive had left a lasting impression.

The sound of his paws tapping against the ground echoed through the room as he swiftly made his way to me, guided by his superior hearing and that keen sense of smell that he was smart enough to never want to lose. As soon as I felt him nudge my hand, I held onto his collar with a death grip, keeping him close.

"They cut the power! They must be here. They don't want us talking to you!" I exclaimed, my voice cutting through the hushed whispers and murmurs of the crowd.

As some members of the audience pulled out their phones and

activated the flashlight function, beams of light illuminated our small corner of darkness. I caught sight of Doc's ghostly face floating towards me. Acting on instinct, I grabbed her arm and pulled her closer as she peered into the darkness, deep in thought.

"There should be contingencies for an event like this," she mused.

Someone called out from the dark. "Stay in your seats, please. Do not panic."

We couldn't see very far, so it wasn't safe to move. All we could do was wait helplessly, rooted to the spot for whatever would come next.

More phones turned on. More flashlights were shone at us, but others were now using their phones, fingers flying over the keys as they Tweeted and Facebooked. I recognized the swooshing sounds as messages were posted in their droves.

I welcomed it all. The photographs and videos being shared were proof of our existence and what we were saying.

Hellen's voice broke through the chaos. "Somebody tell me what's happening? Why haven't the emergency generators kicked in?"

The camera crew bustled behind me, partially illuminated by phone screens as they scrambled to find a solution. Here they were, with the biggest news story this side of the century, but their feed had been cut off. They scampered about, searching for a way to get their spare battery to work.

Marko's voice soared above the panic. "Folks, it looks like we've had some kind of power failure. Please remain seated for your health and safety. Do not panic. We will get this sorted. Just remain in your seats."

The four of us huddled together, feeling helpless. Doc took hold of my arm — I thought for safety — but then she started aggressively pulling me into the dark. I opened my mouth to ask where we were going when a gloved hand suddenly covered my mouth.

Terror spiked through me as I realized that those weren't the Doc's hands on me.

I bucked wildly, trying to throw off whoever my assailant was when I felt an additional pair of hands restraining me.

They had found us!

I heard a muffled squeal and knew that Doc was suffering the same fate. Bandit started barking like crazy, Pixie joining him. I knew that they could sense what was happening even if we couldn't see it.

Hearing the commotion, Hellen's voice called over at us. "Chase? Bandit? Are you guys okay?"

When I didn't answer, she yelled out. "Does anyone have eyes on them? Are they safe?"

I dug my heels in, twisting and flailing my arms in an attempt to break free. When that didn't work, I kicked out at them, but there were so many of them that I was quickly overpowered. With a yelp, I felt myself being lifted and carried backward until we came crashing through the door.

Bright light blinded me, flooding my vision with black spots. I felt, rather than saw, Doc struggling against her own attackers as several more attempted to round up the dogs, but they were so agile and fast, they couldn't be caught.

It was absolute mayhem.

After what seemed like an eternity, my vision finally cleared. My heart sank as I saw about a dozen men in the corridor with us. The ones who weren't restraining us held onto silenced weapons. The men all wore the LA police uniform though, of course, silenced guns weren't something you typically see on cops in any state. And these men moved like ghosts, never uttering a sound or issuing our Miranda rights.

There was no mistaking it — these were Smith's men.

Bandit and Pixie bolted through the doors after us, determined to stay with us, while still giving them the run around. As soon as they were in the corridor, one of the men sprinted to the doors they had crashed through and slid a long, thin metal weapon through the handlebars, effectively blocking the doors and keeping everyone else inside.

Seeing their guns, I renewed my fight against them, desperate that they wouldn't be able to use them on Bandit. The guns weren't pointed at us, however. At any point, they could have shot us and left us for dead, but I guess there were too many people around for them to finish the job. Hence the power cut. They were creating a diversion so they could take us somewhere else.

I remember watching an episode of a talk show once, when I was younger and my mom had been out with whatever guy had been her latest squeeze.

This particular episode had been about personal safety. Opal's guest that week was an expert on personal safety who had warned — women in particular — that the number one rule if you ever were attacked in public was to never, ever let them take you to a second location.

If they managed to move you to a second location of their choice, it was likely to be isolated where they could do whatever they wanted with you.

He had warned that no matter how scared we were, however hurt we might be, if they were able to move us to a different location, it would be much, much worse for us.

Remembering that now, I kicked and struggled like a wildcat.

68

CHASE

I fought so hard that the hand around my mouth slipped a little and I was able to sink my teeth into his fingers. I bit down so hard I went through the glove and hit flesh. The guy screamed in agony. The taste of metallic and salty blood filled my mouth, which I spat out like I was possessed.

Snatching his injured hand away, he backhanded with me with the other one, knocking my head back until I felt my teeth rattle in my skull. A warm liquid began to trickle down my face from my nose, followed by a sharp stinging sensation telling me that he had probably broken it, but so long as I could still breathe, I wouldn't think about it. Every ounce of thought and energy was targeted at keeping us here.

Even if I was fighting a losing battle.

There were just too many of them and they were stronger than us. Bandit was growling so fiercely that had he not been my dog, I could only imagine the fear he would have instilled in me, but he knew not to attack these men, not when their guns could easily be turned on us.

We were stuck in a hard place.

We couldn't stop them. All we could do was delay the inevitable. Our feet beat a frantic rhythm as we neared the exit, and my heart sank at the thought of the waiting vehicles outside. Sully's devastated face flew into my mind only to be quickly replaced with Sam's. When Gideon's image appeared, my heart swelled with all of our recent bittersweet memories until it physically ached.

Tears streamed down my cheeks as I desperately wish that I could have apologized to him. To tell him how sorry I was that he didn't feel he could talk to me, that he couldn't share his pain and grief with me.

I knew that once this was all over he would blame himself for whatever was about to happen to us. The guilt would kill him.

As we reached the exit doors, they were flung open, blinding us with bright sunlight and the blazing Californian sun. As I had predicted, there were several identical vans parked across from us, their dark windows a chilling reminder of how powerless we'd be to their actions once they got us inside.

We were dragged towards them when I suddenly saw the enormous crowd that had gathered outside. They were behind the studio's barriers, which is why I hadn't noticed them right out the gate, but I couldn't miss them now. The crowd stretched on for miles, like they were lining up for a Taylor Swift concert, and they all had their eyes fixed on one point in front of the building.

I strained my neck to see what the commotion was about and realized it must be another big show taping since Jeopardy — celebrity edition or not — wouldn't normally draw this kind of attention. Yet, there was an eerie atmosphere hovering over the crowd. They seemed restless, almost agitated, instead of the typical excited energy that comes with being at a live show. It was like a storm brewing just beneath the surface.

Before I could fully process the strange behavior of the crowd, the fake cops pressed their guns against our backs, forcing us toward the vans.

But then, a loud shout pierced through the tense air: "There they are!"

Suddenly, every single person in the crowd turned to face us. Rows upon rows of faces staring intently at us. I froze in shock, unable to move or even utter a sound.

Thankfully, someone took action for us.

"Leave them alone!" A voice shouted from the midst of the crowd. Others joined in, chanting in unison: "Let them go!"

The icy fear that had me frozen inside suddenly lifted. Was it possible? Were these people here *for us*?

The members of the crowd closest to us hopped the barriers, sprinting toward us with a sense of urgency. As they reached the cops, they lunged at them, attempting to free us from their grasp!

One man at the front raised his weapon and shouted, "Stay back! This is a police matter! Back away or I'll shoot!" But instead of cowering in fear, the crowd bristled with fury.

A woman wearing a bright In N Out uniform fixed him with a steely gaze.

"Hell no! You're threatening us? What kind of police officer would threaten a member of the public like that? We're not committing any crimes, but we're also not letting you take that girl and her dog."

The crowd roared in agreement, pushing forward with even more determination. The armed men were taken aback. There was no way they could stand against the thousands of outraged people that were out here.

A burly man in a builder's helmet and hi-vis vest, still covered in dust from a recent demolition job, brandished his fist at the officers.

"What kind of police use unlicensed vehicles? Where are your squad cars? Why are you using unmarked vehicles?" Turning towards the crowd, he bellowed, "These aren't the real cops. The girl's right, they're after her and her dog!"

More rumbles of discontent surged through the crowd, the air thick with tension. The men hesitated, their bodies bunching together to form a human shield. On an unspoken signal, they took aim at the crowd. One of them fired two warning shots into the sky.

A woman's scream pierced through the chaos, causing the crowd to take a collective step back in fear. They wanted to help us, but they wouldn't risk their lives for a bunch of strangers, even if they believed they were innocent. All they could do was yell helplessly as we were forced towards those waiting vans.

Bandit and Pixie were still beside us. Still barking, their yowl's growing more and more intense. I thought I must be going mad suddenly as I began to hear more barking from further away, yet seemingly all around us too, until the sounds of barking filled the air, growing louder and more intense with each passing second.

I had no idea where the noises were coming from — whether they were only a figment of my stressed mind or actually real. My heart thudded fearfully as we reached the van. The doors slid open and I caught a glimpse of several more fake cops inside when a dog burst through the crowd toward us.

It was a Golden Retriever, known for how friendly and mind-mannered they usually were, but this one showed remarkable aggression as she charged up to the men, snarling ferociously at them.

It took me a moment to realize that all of that aggression was not aimed at us, but at our captors.

A rush of barks and yelps filled the air as another dog burst through the crowd, a Boxer with a sleek coat and muscular frame. It was followed by a tiny Poodle, its fluffy white fur bouncing with each step. More and more dogs appeared, pushing their way through the throng until ten of them stood in a protective circle around us.

The crowd had fallen into a hushed awe, watching in astonishment as the dogs stood guard over us.

And then, amidst the sea of furry faces, I saw one that I recognized — a majestic German Shepherd with piercing amber eyes.

It was the first dog I had saved in Platinum Industries! My gaze shifted over to Doc, whose beaming smile confirmed my suspicions.

"They actually came," she whispered in disbelief.

"But how? What are they doing here?" I babbled, my mind racing to make sense of this unexpected reunion.

Doc's expression softened as she explained, "There were so many dogs we had to find homes for after shutting down Platinum Industries that they were sent to families all around the country. But these dogs were homed here, in LA... and their owners must have brought them to the studio to help us!"

The crowd were pointing their phones our way. If we were lucky, this moment would be broadcasted for all to see — making it nearly impossible for anyone to harm or kidnap us.

Meanwhile, it was the men who were now frozen in fear, exchanging panicked looks as they tried to work out their next move. Each time they tried to step forward, the dogs would lunge toward them, snapping their jaws so close to their hands that the men jumped back. I saw the alarm on their faces and felt a twisted sense of satisfaction.

One of them spoke, his voice strained. "We can't kill them with the whole world watching."

I wasn't sure if he was referring to us or the dogs, but either way, I was grateful for the sentiment.

Doc pointed behind us. I turned to see that it wasn't only the crowd who had a ringside seat to the show, but the massive screen above the studio which previously had advertised trailers of their upcoming movies, now displayed a live feed of all of us in the parking lot. Our faces, the dogs, it was all being broadcasted across the nation!

And then right at the back somewhere, perched on top of a car, I saw Marko, Alicia, and their trusted EN crew filming. Their cameras aimed at us as they captured every moment. Marko flashed a thumbs up at me and I had to smile.

Against the overwhelming tide of fear, hope was beginning to take hold. Here were all these people who believed in us, who were rooting for our survival. I was overwhelmed by their support and found myself thinking that maybe we would make it out of this mess alive.

Suddenly, the piercing screech of sirens filled the air. Several police cruisers careened into the parking lot, horns blaring at the crowd to let them pass.

The police got out of their cars, weapons drawn and aimed our way, but they looked on in total confusion. Marko and his crew were hustling toward them at breakneck speed, desperate to head off an attack that might see us dead, but they struggled to get through the thick crowd.

The cops didn't know what to do, frozen in indecision. One of them could be heard asking clearing over the commotion.

"What do we do? Do we shoot the dogs, the kid, or what?"

Personally, I thought the choice was obvious, but apparently, it wasn't to them. We all stood, rooted to the spot, waiting for their next move.

69

SULLY

The RV burned rubber, hurtling down the highway.

Sam, Gideon, and Emma were huddled together next to me, staring at Elora's iPad in utter horror as the scene unfolded before them.

The bright lights of an enormous crowd surrounded Chase, Elora, and the dogs like a cage, while a group of armed police pressed in on all sides. Although there must have been at least a dozen of them, their faces blurred into one. They were all white, of average build and features, and no facial hair. In fact, there wasn't a discernible detail on any one of them.

Which I was certain was by design.

I met Smith's eyes in the rearview mirror. "Those are your men, aren't they?"

"Yes."

His reply was surprisingly honest and direct. Since I'd taken back the RV, those were the first words he had said, though his sharp eyes never left us and studied our every move. On the screen, Chase was being forced toward those waiting vans. Sam's grip on my hand tightened in response.

"Isn't anyone going to stop them!" Seeing Chase in danger had snapped Gideon out of the stupor that had clouded his eyes since our arrival.

"They still think we're terrorists." As ludicrous as it seemed that a young girl and her dog would pose a national security threat, I knew that not everyone used their common sense before pulling a trigger. The situation felt more dire than ever.

A look of disbelief came over Gideon's eyes. "I can't believe this is happening."

With things spiraling as they were, I couldn't believe I had agreed to this plan, either.

Stupid Sully. Stupid.

"She looks so small and there are so many of them," Emma's normally confident demeanor faltered for once as she murmured, genuinely scared for someone other than herself for once.

"That girl of yours is quite something."

I didn't know how I felt about Smith's admiration for Chase. He had no idea of the doubts that were plaguing my mind, impressed only with the fire inside my girl even when the odds were stacked against her.

Never give up. Never Surrender.

Her voice echoed inside my head with the slogan of one of her favorite movies, Galaxy Quest. I knew I needed to take a leaf out of her own book.

"That she is," Sam replied. Despite the motherly pride evident in her eyes, it couldn't conceal the underlying fear that gnawed at her. As a sheriff and law enforcer, she held the responsibility of upholding the law, yet she now found herself powerless to protect her two of her own kids.

We were flooring it to LA now, though it would be awhile — much longer than I'd like — until we got there. I needed to buy Chase some time. Appeal to Smith's good sense, maybe. He met my troubled gaze.

"You have no idea what she's gone through. That dog was the first person — and yes, to us he is a person — who showed her any love. He was the first family she ever had who gave a damn about her and she would do anything for him."

"I didn't know that," Emma revealed quietly. "I didn't know about her life before she met you."

"She was alone for a very long time," Sam answered. "Her mom never looked after her and her step-father was abusive. It wasn't until she ran away that she felt safer. Imagine feeling safer living on the streets on your own at only fourteen years old." The weight of Sam's words lingered, painting a poignant picture.

Overcome with emotion, Emma lowered her gaze back to the tablet, staring intently as if she were trying to reconcile that version of Chase with the girl she knew.

Even Smith displayed a rare look of shame. "I take no joy from any of this."

I thought of his own family and the love he held for his own children. As alien as it seemed, I was reminded that this man was also a father.

"Then stop this madness. You can't win. Your orders were to get rid of us quietly so no one would even know we existed. Well, now everybody knows. There's no point in you coming after us anymore."

He remained silent, his expression stoic, but I could see a slight twitch in his jawline, indicating my words were chipping away at his resolve.

"Can't you get them to stop? This can't be the result your boss wanted. If secrecy is what they're after, that's all been shot to hell. Isn't there something you can do?"

A pause lingered, tension hanging in the air, his gaze locked onto me with laser-like intensity. Time seemed to stretch, and then, after what felt like an eternity, he broke his silence. "Give me your phone," Smith asked curtly.

"My phone?"

"Yes," he confirmed. "I'll call my men off."

My brows raised so high they almost shot off my head.

"It's not my style to lie, Sullivan. My orders were to keep this a covert mission, but that ship has sailed. My bosses can't risk being exposed. They will want us to retreat. But I can't call my men without a phone."

"Would you like fries with that?" Gideon snapped, his hackles raised. "Do we look that stupid?"

I shot him a warning glance before turning to Sam. She stared at me, her troubled eyes reflecting my own indecision. While I wanted nothing more than his men to leave Chase and Bandit alone, this could be a ploy. The stakes were high, and the shadows of doubt loomed over the decision I was about to make. Trusting the sincerity of Smith's words felt like navigating a treacherous path, but I was desperate enough to call his bluff.

"You're not using any of our devices. I'm taking you to a public phone."

"Fine," Smith responded blandly, as if he'd just agreed to a black coffee instead of white.

Gideon balked at us. "Are you insane? Why would you trust him to keep his word?"

"Because we don't have a choice. If there's a chance this will keep them safe, we have to do it."

Emma's brow furrowed in worry as she spoke up. "Can we please discuss this? I want to help Chase and Bandit, but this doesn't seem very smart," Emma asked.

"This doesn't involve you so it's not up for discussion," I replied without thinking, only to see the stark flash of pain in her eyes. She was trying so hard to be a part of our family, yet I had just dismissed her without a second thought. A dark cloud of guilt washed over me.

Sam sent a watery smile my way, understanding what that must have taken. As Emma's shoulders shook with silent tears, she turned and retreated to the bedroom, with Sam staring after her.

"I'll talk to her after we've made the call."

"You will?"

"Yeah. I'm finally starting to understand how she must be feeling. This whole time, I was scared and even a little jealous of your connection… but it's not really her, is it? I was so afraid you would choose her over me that I never saw how difficult this must all be for her until now."

A sudden bolt of realization shot through me, like an electric shock.

"You thought I'd leave you for her?" I asked, my voice tinged with disbelief.

She nodded, a sheepish blush staining her cheeks. "I knew we rushed into things, that a part of you hadn't truly let go of her yet. So when she returned… I figured it was just a question of time."

I squeezed her hand tightly, trying to relay everything I felt for her through that single gesture. "That was never an option, Sam. You're the one. You're my person. I don't want anyone else. Not even Emma."

She gave me a brilliant smile that lit up her face and, for the smallest fraction of a moment, everything felt right in the world.

We continued driving until we reached a rest stop. Conscious of not drawing attention to ourselves — after all, we were still labeled as terrorists — Gideon stayed in the motorhome with Emma while Sam and I escorted Smith to a nearby payphone. She kept her gun concealed within her jacket, but aimed on him at all times.

Handing Smith some coins, I watched as he dialed a number with the Washington area code. A thought filled my head, so dark, so outrageous that I dismissed it quickly. Surely his bosses weren't so high up that they were connected to a certain White House…

"It's Smith," Smith said into the phone, his voice heavy with urgency and the most amount of emotion I'd heard from him since we'd met. "Tell Alpha team to retreat. Disengage immediately until we receive further orders."

Smith looked as if he was hanging up the phone when, with no warning, he swung the phone with brutal force, connecting solidly with the side of my head. An explosion of pain erupted above my left eye, sending shockwaves through my skull. Staggering backward, my vision became a chaotic constellation of stars, blurring the surroundings in a disorienting haze.

"Sully!" Sam's urgent shout penetrated the fog in my head as she launched herself at Smith, attempting to grapple him. Struggling to regain my composure, I attempted to help, but my vision was still obscured by the stars dancing in my eyes. The sounds of their scuffle were distorted, like distant echoes in a cavern.

Someone fell heavily to the ground — Sam.

It took me a moment to fully regain my senses and help Sam up. Relief washed through me as I saw that she was only a little banged up. By then, Smith had already vanished into the darkness.

Gideon rushed out of the RV, Elora's iPad grasped in his hands. I thought he must have seen Smith attack us and was coming to help, but his eyes were glued to the screen.

"It worked, Sully! Those men are backing away!"

Sam and I hurried over to him, crowding around his shoulder to watch as the footage on the screen showed the ten disguised men who held Chase hostage suddenly retreating in their blacked-out vans, leaving Chase, Elora, and the dogs alone.

70

SULLY

After what seemed an eternity of driving, we finally arrived at the studio, our car weaving through the chaos of crowds and flashing lights.

To my surprise, the masses had only grown larger since we left. The sky was littered with helicopters, each emblazoned with the logos of various news channels. A giant TV screen displayed live footage from NBC's stations, cycling between shots of the frenetic scene below.

And right there, at the epicenter of the commotion, was Chase and the others.

They were surrounded by camera crews and reporters, their faces projected on nearly every channel. Custom hashtags scrolled across the bottom of the screen, including #geniusdog, #geneticbreakthrough, and #jeopardydog -- all trending. There was even one called #savethedogsavetheworld which Gideon had to explain was a play on a slogan from an old TV series called Heroes. Social media was also exploding, with Facebook, Instagram, YouTube, and Twitter all streaming events.

The word was well and truly out now.

As we tried to navigate through the throngs of people, I abandoned any hope of parking our RV. The streets and parking lot were packed with vehicles and eager bystanders. I got us as close as we could to then the four of us tried to make our way through the crowd but people refused to move aside. Several even turning hostile toward us.

"We're their family! Let us through!" I finally started yelling.

No one responded, not until the others took up the call.

"That's my daughter!" Sam suddenly roared in a commanding voice. "Move aside!"

Like magic, a path miraculously opened for us amidst the sea of bodies.

"Chase! It's me!" I yelled with everything I had, but my voice couldn't carry over the crowd.

Police — the real police — were still in the area and looking bewildered. They didn't seem to know what to do either until a call came over their radios ordering them to stand down. Someone high up must have given the order, but who? For a fleeting moment, I couldn't help but wonder if Smith's powerful employers had reached out their long arms and interfered with this situation. Could they have that much control and influence?

Driving those thoughts from my mind, we continued wading through the bedlam until we finally reached the ring of dogs surrounding Chase and her captors. The menacing snarls and sharp teeth made it clear that they were not going to let us pass easily. The German Shepherd closest to me turned, snarling a warning for me to stay back, but when she got a good look at me, her tail started to wag.

She whimpered a friendly greeting. I reached out a hand so she could smell Bandit's scent on me and know that I was a friend as I suddenly placed her as one of the dogs we'd saved from the lab. I vividly remembered the videos of her torture — hadn't been able to forget them, in fact.

She looked the picture of health now. Glossy black and brown coat, a healthy weight, but it was eyes that told me the most — once filled with a desperate fear and sadness, they were now bright with happiness. It was clear that her new family was taking excellent care of her. I stepped past her at the same time that Chase suddenly noticed me. The anxious, worried expression on her face instantly melted away into a wide smile that lit up her entire being.

"Sully! You're all here!"

I staggered into the circle as she ran into my arms. Bandit barked joyously, jumping up and down as he sniffed me, reassuring himself that I was well. Pixie a-wooed, an endearing sound as her nose pointed to the sky, equally delighted by our arrival. Bandit barked something at the dogs, a command, and suddenly, they moved aside, forming a gap that the others could walk through.

I had witnessed this particular skill of Bandit's before, back at my clinic when he had commanded the dogs there to attack Forbes's men before escaping to safety, but for Sam, Gideon, and Emma who joined us in the circle with wide-eyed amazement, it was their first time seeing it in action. As soon as they were clear, the dogs repositioned themselves, closing the ring and providing us with a wall of canine protection.

And the best of it was, the entire thing was captured by the cameras. There could be absolutely no denying that the dogs were obeying Bandit's command.

That he was every bit as special as we were saying he was.

I clung tightly to Chase and Bandit, wrapping my arms around their strong bodies as if they were the only things keeping me anchored to the ground. I knew in that moment that I would never let them go again. I felt a hesitant tap on my shoulder and turned to see Gideon standing there, his expression filled with shame and regret. He reached out to embrace Chase, who released me in order to return the hug.

"I'm sorry," he whispered to her.

"I know. It's alright. I understand."

They held each other, her face resting on his chest. Seeing them like that, I realized their relationship had changed and was no longer of the step-siblings kind. Their feelings had transformed into something deeper and more meaningful.

A hand wove itself through mine as my own love laid her head on my shoulder.

Emma stood off to one side, relieved that our family were reunited, yet also feeling like an outsider in this intimate moment. Without hesitation, Sam reached out and took her hand in hers, clasping it tightly and letting her know that she was not alone anymore.

Not now that she had us.

As I looked around at our united family, I couldn't help but feel hopeful about our future. We may not know what lay ahead, but with our bond stronger than ever before, we were ready for whatever challenges came our way.

And most importantly, we would face them together — no one left behind or forgotten.

71

CHASE

As I gazed into Gideon's eyes, relief washed over me like a warm ocean wave. He was alive and safe, and holding me tightly in his arms. It seemed absurd to think how long it had taken for us to realize our love for each other.

We shared everything with one another, the good and the bad. He had always been there for me, even when others weren't. How could I have been so blind to our feelings? I searched his eyes, still looking for the answers to the lingering question that bothered me.

"Why wouldn't you talk to me? I wanted to help you, but you wouldn't let me."

His eyes turned suspiciously bright. "I was a mess. I wasn't trying to push you away. I just felt so angry at the world, I took it out on you the most because… because I love you. I'm sorry I hurt you. That was the last thing I wanted."

Hearing those words come out of his lips, my heart sang, overflowing with joy.

"I love you too. Just maybe, try talking to me in the future first, you know, before you do anything stupid."

His lips curved into a smile. "I deserved that."

"Yes, and I'm not sure when you're going to be hearing the last of it so you should prepare yourself."

He stared so intensely at me that it seemed the most natural thing in the world when his head dipped closer and he lowered his lips onto mine.

A cheer erupted through the crowd as I suddenly remembered that giant TV screen. Half filled with horror, I turned to see — yup. Our faces blown up as big as a billboard. My cheeks flamed red.

I felt a rumble of laughter in Gideon's chest and had to punch him for it.

***

After half an hour, I found myself back inside the EN News stage, but this time, everything had changed. The once empty room was now filled with seven chairs arranged in a semi-circle, waiting for us. Even Emma was there, sitting among us.

There had been some debate on whether letting her loose on camera was a sensible thing, but in the end, we realized that, like Bandit, exposing the truth might be the only way to keep her safe. The world would be getting the entire Emma experience, whether they were ready for it or not.

Marko and Alicia were kind and compassionate as they led the interview. We spoke honestly and openly, revealing every sordid detail of our story.

I started with how I'd been living on the cold and unforgiving streets until I met Bandit. Every now and then, Bandit would chime in with his own memories, like how excited he had been the first time he was able to communicate with me. Other highlights for him had been when he had learned how to spell a word, and how his first sentence had been: "Hello. My name is Bandit and I love you."

Those were the exact first words my Muttface had said to me.

I could almost hear the collective sigh around the world when that little detail had been revealed. Our story had touched so many hearts.

As the viewers were so invested in our story, we were taking questions from them. The co-hosts picked random questions that were Tweeted in. Some were just plain crazy, like, how did we know Bandit wasn't going to kill us in our sleep and that he wasn't dangerous. I had replied by rolling my eyes and saying the same way the average pet owner knew their dogs weren't going to do that.

The outpouring of support was overwhelming. People from all over wanted to show their solidarity with us and make sure we were never hunted again. A funding page was even started, apparently hitting half a million bucks within an hour!

Doc probably had the hardest time of all. People didn't take kindly to her connection with Forbes and her previous line of work, making her the target of some seriously harsh criticism. It wasn't until Sully explained all the good she had done since, and Bandit publicly stating that she was his friend and had always been nice to him, that some of the hate lessened.

Emma didn't say very much. She was asked a few questions, but since she didn't know very much, she wasn't an exciting interviewee. We hadn't had time to tell Emma the truth about what she was just yet, and it didn't seem right to reveal that information live on air, so we had decided to save that conversation for later.

The entire interview took several hours. The other dogs sat around eagerly listening, joined by their new owners now. I wasn't actually sure how much of it the dogs actually understood, but they seemed happy just to be in Bandit's presence. I guess he was their version of a rock star.

When the cameras flashed off, Alicia gave us all a warm smile.

"You all did amazing. Thank you. Especially you, Elora. I know this couldn't have been easy for you."

"It wasn't, but it needed to be done. If it helps to keep them all safe, then some uncomfortableness on my part is worth it."

Someone came by and unclipped the mic that was attached to my shirt. "What now?" I asked.

Marko grinned at me. "Since we've finished recording, we normally celebrate with a wrap party."

"I don't know that we're up for a party," Sam said. "I mean, we've been through the wringer today…"

"Ah, my apologies for the industry term. It's not always a party per se. Usually, we just have a lot of food."

Bandit's and my ears pricked up immediately. "What kind of food?"

"Free food," he replied, grinning.

My lips stretched into a giant smile, mirroring Bandit's expression.

"Well, that just happens to be our favorite kind!"

72

—————

SULLY

As I gazed out at the familiar landscape of my childhood home, I couldn't help but feel a sense of nostalgia for simpler times. The border of towering oaks that I used to ride past every morning stood stoically in the distance. Beyond the fields of lush green grass, a vast pasture stretched out, dotted with grazing horses. At the far end of our property, a crystal clear creek snaked its way through, providing a cool drink for our beloved equine friends. These sights were all so familiar to me, yet now they seemed like distant memories.

After being back in Montpelier for a week, our world had been turned upside down, and not only for losing a beloved member of our family in such a traumatic manner. The home I grew up in, the home where our extended family had come together — that was all gone. The scaffolding that now covered every inch of our ranch was evidence of the significant changes taking place. Even at this early hour, workmen swarmed around like busy bees, their tools and equipment creating a constant hum of activity.

Since our story had made headlines, help had arrived from some of the unlikeliest of places. Thanks to the generosity of strangers, that funding page had swollen to such numbers that none of us ever needed to work again if we didn't want to. However, whenever I made a crack about retiring early, Sam would give me this pointed look. It wasn't a threat, not exactly, but my lady would not be impressed if I became a kept man. The money we had received had been a real blessing, coming in handy as our home had been reduced to rubble.

The sounds of hammers and saws echoed through the neighborhood, evidence of the builders working tirelessly to restore our house. In the meantime, Mobile Travelers, the largest RV company in the world, had graciously provided us with two state-of-the-art motorhomes to use as temporary shelter. And the most surprising part? They didn't charge us a cent. It seemed that our story had touched their hearts and they wanted to show their support. If we wanted to show a little appreciation their way, all we'd need to do is pose with the motorhomes for some photographs making sure that Bandit was center stage.

Yes, we had all been overshadowed by a dog.

It hadn't been all fun and building games, however. A team of stern-faced FBI agents had come to question us about our mysterious government department and elusive accomplice, Smith. Despite going over our story multiple times, they remained adamant that no such department existed and claimed ignorance about Smith's identity.

Not that I was surprised.

Maybe one day, we'd be able to flush them out, but until then, I was content with living our lives and enjoying what little moments of peace we could find.

I felt a presence beside me and smiled.

"Are you checking me out?"

Sam laughed, a throaty, delicious sound that tickled me all over. I felt her arms weave around my waist as she stepped in close to me.

"Nothing I haven't seen before."

"Yet, you're still here. You must be a glutton for punishment."

She turned to face me, her eyes sparkling with love and mischief.

"For better or worse, right? You're not getting rid of me that easily."

She smiled at me, though I could sense that there was something weighing on her mind. "Have you thought about what we are going to do about Emma?"

Some of the light went out of my eyes. This had been the one ongoing problem we still hadn't solved. She still lived with us and although she and Sam had resolved their differences, none of us quite knew what to do next.

"That's going to require a little more thought."

Sam nodded, eminently patient. Not for the first time, I was grateful for her understanding: how many other women would be the same in her position? "The other day, you asked what I would do if Emma — my Emma — came back."

Sam's shoulders tensed, the only outward sign of her tension. I brushed a stray lock of her blonde hair out from her face.

"If she came back today... I would still choose you. What we have is just as real and meaningful as what I had with the previous Emma, but that chapter is over now. My life is with you, and you alone. You are my everything."

Smiling that stunning smile of hers, my wife kissed me with the heat of a thousand suns.

73

CHASE

As the sun rose on a new day, we were greeted by an unexpected surprise visitor.

Well, actually, we've had lots of surprise visitors since we arrived home. It seemed that every single person we knew in the world — and quite a few who we didn't — wanted to swing by to talk to Bandit .

He had always been a star, but now the rest of the world had cottoned on.

My little star wasn't so into all the attention, however, and wanted to be left alone with his family as we started building the next stage of our lives together. As I sat down for our usual morning game of Jeopardy, I couldn't help feeling a flash of irritation when an SUV pulled up outside. I assumed it was yet another paparazzi or fan looking for a photo or autograph.

But to my surprise, the person standing on our doorstep was a familiar and welcome friend. She flashed me a warm smile as I opened the door.

"Hey Doc, we're just having breakfast. You want something to eat?"

"I'd love some coffee, actually," she replied. "I rushed over here so quickly that the only breakfast I had was a coffee from a gas station that was more like sludge than anything else. Does Sully have some of his famous brew? I could really use a cup."

A wide grin spread across my face as I turned to her, chuckling. "Well, sure if he didn't drink it all already. I swear he's the reason the coffee industry stays in business."

As soon as he heard her voice, Bandit came bounding over to greet her. Pixie weaved through Doc's legs and the two dogs did a happy little dance together, followed by the regulatory sniffing of each other's butts, proving that all dogs were weird, even the super smart ones.

I thought it was pretty adorable how the two were friends now, especially when it wasn't even a month ago when they were mortal enemies.

"Excuse the chaos," I said, gesturing around the makeshift space. "The house is still being rebuilt, but the coffee maker works fine."

Leading her to a small table by what would eventually be our new kitchen, I pointed out the window overlooking the backyard.

"This will be our view," I said with a smile. Currently, the room was a disorganized maze of half-finished tasks. The new oven sat unconnected to the gas mains, and there was no sink in sight. Only some of the cupboards had been installed, lacking any doors, of course. Our old counter had been replaced by a sleek marble one that Sam had always dreamed of having. Though I found it a bit cold to the touch, seeing how happy it made her made it all worth it. Who was Sully to deny her this simple luxury?

Pouring Doc a cup of steaming coffee, I felt the warmth radiating through my palms. Handing it to her carefully, we all made our way out onto the porch where the others now sat around a table. The crisp morning air greeted us as we settled into our seats, surrounded by the peaceful countryside. There was a chorus of

"Helloes" and "What's Up Doc?" — the latter of which sent my dog into what I think was peels of laughter.

He rolled around on the wooden deck with his paws in the air, making a weird snorting sound through his nose. We'd recently started watching the old Warner Brothers cartoons, and apparently, this slogan tickled his funny bone.

From her spot on the bench, Emma watched with cautious curiosity. She scooted all the way to one side so Bandit wouldn't accidentally get her with those roving paws of his. She still tended to be uncomfortable around him, though she had lost that initial animosity she'd had toward him.

Bandit didn't seem to mind though. In fact, he'd tried being friends with her. I even caught her awkwardly patting him on the head once when she thought no one was watching, only to frantically scrub her hands in the sink after, as if she didn't want to catch his cuteness.

Taking a seat beside Sam, Doc addressed us all with a warm smile on her face.

"I've been in communication with various branches of the government. Unsurprisingly, they still refuse to admit that there was ever a department like the one you mentioned. I doubt we will ever discover the truth of the matter. However, I do have some very good news that I couldn't wait to tell you. Despite their initial denial, I have convinced them to fund a new department that will investigate Xavier's work. And even better, they have granted me permission to oversee it, so I can make sure that no dogs or any other animals will ever be harmed again."

"That's not good news, Elora. That's fantastic news!" Sully grinned.

Doc turned to Emma, her expression softening as she spoke in a gentle tone.

"They also authorized me to delve into your origins, but only if you give your full consent. If you want to be left alone, I can do that, but you are a scientific marvel and one of a kind. There is so much we could learn from you if you trust me enough to work with me."

Before Emma could even respond, Sam interjected, her voice laden with concern. "You don't mean to use her for experimentation, do you? Because I won't allow that to happen."

Emma looked at Sam, unable to hide her shock. "You're defending me?"

"You're new to all of this, and it's all of our responsibility to look out for you, especially when you're family."

Emma's eyes widened into round circles of surprise that glimmered with unshed tears. She clutched her hands tightly in her lap, her fingers interlocking like a puzzle. Considering her next words carefully, she spoke to Sully.

"In the last few days… I've seen how happy you and Sam are, and even though you have all been kind to me, I know I don't belong. Even if you didn't have Sam, I'm not the same person you married, but I am a constant reminder of her. I think I do care about you, as much as I know how to care about anyone, so perhaps it would be best for me to leave you in peace."

She turned toward Doc and gave a solemn nod. "Yes, I'll be happy to come back with you. I want to understand more about myself."

Sam strode over to Emma, her gaze fixed on her face. "Are you sure?"

A small smile crept across Emma's lips, the first genuine one that had graced her features since arriving home.

"I'm positive."

The next few hours were a flurry of activity as we sorted through Emma's departure.

She didn't have much, so it wasn't so much a case of us packing her things — everything she had fit in the one bag — but we wanted her to know that even though we hadn't always gotten along, we were her family now and would always be there for her.

After her sudden decision to leave, Emma and Sully disappeared for a walk around the property. The sight of them heading off together actually tugged at my heartstrings.

From that fateful night when I had arrived at Sully's door covered with Bandit's blood, I could never have predicted any of this. That Sully had been a shadow of the person he was now. He had been hanging on by a thread... but now, inexplicably, that thread was back only for him to finally let her go.

The sound of joyful barking pulled me from my thoughts. In the distance, I could see Bandit bounding across the grass with Pixie close behind. They weaved and dodged under the sun's warm rays, their paws kicking up fresh blades of grass as they playfully chased each other through the yard, having a whale of a time.

A warm, contented smile spread across my lips as I watched them play with such delight. Bandit was such a special dog that I often forgot he wasn't very old in dog years, not even a teenager yet. But despite his intelligence, he still loved to play with all the carefree abandon of a puppy. It was thrilling to see Pixie come out of her shell too, her cautiousness forgotten in the presence of her furry best friend. The two of them had gone through so much together.

As I stood there, basking in the joy radiating from their playful antics, it suddenly struck me how much these two had in common.

Both had been subjected to cruel experiments, but while Bandit had been rewarded for his cleverness, Pixie had endured years of torture at the hands of a cruel and sadistic man.

Wrapping my arms around myself, I let myself revel in their heartwarming bond. Their joyful energy filled the air until all too soon, it was time for Doc to leave.

She waited patiently by the car while the rest of us said our goodbyes to Emma. Gideon gave her a quick hug that she returned. The two of them had never really seen eye-to-eye, but I knew he only wanted what was best for her.

I hugged her next. "I hope you find the answers to all of your questions."

"And I hope you find a cure for your snoring," Emma replied. It took a moment before I saw the corners of her mouth twitch.

"Did you just make a joke?"

"Why would I do that? I take my sleeping very seriously." But there was something different in her eyes, a mischievous glint that hadn't been there before.

Sam stepped forward, smiling warmly at her. "Good luck. And remember, whatever happens, you always have a home here with us."

Emma didn't reply, but those eyes of hers grew brighter. She gave her a small and grateful nod, seemingly overwhelmed with emotion, as Sully came around from the trunk of the Doc's car. Opening his arms to her, she stepped into them.

He held her close for a few moments, but I could see the love that he had for her was different from what he shared with Sam. It seemed almost parental, like the love he had for Gideon and me.

"Elora will look after you. Stay in touch with us. We want to know how things are going and not only when you have news. Call or write, any time."

Nodding, she swallowed the lump that was in her throat and got into the car. Bandit came around to bump her hand under his head.

"See you later, smelly pants," she said.

He chuffed, his face breaking out into a goofy, lopsided grin. Doc climbed into the driver's seat only to realize that they were one short.

"Pixie, come on," she called out.

But her only response was a distressed whine. Bandit's smile instantly disappeared as Pixie pressed up against him. The two of them stared up at us, two identical pairs of pleading eyes as Pixie made no move to get into the car.

Bandit had left his iPad inside while he was playing (and while the builders were all around), but I didn't need an electronic device to translate their meaning.

"Um Doc… I think Pixie wants to stay," I broached the subject gently. Doc climbed out of her car, her forehead wrinkled with surprise.

"Is that true? Do you want to stay here with Bandit?"

Pixie barked once in response, then lowered herself onto her stomach as if to emphasize her decision. Doc's face became flustered, clearly caught off guard by this.

"I suppose she has made her choice known. Are you all comfortable with that?"

We barely even gave it a moment's thought. Sully nodded. "Sure. If that's what Bandit wants, too."

Now it was Bandit's turn to bark. Moving to Pixie, Doc bent down until her she was eye level with the dog. Reaching out, she gently cupped Pixie's head in her hands.

"You have been such a brave and good girl. I know you'll be well looked after here."

Pixie's tail wagged furiously and she let out an affectionate bark at Doc's words. Then her tongue darted out and she showered Doc's face in wet kisses until she laughed.

"I love you too."

Climbing back into her car, Doc rolled down the window and waved goodbye to everyone.

"I'll see you all again soon."

"Don't make it too long," Sully called out.

She gave them one last wave and then the Doc and Emma were gone.

74

SULLY

T he golden rays of the setting sun bathed the land in a warm and peaceful light, casting long shadows across the grassy fields.

The builders we had hired to repair the ranch the way we wanted it had left, knowing we needed this time to ourselves today.

With solemn faces and heavy hearts, the family gathered around the grave Gideon and I had dug, the rich smell of the fresh earth filling my nose. We had prepared for this day all week, but hadn't been ready to see him off until now.

With Elora and Emma gone, and now Pixie becoming part of the family again, the time felt right.

We were ready.

Dad's body had been preserved in a nearby funeral parlor while we deliberated on what to do with his remains. He had left no instructions, but I knew he would want to be buried beside my mother on our property — it was their favorite spot with the best view.

As we lowered his coffin into the ground, each of us took turns dropping a handful of soil onto his casket as a final farewell.

When it was time for Gideon to step up, he faltered. Chase made a move toward him, but I stopped her. This was something I needed to do for him — to show him that I would now be there for him the way my father had been.

Throwing my arm around Gideon, I lent him my strength.

As the sun slowly dipped below the horizon, I read over the carefully chosen inscription on the gravestone one last time:

Here lies Zebediah Sullivan.

1947 - 2019

You will be sorely missed by your sons and family.

75

—————

CHASE

Despite the months of turmoil and danger we had faced, there was finally a sense of peace settling over us. The rebuild of the ranch had been completed, but it wasn't for our whole family's use anymore. The once humble barn now stood tall and grand, having undergone its own extensive renovation to become our very own office space.

That's right, Bandit and I had our own office now.

And before you go thinking what a ridiculous waste of a nice barn that was, just know that this was totally necessary. Every single day, offers came flooding through from film studios and television companies. Some wanted to film a docu-drama about our lives (we even had an offer from the same network who produce the Kardashian show though the last thing we wanted was to live under more scrutiny), while the studios were trying to get us to agree to not one, but an entire *franchise* of movies based on our adventures.

The world was going mad for Bandit, and they all wanted to capitalize on his fame.

The idea of having movies made of our story was kind of fun. I guess we hadn't entirely dismissed the idea, although I don't think neither Bandit nor I really wanted to be movie stars. That kind of stress wasn't for us, although we were happy to make the odd appearance on a chat show — those were kind of a blast.

They would send a private plane for us, fly us all out to LA. Just the thought of flying somewhere on a private jet blew my mind, especially since I had never been on a plane before. Did you know they have entire bedrooms on planes, with a double bed, ensuite bathroom and everything? It was like a luxury hotel in the sky.

Hellen had featured us several times on her show already. Being such a huge lover of animals, she had raised a ton of money, setting up a charity to make sure that all those other dogs who were experimented on would never lack for anything. Even more than that, she also established a foundation dedicated to finding humane alternatives so that no animal would ever have to endure testing again.

The appearances were so much fun that we would have done them all for free, instead; we were making so much money for them. I'm talking A LOT a lot. Forget worrying about whether I could afford to eat again. Now I could have those little melt-in-your-mouth meringue thingies shipped in from France *daily* if I wanted.

If Sam would let me, anyway.

She set limits on what she deemed too outrageous. Killjoy.

Sam continued to be a sheriff because she loved her job and wouldn't be a 'kept woman,' even if it was the kids who were paying for everything. Sully chose to stay home with us, still reeling from the aftermath of everything that had happened.

He didn't want to be away from his family again, not after facing such terrifying circumstances. He said he couldn't go through that kind of worry again and so we spent most of our time at home, enjoying each other's company. Sully had been contemplating starting something up on our property — he had been researching local plans and permits, trying to figure out what options were available to him. At first, I thought he might open another veterinary practice but in the end, he surprised me by revealing his true passion: opening a rescue center for animals that had been subjected to cruel lab experiments. His goal was to rehabilitate these poor creatures and find them loving homes.

This was his big mission now and one we were all on board with, especially Gid, who had quit his job with Warrey (well, technically, he'd been fired as he hadn't turned up to work for days on end).

When our first paycheck came through, I admit I might have gone a little nuts. I mean, who knew there could be so many zeroes? I spent a ridiculous amount on toys and treats for the dogs, as well as an entire room that was made out of interactive quizzes for Bandit to lose his mind in. For me and Gid, I built a cool new gaming center (Sully had finally relaxed his stance on video games after much, much persuasion from the two of us). And for Sully and Sam, I fulfilled their lifelong dream of having a swimming pool in the backyard. Even after all of these lavish purchases, I was left with a ton of money.

But there was one thing I knew I wanted to get — and it wasn't even for any of us.

Ever since I knew I would have large sums of money coming to me, I'd been giving a lot of thought to what I would spend it on. Turns out, that since I'd managed to go without for so long, I only really thought about the necessities. Subsequently, I didn't really have a long wish list for myself, but when I'd been messing around on the internet, I suddenly remembered a particular property I was interested in.

With my newly acquired wealth, I was able to locate it fairly easily. It hadn't been for sale, but after offering the current owners a big enough incentive, they finally sold it to me for an extortionate price. But I knew it would be worth every cent.

Legally, I couldn't purchase the place on my own as I was

underage, so Sully had to co-sign for me. His face had been quite the picture when I had told him I wanted help buying a house.

"Are you planning on moving?" he'd asked, looking kind of sick by the idea.

"No," I was quick to reassure him. "It's not for me."

"Then who are you buying houses for?"

"It's a surprise."

Suffice to say, I had piqued his interest, which is why he had followed me into my office today. I had just dialed the number for the lucky new owners. After a few rings, the phone was answered by an elderly male voice.

"Hello?"

"Hi," I began hesitantly. "I don't know if you remember me, but you and your wife helped me a few months ago."

I sounded like an idiot. Feeling like a nervous wreck, I wished I had practiced this conversation in front of a mirror before making the call. The phone line crackled with static as I waited for a response. Finally, there was a sharp gasp on the other end.

"Chase? Is that really you?"

A wave of relief washed over me at the sound of Harold's voice. "You remember me?"

"Of course I remember you, dear. Why, we've been following your incredible adventures in the news! Wait, one second will you? I have to get my wife. She won't want to miss this call!"

Harold hurried off to fetch his wife Margaret, leaving me with my thoughts. I twisted a strand of hair between my fingers while I pictured their warm smiles and gentle demeanor.

When Xavier had kidnapped Bandit and left me in that forest, I might have struggled for days if it wasn't for Harold and his wife stopping their car to rescue me. And their kindness hadn't ended with them taking me to a phone where I could call for help.

Seeing my state, and knowing how long it had been since I had eaten, the two had paid for several rounds of food for me. When

Gideon had finally arrived, they wouldn't accept a penny from us, not even when I found out how pressed for cash they were.

I had been so deeply touched by their kindness, especially when I had learned that they had tragically lost a son. Yet, despite their pain, they still believed in God and practiced giving without expecting anything in return. Their unwavering compassion had stayed with me ever since that fateful day on the road.

The weight of their decision to sell the house they had raised their children in still weighed heavily on them, especially now that their son was gone. The walls held echoes of the laughter, tears, and memories they cherished. But the medical bills had piled up, leaving them with no choice but to sell their home.

But now, it was my turn to do something for them.

"Chase?" Margaret's delighted voice came over the phone. "We're so thrilled you're calling! We were so worried when we saw what was happening in Los Angeles on the news, but then that Jeopardy show! There will never be another one like it!"

We shared a laugh as Sully listened in, a smile on his face as he already knew where this was heading.

"We had no idea that what was happening. What a terrible time you have had." It was Harold again. I could almost picture the two of them huddling over the one handset as they both tried to talk to me.

My chest tightened at the genuine concern in their voices. "I know. I'm sorry I couldn't say anything to you at the time. I didn't want to lie or keep things from you. I hope you understand."

"Of course we do, dear," Margaret exclaimed. "I have to admit, we would have loved to meet your talking dog! What a sweetheart he is!"

"We are so glad to have been able to help you, Chase. Had we known what you were going through, we would have done much more for you," Harold chimed in.

I felt a lump in the back of my throat. I had barely said hello yet here they were, wishing they could have done more for me — a complete stranger that they had picked up on the street.

"I really appreciated your help. I've never forgotten your kindness, especially when I learned about your own problems. The thing is, I've now found myself with a good amount of money, and I don't even need much because I have my family around me. So, I spent some of the money we've earned… and I bought you your old house back."

There was a sudden silence over the phone. It was so quiet you could have heard a pin drop. In fact, they were so quiet I wondered if we'd been cut off.

"Hello? Are you both still there?"

Harold's overwhelmed and confused voice spoke again. "I'm sorry, Chase. These old ears aren't what they used to be. For a moment there, I thought you said you'd bought us our old house back."

"That is what I said. I know how much you love that house because it's where you raised all your children. You mentioned how all the memories you have of your son who passed away were in that house, and I just wanted you to have that again. These past few months, I've really learned how much our memories can mean to us, especially when we lose a loved one. And I want you to have him back again, so I hope you'll accept this."

"You didn't need to do anything, Chase! Any decent person would have helped you. All we did was buy you breakfast. You don't have to buy us a house!" Margaret exclaimed, touched beyond belief yet unable to accept this tremendous gift that I was offering.

"But I want to do this for you. You said to me once that God will always provide for you and this is his way of doing that — through me. So please take this house because I don't need it. I'm giving it to you. Please say you'll take it."

Several more moments of silence greeted me. "We… we would be honored," Harold finally answered, choking up.

I felt relief wash over me as they accepted my offer.

"Fantastic! The deeds and the keys will be on their way to you in the next few days, so keep an eye out for them. They will be couriered directly to you."

I'm not sure what Margaret said next because suddenly she was sobbing down the phone while Harold tried to comfort her. I strained to hear their words amidst the chaos until they finally came back on the line.

"Thank you so much, Chase. You have no idea how much this means to us. God bless you. God bless you, your dog, and your whole family," Margaret choked out between tears.

A lump formed in my throat as I hung up the phone, tears stinging at my eyes, but I also had the biggest smile on my face. I had no idea giving could make you feel so good. I had spent so much of my life desperately wanting for everything that now that I was in a position to give, it felt *amazing*.

"Kid, you really are something," Sully said, beaming with admiration and love.

Clapping my hands together, I looked at him then Bandit, laying by my feet, his tail thumping the floor in excitement.

"That was amazing! I want to do it again. Who else can I buy a house for?!"

EPILOGUE

Gideon, Bandit, and I sat in our cozy office, surrounded by shelves of books and mementos from our adventures. The latest draft of a manuscript lay open on the desk in front of us, its crisp white pages filled with words that told our story.

Months of careful consideration and countless meetings had led us to this moment. We were faced with multiple movie offers, each one tempting but also threatening to take away our creative control. But after much discussion, we made a bold decision: we would hire our own ghostwriter to pen our story, which we would then turn into movies ourselves.

Yes folks, the three of us were going to produce our own movies!

Excitement bubbled inside us as we envisioned bringing our story to life on the big screen. Our three heads leaned close together as we poured over the manuscript, already dreaming up scenes and casting choices.

The ghostwriter we had hired was a talented writer from London, who had been working closely with us for months to capture the essence of our journey. We wanted the world to know what had happened to us — the joy, the pain, and the lessons learned.

But for Bandit, it was about more than just our story. He hoped that by sharing it with the world, people would come to care about all animals and work towards protecting them from harm.

As for me?

I guess I just wanted anybody out there who had ever felt unloved, who didn't come from a fairytale family like the ones you see in Christmas movies, I wanted them to know that there was hope: their family — the one they should have — could still be out there. They just have to keep the faith and never give up searching. I honestly believe that we can all find the love and support we each need and deserve.

A knock sounded on the door, followed by the appearance of Sully and Sam. Sully's phone was clutched tightly in his hand and he wore a serious expression. It seemed like there was something important he wanted to tell us.

"You guys got a minute? We just received an email from Emma," he said, motioning for us to gather around.

"I think you'll want to hear this," Sam finished, smiling at us.

I pushed back from the table, swinging my chair to face him. "What's it say?"

Sully perched himself on the edge of the table, taking a deep breath before starting to read aloud.

"Dear Everyone,
I'm having so much fun with Elora. She's been teaching me so many things, including how to be human again — actually, I guess again isn't the right word since I wasn't really here before, not in this body anyway.

After lots of testing (none of it painful, though a few were uncomfortable and involved some very long needles!), they have confirmed Elora's original diagnosis: I am a clone of your Emma, Sully.

I finally received the confirmation yesterday. This makes so much sense now. Things are falling into place and I finally don't feel so strange. Everything I thought I knew had come externally from videos and photographs that Xavier had fed to me. He wanted me to have a link with you, Sully, in hopes of causing confusion between you and Sam. Which I did really well, for a while there. I'm sorry to say.

Elora and her team (who are all really nice) think that I can help millions of people. They say that by using the technology that brought me to life, they will be able to clone healthy organs to replace those eaten away by diseases like cancer.

In fact, Elora thinks we should be able to help people with the same cancer that killed your Emma."

Sully's voice cracked at this part and he wasn't able to continue. Sam took the phone from him, reading the rest of the email out loud.

"I now feel as if my life has meaning, and I'm so happy that I can help all these people, including you. I really am sorry that I complicated your life but I have finally found a place in the world again. With love, Emma II."

I think we all got a bit emotional after that email. Sully looked like he might burst into the ugly cry at any second, but somehow, he managed to keep it together. Taking sympathy on him, Sam looked at the three of us and changed the subject.

"Have you guys come up with a name for your book series?"

I looked over at Bandit. He tilted his head at her, nodding like a human.

"We're thinking of calling it the Chase Ryder series. I wanted to go with the Chase and Bandit series, but he said it sounded cooler with just my name. He insisted that having one main protagonist would make for a stronger story, something all the writing books he had been devouring lately were saying, but I don't agree. I mean, this is all our story, not just mine."

Sam laughed, shaking her head.

"You guys kill me, you know that?"

Gideon stretched and let out a deep sigh, squeezing the muscles on the back of his neck.

"Is it break time yet? We've been at this all morning already."

"Twist my arm," I answered, already jumping up and heading into the house where the snacks lived. The second I stepped through the door, pandemonium greeted me.

Pixie lay in a basket by the crackling fireplace where a dozen brown and white puppies wriggled around her. She had surprised us by getting pregnant very soon after moving back in with us, and the puppies were just under four weeks old now.

We couldn't have been more thrilled, even with the unexpectedly large litter, which Sully explained rarely happened for a first-time mom. Then again, the parents were extra special. And Bandit couldn't have been a better dad. He seemed to have endless patience as they climbed all over him, these wriggling furballs of energy. Literally everything excited them.

As Sully kneeled beside me, he couldn't resist reaching out to pet the nearest pup. It was a tiny ball of fur with a big brown patch over one eye and a wagging tail that never seemed to quit.

"Have you got names for them yet?"

I pointed at the one in his hand while Bandit said. *"That's Patch"*

"Because of his eye, obviously," I filled in.

Hearing the name, Patch suddenly squirmed out of his hands

and bolted for Bandit, but his little paws couldn't quite get purchase on the smooth new floor and he skidded all the way across the room until he bumped into Bandit at a sudden stop. Shaking his head, he looked up at Bandit with intelligent eyes, then sat, waiting for further instructions.

Sully and I shared a look.

They were too young to know their names, or much more than that, but it definitely seemed that Patch already knew his name and was now waiting for Bandit to begin a game or activity.

I pointed at a different puppy, one with a white shape on his rump.

"That one's Star." Bandit said.

The minute the iPad said *his* name, Star's head shot up, then he too bounded over to sit beside his brother.

Sully's mouth fell open. "No way. They're much too young to behave like this."

Feeling a wave of excitement building inside, I watched as Bandit finished calling his kids.

"Panda, Ace, Champ…"

As he called their names, each puppy jumped to attention, coming to sit in a neat row in front of Bandit until all twelve were in a neat line in front of him.

I turned my head sharply to look at Bandit. His eyes seemed to sparkle with amusement as he glanced back at me.

"Did you know about this?" I asked, feeling a mix of shock and excitement. "Did you know they were super smart, too?"

He snorted out of his nose, laughing at our shock. Sully and I exchanged a quick glance, the same startled expression in our eyes.

"But…" was all Sully could say.

I at least managed two whole words before the full ramifications of an entire household of super smart dogs could hit me.

"Oh boy."

THE END

A NOTE FROM THE AUTHOR

If you've got this far then hopefully you've liked this book, maybe even loved it (yay!) in which case can you please take a few minutes to review this book and the series?

I'm an indie author which means I write on my little computer from my little rental home (London is expensive, y'all). The websites, paperbacks, advertising… everything is done by me so if you love my books and would like to see me become successful as an indie author, and you know, maybe finally buy myself and my cats a little home that I own, please help by <u>leaving your reviews</u>.

The more people that know about my books, the better they will do and the more time I will have to write you more books!

And if you would like me to continue this series, do let me know in your reviews and FaceBook ad comments. This is how I judge what projects to focus on next.

Thank you so much for reading!

— Jo

WE'RE NOT DONE YET!

Jo has another series that you might like!
Continue reading for a sneak peek of her romantic suspense series,
SILVER SCREEN SECRETS, also starring an adorable dog!

Fans of Nora Roberts, the glitz and glamor of Hollywood and of
course, dogs, will love this suspenseful series!

(Available as ebook, paperback, and audiobook)

UNTIL THE STARS DON'T SHINE, SILVER SCREEN SECRETS BOOK 1

When a former marine and his highly trained dog are hired to protect the daughter of a Hollywood star, love was the furthest thing from their minds.
But when it becomes clear that she is in danger, how far will he go to save her?

Perfect for fans of Nora Roberts, heartwarming romantic suspense, and dog lovers everywhere!

Kane Turner is a simple man who cares nothing for riches. Scarred both physically and mentally from his tours as a marine, all Kane cares about is his bike, beer and dog Bud – and not necessarily in that order. He lives in a trailer on the beach, working security detail for his friend's company, protecting some of the wealthiest (and most superficial) people in the world with loyal Bud at his side.

Ask anyone and they'd tell you that Lexi Gray-Rockefeller has it all. The daughter of Hollywood royalty, she's rich, one of the most stunning women in the world with parents who dote on her. Yet

Lexi is lonely. All she wants is to work with animals. She doesn't care for the LA lifestyle having struggled to make any lasting relationships: people are generally too in awe of her family or befriend her only for what they can get.

Following a series of threats, Kane is hired to protect Lexi, yet despite their world of differences the two of them find themselves falling in love. In Kane (and his dog Bud), Lexi has found an authentic soul who doesn't care who her parents are or how wealthy she is, while Lexi is the one person who can seemingly heal Kane's wounds.

When Lexi is kidnapped, Kane only has a short time to save her. Can he find her before time runs out?

Heat level: a hint of steam - nothing graphic.
This book also covers billionaire and military themes.
This is a standalone book with no cliffhangers though you'll get the best experience by reading the series in order.

Read the first chapter of this series —>

PRELUDE

He had just come off a trying assignment and was looking forward to some R&R when the call had come, smack in the middle of what constituted packing.

A few shirts, his trusty camo shirts, briefs, and cargo pants as beat up and put through the ringer as he was, were being shoved into a canvas backpack when his phone had buzzed.

The melodic rap by D'angelo that had been blasting from the old school sound deck that provided his one luxury in life stopped playing, replaced by that annoying ringtone that seemed to reverberate around the tin walls of the Airstream Travel Trailer he called home.

Though it was only thirty-feet long, the trailer had everything he needed for full-time living: a bedroom with a double bed that connected to a small but serviceable living room that also doubled as his kitchen and office, with a shower room and laundry at the other end of the trailer. And it came with one of the most glorious views of the Malibu ocean that he would never be able to afford in his lifetime if he wasn't living in a mobile home.

Truly, it offered the best of both worlds and the icing on the cake? When he inevitably felt that siren call to move, he could simply shift his home and his life by attaching it to his truck and hauling it off to the next place.

The ringing continued its insistent call, interrupting his thoughts. Lips turning down with disapproval, he looked for the phone but couldn't locate it anywhere near him.

"Bud," he called out. "Fetch my phone."

The German Shepherd who had been snoozing by the bed sprang up and raced into the lounge, letting the rings guide him. When he padded back, the phone was gripped carefully between those two strong jaws of his. Intelligence shone out of his brown eyes as he looked up at his owner for approval.

"Thanks, boy."

He took the phone from him and ran a hand over his dog's smooth head in the way that he liked. Bud chuffed happily, lifting first one paw then the other before returning to his position by the foot of the bed, circling round in the way that dogs do before lying back down.

The man stared down at his phone, at the name of the lowlife who dared to interrupt this most holy of times — that of vacation.

He'd worked long and hard, and this downtime was due him. People knew better than to bother him when he could almost taste the grit in his teeth and feel the desert air whistling through his hair.

It was going to be him, his bike, his trusty dog and the unforgiving outback of the desert.

Which was just how he liked it.

His eyes slid over a shelf of framed photographs and nicknacks collected from a lifetime of experiences. Landed on the only picture he had kept from high school, back when he hadn't been half as tough or rugged as he was now.

The two teens in the picture were skinny things, all arms and legs with glasses and unfortunate zits that were the cause of many a beating from the jocks that'd had their run of the school.

After a pretty miserable childhood being bullied and living under the roof with a drunk for a father, and a drug addict for a mom, when Kane Turner suddenly grew two feet — seemingly each way — he'd fled to the marines as soon as was feasibly possible.

Disciplined, driven, and relieved to be getting out of his crummy home situation, he advanced up the ranks quickly due to formidable physical skills and an almost sixth sense for danger.

Didn't matter if he was in the sketchier parts of downtown or conducting a dawn patrol in Afghanistan, Kane always knew moments before contact with a hostile was initiated. It was this uncanny ability that had kept him alive throughout each of his tours when so many of his brothers had fallen by the wayside.

Despite being so good at his job, he never enjoyed it.

It was in his blood to protect and serve, but he didn't like fighting people, didn't like hurting them, however misguided they were. Still, he would have stayed a marine if it wasn't for the devastating loss that occurred in Operation Condor.

It was supposed to have been a routine expedition.

A simple patrol in a small town in the middle of nowhere where only a handful of people lived. They were to show their faces, let the locals see that the US controlled the region when an IED went off as they neared.

The car ahead had flipped over though luckily, Kane had felt that tingle in the back of his neck, that flutter in his stomach that had warned him something was amiss.

Slowing down his vehicle as he scouted the area, he had been far enough back that the bomb only did surface damage. The wounds he sustained would leave a few wicked scars, though they were nothing compared to the devastation his marine brothers faced.

Suffering through weeks of agony, their injuries finally proved too great as a number of them died one after each other. Those who clung on to survival did so by a thread: tormented by PTSD, they only made it through the day by medicating themselves with whatever was to hand.

And those were the lucky ones.

Unable to work or return to normal civilian life, a few became homeless, sleeping rough on the streets before vanishing off the face of the earth completely.

Kane hadn't wanted that for himself.

He hadn't survived his childhood to let that be the end of his story. He knew he had to quit before his number ran out.

After he returned to civilian life, Kane flitted around from city to city, working various manual jobs from construction to bar tender to a stint as an Uber driver, until his high school buddy Wilson had called, offering to employ him.

The class nerd, Wilson had gone on to make a major success of himself and now ran one of the most sought-after VIP security services. Having heard that Kane was struggling, he wanted to help the one person who hadn't made his life a misery at school.

The money was decent, and it was fun to mix with the Hollywood elite who were as eccentric, as out of control as a person would expect. From well-organized "sleepovers" featuring some of the country's best-known faces to basement S&M dungeons, Kane had seen it all.

Despite some of the crazy things he'd witnessed and how he could likely fund the rest of his life if he would only pen a book detailing the madness he'd been privy to, Kane was a consummate professional and would never betray his employer's trust.

This kind of integrity was a quality often missing in LA, and so he found his services in constant demand, particularly when the employer happened to be a bored and lonely housewife.

Many fell for his brooding good looks, while others simply loved the challenge.

Kane frequently found himself in uncomfortable situations where he would catch his client walking around in nothing more than a thong and a smile.

He never took advantage of the moment.

The women who threw themselves at him? He never found them attractive. He didn't like their too-tight facial features so often caused by surgery, or the voluminous breasts that never moved. The fake tans made him think of overcooked frankfurters on a grill. In fact, he hated fakeness in general, which was why, although he was seen as a catch, he still hadn't found The One.

Not that he believed in that kind of thing.

Having seen what a loveless marriage could do to two people, he had sworn off the idea which was just as well, as none of his previous relationships had been at all successful with an average lifespan of only a few months — if that.

He knew he was far from perfect, but he'd considered himself above average in many respects and most of the women he came across tended to agree… until they came home with him for the first time.

Apparently, his tiny tin home didn't hold quite the same appeal for them as it did him.

After the first night, many didn't bother returning while the ones who hung in there he would inevitably find fault with.

What was it about the women in this town that made them all so focused on fame and money?

He'd lost count of how many celebrity parties he'd worked at where women initiated conversations with potential "love" interests by asking them what job they had or how much square footage their house contained.

It all left a bad taste in his mouth.

Having finished a trying job with a diva pop star who'd acted very badly when Kane had rejected her drunken advances, he had packed a bag and was ready to take off on his Harley for a week in the mountains but now the one person in the world he couldn't ignore was calling.

"Wilson," Kane answered his phone. "I'm literally walking out the door so this had better be good…"

"I know, but this just came through," Wilson responded with uncustomary excitement.

Mack "Stonewall" Rockefeller, the well-known movie mogul who owned Pinnacle studios, was receiving death threats. This wasn't unusual in and of itself — the rich and famous were always being targeted by money grabbers and weirdos — however Wilson was particularly concerned as the threats were coming from the same source…

And they seemed to be escalating.

The Rockefellers had a daughter who they had managed to keep out of the limelight for most of her life. Not much was publicly known about her other than she was about to turn twenty-five and an enormous yet "private" party was being thrown to celebrate the occasion.

Wilson explained how bad an idea that would be: Stonewall would essentially be opening his home to thousands of strangers. If anyone wanted to do something to them, there wouldn't be a more perfect opportunity.

Stonewall and his movie star wife Mandy were resisting, however, and were in the process of finalizing the firm they would go with for the job. In particular, they were looking for a body-guard for their daughter. Wilson had fought for their business for years. The literal King and Queen of Hollywood, if he was able to win this contract, it would set up the company for life.

"So what's the problem?" Having had all this explained to him, Kane wasn't sure the point of his call.

"I'm stuck on this detail in DC right now and none of my usual men are cutting it. I need someone different, someone who might shake things up."

Kane ran through what he'd been told about the family in his head. "They sound high maintenance and I just got done with a job like that."

"Just meet them. Talk to them like you would any other client. If they don't go for you, fair enough. But I'm telling you, every firm I know is fighting to land this gig. It would mean a tremendous amount if we could win the account."

Kane glanced over at Bud. His ears were pricked high as he listened keenly, picking up on his reluctance.

"I already told Bud we were going. You know I hate disappointing him."

As if he understood, Bud sighed, staring at him with sad, accusatory eyes designed to pull at his heart. He tossed a rubber bone at him that Bud snatched out of the air with his jaws.

"Tell him there's a giant marrow bone in it for him if he'll wait just a little longer." Wilson sounded hopeful, knowing his pleas were working.

"Tell him yourself," Kane grumbled, shaking his head. He looked longingly out of a window, at the faint outline of the mountains that seemed to be moving further away into the distance.

"Thanks man. Appreciate it. Get the job and you can have a long break after. As long as you want."

"Don't forget the marrow bones," Kane reminded him, determined that Bud would not lose out.

"I'll have a box shipped over," Wilson laughed. "You'll need to get there this afternoon. Go flash them some of the Kane charm. Clara will collate a file and send it over to you ASAP."

Clara was Wilson's assistant. She'd worked with him for close to five years now. She wasn't the quickest, but Wilson swore she was loyal and could be trusted with anything.

Kane hung up the call and sent Bud an apologetic look.

"So… it looks like we're going to have to put a pin on that vacation I promised you…"

Bud responded by groaning and covering his eyes with a paw.

"Don't be such a drama queen. At least you've got bones coming."

At that, Bud perked right up. His tail thumped against the laminate floor tiles.

"Let's grab a walk before we head over there. I've got a feeling this job is going to be rough."

Barking with the kind of excitement that would make a person think he had never been out on a walk before *in his life*, Bud raced to the door, jumped up to the handle and tugged on it with his mouth. The door swung open. Light and sea air flooded into the trailer that had his mouth opening to capture it all, but he stopped short of going outside.

He was too well trained too not to.

Kane nodded, giving a hand signal. "You can go."

At that, Bud bounded outside, yapping and barking like he was a puppy again and not the grown-up three-year-old that he was.

Rolling his eyes at his dog's antics, Kane joined him outside.

AFTERWORD

There are many reasons why I wrote this particular series.

It all started when Chase and Bandit's characters came into my head one day, and despite my common sense telling me that it would be a tough sell — genius dogs in a thriller! — I couldn't stop thinking about them. I fell in love with these two almost the second that they were born.

I hadn't written any books at the time so the idea of writing one was incredibly daunting. English wasn't always my first language — I actually didn't know how to speak it until I was around five or six when I was sent to summer school as I kept speaking Cantonese in class.

When I was finally able to read English properly, reading became my passion. I was a voracious reader, reading up to fourteen books a week (the maximum I was allowed to take out at the local library using two library cards — I'd signed my mom up for one just so I could use her card!).

I read anything and everything. I had no idea what author was who as I was the only real English speaker in my house so I simply worked my way through the bookshelves starting from A. One thing I quickly learned about myself: I simply LOVED stories about families particularly if they featured a young character as a main protagonist, and if it had a lovable animal in there too… oh boy!

I think you can see where this is going.

Bizarrely, though I had worked as a professional screenwriter for over a decade before I ever wrote a single word of Wanted, I was filled with doubt over my ability to not only finish a novel but to do a good job of it. Having trained myself to write in the usual screenwriting style where the economy of words is king — why use five words to describe something when you can use one? — I found the whole idea of being able to write how a character *felt* and *thought* (both no-no's in screenwriting) freeing, but also incredibly daunting.

So, to finally have arrived at this point, seven or so years after I first began the series, to have just typed the words "THE END," the feeling is indescribable.

As thrilled as I am, I am also at a loss. These characters had become part of my family. I lived through every one of their heartbreaks. I laughed and cheered as they rose above their problems to become the unit we now know.

Thank you for taking these characters into your hearts and for letting me know how much you have loved their story.

If you'd like to help me turn this into a film or television series, please *leave your reviews* for these books and help spread the word. The more love there is for these books and the more demand there is for a show / movie, the more likely it is to happen.

My thanks go to my wonderful proofreader and grammar guru, Janice Harris for her support and insightful work. Thank you also to Dawn for being my sounding board for all things fictional and in life.

- Jo

ALSO BY JO HO

SERIES

The Twisted Series, YA Urban Fantasy

(Available as ebook, paperback, audiobook)

Perfect for fans of The Mortal Instruments, The Vampire Diaries, and Pretty Little Liars!

Read it three ways!

As the single editions:

What Doesn't Kill You (Book 1)

Beware The Signs (Book 2)

See No Evil (Book 3)

The Blood That Binds (Book 4)

When Trouble Comes (Book 5)

Bad Habits (Book 6)

Left Behind (Book 7)

Hell Hath No Fury (Book 8)

In Her Skin (Book 9)

First Date Jitters (Book 10)

Grave Matters (Book 11)

Plus lots more to come!

TWISTED MAGIC 1

A specially discounted box set edition containing all 11 of the first Twisted books.

TWISTED SAGAS

Discounted 3 - book box sets of the Twisted series

The Chase Ryder Series, YA Thriller

- Winner of a Readers' Favorite Gold Medal Book Award -

(Available as ebook, paperback, hardcover, large print, audiobook)

Love stories the entire family can enjoy? Love dogs?

Then you'll love this series!

Wanted, Book 1

Haunted, Book 2

Hunted, Book 3

STANDALONES

(Available as ebook and paperback)

A new town, a new place, and a new mystery…

The Boy Next Door (YA Mystery)

Books are available as ebook, paperback, and audiobook

For purchase links please visit Jo's website at
www.johoscribe.com/buy-now

ABOUT THE AUTHOR

A proud geek and video gamer, and champion of complex female protagonists, Jo brings her page-turning screenwriting style to books to weave well-crafted, suspenseful stories with twists you don't see coming.

A self-taught screenwriter, Jo's writing life began when she created the ground-breaking, critically acclaimed CBBC action fantasy television series, "Spirit Warriors," which introduced leading actress, Jessica Henwick ("Game of Thrones," "Star Wars: The Force Awakes") to the screen. Granted the biggest budget ever given to a CBBC show at the time, it was nominated for "Best Children's Program" at the 2011 Broadcast Awards, with Jo herself, going on to win the Women in Film & Television's "New Talent" Award in 2010. Jo even made history for being the first Asian person — man or woman — to create a British television drama series.

Since then, Jo has worked with some of the most acclaimed producers in the world with several television shows and movies currently in development. It is her dream to bring her Twisted series to screen and she believes she can make it happen with her readers' help!

Jo lives in London and hopes one day to travel across America in a super kitted out, Zombie-apocalypse-ready RV, with her lovely fella, Matt, and three equally lovely kitties.

Sign up to her mailing list for updates, book release details and offers at www.johoscribe.com

Join Jo's Newsletter to be first to hear about her books.

For a complete list of Jo's books, visit her website.